'Something special . . . [   ] and the story grips from the astonishing opening sequence to the unexpected conclusion'
The Times

'Two pages into *Farlander* I was hooked . . . I'll certainly be reading the next book, for I have a feeling that it's going to be even better. Nice one Mr Buchanan'
Neal Asher

'A[n] impressive debut . . . Farlander is a well-imagined book which stands out nicely from the usual fantasy fare'
BookGeeks.co.uk

'[...ing] old-school epic fantasy with a few modern twists . . . [Buchan]an writes with an effectively ruthless but concise style which is still gripping'
The Wertzone

'[Th]e world of *Farlander* is a rich one and Col Buchanan [has g]reat talent . . . exceptional storytelling, comprehensible [en]joyable characters and a story which puts assassins in a new perspective'
Only The Best Sci-Fi/Fantasy

'[...da]ring new fantasy series that sets the blood pumping . . . [f]earless in execution, exhilaratingly new and with a steely [inten]sity . . . *Farlander* has staked its claim vociferously – this is a series to be reckoned with. Everyone take note'
TheTruthAboutBooks.com

Farlander

Col Buchanan is an Irish writer who was born in Lisburn in 1973, and now lives on the west coast of Connemara. In recent years he has mostly settled down, and loves nothing more than late-night gatherings around a fire with good friends. *Farlander* is the first of the Farlander novels.

By Col Buchanan

The Farlander novels

FARLANDER

STANDS A SHADOW

THE BLACK DREAM

COL BUCHANAN

Farlander

THE FARLANDER NOVELS

Book One

TOR

First published 2010 by Tor

This edition published 2015 by Tor
an imprint of Pan Macmillan, a division of Macmillan Publishers Limited
Pan Macmillan, 20 New Wharf Road, London N1 9RR
Basingstoke and Oxford
Associated companies throughout the world
www.panmacmillan.com

ISBN 978-1-4472-6185-8

1 3 5 7 9 8 6 4 2

A CIP catalogue record for this book is available from
the British Library.

Typeset by Ellipsis Digital Limited, Glasgow
Printed and bound by CPI Group (UK) Ltd, Croydon, CR0 4YY

For my wife, Joanna

A heartfelt thank you to my agent Louise Burns
and my editor Julie Crisp.

To my early test readers
Ben Fox, Ian Chapman and Art Quester.

To all the folk at FD,
especially the ever-supportive Michael Duffy.

And to Deborah, for old times' sake.

The son breathes,
the father lives.

ONO, THE GREAT FOOL

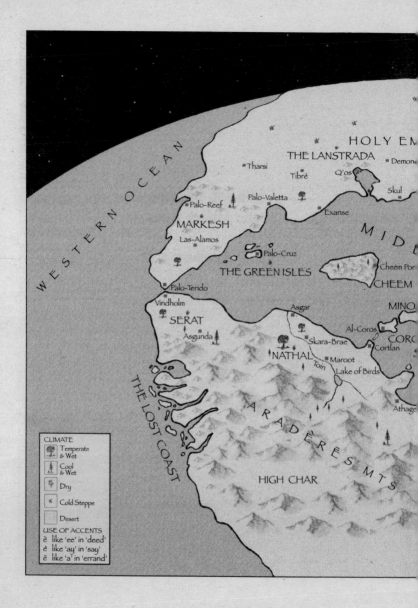

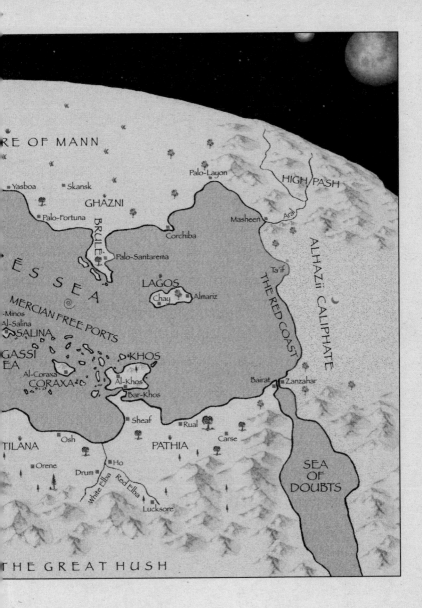

Big Boots

Ash was half dead from exposure when they dragged him into the hall of the ice fortress and threw him at the feet of their king, where he landed on the furs with a grunt of surprise, his body shaking and wanting only to curl itself around the feeble heat of its heart, his panting breaths studding the air with mist.

He had been stripped of his furs, so that he lay in underclothing frozen into stiff corrugations of wool. His blade had been taken from him. He was alone. Still, it was as though some wild animal had been thrown into their midst. The villagers hollered amid the smoky air, and armed tribesmen jabbered for courage as they prodded at his sides with bone-tipped spears, hopping and circling with caution. They peered through the steam that rose off the stranger like smoke; his breath spreading in clouds across the matted surface of lice-ridden skins. Through gaps in these exhalations, droplets of moisture could be seen running down his frosted skull, past ice-chips of eyebrows and the creased-up eyes, dripping free from sharp cheek bones and nose and a frozen wedge of beard. Beneath the thawing ice on his features, his skin looked black as night water.

The shouts of alarm rose in volume, until it seemed the frightened natives would finish him there and then on the floor.

'*Brushka,*' growled the king, from his throne of bones. His voice rumbled from deep within his chest, echoing around the columns of ice arrayed along the length of the room, and rebounding back at him from the high-domed ceiling. At the entrance, tribesmen began to shove the wide-eyed villagers back through the hangings that veiled the archway. They resisted at first, voicing their complaints; they had been drawn there in the wake of this old foreigner who had staggered in

1

from the storm, and felt compelled to see what would happen to him next.

Ash was oblivious to it all. Even the occasional jab of a spear failed to draw his attention. It was the sensation of nearby heat that roused him at last, causing him to lift his head from the floor. A copper brazier stood nearby, with bones and cakes of animal fat smoking and burning in its innards.

He began to crawl towards the heat, as clubbing spears tried to deter him. The blows continued as he huddled against the brazier's warmth and, though he flinched under every blow, he refused to move from it.

'*Ak ak!*' barked the king, and his command finally forced the warriors to draw back.

A silence settled in the hall, save for the snapping flames and the tribesmen's heavy breathing as though they had just returned from a long run. Then, through it all, a groan of relief sounded loud and clear from Ash's throat.

I still live, he thought with some wonder, in something of a delirium, as the glow of the brazier seared through him. He clenched numb hands into fists to better feel the precious heat held within them. He felt the skin of his palms begin to sting.

At last, he looked up to take in his situation. All around he saw the gleam of grease on bare skin, blankets worn like ponchos over bodies half-starved in appearance, faces pierced with bone, gaunt and hungry-eyed; a little desperate.

He counted nine armed men in all. Behind them, the king waited.

Ash gathered himself, though he doubted he could manage to stand just then. Instead, he shuffled on to his knees, to face the man he had ventured all this way to find.

The king studied him as though considering which part to devour first. His eyes were like flints nearly lost in the fleshiness of his face, for he was a huge man, so grossly inflated with fat that he required a girdle of stiffened leather slung across his lap to support the sag of his belly. Otherwise he sat there almost naked, his skin agleam with a thickly applied layer of grease, with only a necklace of leather hung against his chest, and his feet bound in a massive pair of spotted-fur boots.

The king took a drink from an upturned human skull, and

smacked his lips in leisurely appreciation. A belch erupted from his gullet, the flab of his neck quivering, then he produced a long, self-satisfied fart that quickly polluted the smoky air with its tang. Ash remained silent and unperturbed. It seemed that all his long life he had been confronting men like this: petty chiefs and Beggar Kings, once even a self-proclaimed god: figures who sometimes hid behind the glamour of status, or even a semblance of polite gentility, but remained monsters all the same – as was this man before him, and as all self-made rulers must be.

'*Stobay, chem ya nochi?*' the king asked of Ash, his gaze moving over him with a ponderous intelligence.

Ash coughed life back into his throat. His dry lips cracked open and he tasted blood on them. He stroked his neck in a gesture of need.

'Water,' he finally managed.

A royal nod. A water sack landed at his feet.

For a long time, Ash drank greedily from it. Then he gasped, wiped his mouth dry, leaving a smear of red on the back of his hand.

'I do not speak your language,' he began. 'If you wish to question me, you must do so in Trade.'

'*Bhattat!*'

Ash inclined his head, though he did not respond.

A frown creased the king's face, muscles trembling as he barked an order to his men. One of the warriors, the tallest, strode to one side of the great chamber, where a box sat by the wall of carved ice. It was a simple wooden chest, the kind used by merchants to transport chee or spices. All eyes in the hall looked on in silence as the warrior unbuckled a leather latch and wrenched open the lid.

He stooped and grabbed something up in both hands. Without effort he pulled it out – a living skeleton still clad in flesh and tattered clothing. Its hair and beard were overgrown and matted, and it peered about with red-rimmed eyes that squinted against the light.

Bile surged in Ash's gut. It had never occurred to him there might still be survivors from last year's expedition.

He heard the grinding of his back teeth. *No. Do not become attached to this.*

The tribesman held the starving man upright, until his stick-like legs had stopped shaking enough to support his weight. Together, slowly, they approached the throne. The captive was a northerner: one of those desert Alhazii, judging from what grim looks were left to him.

'*Ya groshka bhattat! Vasheda ty savonya nochi,*' the king ordered, addressing the Alhazii.

The desert man blinked. His complexion, once swarthy like all his people, was now as yellow as old parchment. By his side, the tribesman nudged him until his gaze came to rest on Ash. At that his eyes brightened, and some flicker of life returned to them.

He opened his mouth with a dry clucking noise. 'The king . . . would have you speak, dark face,' he rasped in Trade. 'How did you come to this place?'

Ash could see no reason to lie, just yet.

'By ship,' he said, 'from the Heart of the World. It still waits for me now on the coast.'

The Alhazii recited this information to the king in the tribe's own harsh tongue.

The king waved a hand. '*Tul kuvesha. Ya shizn al khat?*'

'From there,' translated the Alhazii. 'Who helped you to come from there?'

'No one. I hired a sled and dog team. They were lost in a crevasse, along with my equipment. After that, I was caught in the storm.'

'*Dan choto, pash ta ya neplocho dan?*'

'Then tell me,' came the translation, 'what is it you will take from me?'

Ash narrowed his eyes. 'What do you mean?'

'*Pash tak dan? Ya tul krashyavi.*'

'What do I mean? You come here from a long way.'

'*Ya bulsvidanya, sach anay namosti. Ya vis preznat.*'

'You are a northerner, from beyond the Great Hush. You come here for a reason.'

'*Ya vis neplocho dan.*'

'You come here to take something from me.'

The king jabbed a sausage-sized thumb at one of his sagging breasts. '*Vir pashak!*' he spat.

'That is what I mean.'

Ash might have been a rock carved in the perfect likeness of a man, for all the reaction he now gave to the question hanging between

4

them. A frigid gust whistled in from outside, flapping the heavy furs draped across the entrance archway behind him, causing the flames of the brazier to recoil. The storm reminding him of its existence, and that it was waiting for his return. For a moment – though only for a moment – he wondered if perhaps now was the right time to introduce a few choice lies. It was not in Ash's nature to ponder overly long on matters of consequence. He was a follower of Dao – as were all Rōshun – therefore better to remain calm and act spontaneously, guided by his Cha.

Internally, he followed the steady flow of air as it entered his nostrils, infiltrated stinging cold into his lungs, then emerged again as warmth and steam. Stillness came upon him. He breathed and waited as the words of his answer formed themselves, then listened as he spoke them, as intrigued by them as everyone else.

'You wear something that belongs to another,' rang out Ash's voice as he raised a finger to point at the necklace hanging between the king's drooping breasts – and he thought: *the direct path, I might have known.*

The object strung on a length of twine was the size and shape of an egg cut vertically in half. It was the colour of a chestnut, and wrinkled like old leather.

The king now grasped it like a child.

'It is not yours,' Ash repeated. 'And you do not know what purpose it serves.'

The king leaned forward, his throne of bones creaking.

'*Khut,*' he said, quietly.

'Tell it,' the Alhazii supplied.

Ash stared at him for the length of five heartbeats, studying the flakes of skin in the man's thick eyebrows, the crusts of sleep in the corners of his eyes. His black hair, saturated with grease, hung in a sheer curtain to his shoulders, like a wig.

In the end, Ash nodded. 'Beyond the Great Hush,' he began, 'in the Midèrēs, what they call the Heart of the World, there is a place which man – or woman – can call on for its protection. With coin, a large amount of coin, they buy from it a seal like the one you wear now, to hang from their necks so that all might see it. This seal, Old King, offers them protection, for if they die, then it dies with them.'

The Alhazii's subsequent translation rolled and chattered over these words. The king listened, rapt. 'That seal you wear now was worn by Omar Sar, a merchant, a venturer. It has a twin, which we watched, as we watch all of them, for signs of death. Omar Sar travelled here many moons ago on a trading expedition. Rather than allow him to trade here, amongst the settlements of your . . . *kingdom*, you thought it better to murder him and all his men, and seize what goods he had brought with him. But you did not realize that his seal protected him. You did not know that if he was slain, then his seal would die too, and its twin would also die, and more than that . . . the twin would point to the one who had killed him.'

Slowly, his knees and hips exploding with pain, Ash unfolded himself from the floor to stand before the king. 'My name is Ash,' he declared. 'I am Rōshun, which in my tongue means "autumn ice" – *that which comes early*. It means I come from that place of protection where all Rōshun come from, for that place is where we carry forth vendetta.'

He paused to let his words sink in, then continued, 'So you are correct, you fat pig, I have come here to take from you. I have come here to take your life.'

As the translation rattled nervously to a stop, the king roared in outrage. He shoved the Alhazii away from the throne, sending the man spilling to the floor. With blazing eyes, the king hefted the skull in his hand and launched it at Ash.

Ash swayed slightly to one side, and the skull shot past his head.

'*Ulbaska!*' The king bellowed, the excess flesh of his face quivering in time to the syllables.

His tribesmen stood frozen for a moment, fearing to approach this black-skinned old man who dared to cast threats at their king.

'*Ulbaska neya!*' he roared again, and then the warriors converged on Ash. The king sat back, ample breasts heaving, and unleashed a torrent of angry words as the spear points settled against Ash's flanks. From the floor, sprawled on his back, the Alhazii pattered out the royal diatribe in Trade, like a clock that could not be stopped.

'You know how I came to be ruler here?' the king was demanding. 'For a whole dakhusa I was sealed in the ice cavern, with five other men and food for none. One moon later, when the sun returned and melted the entrance, out came me. Me, alone!' And he pounded his chest as he finished this, producing a heavy, fleshy, animal sound.

'So threaten me if you will, old man fool of the north,' – and the Alhazii paused even as the king paused, both drawing in a lungful of air – 'for tonight you suffer, you suffer hard, and tomorrow, after I awake, we will make good use of you.'

The tribesmen gripped Ash tightly, with shaking hands. They stripped him of his underclothing till he stood naked and shivering in the frigid air.

'Please,' whispered the Alhazii from the floor. 'Sweet mercy, you must help me.'

The king gave a jerk of his head, and they hauled Ash away.

Through the hangings they went, where the fighting men stopped long enough to pull on heavy skins, and then he was dragged along the passageway and beyond.

Outside, the storm still tore through the night. Ash's heart almost stopped with the cold shock of it.

The wind pounded him relentlessly, shoving him even as the warriors shoved him. It howled for his body heat as snow lashed against his bare skin like fire. Pain entered his bones, his internal organs, his heart that was skipping and hammering in disbelief.

He would die in just moments, this way.

The grim-faced men pulled him across the snow towards the nearest of the ring of ice huts. The tallest took the lead, ducking inside, while the others came to a stop. They held their spears aimed at Ash, ready to thrust if need be.

Ash hopped about on his feet, arms wrapped about himself helplessly as he treaded snow. He turned slowly, offering one side of his body to the wind, and then the other. The men around him laughed.

From the entrance of the ice hut emerged a couple carrying bundles of their sleeping furs. They cast dark looks of resentment at the tribesmen, though they said nothing as they stumbled off towards another dwelling nearby. The tall warrior backed out next, pulling with him the skins that had covered the floor of the hut, before he yanked off the further skins that shielded its tunnel-like entrance.

'*Huhn!*' grunted the leader, and the warriors bundled Ash inside.

It was black as a pit within, and quiet, but the air felt warm in comparison to the gusting winds outside. Without any clothing, though, he would soon be freezing again.

Behind him, they set about sealing the entrance with blocks of ice.

Ash heard water being splashed against it, and waited without moving until finally he was trapped inside.

He kicked at the wall of the hut with the side of his foot, but it was like kicking stone.

Ash sighed. For a moment he swayed on his feet, close to fainting. In that instant he could feel, pressing down on him, the crushing weight of his sixty-two years.

He collapsed to his knees on the hard-packed floor, ignoring the burn of ice against his shins. It took all his focused will not to simply lie down and close his eyes and go to sleep. To sleep now would be to die.

Cold. So cold he was likely to shake himself apart. He blew into his cupped hands, rubbed them vigorously, slapped his body with stinging palms. It roused him somewhat, so he slapped his face too for good measure. Better.

Noticing his scalp was cut, he pressed a ball of snow against the wound until it stopped bleeding. After a while his eyes began adjusting to the dark. As the ice walls brightened, they seemed to become infused with the faintest milky light.

Ash exhaled purposely. He clasped his hands together, closed his mouth to stop his teeth from chattering. He began a silent mantra.

Soon, a core of heat was pulsing outwards from his chest, seeping its steady course into his limbs, his fingers, his toes. Vapour began to rise from his goosebumped flesh. His shivering stilled.

High above his bald head, the wind keened through a small air-hole in the dome-like ceiling, as if calling to him, carrying with it the odd flake of snow.

*

He imagined he had erected his heavy canvas tent, and was now huddled inside it, safe from the wind, warming himself at the little oil stove made of brass. Broth simmered with smoky cheer. The air was steamy, heavy with the stench of his thawing clothes, the sweetness of the broth. Outside, the dogs moaned as they hunkered down in the storm.

Oshō was with him in the tent.

'You look bad,' his old master told him in their native Honshu, lines of worry creasing ancient skin as dark as Ash's own.

8

Ash nodded. 'I'm almost dead, I think.'

'You are surprised? All of this, at *your* age?'

'No,' confessed Ash, though for a moment, chastised by his master, he did not feel his age.

'Broth?' Ash, asked, as he scooped some into a mug, though Oshō declined by raising a single forefinger. Ash drank on his own, sipping loudly. Heat trickled down into his stomach, revitalizing. From some-where elsewhere a moan sounded, as though in longing.

His master observed him with interest.

'Your head,' he said. 'Any pains?'

'Some. I think another attack might be coming on.'

'I told you it would be this way, did I not?'

'I'm not dead yet.'

Oshō frowned. He rubbed his hands together, blew into them.

'Ash, you must see how it is time, at last.'

The flames of the oil stove sputtered against Ash's sigh. He looked about him, at the noisy flaps of the canvas, at the air rolling visible from the broth. His sword, perched upright against his leather pack, like the marker of a grave. 'This work . . . it is all I have,' he said. 'Would you take it from me?'

'Your condition does the taking, not I. Ash, even if you survive tonight, how much longer do you think you have?'

'I will not lie down and wait for the end, no purpose left to me.'

'I do not ask you to. But you should be here, with the order, and your companions. You deserve some rest, and what peace you may find while you still can.'

'No,' Ash responded hotly. He glanced away, staring far into the flames. 'My father went that way, when his condition worsened. He gave in to grief after the blindness struck him, and lay weeping in his bed waiting for the end. It made a ghost of him. No, I will not squan-der what little time I have that way. I will die on my feet, still striving forwards.'

Oshō swept that comment aside with a gesture of his hand. 'But you are in no shape for this. Your attacks are worsening. For days you can barely see due to them, let alone move. How can you expect to carry on in this way, to see a vendetta through to the end? No, I cannot allow it.'

'You must!' roared Ash.

Across the sloping confines of the tent, Oshō, head of the Rōshun order, blinked but said nothing.

Ash hung his head, then breathed deeply, composing himself.

Softly came the words, offered like a sacrifice on an altar: 'Oshō, we have known each other for more than half a lifetime. We two are more than friends. We are closer even than father and son, or brothers. Listen to me now. I need this.'

Their gazes locked: he and Oshō, surrounded by canvas and winds and a thousand laqs of frozen waste; here in this imaginary cell of heat, so small in scale that they shared each other's breath.

'Very well,' murmured Oshō at last, causing Ash to rock back in surprise.

He opened his mouth to thank him, but Oshō held up a palm.

'On one condition, and it is not open for debate.'

'Go on.'

'You will take an apprentice at last.'

A gust pressed the canvas of the tent against his back. Ash stiffened. 'You would ask that of me?'

'Yes,' snapped Oshō. 'I would ask that of you – as you have asked of me. Ash, you are the best that we have, better than even I was. Yet for all these years, you have refused to train an apprentice, to pass on your skills, your insights.'

'You know I have always had my own reasons for that.'

'Of course I know! I know you better than any soul alive. I was there, you recall? But you were not the only one to lose a son in battle that day – or a brother, or a father.'

Ash hung his head. 'No,' he admitted.

'Then you will do so, if you make it safely out of this?'

Still he could not look directly at Oshō; instead his eyes were filled with the scattering brilliance of the oil stove's flames. The old man did know him well. He was like a mirror to Ash, a living breathing surface that reflected all that Ash might try to hide from himself.

'Do you wish to die out here alone, in this forsaken wilderness?'

Ash's silence was answer enough.

'Then agree to my offer. I promise you that, if you do, you will make it out of this, you will see your home again – and there I will allow you to continue in your work, at least while you train another.'

'Is that a bargain?'

'Yes,' Oshō told him with certainty.

'But you are not *real*. I lost this same tent two days ago . . . and you were not journeying with me when I did. You are a dream. An echo. Your bargain means nothing.'

'And yet still I speak the truth. Do you doubt it?'

Ash gazed into the empty mug. The heat had faded from its metal curvature, leaching the warmth from his hands.

Ash, long ago, had accepted his illness and its eventual, inevitable outcome. He had done so in much the same way as he accepted the taking of those lives he took in pursuit of his work; with a kind of fatalism. Perhaps a touch of melancholy was the result of such a vantage, that the essence of life was bittersweet, without meaning save for whatever you ascribed it: violence or peace, right or wrong, all the choices one made, though nothing more – certainly nothing fundamental to a universe itself purely neutral, seeking only equilibrium as it unfolded for ever and endlessly from the potentials of Dao. He was dying, and that was all there was to it.

Still, he did not wish to end it here on this desolate plain. He would see the sun again if he could, with eyes and mouth open to savour its heat; he would inhale the pungent scents of life, feel the cool shoots of grass against his soles, listen to the flow of water over rocks, before that. And here, in his dream fantasy, Oshō was a creation of that same desire: in that moment, Ash dared not hope that he could be anything more.

He looked up, speaking the words as he did so. 'Of course I doubt it,' he replied to his master's question.

But Oshō was gone.

*

It was a slow, nauseous pain that now came upon him, sickness washing his vision. The headache tightened its vice-like grip against the sides of his skull.

It drew him out of his delirium.

Ash squinted through the darkness of the ice hut. His naked body shook, convulsed. Minute icicles hung from his eyelashes. He had almost fallen asleep.

No sounds intruded through the hole in the roof. The storm had ceased at last. Ash cocked his head to one side, listening. A dog barked, followed by others.

He blew the breath from his lungs.

'One last effort,' he said.

The old Rōshun struggled to his feet. His muscles ached, and his head contracted with pain. He could do nothing about that, for now, since his pouch of dulce leaves had been taken from him, along with everything else. No matter, it was hardly a serious bout yet; not like the attacks he had experienced on the long voyage south, confining him in agony to his bunk for days on end.

Ash stamped his feet and slapped his body until sensation returned. He breathed hard and fast, gathering strength with every inrush of breath, purging exhaustion and doubt as he exhaled.

He panted into each palm, clapped twice, then leapt upwards. He slipped a hand through the ventilation hole so that he hung there with his legs dangling below him. With his other hand he began to stab at the ice around the hole, each strike delivered with a low '*Hu!*' that was more a gasp than a word. Each impact sent a sickening shock along the bones of his arm.

Nothing happened at first. Again he was reminded of futilely striking stone.

No, he would get nowhere like this. Instead he thought of melting ice covering a pond, its crust thin enough to break through. As air whined through his nostrils, he became light-headed, making him focus that much harder.

A sliver of ice at last broke free. He allowed this moment of triumph to wash over him, without pausing in his efforts. More chips of ice loosened, until shards of it were raining down against his face. He squeezed his eyes shut to clear them of sweat. But it was more than sweat: his hand was darkly bloody from the work. Drops of blood splashed on to his forehead, or fell to the ground, to freeze there before they could soak in.

Ash was wheezing heavily by the time he had cleared a hole large enough to see a portion of night sky. For a moment he stopped and simply dangled there, to catch his breath.

As the moment lengthened, it took another effort of will to rouse himself. With a grunt of exertion, he hauled himself through the opening, scraping naked flesh as he went.

All seemed quiet throughout the settlement. The sky was a black field scattered with stars as small and lifeless as diamonds. Ash slid to the ground and crouched knee-deep in the snow, not looking back at the line of blood that now streaked the domed roof of the ice hut.

Ash shook his head to clear it, then took his bearings. Ice houses lay all around him half buried in snowdrifts. Small mounds shifted where dogs lay sleeping for the night. In the distance, a group of men prepared a sled team for the morning hunt, unaware of the figure watching them calmly through the dimness.

Keeping low, Ash took off towards the ice fortress, his bare soles crunching through a fresh crust of snow.

The structure loomed against the stars as he approached.

He did not slow his pace, kept running to the tunnel entrance, snapped his way through the hangings into the passage within. He startled the two tribesmen standing guard there beside a burning brazier. The space was small, no room to move easily. Ash drove his forehead straight into one guard's face, cracking the man's nose and knocking him, stunned, to the floor. Pain flashed through his own head, at which point the other guard almost caught him with a lunge of his spear. Ash ducked in time, felt the carved bone tip slide across his shoulder. Muted grunts, then the slap of flesh against flesh, as he sent a knee into his opponent's groin, his pointed knuckles slamming into the man's throat.

Ash stepped over the two prone bodies, narrowing his eyes as he ventured within.

He stood in a constricted passageway. Ahead lay the main hall, its entrance covered in skins. Behind the hangings all seemed quiet. But, no, not entirely quiet. He could hear snoring beyond.

My blade, Ash thought.

He darted left through a different archway. It lead into a small space thick with smoke, lit only by a small brazier standing in one corner, a red glow emanating from the fatty embers it contained illuminating the room for a few feet of air all around, and then darkness.

A pallet bed lay next to the brazier, where a man and a woman lay asleep, pressed against each other. Ash remained a dark shadow as he padded over to the far wall, where his equipment had been piled. It was all still there.

He fumbled through his furs until his hands came upon the small leather pouch of dulce leaves. He took one out, then thought better of it and took out two more, stuffing the brown leaves into the side of his mouth, between teeth and cheek.

For a moment he sagged against the wall, chewing and swallowing their bitter flavour. The pain in his head lightened.

He ignored his furs. Steel glinted as he drew his blade from its sheath. The couple slept on regardless as he padded back towards the entrance to the main hall.

Light spilled across his bare toes from the gap beneath the hangings. Ash sucked in a bellyful of air. Exhaling through his nostrils, he stepped through, still as naked as the blade held low in his grip.

The king sat asleep on his throne at the far end of the hall. His men, some partnered with women, lay in heaps on the floor before him. To one side of the entrance a tribesman leaned on his spear, half dozing where he stood.

Ash no longer trembled. He was in his element now, and the cold became something he wore like a cloak. He was not afraid, fear was a distant memory to him, as old as his sword. His senses heightened in that moment just before he struck. He noticed an icicle, high on the ceiling above a brazier, a soft hiss each time it loosed a drip into the flames below it; he scented the sharp odour of fish, sweat, burning fat, and something else, almost sweet, that made his stomach rumble. He felt his muscles sing in rising expectation.

Movement had caught the guard's eye, stirring him to wakefulness where he stood. The tribesman looked up in time to see Ash sweeping down on him with bloodied face and bared teeth. The blade swung towards him. It cut an arc through the smoky air and met the brief resistance of the man's chest. He choked out a cry even as he fell.

It was enough to wake the others.

The tribesmen reached for their spears as they struggled to their feet. Without order, they rushed at Ash from all sides.

He scattered them as though they were children. With single strokes of his blade, he butchered each tribesman who came across his path, no sense of self in what he did. He was silence in the midst of confusion, his motions propelled by their own trained instincts to advance, and only to advance, his slashes and thrusts and swerves timed in a natural rhythm with his steps.

Before the last tribesman had fallen Ash was in front of the throne, a mist rising behind him from the floor of leaking corpses.

The king sat there trembling with rage, his hands straining against the bone arms of his chair as though he was trying to stand. He was drunk, the stench of alcohol thick on his breath. His lungs heaved as though he needed more air, and a thin drool ran from his parted lips as he watched, with half-lidded eyes, the Rōshun now standing before him.

He looks like an angry child, thought Ash, before casting the notion aside.

Ash flicked blood from his blade, settled its point beneath the chin of the king. The king's breathing grew visibly faster.

'Hut!' snapped Ash, pressing the blade until it broke the skin, forcing the king to raise his head so that their gazes met more clearly.

The king glanced down at the blade held to his throat. A rivulet of his own blood coursed down the groove in the steel without resistance, like water trickling over oiled canvas. He looked up at Ash and, beneath his left eye, a muscle twitched.

'*Akuzhka,*' the king spat.

The blade suddenly pierced up into his brain. One moment the gaze of hatred was there; in the next, all life had faded.

Ash straightened up, gasping for breath. Steam billowed from around the throne, as the contents of the dead king's bladder suddenly splashed to the floor.

Ash removed the seal from the king's neck, dropping it over his own head. As an afterthought, he closed the man's eyes.

He moved next to the wooden chest by the wall and opened it, hauling out the Alhazii curled within.

'Is it over?' the man croaked, gripping hold of Ash as though he would never let go of him.

'Yes,' was all that Ash replied.

And then they left.

CHAPTER ONE

The Shield

Bahn had climbed the Mount of Truth many times in his life. It was a green, broad-shouldered hill with gentle slopes, not overly high; yet that morning, hiking up the path that wound its way towards the flattened summit, it seemed steeper than it ever had before. He could not fathom why.

'Bahn,' said Marlee by his side, her hand in his tugging him to a stop.

He turned to find his wife was gazing back along the path, her other palm shielding her eyes from the sun. Juno, their ten-year-old son, struggled some way behind. He was small for his age, and the picnic basket he carried too bulky for his short arms. Still, he had insisted on carrying it on his own.

Bahn wiped sweat from his brow. In the moment his hand drew clear, and cool air kissed his forehead, he thought: *I do not wish him to see this today*. And he knew then that it was not the hill itself that was steeper that morning. It was his own resistance to it.

An apple toppled from the basket, red and shiny as lip paint, and began to roll down the foot-polished stones of the path. Both parents watched as the boy stopped its progress with his boot, then bent to pick it up.

'Need a hand?' Bahn called back to his son, and tried not to dwell on the money it had cost him for that single apple, or the rest of their precious picnic.

The boy replied with an angry glare. Dropping the apple back into the basket, he hefted the load before continuing.

Thunder rumbled in the far distance, though there were no clouds in the sky. Bahn looked away from his son, tried to exhale the worry that seemed always to curdle in his stomach these days. He forced a smile on to his face, in a trick he had learned during his years of fighting in the Red Guard. If he stretched his lips just so, his burdens would seem to grow a touch lighter.

'It's good to see you smile,' said Marlee, her own brown eyes creasing at the edges. On her back, in a canvas sling, their infant daughter hung open-mouthed and asleep.

'It's good to have a day away from the walls, though I'd rather we spent it anywhere but here.'

'If he's old enough to ask, he's old enough to see it. We can't shelter him from the truth forever, Bahn.'

'No, but we can try.'

She frowned at that, but squeezed his hand harder.

Below them, the city of Bar-Khos roared like a distant river. Gulls soared and dipped above the nearby harbour, wheeling in their hundreds like a snowstorm in the far mountains. He watched them, a hand across his forehead to shade his eyes, as they took turns to speed low and fast across the mirror-flat water, their reflections flying upside-down between the hulls of ships. Sunlight speared back from the surface, the dazzles painting it in burning gold. The rest of the city lay beneath a glamour of heat, the figures of people small and indistinct as they made their way through streets cast into deep shadow. Bells rang from above the domes of the White Temple, horns sounded from the Stadium of Arms. In air hazy with dust, mirrors flashed from the baskets of merchants' hot-air balloons tethered to slender towers. Beyond them all, beyond the northern walls, an airship rose from the pylons of the skyport, and began heading east on its hazardous run to Zanzahar.

It seemed strange to Bahn, even now, that life could carry on seemingly as normal while the city teetered on the brink.

'What are you waiting for?' Juno panted, as he caught up with them.

Bahn's smile was now a genuine one. 'Nothing,' he replied to the boy.

*

On days like this one, a crisping hot Foolsday at the high point of summer, it was common for people to climb their way out of the baking streets of Bar-Khos to seek refuge on the top of the Mount of

Truth. There a park rose in terraces around its flattened summit, and a breeze blew constantly fresh from the sea. The path levelled off as it reached the park itself. Young Juno, feeling more confident now with his load, took this opportunity to increase his pace, overtaking his parents before dodging past others who were strolling more sedately. Together, they skirted a narrow green where, amongst a group of children playing with a kite, a fight was breaking out over who should fly it next. Beyond them, on a bench overshadowed by a withered jupe tree, an old beggar monk sat with his bottle of wine while talking incessantly to his dog. The dog seemed not to be listening.

Again, a peal of thunder rolled through the air, sounding more distinct now they were closer to the city's southern walls. Juno glanced back towards his parents. 'Hurry up,' he urged, unable to contain his excitement.

'We should have brought his kite along for later,' said Marlee, as behind them the children ceased their squabbling long enough to send their box of paper and featherwood sailing into the wind.

Bahn nodded, but said nothing. His attention was fixed on a building that stood on the summit of the hill and occupied the very centre of the park. Surrounded by hedgerows, its tall walls were dotted with hundreds of white-framed windows, reflecting either sky or blankness depending on where he looked. Bahn himself reported to that building almost daily, in his capacity as aide to General Creed. Even without choosing to, he found his gaze running across the flank of the Ministry of War, to where he knew the general's office was located. He sought sign of the old man perhaps watching from one of the windows.

'Bahn,' chided his wife, as she tugged him onwards.

At last they came to the southern fringe of the park. Juno moved ahead, weaving his way between the crowds of people sitting amongst the long grasses, but slowing with every step as he took in the vista appearing below. Finally he stopped completely. After a moment, the basket tumbled from his hands.

Bahn went over to join him and began to gather up the spilled contents of the basket. All the while, he watched his son closely, much as he had once watched him take his first tentative, risky steps as a young child. The boy had always been banned from visiting the hill on his own, but in the last year he had begun to ask and then to plead to be brought here, fired up on the stories told by his friends. He had wanted to see for himself why the hill was named the Mount of Truth.

Now, from this moment on, he would always know.

On this southernmost edge of the tallest hill of the city, the sea could be seen to run both east and west along the coastline – and directly ahead, the long, half-laq-wide corridor of land known as the Lansway, reaching out like a road towards the continent lying beyond, which today was a mere suggestion of contours and cloud barely visible in the distance.

Across the waist of this isthmus, in sheer grey stone, rose the great southern walls of Bar-Khos known as the Shield.

Those walls – which had protected the city from land invasion for over three centuries, and therefore the island of Khos, breadbasket of the Mercian Isles – towered some ninety feet in height, and taller still where turrets rose from the battlements. They were old enough to have given the city its name of Bar-Khos – 'the Shield of Khos'. There were six bands of wall in all, or at least there had been until the Mannians had arrived with their flags waving and their declarations of conquest. Now just four stood blocking the Lansway, and two of those were of recent construction. In the original outermost one still standing, no gates or gateways remained: all such entrances had been sealed up with stone and mortar.

The Mount of Truth offered the highest vantage point in the city. It was from here, and here alone, that the ordinary citizen could witness what confronted the walls on the other side. The boy, doing so now, blinked as his gaze roved out from the Shield towards the Mannian besiegers arrayed like a white flood across the plain of the isthmus; the full might of the Imperial Fourth Army.

His young face grew pale, his eyes widening with every new detail they absorbed.

The Lansway was entirely covered by a city of bright tents, neatly arranged in rows and quarters by the streets of wooden buildings dividing them. The tent city faced the Shield from beyond countless lines of earthworks – ramparts of dirt raised up across a plain of dusty yellow – and meandering ditches choked with black water. Behind the closest sequence of these earthworks, like creatures basking in the heat of the sun, squatted the siege engines and cannon, belching smoke and constant noise as they fired at the city in a slow, unending regularity that had lasted – beyond everyone's expectation – for the last ten years.

'You were born on the very first day they assaulted the walls,' Marlee said from behind them, in a voice seemingly calm, as she unwrapped a loaf of honeyed keesh from their basket. 'I went into labour early, and you came out no bigger than a farl. It was due to the shock of losing my father, I think, for that was the morning he fell.'

The boy gave no impression of hearing her; what lay before him had seized his full attention. Yet, in the past, Juno had asked more than once to be told about the day he was born – only to be given the barest facts possible. Bahn and his wife each had their separate reasons for not wishing to recall it.

Give him time, Bahn thought, sitting himself on the grass to study the vista with his own more experienced eyes. Memories were stirring, unbidden, in the wake of his wife's words.

Bahn had been just twenty-three when the war had begun. He could still recall exactly where he had been when news had first arrived of refugees flooding towards the city from the continent. He had been seated in the taproom of the Throttled Monk, still thirsty after his fourth black ale, and drunk already. His mood had been foul that afternoon: he'd had altogether enough of his job as a shipping clerk at the city skyport, putting up with a foreman who was a stumpy-legged little dictator of the worst kind, and all for a wage that barely saw him and Marlee through to the end of each week.

The news, when it broke, was delivered by a fat skins merchant just returned from the south, the man's portly face a bright scarlet, as though he had run all the way home just to say what he revealed next. Pathia had fallen, he declared to them all breathlessly. Pathia, their immediate neighbour to the south, was the traditional enemy of Khos – the very reason the Shield had been built in the first place. Around the taproom his words fell upon a sudden silence. As they now listened, shock and wonder grew in equal measure. King Ottomek V, despised thirty-first monarch of the royal line of Sanse, had been foolish enough to be captured alive. The Mannians had dragged him screaming, twisting and turning through the streets of conquered Bairat behind a galloping white zel, until the skin had been flayed almost entirely from his body – along with his ears, his nose, his genitals. Near death, the king had then been cast down a well, where he had somehow clung on to life for an entire night, while the Mannians laughed down the shaft at his cries for mercy. At dawn, they had filled the well with rocks.

Even amongst the most hardened men in the taproom, such a fate drew muttered oaths and shakes of the head. Bahn grew fearful: this was bad news for them all. For the full length of his life, and more, the Mannians had been conquering nation after nation around the inland sea of the Midèrës. Never before, though, had they been so close as this to Khos. Around him, the debate rose in volume: shouts, arguments, thin attempts at humour. Bahn pushed his way outside. He hastened for home, back to his wife of barely a year. There he rushed up the stairs to their small damp room above the public bathhouse, and blurted all of it out in one desperate, drunken tirade. She tried to soothe him with soft words, then she made him some chee, her hands remaining miraculously steady. For a time – Bahn's mind needing a release from itself – they made love on the creaking bed, a slowly passionate affair, her gaze fixed constantly on his.

Together, later that night, they stood on the flat roof of the building, and listened with the rest of the inhabitants of Bar-Khos to the cries of the refugees pleading to be let in, thousands of them huddled beyond the walls. From other rooftops, people shouted for the gates to be opened; others demanded, in hot anger, for them to let the Pathians rot. Marlee had prayed quietly for the poor souls, he remembered, whispering under her breath to Erës, the great World Mother, her painted lips moving blackly under a strange light cast by the twin moons hanging over the south. *Oh mercy, Sweet Erës, let them in, let them have sanctuary.*

It was General Creed himself who had ordered the gates to be opened the next morning. The refugees flooded in bearing stories of slaughter, of whole communities put to the torch for their defiance against the invaders.

Even confronted with such alarming accounts, most in Bar-Khos considered themselves beyond harm. The great Shield would protect them. Besides, the Mannians would be busy enough with the newly conquered south.

Bahn and Marlee carried on with their lives as best they could. She was expecting again, and therefore taking it easy, cautious of risking another miscarriage. She drank infusions of herbs the midwife gave her and would sit for hours watching the busy street below, a hand splayed protectively over her belly. Sometimes her father would visit, still clad in his reeking armour, a giant of a man, his face hard, without flex, squinting at her with eyes dimmed by age. His daughter was precious to him, and he and Bahn would fuss over her until she finally snapped and lost her temper. Even that did not dissuade them for long.

Four months later, news came of an advancing imperial army. The mood in the city remained much the same. There were six walls after all, tall and thick enough to protect them. All the same, another call went out from the city council asking for volunteers to fill the ranks of the Red Guard, which had thinned considerably during the previous decades of peace. Bahn was hardly cut out to be a soldier, but he was a romantic at heart and, with a wife and child and a home to protect, in his own way he was stirred to action. He quit his job without fuss, simply not turning up one morning – a warm thrill in his belly on thinking of the foreman having a tantrum at his absence. That same day Bahn signed up to defend his city. At the central barracks, they handed him an old sword with a chipped blade, a red cloak of damp-smelling wool, a round shield, a cuirass, a pair of greaves and a helm all much too large for him . . . and a single silver coin. He was then told to report every morning to the Stadium of Arms for training.

Bahn had barely learned the names of the other recruits in his company, all still as green and untrained as he was, when the Mannian herald arrived on zelback to demand the city's surrender. Their terms were simple enough. Open the gates and most would be spared; but fight and all would be slain or enslaved. It was impossible, the herald announced to the high wall looming before him, to resist the manifest destiny of Holy Mann.

A trigger-happy marksman on the ramparts shot the herald off his mount. A cry rose up from the battlements: first blood.

The city held its breath, waiting for what was to come next.

At first their numbers seemed impossible. For five days the Imperial Fourth Army assembled across the width of the Lansway, tens of thousands stamping into position in an ordered procession, then spreading out to erect their colony of tents, earthworks, guns in numbers never seen before, mammoth siege towers – all before the collective gaze of the defenders.

Their barrage finally began with a single screeching whistle. Cannon shots pounded into the wall; one arched high and landed in a shattering explosion among the reserves of men behind. The defenders on the parapet hunkered down and waited.

On the morning of the first ground assault, Bahn was standing with some other raw recruits behind the main gates of wall one, the heavy shield hanging from his arm, a sword in his trembling hand. He had not slept. All night the Mannian missiles had crashed down around them, and horns like wild banshees had sounded from the imperial lines, fraying his nerves to tatters. Now in the early dawn he could think of only one thing: his wife Marlee at home with her unborn child, worried sick over both her husband and her father.

The Mannians came like a wave cresting over cliffs. With ladders and siege towers they attacked the ramparts in a single crashing line; Bahn, from below, watched in awe as white-armoured men launched themselves over the battlements at the Red Guard defenders, their battle cries like nothing he had ever heard before, shrill ululations that seemed barely plausible from human throats. He had already heard how the enemy ingested narcotics before battle, primarily to dispel their fears; and indeed they fought in a frenzy, without any regard for their own lives. Their ferocity stunned the Khosian defenders. The lines buckled, almost broke.

It was butchery, murderous and simple. Men slipped and pitched headlong from the heights. Blood flowed from the parapet gutters like the run-offs of a crimson rain so that soldiers had to run from underneath them with shields held over their heads. His father-in-law was up there somewhere, in amongst the grunts and hollers of collision. Bahn did not see him fall.

In truth, Bahn failed to use his sword even once that day. He did not even come face to face with the enemy.

He stood shoulder to shoulder with the other men of his company, most of them strangers to him still, every face that he saw a stark white, drained of spirit. The din of the battle robbed him of breath; he felt a sickness take hold of his body, like a dizzying sense of freefall. Bahn held his sword in front of him like a stick. It may as well have been a stick, for all he knew how to use it.

Someone's bowels had loosened nearby. The ensuing stench hardly inspired courage in the other men; it inspired only an urge to run, to be away from there. The recruits trembled like colts wanting to bolt from a stable fire.

Bahn did not know what it was that breached the gates in the end. One instant they were there before them, massive and stout, seemingly impregnable. Rall the baker was jabbering by his side, something about his helm and shield being his own, how he had bought them from the bazaar, a jumble of words that Bahn could barely hear. The next instant, Bahn was sprawled on his back, gasping for air, his mind stunned to numbness, a high-pitched ringing in his ears as he tried to remember who he was, what he was supposed to be doing here, why he was staring at a milky blue sky obscured with rolling clouds of dust.

As he lifted his head, grit pattered down all around him. Old Rall the baker was shouting in his face, eyes and mouth open wider than they had any normal right to be. The man was holding up the stump of his arm, the hand still dangling from a narrow length of tendon. Blood jetted in an arc that caught the slanting sunlight, becoming almost pretty in that moment. Pain descended on Bahn then. It stung the torn flesh of his cheeks, and at once he could feel the explosion of breath from Rall's screaming against his face, though he still could not hear him. He looked over to the gates, between the legs of men still on their feet, and found himself staring over a carpet of raw meat, of gristle, with hideous movement in amongst it. The gates were gone. In their place stood an unfurling curtain of dark smoke, parting here and there where white figures slipped through, howling as they came.

Somehow, he staggered to his feet as survivors from his company ran forward to fill the breach. That seemed like madness to Bahn: farmers and stall-keepers in ill-fitting armour rushing straight at killers intent on hacking them down. His eyes burned with what he saw: the impetus, the nerve of those men, when all about them their comrades lay exposed to the sky, or stumbled about, unhinged from their senses, jostling to get away. It roused something within Bahn. He thought of the sword in his hand, and of running to help those fellows, too few of them trying to stop the tide.

But, no, he no longer held his sword. He looked about for it, frantic, and saw old Rall again, on his knees, screaming up at him.

What does he want of me? Bahn had thought wildly. *Does he expect me to fix his hand?*

At the gates themselves, the defenders were being cut down like wheat. They were inexperienced recruits. And the Mannians were not. Somewhere behind Bahn, a sergeant yelled for the men to stand firm, spittle flying from his mouth as he shoved at their backs and tried to form them into a line. No one was listening to him, and those around Bahn were pushing against him, cursing, crying out, wanting only to flee.

He knew it was hopeless then; besides, he couldn't find his sword. There were other blades lying amongst the debris, but not one with the right number on the hilt – and it was vital to him, for some reason just then, to find the right one. Perhaps if he had done so he would have died that day. Instead, in those scattered moments he spent searching in vain, the urge to fight drained out of him. Instead, he wanted more than anything else to see Marlee again. To see their child when it was born. To live.

Bahn grabbed old Rall and hauled him clumsily over his shoulder. His knees buckled; but fear loaned him extra strength. With the rest of the panicking men, he allowed himself to be jostled back towards the gates of wall two, faces glancing back over shoulders, over Bahn's shoulders, no talk or shouting from them now, simply wordless panting. Even Rall stopped yelling and began thanking him, would not stop thanking him. His words emerged jerkily to the bounce of Bahn's footfalls.

It was a full rout, as hundreds of men raced back across the killing ground, casting their weapons and shields aside as they went. The distance was several throws to reach the safety of wall two. The old baker grew heavier on his back, so that Bahn's stride unevitably slackened and he fell behind the main mass of escapees. Rall shouted for him to move faster, warning that the enemy were close behind. Bahn hardly needed telling. He could hear the Mannians baying in hot pursuit.

They were the last to get through, just before the gates were slammed shut and sealed. Less fortunate men remained trapped on the other side. They pounded for the gates to be opened. They shouted of how they had wives and children at home. They cursed and pleaded. The gates stayed closed.

Bahn lay in a heap and listened to the shouting on the other side, more grateful than anything else in his whole life that it was not him still out there.

He had closed his eyes, overwhelmed. For a long time, lying face-down in the dirt, he had wept.

Now a gust of wind swept across the Mount of Truth, warm and humid. Bahn exhaled a breath of stale air and returned his attention to the hill and the summer's sunlight, and his son staring down at the walls.

'Drink?' asked Marlee, as she handed her husband a jug of cider, her motions slow and careful so as not to wake the child on her back. Bahn's mouth was parched. He took a drink, held a mouthful of the sweet liquid before swallowing. He then followed his son's gaze.

Even now, as he and the boy silently watched, an occasional missile struck or rebounded off the still intact outermost rampart facing the imperial army. A giant glacis of earth fronted the entire wall now, deflecting or absorbing such shots – one of the inspired innovations that had allowed them to draw out the Mannian siege for this long. Still, this rampart was sagging in places, and the battlements behind it gaped like toothless mouths where sections of stone and crenellations had fallen. Along these ragged defences, an almost imperceptible line of red-cloaked soldiers huddled behind the surviving cover; amongst them, crews operated squat ballistae and cannon, constantly firing back at the Mannian lines.

Behind the other three inner walls, more heavily garrisoned in comparison, cranes and labourers could be seen erecting yet another one. So far, four walls had fallen to the never-ending barrage of the enemy – at a staggering material expense to the Mannians. In response, the defenders had succeeded in building two new ones to replace them, but they could not hope to erect ramparts indefinitely. The latest construction lay close to the straight channel of the canal which cut across the Lansway to connect the two bays. Not far beyond this canal, the Lansway ended at the Mount of Truth, and beyond that sprawled the city itself. It was clear they were running out of room.

Bahn's son was peering down at the wall currently under fire.

Along its battlements, between the cannon, ballistae, and the occasional long-rifle firing in reply, men laboured with cranes as they raised great scoops of earth and rock. Some kept dropping out of sight as they were lowered on ropes over the far side, while others merely tipped the contents of the cranes' scoops over the outer rim. Even as they watched, a group of men pulling on ropes collapsed amidst a cloud of flying debris.

Juno gasped.

'Look there,' said Bahn, quickly drawing his son's attention away from the sight, and instead pointed out various structures dotted around the prospective killing grounds between the walls. They looked like towers, though they were open on all sides and not very tall. 'Mine shafts,' he explained. 'The Specials are fighting every hour down there, trying to stop the walls from being undermined.'

At last Juno looked down at his seated father.

'It's different, from what I was expecting,' he said. 'You fight there every day?'

'Some days. Though there are few battles any more. Just this.'

His words appeared to impress the boy. Bahn swallowed, turning away from what he recognized as pride in his son's eyes. Juno already knew that his grandfather had died defending the city. Even now he wore the old man's short-sword about his waist; and, when they returned home, he would no doubt insist that his father give him further lessons in its use. The boy talked often of how he would follow in his father's footsteps when he was old enough, but Bahn did not wish to encourage such ambitions. Better his son ran off to be a wandering monk, better even to sign up on a leaky merchanter, than stay here and fight to the inevitable end.

Juno seemed to read his mood. Softly, he asked, 'How long can we hold them off?'

Bahn blinked, surprised. That was the question of a soldier, not a boy.

'Papa?'

Bahn almost lied to his son then, even though he knew it would be an insult to the boy's growing maturity. But Marlee was sitting just behind them, his wife who had been raised to face the truth no matter how unpalatable it might be. He could sense her ears listening keenly in the silence that awaited his reply.

'We don't know,' he admitted, as he shut his eyes momentarily against another gust of wind. Bahn tasted salt on his lips, like the remnants of dried blood.

When he reopened them, it was to see Juno staring again at the walls, and the Mannian host that confronted them. He appeared to be studying the countless banners that were visible: to one side, the Khosian shield or the Mercian whorl on a sea-green background, dozens of them fluttering along the ramparts; on the other side the imperial red hand of Mann, with the tip of the little finger missing, emblazoned on a field of pure white – hundreds of them staked out across the isthmus. Intent on this scrutiny the boy's skin clung thin and tight to his face.

'There is always hope,' said Marlee reassuringly to her troubled son.

Juno looked to his father once more.

'Yes,' agreed Bahn. 'There is always hope.'

But even as he said these words, he could not meet his son's eyes.

CHAPTER TWO

Boon

The foot prodded him again, more insistent this time.

'Your dog,' came the voice through the thin material of his blanket. It was female, and sour. 'I think it's dead.'

Nico forced his eyes open a fraction, so that a glimmer of early sunlight tangled within his lashes. Too bright, he thought, as he hunkered further into the warmth of his own body. Too early.

'Leave me be,' he mumbled.

The blanket swept away, leaving him beached in the daylight. He clamped a hand over his eyes, squinted through the crack between his fingers, to see the girl standing over him, her hands on her hips. Lena, he recalled.

'Your dog, I said. I think it's dead.'

It took a few moments for her words to make sense. He was a poor riser these days; mornings were always a sombre, unwanted affair, and he did not like to face them.

'What?' he said, as he sat up and frowned at the girl, frowned also at a sun that shone several hours old in the sky. Boon was by his side where he had lain down last night. The old dog was still sleeping, surely, but flies were climbing over his muzzle, his blond fur. 'What?' said Nico again.

He scattered the flies with his hand, and ran it along Boon's coat. The dog did not stir.

'He was like that when I woke up,' came Lena's distant voice. 'I tell you, we'll be next if we don't get some proper food into us.'

'Boon?'

The dog looked terribly thin in the bright daylight. Ribs protruded along his side; his spine was a sharp ridgeline of bone. Nico expected an ear to twitch, or maybe a sudden sigh inspired from some animal dream. There was nothing.

He lay back on the grass, pulled the blanket over his head. Then he rested an arm across his old friend.

*

The summer drought had hardened the ground, so Nico used his knife to loosen it before digging the grave with his bare hands. He had chosen a spot beneath an old jupe tree on a hill just to the south of the park, not far from where they had been sleeping. Gaunt faces watched him as he worked. More than once during months past, he had fought away people trying to kill his dog, people desperate enough to crave the animal's flesh. Nico had shouted at them and thrown sticks, while Boon stood snarling at his side. Now he glared at them defiantly, the mud on his face streaked with tears. *I'll kill anyone who touches him*, he swore to himself miserably.

Boon weighed no more than a sack of sticks as Nico lifted him and laid him out in the shallow grave. For a while he knelt over him, stroking his golden fur. The flies were gathering again.

Boon had been just a pup when Nico's father had first brought him back to the homestead, Nico himself only a few months old. 'A companion to look after you,' his father had explained when Nico was years older. Boon by then had grown into an oversized hound, and the two of them were now inseparable. His kind had been bred for baiting deer and bear; for coursing upon open plains and forested slopes. This last year, living rough in the streets of the city, with so little food, had not been kind to him.

It was hard, pushing the dirt back into the hole, and then covering him with it.

'Goodbye, Boon,' he said at last, patting the earth flat, and his young voice emerged as a dry whisper, lonely as the sky.

He stood up, placing his straw hat on his head, wishing he had more to say. Words normally came easily to his lips.

His shadow lay across the grave: a solid form, its legs parted, hands clenched like balls, its head made bulbous by the hat. Its presence turned the dry, upturned earth black.

'I'm sorry I let you come to the city with me,' he said. 'But I'm glad you were here, Boon. I never would have survived this long otherwise. You were a good friend.'

Nico felt subdued as he shambled, with his pack, down to the great pond. He found himself a space amongst the other park-dwellers crowding the water's edge. There he washed his hands to clean the dirt from them, though his fingernails remained embedded with earth. He had torn the skin around them with his digging, and for some time he watched his blood seep in small clouds into the murk of the pond.

Nico swept the water clear of surface scum, took his covestick from his pack, and scrubbed his teeth. He was aware of the rank taste of the water on his lips, like silage he always thought, and was careful not to swallow any. Sunlight blinded him. Way out in the middle of the pond, the sun glowered in a fiery reflection. For a while he stared at that too, long enough for his eyes to hurt.

Lost, aimless, his thoughts returned to him slowly, settling down with care. *Just walk*, they said to him. *Get on your feet and walk.*

Nico stood and hitched his pack, all that he owned, on to his back. The blood rushed from his head and he swayed for a moment, feeling nauseous and weak. Around him the park was choked with refugees, its lawns of yellowgrass long since trampled to bare earth, its trees cut to stumps that poked in sorry isolation from the ground. He placed a foot forwards, allowed himself to fall into the rhythm of a forward stride. It was without haste or even purpose that he picked his way between wooden lean-tos and patched tents stitched out of old clothing. He passed groups of dirty children, as thin as sticks, and men and women with blunted looks in their eyes, struggling to bear up to more than just the present. Some were Khosian by appearance, but many more were refugees from the southern continent, Pathians and Nathalese; or more recent arrivals from the north, from the island of Lagos or from the Green Isles. They were strangely quiet, for so many people. Dogs barked, of course. Babes howled for mothers' milk. But, overall, they saved their energies for things more important than talk.

Nico's stomach growled at the scents of their cooking. For two weeks now he'd eaten nothing but beggar's broth – hot chee with hunks of keesh bobbing in it. No one could hope to live for long on a diet like that, and already his breeches hung slack from the belt he had re-notched tighter just a few days ago. As he moved, he could feel his protruding bones rub against the coarseness of his filthy clothes. The girl Lena was right: if he did not eat properly soon, he would lie down and die, just like Boon.

Just walk, soothed his mind.

Nico pressed through the main gates of Sunswallow park into the district beyond. There, in the streets, people walked without hurry, chatting or lost in their private thoughts. Man-drawn rickshaws rattled noisily over the cobbles, bearing single passengers of every kind. From the south, Nico could hear the grumble of guns, just over a laq away.

He took off towards the heart of the city, in the direction of those guns, his loose soles slap-slapping against the cobbles, his head thrust forward. A few blocks later he rounded a corner and emerged into the Avenue of Lies. The noise was overwhelming, like stepping out of a deep cave into a roaring torrent. Shouting was more common than ordinary talk. Hordes of street performers rang bells or played flutes for small change; wind chimes strung across the streets clattered in the breeze. It was as though the populace of Bar-Khos wished to make as much clamour as possible, so as to drown out any reminders of the ongoing siege from their daily lives.

Trees lined much of the avenue. In one of them, on a bare branch that twisted and drooped its way towards the street, a black and white pica sat watching the traffic below. From habit, Nico found himself tipping his head to the bird.

The mere act reminded him of a different morning. Of the day he had left home for good.

He had seen a pica then, too. It had laughed down at him from the roof of the cottage as he took off into the early glow of dawn, his pack on his back and his head filled with naivety. He had disliked that particular bird about as much as he disliked senseless superstitions, yet he had nodded to it anyway, as his mother always did, and set his feet to the path that would lead him down to the coast road and, from there, a four-hour march to the city. He had not wished to tempt fate on that of all days.

That same morning he'd found that leaving home was hardly the joyous occasion he had dreamed about. With each step, his sense of guilt had grown ever sharper in his chest. He knew his mother would be distraught at finding him gone in this way. And Boon . . . Boon would pine in his own canine way.

He had gently stroked the dog as he slept on regardless on the old rag blanket beneath Nico's own bed, the hound being too old, by then, for early rises. Boon had whimpered in his sleep, like a young pup, and quietly farted.

'I can't take you with me,' Nico had whispered. 'You wouldn't like it in the city.'

He had then departed quickly, before he could change his mind.

Guilt had not stopped him from walking away, though, as he carried onwards down the path, it had struck him, with unexpected force, how he was facing more than just the groves of cane trees and swaying redgrass and the gently winding track immediately ahead. In front of him now stretched a great expanse of the unknown, a future that was daunting and without bounds. The thought might have been enough to turn him back there and then, if he'd had any suitable alternative – but he did not. Better to run away than remain in the oppressive atmosphere of the cottage with Los, his mother's latest lover. A scoundrel, Nico considered. A man he despised.

Nico had been sixteen years of age that morning. Turning the corner, losing sight of the cottage and his childhood home, he had never felt such trepidation and loneliness before then, such a bleak isolation of his spirit.

When he heard the padded footfalls of Boon approaching behind him, he had smiled within, despite himself.

Boon had appeared at his side, tail thrashing in excitement.

'Go home!' Nico had hissed without much sincerity.

Boon panted without concern. He had no intention of going anywhere that Nico was not.

Again, he had tried to shoo the dog away. His heart was hardly in it though. He ruffled the fur of Boon's neck. 'Come, then,' he had told him.

Together, with the day brightening, they had continued on their long trudge towards the city.

Nico now smiled at the memory. It did not seem a mere year ago. Rather, it seemed like a lifetime had passed since then. Change was the true measure of time, he had come to realize. Change and loss.

He was currently heading south, following the general direction of traffic moving towards the bazaar or the harbour. He did not yet know which destination he would choose; for he did not yet have one in mind. On either side of him, buildings rose three or four storeys high, drawing Nico's gaze upwards to rooftops overgrown with greenery. High above their chimneys, merchant balloons hung in the air, tethered by lines of rope. Wicker baskets dangled underneath them, and in one he spied the tiny face of a young boy. The lad was shielding his eyes as he gazed out towards the coast, watching the distant signal platforms for signs of approaching merchanters. Beyond him, the blue wash of sky thinned to white under the sun's blinding glare. Gulls wheeled up there, mere specks.

Nico instinctively turned left, into Gato's Way. The bazaar then. He wondered at himself and the unconscious choice in that. The bazaar held few attractions for someone starving and without means. Yet it was also where he and his mother used to come to sell their home-brewed potcheen once a month, travelling to the city in their rickety cart to earn what little money they could. Those trips had been the high point of his month, when he was younger; exciting yet still safe in his mother's presence.

A man pulling an empty rickshaw veered past him as Nico stepped into a riot of noise. The bazaar was a rolling mishmash of a place. Its great square, so vast that its furthest edges were obscured by smoke and haze, was open on one side to the sea front and the grey stone arms of the harbour, where masts swayed as thickly as trees in a forest. On the other three sides the space was enclosed by the shady porticos of chee houses, inns, and temples dedicated to the Great Fool. A maze of stalls stretched between them; people in their thousands jostled or bartered or perused the goods for sale. Nico, suddenly eager to lose himself amongst the press, allowed himself to be swept into it all.

Everywhere, colours shone sun-soaked in the heaving spaces. Nico swiped flies from his face, inhaled the damp reek of sweat, pungent spices, animal dung, perfumes, fruits. His stomach was on fire now. It was eating itself, and the rest of his emaciated body, with every step that he took. He felt dizzy, unreal. His eyes were interested only in the foodstuffs all around him, on the stalls already half empty of goods. Thoughts of snatching an apple, a stick of smoked crab, filled his mind. He fought against such thoughts, since he knew he did not have the strength to run if it came to a chase.

For a time, simply to distract himself from these rising temptations, he stopped in the lee of one stall to listen to some street traders singing out with gusto over the heads of the passers-by. Their melodies were pleasing to hear, even though they sang of nothing more profound than goods on offer and prices for the day. On a whim, Nico asked several of them for food in return for work. They shook their heads: no time for him. They were barely surviving themselves, their expressions said. One old woman, on a stall selling sheets of gala lace next to baskets of half-rotten potatoes, chuckled as though he had made some kind of joke . . . though she checked herself when she noticed his brittle gaze, his gaunt appearance.

'Come back in a few days,' she told him. 'I'm not promising you anything, mind, but I might have some things needing done. Come and see me then, yes?'

He thanked her, though this was of little help to him. In a few days he might be too far gone.

Maybe, Nico reflected moodily, it was time to go home. What was left for him in the city now? The Red Guard wouldn't have him; he'd tried more times than he could remember to enlist like his father before him, but he looked his youthful age and could not pass for being any older. And there was little casual work here in Bar-Khos. Over the past year he had been lucky if he had gained a few days' labour here and there, mostly on the docks sweating under heavy loads for a pittance. In between, nothing but daily desperation. There were simply too many people available for too few jobs. Along with the worsening food crisis due to the siege, it was becoming ever more difficult to survive here.

The loose confederacy of islands known as Mercia was still free, certainly, but it was effectively besieged by Mannian sea blockades, in the same way that Bar-Khos was besieged by the Imperial Fourth Army. No safe passage existed anywhere in or out of the isles themselves. Since every nation of the Midères had fallen save for the desert Caliphate in the east, all foreign waters were patrolled by imperial fleets. Only a single foreign trade route remained open to Mercia, and that was the Zanzahar run, as perilous a route for convoys as could be, hard fought over every day and with their shipping harried constantly by the enemy.

The blockades were slowly choking the life from the Free Ports and, as a consequence, many survived now on nothing more than the free keesh handed out by the city council, or what they grew on their rooftops or in small vegetable plots, or by resorting to crime and prostitution, or by masquerading as monks of the Dao, the only ones still legally allowed to beg in the streets. Or else they starved, like Nico.

At least back home he would have some food in his belly, a roof over his head. Besides, knowing his mother, by now she had likely thrown Los out of the cottage after finally opening her eyes to him; or, if not, then Los would have run out on her, no doubt taking everything valuable she owned, and either way some new man would now be occupying the place of his absent father.

Still, he loathed the thought of returning to his mother as a failure, having to admit he was unable to stand on his own two feet.

But you are a failure. You couldn't even take care of Boon. You just let him die.

He wasn't ready for that thought. He swallowed it down, blinking hard.

It was now almost noon, and the asago had begun to lift the canopies with its hot breath. It came always at that time of year, and especially at that hour. Soon enough the rising heat was driving many people into the cooler environment of the surrounding chee houses, where they might sit out the siesta in moderate peace and comfort, and compare business or play games of ylang while they sipped from tiny cups of thick chee. Nico barely noticed the heat, as he made the most of the dwindling crowds and struck out unimpeded for the south-west corner of the vast square where, like a great exhalation of relief, it opened out on to the wide expanse of the harbour.

It was there that Nico found the street performers set up for the day. They stood or sat in whatever spaces they had found between the steady flow of longshoremen that passed from harbour to bazaar. Many were packing up for the siesta, though the hardier – perhaps the more needy – were opting to stay on in spite of the heat. Nico scanned the jugglers and the tongue readers, and the begging monks seated before their bowls – fake monks, his mother had always claimed – until at last he came to a group of performers barely visible for the surrounding crowd. He pushed closer for a better view of them.

They were a troupe of actors, two men and a woman he had never seen before. Without further thought, he squeezed through the crowd until he stood at the fore.

The play was a simple affair, the story of a poor seaweed farmer and his love for a beautiful witch of the sea. It was *The Tales of the Fish*, and narrated by the younger of the two men, himself no older than Nico, in that simple style of prose that was increasing in popularity these days over the long-winded sagas of old.

In a shaky, high-pitched voice the young man was recounting the story, while the woman and the older man played their parts in mime. It was obvious why they had attracted such a large audience. The woman, tall and lithe and wonderfully bronzed, played the sea-witch in appropriate costume, which meant she was naked, save for her straight golden hair and the strips of seaweed wrapped around a few select parts of her body. They were distracting, those delicate flashes of thigh and nipple, and kept snagging Nico's eyes as he tried to focus on the performance itself.

Nico liked to watch performers wherever he could find them, and he judged this woman a fine actress, whose subtle skills contrasted noticeably with her partner's lesser talents, which seemed few. The man was too pronounced and swaggering in his role, and few of the audience seemed to be paying him much heed. They were all ogling her flesh, like he was.

Nico was still gazing enraptured when a round of applause heralded the tragic end to the story – the seaweed farmer having swum to his death while pursuing his beloved out to sea. As the young narrator moved round the crowd with an empty hat, in search of donations, Nico found that his mouth was hanging open, and closed it with a snap. The actress meanwhile slipped a thin robe over her shoulders, and shucked the seaweed off from underneath it into a wooden pail. As she swept her hair back, she glanced around the crowd and caught his eye. Her gaze lingered.

A year ago Nico would have lowered his gaze straight to his feet in embarrassment. This past year, though, living in the city, he had gained more practice in meeting such glances, for he had received his fair share of them. He did not know why. Nico did not consider himself particularly handsome; even properly fed he had always been thin. And his face, whenever he had studied it in his mother's tarnished vanity mirror, had always looked strange to him: his nose turned up slightly at the end, he had lips too wide and full, his skin was freckled like a girl's, and, if he looked closely enough between his eyebrows, where once he had scratched at the childpox, he would see not one circular scar, but two.

In truth he did not understand why the actress's long-lashed eyes stayed fixed on his for so long. At least he was able to meet her calm appraisal for a while, sufficient time at least to be counted in seconds, before her confident gaze wore down his own and, his courage breaking, he looked away.

'You're blushing,' came a voice nearby.

It was Lena, standing right behind him in the crowd, her eyes narrowed against the sunlight. She looked pretty like that, without the usual frown cooling her Pathian features.

'It's hot,' he told her, and Lena's thin lips curled at the corners. With a tone of suspicion in his voice, he continued: 'I didn't notice you standing there.'

'I was following you,' she admitted, matter-of-factly. 'To make sure . . . you know . . . that you were all right.'

He did not believe that. So far, Lena had not shown herself overly concerned with the welfare of others. He wondered what she was after.

'Listen,' she continued, 'I'm sorry about your dog. Really. But we need to do something, Nico. We need to eat soon.'

He shrugged. 'They won't be handing out any more keesh until tomorrow. Anyway, I'm thinking it might be time for me to go home.'

'You don't really want to do that, do you?'

'Hardly.'

'Good, because I have a much better idea, if you're interested. A way for us to make some money.'

Ah, he thought. *Here it comes.*

She was standing close enough for one breast to brush across his front. That shocked him, physically, even more so because he suspected it was no accident. Nico studied her from beneath the brim of his hat, wondering, not for the first time, what it might be like to kiss her.

'Why do I have a feeling I won't like this?' he asked, his voice sounding coarse.

Lena swiped a lock of dark hair aside from her face, and spoke softly, intimately. 'Because you won't. But we don't have many choices left to us, do we?'

*

The asago rasped across the rooftops of Bar-Khos, bearing with it the fine grains of the Alhazii desert six hundred laqs to the east. The dust stung Nico's eyes and he squinted, grimacing, wanting to be down from here. He was not comfortable with heights.

Nico could clearly see the Shield from his rooftop vantage, and the Mount of Truth topped with its scalp of parkland, amid which rose the tall, many-windowed bulk of the Ministry of War. For a few welcome moments the breeze dropped, giving the sensation of an oven door closing. From the distance, he heard the regular percussion of cannon fire, followed by a scream, barely audible.

'This is crazy. What if we get caught?'

'Look,' she snapped from behind him, 'it's either this or I go down to the docks and lift my skirt for whoever will pay me. You'd rather I did that instead?'

'You don't even own a skirt.'

'Maybe after a few hand shanks I'd be able to afford one. You could become my pimp then. I'm starting to think you'd even like that – standing back, doing nothing.'

He sighed, and kept moving.

Nico had taken his shoes off, to carry in his hands, as suggested by Lena for better footing on the roof tiles. It worked, for sure, but the tiles were blisteringly hot against the bare soles of his feet. He was almost dancing across them. 'My feet,' he complained, 'they're burning.'

'You want to fall and crack your skull?'

'I want to get off this roof, Lena. That's what I want.'

She didn't respond.

They were working their way across the sloping roof of a taverna, three storeys above the streets of the city. The taverna encompassed two buildings, one taller than the other, and the remaining two storeys of the second rose up ahead, a wall of crumbling whitewash punctuated occasionally by narrow windows. Some of those were shuttered tight; others were open, flowing with curtains of fine gala lace.

Around Nico's feet, lizards sprawled across the hot tiles, casting ancient, baleful stares as Lena took the lead, her own eyes quick and nervous. She peered through one of the open windows, ducked away at the sound of voices inside. Crouching, she padded up to another, checked inside and rejected it, padded on to yet another.

Nico hopped from one foot to the other, the pain too much to bear. He slipped his shoes back on, wondering what in Erēs he was doing here with this girl, wondering too if she had done this somewhere before. They were risking a public flogging if they were caught.

'This one,' she whispered, as Nico approached the window she had finally selected. 'Inside with you, and search the bag for a purse.'

Me? mouthed Nico.

'Yes, you. You haven't done anything yet but complain.'

'Lena, I mean it, let's go before it's too late.'

The scowl on her face tightened. 'You want to eat today or not?' she demanded.

'Not if it means going through with this business. Do as you wish. I'm leaving.'

She caught him in her grip as he turned to go.

'I mean it,' she hissed. 'If we don't do this, then I'm heading for the docks. Whatever it takes, I don't care. I won't starve to death like your dog did.'

Her words and grip seemed to hold him in a sudden spell. His stomach rattled, urging him on. He nodded dumbly.

She released him, offered him a foot-lift. He barely knew what he was doing as he gritted his teeth and scrambled upwards.

Awkwardly, he passed through the swaying lace curtains, trying to keep as silent as he could. His body trembled, and the whitewashed sill was warm against his palms. Inside, he lowered his feet towards the stone floor. His soles settled quietly, he straightened – then froze.

On the bed lay a figure clad in a dark robe.

Nico's throat made a good attempt at choking itself. His heart seemed to be causing such a racket, he was sure it could be heard by anyone within earshot. The figure was asleep, though, his chest rising and falling in a regular, shallow rhythm.

The man's skin was pure black. A farlander, decided Nico – an old farlander with a bald head and a tough, lean face etched with lines.

And something else there, on the cheeks, glistening bright in a ray of sunlight that slanted through the swaying lace.

He's crying in his sleep, realized Nico.

Lena glared at him from the window. There was no way of getting past that face. Nico swallowed his fears and a sudden rising sense of guilt. He squeezed his sweating fists and stole across the room to where a chair sat. Carved from twisted driftwood, it was laden with a leather backpack. He reached it without causing noise. From the window Lena bared her teeth, her hand flapping in a signal to hurry.

It was a fumbling, sweaty business searching through the leather pack, and Nico's hands moved clumsily as the sweat stung his eyes. For a moment he heard voices outside the room, and floorboards creaking as someone walked past outside the door. That only made him work faster, till at last he found a purse, fat and heavy with coinage.

Lena flapped her hands again. The old man slept on.

Nico was just about to leave, when he noticed something hanging from the same chair. It was a necklace of some kind, though not a pretty thing fashioned with jewels or silver. This was distinctly ugly, with the appearance of a large leathery nut, and it was coated in something that looked like dried blood.

A seal, realized Nico. *That old man wears a seal.*

Almost of its own accord, his hand reached towards the pendant. Behind him, the old man groaned suddenly in the bed. Nico stopped himself in time, pulled his hand away. What was he thinking of?

He turned to go, and almost dropped the purse in alarm. The old farlander was sitting upright, blinking at him with strange folded eyes.

Nico felt his bowels loosen. He could not move. He looked to the door, to the window, and licked his dry lips.

The old man turned his head, looking from one side of the room to the other. It was as though he could barely see.

'Who's there?' he croaked.

Nico was past containing himself any longer. With six quick strides he was across the room, and clambering out through the window.

'He's awake!' he hissed as they scuttled back across the sloping rooftop, the lizards regarding them as they hurried from the scene.

'And half-blind by the sound of it,' Lena replied, moving onwards. 'Hurry up!'

Nico followed more slowly, focused on negotiating the tiles without slipping.

They reached the end of the rooftop, where it dropped a few feet on to that of another building.

'Here,' said Lena, turning back to him. 'Give it here,' she demanded, eying the purse in Nico's hand. He pulled up short, the purse clutched to his chest.

Nico did not want this money. Somehow, though, he did not want Lena to have it either.

She made a snatch for the purse, but Nico jerked backwards.

It was then that his left foot slipped out from under him.

He fell sideways, catching a glimpse of Lena's hands grabbing desperately towards him – for the purse, no doubt – before he slammed against the tiles in a scattering of lizards and expelled breath, and that was that – he was rolling and clattering down the side of the roof, all the way to its edge, where his legs swung out high over the cobbled street, a gasp in his throat and his fingers scrabbling for a hold that never came.

He fell off.

Nico screamed with all the remaining force of his lungs. His shoulder glanced the sign of the taverna, and his entire flopping body spun once before he continued plummeting face-down towards a canvas awning, hollering as he crashed through it, still screaming as the hard cobbled street lurched upwards, his arms throwing themselves over his face for protection as he smashed through one of the tables positioned outside the taverna.

Winded, Nico lay amidst the debris of awning and table, as chippings of wood and paint and fabric fell like snow all around him. After a pause, a fat old lady moved forwards to help him; other folk sat in shock with cups of chee still half-raised to their lips. Nico was stunned, unable to draw a breath. He could see his straw hat resting in front of him. He could barely believe he was still alive.

Of all the luck, though: the purse full of money must have fallen from his grasp as he slid down the rooftop, and it must have since been making its own slower, more complicated, though just as inevitable progress off the edge. As the old women bent to give aid the purse exploded on the cobbles right in front of Nico's face, its silver and gold coins scattering across the street in a horrifying riot of noise and sunlit reflections. The old woman clamped a hand to her mouth. Passers-by turned to stare at the scene. Eyes took in this boy, this fortune in money, this fall from the roof of a taverna, and within moments the cry was raised.

'Thief!' they shouted, with Nico still too winded to even move. 'Thief!' they shouted in chorus, as he flopped on to his back and stared up at the roof he had just pitched from, to see that Lena was gone, and only the sun remained to glare down at his ill fate.

In his daze, Nico was hoping that this was all a dream, a nightmare dream that he would soon awaken from. But a pair of rough hands were soon shaking that fantasy out of him. And, as he was dragged to his feet, reality impacted with a greater force than even the ground itself. *Oh sweet Erēs* . . . his mind yelled at him . . . *this is real . . . this is actually happening!*

And then he passed out.

CHAPTER THREE

Visitations

He had never seen a gaol before, let alone spent the night in one.

The place was an open affair, and most of its inmates could wander freely within its walls. There was even a taverna of sorts for those with the money to frequent it, and a cantina that sold better food than the gruel slopped out in the yard. On the whole the guards – mostly prisoners themselves – kept out of the way and left the other inmates to themselves.

Nico settled in the corner of a cell, one of many to be found in the labyrinth deep beneath the main yard. He sat on a layer of mouldy, lice-infested straw, a single oil lamp hanging above the doorway for light. The straw reeked of stale urine, and he could see cockroaches scurrying within it.

The same was occupied by other thieves and debtors of various ages, some of them as young as Nico or even younger. His fellow inmates paid him little notice; mostly they came and went and rarely stopped there for long. Nico was grateful for that as he sat in his corner, nursing his bruised and aching body, his thoughts circling like dark flapping birds intent on tormenting him. Try as he might, he could not help but think of home and his mother.

She would be distraught if she ever heard of what he had become: a common thief caught in the act. She would be angry with him beyond words.

But then, his mother was hardly without fault herself. After all, if he traced his present predicament back a whole year or more, then she was as much to blame for it as he. She was the one who had needed to fill her empty life with a string of ill-suited lovers. She was the one who had chosen to ignore the antagonism between Los and her son, causing Nico to be driven out as a consequence; then driven to this.

Los had been yet another in a long line of his mother's poor choices. On the first night she had brought him home from the crossroads taverna, dressed in fine clothing that was much too loose on him – clearly stolen – the man had eyed the contents of the cottage as if to assess what they were worth, including his mother. It was obvious he had set about catching her that night; the couple had made so much noise in the bedroom that Nico was forced to drag his bedding out to the stable and bed down with their old zel, Happy.

He resented her for it, this weakness regarding men. He knew she had her reasons, knew too that she was hardly the one he should be resenting for what had become of them both, mother and son. But there it was, and he could not help it.

This had already been the worst day of his life, and the rest of it passed in numb shock, timeless and awful. With the falling of night, marked here not in fading daylight but by the snuffing of the lamps and the slamming of distant heavy doors, the stench within the place grew even more fetid, a drifting, clogging miasma that bore with it the smells of the human animal caged too long in its own squalor. It became so bad that Nico tied his kerchief around his mouth and nose. It helped little though, and he would occasionally have to lean to one side and lift it in order to spit from his mouth the rank taste that had accumulated on his tongue.

It seemed that whatever truce existed between the inmates during the hours of daytime vanished during those long ensuing hours of blackness. A fight broke out in another cell, shouts and catcalls and then the long keening howls of a man in pain, which dimmed to the occasional sob and then to nothing. For a time, a dull thudding penetrated the stone wall at his back, as though someone was crashing his head against the other side, while shouting out with each impact muted words that might have been, *let me out, let me out.*

Nico could not bring himself to sleep in such a place. Still, he was tired, exhausted from the day's events, and the thought of those still to come. So he lay awake listening to the snores of his cellmates, swiping the odd cockroach from his body, and cursed himself for ever coming to this city, for bringing Boon along with him, for getting involved with Lena and her fool ideas.

He had known that she was not to be trusted, having displayed few signs of scruples in his company. What was she doing now, at this same moment, he wondered? Did she even care that he had been seized by the Guards and thrown in the city gaol to await his punishment? He doubted it.

Nico stared into the gloom, only too aware of what they did to thieves in the city. It was this fate he was trying most of all not to think about. Last Harvest Festival he had seen a thief flogged and branded for his crime, and the young delinquent had not been much older than Nico himself.

Nico did not know if he could bear such punishment.

*

Sometime later in the night he jerked from a daze to find a hand pressed against his leg and a face breathing foul air into his own. He jerked upright, shoved the unseen man's weight away from him, shouted something that was more a cry of fright than distinct words. A muttered curse in the darkness, the scraping shuffle of someone retreating.

He rubbed his face to wake himself fully, then hunkered back against the wall.

He needed to get out of this place. He could barely breathe, in this airless, roiling stench. The blackness pressed down on him like a blanket of heavy velvet. He felt trapped, knowing that till morning he could not simply stand up and walk outside of his own volition, not even to see the sky, feel the fresh air upon his face. A memory that was more a recollection of sharp emotion came to him then: that time he had found the snare while walking in the hills overlooking their cottage – the tightened loop of wire holding the severed limb of a wild dog, flesh still hanging in shreds from the leg bone that had been chewed clean through.

A sound of shuffling feet in the darkness: someone approaching again. Nico tensed, ready to lash out.

I will tear off your flesh with my teeth, he thought, *if you do not back away from me.*

'Relax,' came a voice. 'I'm a friend.'

A man sat down next to him, the sound of his hands fumbling within his clothing.

A flame ignited in the darkness, at first too bright to look at. Nico squinted with a palm shielding his face. For a moment the flame sizzled and curled, as the blackened end of a cigarillo burned and glowed red. Then the man blew out the match, plunging them into a darkness even deeper than before.

'You know, I've been lying awake all night trying to figure how I recognize your face.' The red tip of the cigarillo smeared through the air and crackled into renewed brightness as the man inhaled, lighting up the extremities of his face while casting its hollows into shadow.

'Your father,' he said, exhaling. 'I used to know your father.'

Nico blinked, his eyes still swimming with spots of colour.

'Of course you did,' he said, sarcastically.

'Don't call me a liar, boy. You're his spitting image. Your father was married to a redhead by the name of Reese. A fine-looking woman, if I recall.'

Nico let his hand drop from his face, sheathing his anger for the moment. 'Yes, my mother,' Nico agreed. 'You truly knew him, then?'

'As well as any man. I fought with him under the walls for two years.'

'You were a Special?'

'Surely. Though it seems a lifetime ago now, thank the Fool. I make a living now, a small one, playing rash. Rest of the time, when I can't repay my debts, I'm obliged to linger here.' The man rubbed a hand across the stubble of his chin. 'And what of you? What brings you to this condition?'

Nico had no wish to get into the whole sorry affair. 'My healer said it would be good for my lungs, so I come down here from time to time.'

'Your father had wit, too,' the voice replied without the merest hint of humour. 'It was the one thing I liked about him.'

There was an edge to his voice as he said this. Nico heard it, and waited for him to say more. The tobacco smoke curled about his face for a moment, the scent pleasant here in this foul place. It reminded him of nights sitting around a campfire in some park or empty building, with Lena and the others he had come to know while without home or shelter, Nico cracking jokes and watching the bottles of cheap wine and the tarweed roll-ups pass freely between them, their laughter raw, while the warm circle of light held at bay the hard day that was inevitably to come.

'We didn't see eye-to-eye on occasion,' the man continued in his sour drawl. 'He accused me once of cheating at rash. Though he couldn't leave it be at that, of course. Had to go and catch me out in front of the whole squad. Cost me a lot of money, did your father. I got the man back, though.'

A cough followed that might equally have been dry laughter.

'To be honest with you I wasn't hardly surprised when he lit out on us, and deserted like he did. The last time I saw those scared eyes of his, I knew what he was thinking. Clear as day I saw it.'

Nico's jaw clenched tight. His nostrils flared. He took a breath and said, coolly, 'My father was no coward.'

Again that cough. 'I don't mean anything by it. Everyone's a coward when it comes down to it, save for the crazy ones. Some are just more scared than others, is all I'm saying.'

Nico's breathing was now loud enough to be heard above the snoring of the other men.

'Easy now, it's only talk, and talk's not worth a damn. Here, have a draw.'

Nico ignored the burning end of the cigarillo held before his face.

He thought of his father instead: a tall, straight-backed figure in his memory, long-haired and kind of eyes, and his words softly spoken. The same man laughing wildly, with a pitcher of ale in his hand, while grabbing his mother by the waist to dance with her, or snatching up his jitar to pluck them some poorly composed song. A hike the two of them had made together in the lonely hills. A sunny Foolsday when he had taken Nico to some beach so that he himself could gaze out to sea while Nico played down by the shore line.

Nico had been ten when his father enlisted with the Specials. The enemy was pushing harder than ever before, it was explained. Every day some new Mannian tunnel was encountered, or the Mannians themselves broke through into the underground works of the defenders. The Specials were taking heavy losses, and they needed volunteers.

For a month at a time his father would go off to the city and fight beneath the walls of the Shield, then come home a slightly different man. With every return he seemed quieter, and less handsome in appearance.

On one visit home he had lost a whole ear, so that only an orifice remained on that side of his head. Yet Reese still embraced him and whispered soft words in his damaged ear loud enough for Nico to overhear, telling his father how relieved she was to see him still alive. Another time, his father arrived at the door with a bandage wrapped all around his head. When he took it off some days later, it looked as though his remaining ear had been chewed by a dog. Over time his eyebrows faded to nothing. His long hair became stubble. Scars criss-crossed his scalp, face and lips. He began to hunch his once broad shoulders as though he was permanently cold.

Nico's mother would try to hide her horror at these changes in the man that she loved, but often some unguarded expression would betray her.

When his father had finally returned for his first prolonged leave of absence from the Shield, Nico barely recognized the man who eyed his son as though looking at a stranger, and sat by himself out in the rain, and never smiled, and seldom spoke, and drank heavily. An atmosphere developed inside the cottage. His father would shout over the smallest of annoyances, till Nico grew tense and ever-expectant of trouble.

He took to going outside more with Boon, the two of them wandering the forest and the land around their cottage. When the weather was bad, Nico would stay in his room, with the door shut, and recount in his mind the stories that he knew, or recall *The Tales of the Fish* he had seen in his visits to the city, thus passing the time in idle fantasy.

One night, his father drank himself into a rage so consuming that he attacked Nico's mother, dragging her around the room by the hair while Nico yelled and begged for him to stop. He struck out at Nico and knocked him to the floor. Then, just as suddenly, stopped, blinking down at his son's shocked expression, before he stumbled out into the night.

Returning the next morning, his father packed his personal things and left, while Nico and his mother still slept huddled together in his small bed. Nico felt as though his world had given way beneath his feet. His mother had cried for a long time after that.

Nico now clenched his fists in the close darkness of the cell, and sighed. 'He had his reasons for leaving,' he said to the unseen man.

The cigarillo puffed, puffed, faded.

'Aye, well, scared or not, you'd know better than any I reckon.'

'What do you mean by that?'

'I mean to say the blood of the father most certainly runs through the son. What's true of him will be true of you.'

Nico felt the heat flushing his cheeks. He turned away from the stranger, wanting no more from him.

Shouts echoed from another cell, the words barely intelligible; a madman raving about how the Mannians were coming from across the sea to burn them all alive.

The glow of the cigarillo quickly vanished as the visitor stubbed it out against his palm. He grunted as he rose, and then he paused there, muttering something to himself. As he turned back to Nico, his heavy hand sought his shoulder and patted it once.

'You're all right now, son,' the man said. 'You can sleep now.'

He left with the lingering flavour of the smoke still coiling where he had sat.

No one else bothered Nico after that.

*

His mother came in the morning, dressed all in black as though attending a funeral. Her eyes were puffy from crying and the red hair pulled tight against her head gave a pinched, determined set to her features. It was the first time Nico had seen her in over a year.

Los was with her, clad in his best, pretending to be piously shocked at this thing young Nico had done. It was Los who spoke first, as they stood facing each other through the bars that separated inmate from visitor, in the dim, cool vault that served for these occasions.

'You look a mess,' he said.

Nico was lost for words. His mother and Los were the last people he had expected to see before him.

'How did you know?' he asked her, keeping his voice low.

His mother approached as though to reach out to him, but she was prevented by the bars and anger flashed suddenly in her eyes.

In a cold tone, she replied: 'Old Jaimeena saw you being dragged through the streets by the Guards, and was good enough to ride out and tell me.'

'Oh,' Nico said.

'*Oh?* Is that all you have to say for yourself?'

Her anger was like a breath of air against his own; it fanned embers that had lain dormant in him since the day he walked free from the cottage.

'I didn't ask you to come here,' he snapped. 'Nor him, either.'

Surprise crossed her face, and Los came to her side, all the while fixing Nico with hard eyes.

Nico stared back. He'd be damned if he would be the first to look away.

His mother made to speak, then faltered. All at once her shoulders dropped, her armour shattered. A hand reached through the bars. Nico felt it slide around the back of his neck, fingers gripping him and pulling his head towards her, into an embrace between the cool metal.

'My son,' she whispered into his ear. 'What have you done? I never took you for a thief.'

He was surprised to feel the sting of tears in his eyes. 'I'm sorry,' he said. 'I was desperate, starving.'

She made a soothing sound, stroked his face. 'I've been so worried about you. Every time we came to the city I looked out for you, but all I ever saw were people going hungry. I wondered if you were managing to survive at all.'

He took a shuddering breath. 'Boon . . .' he managed. 'Boon is dead.'

Her grip tightened around his neck. She began to weep. He cried with her, his numbness gone now, his emotions let loose in the shared intimacy of their pain.

The door to the visitor's passage cracked open, and a figure entered. Nico looked up, wiping his eyes clear, and his mouth dropped open.

It was the farlander, the old man he had stolen the money from the afternoon before.

The newcomer stood on the threshold, his head cocked to one side, a leather cup of chee steaming in one hand. He was shorter than he had seemed as he had lain on the bed. With a shaven head and black robe, he had the appearance of a monk, though a strange monk at that, because he carried a sheathed sword in his other hand. Nico's mother broke away to look too.

The man moved smoothly across the stone floor and stopped

before them all, the motion not unlike the swaying surface of chee in his cup: at once contained and settling into itself.

Close up, the farlander's eyes were the colour of dead ashes, though they were intense in their scrutiny. Nico almost took a backward step. There was no trace here of that confused old man awakened from his dreams, blinking around him as though unable to see.

'This is the thief?' he demanded of Nico's mother.

She swept her eyes dry, drawing herself tall. 'He is my son,' she declared, 'and more a fool than a thief.'

The man appraised Nico coolly for a few seconds, as though inspecting a dog he had a mind to buy. He nodded. 'Then I will have words with you.'

He took himself to one of the stools positioned in the centre of the vault, sitting down with his spine straight and his sword resting in his lap. He set the cup on the floor. 'I am Ash,' he announced. 'And fool or not, your boy stole money from me.'

Sensing business of a sort, Nico's mother became her usual calm self once more. She took a stool opposite him. 'Reese Calvone,' she told him.

Los approached to place a hand on her shoulder, though obviously wary. She brushed it away and he retreated to the far wall, as close to the door as he could position himself. He watched them in silence, from the corners of his eyes.

'Your son is to be flogged and branded no doubt,' continued the old man, 'as you people do in these parts. Fifty lashes, I am told, is common for daylight theft.'

Reese nodded, as though it had been a question asked of her.

'It is a hard business that.'

Her green eyes narrowed, and she glanced quickly to Nico before returning her attention to the stranger before her.

'You are taking it well,' he observed.

'Have you come here to gloat, old man?'

'Hardly. To know the son, I would first know the mother. It might help your boy's situation.'

Reese looked down at her hands, and Nico followed her gaze. Coarse working hands, covered in the cuts and scalds of many years; they looked older than her face, which was pretty, even now, despite its tears and worry. She inhaled a deep breath before she spoke. 'He is my son, and I know his heart. I know that he can bear it.'

Nico dragged his gaze from his mother to the old man, whose sharp face offered nothing.

'What if there were another way?'

She blinked. 'What do you mean?'

'What if he did not have to take the whip across his back, or the brand on his hand?'

She glanced at her son again, but Nico was still staring at the figure in the black robe. There was something about this old man . . . something he felt he could trust. Perhaps it was his easy authority – not the authority of one who has been granted it, and learned to adopt it in his ways, but rather something entirely natural, the result of a sincerity, a directness, of spirit.

'What I have to tell you must stay within this room. Your . . . *man* must leave, then I can explain.'

Los snorted. He had no intention of leaving.

'Please,' said Reese, turning to him. Los feigned a look of hurt pride. 'Go,' she insisted.

Los still hesitated; he glanced at the old man, at Nico, then back to Reese.

'I'll wait outside,' he announced.

'Yes.'

Los skulked from the room, casting the old man a final glare before closing the door behind him. Even as the noise of it slamming rebounded from the walls of the vault, the farlander continued.

'Mistress Calvone, my time is short here, so I must get to the point.' But he stopped then, and Nico saw how his thumb stroked the leather binding of his sheathed sword.

'I am growing old,' he ventured, 'as you can see.' A smile, perhaps, in his eyes. 'There was a time when a boy such as yours would have never made it through my window without waking me. I would have cut off his hand even as he reached out for my purse. Now though, I sleep through it all, exhausted by the afternoon heat like the old man that I am.' His gaze dropped to the floor. 'My health . . . it is not what it once was. I do not know how much longer I can continue in this work. In simple terms, and in the tradition of my order, it is time that I trained an apprentice.'

'More likely you're lonely,' replied Nico's mother sharply, 'and in the fancy for a pretty boy.'

He shook his head simply. *No*.

'Then what line of work are you in? You dress like a monk, yet I see a sword in your hand.'

'Mistress Calvone,' he spread his hands wide, as though indicating something obvious, 'I am *Rōshun*.'

Nico laughed then, despite himself. It came out tinged with hysteria and, when he heard it echo back from the curving roof of the vault, he stopped just as abruptly.

Both faces had turned towards him.

'You want me to train as Rōshun?' Nico managed. 'Are you mad?'

'Listen to me,' the farlander said to him. 'If you give your consent, I will speak with the judge today. I will ask for the charges to be dropped, and I will pay him a sum of money for his trouble and that of the gaolers. You will be saved from your ordeal.'

'But what you ask . . .' protested his mother. 'I may never see my son again. He would risk his life in such work.'

'We are in Bar-Khos. If he stays here, sooner or later he may be called upon to risk his life on the walls. Yes, my work is dangerous, but I will prepare him for it well, and when I bring him into the field with me, he will be present only as an observer. Once his apprenticeship is finished, he may choose to commit himself to the profession, or to go anywhere else that he wishes. He will have money by then, and many useful skills. He may even return here to Bar-Khos, if it still stands.'

He watched as she pondered this, then continued, 'Right now, a skyship is waiting for me at the city skyport. In a few days its repairs will be finished, and we will travel to the home of my order. There he will be introduced into our ways, and I assure you, Mistress Calvone, that at all times I will place your son's life before that of my own. That is my solemn oath to you.'

'But why? Why my son?'

The old farlander seemed stopped in his tracks by that question. He ran a palm across the shaven stubble on his head, creating a sound like stone rubbing against the finest of sandpaper.

'He showed skill, and some courage, in what he did. Such qualities are what I seek.'

'But surely that is not all?'

The old man stared at her for what began to seem a long time. 'No,' he conceded, 'that is not all.' And he rocked back on the stool, looking once more to the floor, at the space between himself and Reese. 'I have been having dreams of late, though that will mean nothing to you. Still, they guide me in some way, and I feel they are right.'

Nico's mother squinted at him, still unconvinced.

'I'll go,' announced Nico suddenly from across the vault. Both heads swung towards him again and he smiled, feeling foolish. His mother frowned.

'I'll go,' he repeated, more firmly this time.

'You will not,' she announced.

Nico nodded, a little sadly. He knew what the Rōshun were, everyone did. They killed people, murdered them in their sleep in exchange for the money they had been paid to carry out a vendetta. He could not see himself doing that, not for anything in all the world, but, still, he could leave as soon as his apprenticeship was finished, armed at least with new skills and experiences. Perhaps in its own way, this was it, his chance to make something of himself. Maybe the Great Fool had been right, and in the worst of days were laid the seeds for better times.

Then again, perhaps instead of escaping one punishing ordeal, he was trading it for a much worse one.

He didn't know. He could never know unless he went through with it.

'Yes, mother,' he said with a tone of finality, 'I will.'

CHAPTER FOUR

Flags of Conquest

'I'm hungry,' complained the young priest Kirkus.

The woman lying on the divan opposite gave a smile that almost split her withered features in two, showing a fine set of teeth that were not her own. 'Good,' purred the ancient priestess, while she spiralled a painted fingernail across her gleaming pot belly, tracing the course of old stretch marks and the gold ring pierced in her navel. 'The flesh is strong, Kirkus. But it may only become truly divine when it acts in accordance with the will. Deny your hunger. When next you eat, do so because your will has decided the issue as much as your stomach. That is how we maximize our appetites so that they demand power. That is how we achieve Mann.'

Kirkus grunted in irritation. 'You are starting to bore me. You offer nothing but sermons that I have heard a thousand times before.'

Her chuckle made him think of dry paper being ground purposely underfoot. It only irritated him more. Still chuckling, she shifted her bony frame on the divan, turning over to expose her bare, wrinkled back to the sun. The sound of her laughter spilled over the side of the imperial barge and fell, between the splashing, slow-moving strokes of the oars, into the brown waters of the Toin, before fading, ever so slowly, towards the distant bank of mud – where a crocodile stirred and plunged into the sluggish current in a brief sparkle of sunlight.

Abruptly, her teeth clacked shut.

'But I think you forget yourself, my young man, hmm? Not yet fully cocked, and you think yourself the next Holy Patriarch. Very good, but we are on the grand progress meanwhile, and I *am* to instruct you until you prove yourself worthy of the faith. These things you must know . . . but more than just know. You need to feel them, too, right down in your guts.'

'I already feel them right down in my guts,' he snapped. 'That's the problem, you old crone.'

Her look was one of measured appreciation. Kirkus knew he was her favourite pupil, and sometimes, when she scrutinized him in this way, it made him think of her as some obsessive sculptor, locked in an attic for years, slavering much too lovingly over her latest precious creation. Kirkus looked away from those hungry eyes, partly disgusted. He glared instead at the slave standing behind his divan, cooling him with a fan of ostrich feathers in this private space screened off from the rest of the deck; a thin Nathalese girl, with red hair hanging down around her small firm breasts, her ruined eyes hidden behind a scarf of peach silk, her hands gloved in white in case they accidentally touched the divine skins of Mann. Appetites, Kirkus thought lazily, taking in the slickness of her skin, noting how it stretched to the regular rhythm of her motion. He imagined for a moment what it would be like to take her, right here on the deck – this blind and deaf girl with only the sense of touch – the experience of pain or pleasure – left to her. Suddenly, he was physically responding to the thought of it.

'Patience,' the old priestess declared with mirth, her attention focused all too plainly on the evidence of his sudden enthusiasm. 'We dock at the next city at noon. You have heard of it, I trust. It is called Skara-Brae.'

Kirkus nodded. He had read of it in his studies of Valores's recently published *Account of Empire*, and wished to forestall yet another lecture from her.

'We can find some more playthings for your initiation. And, after that, we will go pay a visit to the city's high priest, and there drink and dine to our stomachs' content.'

'If only it was merely food that I craved,' he remarked gloomily, giving the slave another hard stare.

'You poor, weak child; it will all be worth it in the end. Have faith in an old woman who wishes only the best for you.'

She looked to the river for a moment, her features relaxing as she reflected on some distant memory, perhaps her own initiation as a priestess. Suddenly an expression of youthfulness passed over her features, as though by some glamour of recall. 'By the night of the Cull,' she said, still gazing at the flow, 'you will be so full to bursting that, when you unleash those desires, you will at last know what it is to be divine. I quite guarantee it, my fine boy.'

Another sermon, Kirkus thought to himself. But he swallowed down his annoyance and offered a grunt of acknowledgement, if only to shut her up. Let her savour her vain wisdom, he decided. She had nothing else left to her, certainly not beauty, nor even any real power in his mother's court.

Kirkus tried to think of other things. He scanned the water and the far bank, looking for something of interest to occupy his roving eyes. But there were only birds and buzzing insects, and the occasional white-and-black striped zel sipping from the water's edge. He was bored of it all already, twelve days now on this stinking, torpid river in the hinterlands of the Empire – twelve long months of travel and sightseeing before that – and never once allowed to act freely, on his own desires.

What else could he do, though? The old bitch was his grandmother, after all.

*

The Toin was one of the great rivers of the Midèrēs. It fell from the highlands of the mighty Aradèrēs mountains, first as small rushing torrents that rapidly gathered in tributaries before descending into the Lake of Birds, then, continuing as an ever-widening flow that stretched at some points for over a laq across. The river provided the commercial lifeblood of Nathal, and all of the nation's major cities could be found along its natural course.

As a nation, the Nathalese were a proud people. They had never been conquered by their neighbours – Serat to the west, Tilana and Pathia to the east. For a thousand years their culture had blossomed, uninterrupted, with philosophy, learning, and the arts. Daoism had come to them and they had embraced it also, as they embraced all such new ideas and thinking, adding it to the many other faiths that were practised and nurtured in their lands.

No longer could they feel so proud, though. Fifteen years ago their cherished independence had fallen beneath the studded boots of the Holy Empire of Mann. For a while they had fought a guerrilla war against the occupiers, but even those small flares of resistance had finally been extinguished. The crucifixion of entire towns in retribution for such rebelliousness had hammered even the proud Nathalese into submission. Nathal was now yet another province of the Holy Empire. It was ruled, as all the other fallen nations were ruled, by a hierarchy of administrating priests of Mann, its traditional beliefs outlawed, all concepts and faiths not in accordance with the divine flesh being vigorously censored and destroyed.

As the extravagant imperial barge finally pulled into the docks of Skara-Brae, the riverfront looked like that of any other settlement within the Empire. Signs hung overlarge from the fronts of old and new buildings alike, displaying goods and services for those unable to read in Trade, while outside the stockhouses gangs of unemployed men waited in the hopes of finding employment for the day, and fat patricians and their bodyguards oversaw the loading and unloading of their precious cargoes. Prostitutes and beggars waited in the shadowy openings of alleyways, many of them ill from missing their regular fixes of dross. Everywhere, imperial auxiliaries could be seen maintaining the peace, mostly drawn from the local population, wearing suits of white leather armour and the hard, wary expressions of those despised by their own people.

However loud the Nathalese might cry out for independence, occupation by the Empire had been good for them in one obvious way. Fifteen years ago this riverfront would have been the site of only a sluggish interchange of goods, just like the river it relied upon. Now, business was booming.

As the barge came to a stop, a hush fell upon the riverfront. Sixty oars rose dripping into the air as one. A detachment of Acolytes marched first from the deck, armed with spears and long-swords – even the occasional rifle. They were armoured with heavy suits of chainmail that hung down to their knees; awful to wear in such heat, though these male and female warrior-priests betrayed no signs of discomfort. Masks covered their faces, white and featureless save for a smattering of holes to breathe and see through, and over the mail they wore the striking white robes of the order, with hoods covering their heads, the material thin, embroidered with patterns of white silk thread that reflected the sunlight in subtle, ever-changing ways. From their ranks, a runner instantly set off into the city at a jog, bearing news for its high priest and governor. Like it or not, tonight he would be receiving visitors for dinner.

The Acolytes moved into the crowd with the confidence of fanatics born and raised to a purpose, pushing the locals back to form a large open circle. Once that was established, they forced those standing nearest to their knees. The local auxiliaries began to follow their example – pushing children and wealthy merchants alike to the ground, until the only people left standing were the Acolytes themselves.

That done, two priests emerged, reclining on a heavy palanquin borne by twelve slaves shackled together at the neck by gilded chains. Around them the Acolytes formed up in ranks, while several hundred faces gazed dutifully at the ground, or tried, from the corners of their eyes, to catch a glimpse of these beings who claimed to be divinities. They did not see much: merely two figures reclining on the sedan, their faces masked with gold and their heads shaved bare and gleaming.

With a shout the procession set off into the quieter streets of the city, breaking the previous stillness with the crash of studded boots against cobbles and the occasional bark of command from the Acolyte captain. At its head walked a single young man bearing the imperial banner, displaying the red hand of Mann. Again the Acolytes broke aside in ones and twos to force onlookers roughly to the ground.

'Captain,' the grandmother, Kira, said quietly to the commander of the guards, 'let them be for now. We cannot see them if they are all lying on their bellies.'

The captain nodded and passed on the instruction.

The two reclining priests were clothed in the same white robes as their Acolytes. They sprawled in comfort and nibbled on the occasional piece of dried fruit through the narrow slits of their masks. It was all that Kirkus was allowed to eat for now. Excitement glinted in their eyes, for it had been two days since their last venture into a Nathalese town, and they both needed the distraction it would offer them.

It was Kirkus who first spotted something that caught his attention: a young girl with dirty, bare feet selling sticks of keesh from a basket.

The old priestess eyed her young protégé, aware of his interest. She studied him, waiting, until Kirkus cleared his throat.

'That one,' he instructed, pointing a finger at the girl. The captain gave a command, and a group detached itself from the vanguard to quickly surround her. They threw her basket to the ground and carried her, struggling, back to the rear of the procession. Those townsfolk still on their feet shouted in alarm. A few even made a move to help the girl, though others pulled them back for their own sake, and for everyone's sake.

All they could do was watch as the Acolytes shackled her in chains and led her away to the rear, the girl crying now, looking about her for support. The silent stares of the street folk grew more openly defiant; it was the only protest left to them. But even that would not last long.

It was next the turn of the grandmother, Kira. With a snap of her fingers she set the Acolytes on to the hostile populace. Soon, people were scattering in all directions, away from the sudden violence, as the warrior priests began dragging bodies out of the fray.

'Wonderful,' sneered Kirkus. 'Now you frighten away our sport.'

'It is a large city. It has many streets.'

She was right, of course. Other streets, in different quarters, were calmer than those left in the procession's wake. Word must surely have already reached them, though, for the streets were emptier than might have been expected. Still, people went about their daily business, perhaps figuring rumour for exaggeration, or they were simply not in a mind to be chased from their own ground. By now, no one looked directly at the passing procession.

'Do you see anything else of interest, my child?'

Kirkus shook his head within his sharp-contoured mask. But he stared with fascination, appraising everyone that he saw, waiting for something further to grab his attention.

'I sometimes wonder,' mused Kira, as she studied the young girl captive now walking in chains at the rear, 'if we have not lost something in the gaining of an empire. At least, it seems that way to me sometimes. For every gain there is a loss. And every loss a gain. Once upon a time we had to do this through stealth and deceit: drunks stumbling home from the inns, street children out late, unwary travellers on the road. But that was long ago. In my memory, it seemed somehow better.'

Kirkus was barely listening, his gaze still intense – waiting, waiting. The palanquin finally halted in a noisy market square. This was the city centre, Kirkus knew – for where else would one expect to see a one-hundred-foot rusting spike rising sheer from the stone flagging? He stared at the great pole towering above the marketplace.

His grandmother noticed his wonder. 'It was Mokabi's idea,' she began. 'After the town fell he—'

'*I know.*'

The locals seemed to pay the monument little heed as they went about their business. He could see wreaths of flowers piled around its mottled base, where soldiers stood guard, eyeing the crowds.

The city of Skara-Brae had been the final Nathalese stronghold to hold out during the Third Conquest. Hano, the young queen and military genius of Nathal, having been defeated at last in the field, had bolted here to Skara-Brae with the last of her forces. Archgeneral Mokabi, commanding the Fourth Army, had given chase and laid siege to the city, demanding the gates be opened, else all within would be slain. At this, it was said, the young queen had offered to surrender herself, but her soldiers and the city's population refused to let her go. They paid the ultimate price for their defiance.

When the city finally fell, at great cost to the Fourth Army, Archgeneral Mokabi decided to hold a celebration for his conquering troops, one befitting those who had sacrificed so much during the campaign. First, they turned the town into an open brothel, slaying what they finished with or did not want in the first place. Then, in a stroke of inspiration, the archgeneral ordered a great spike to be forged from the melted armour of all those men of his army who had fallen during the siege. Fashioning a spike running a hundred feet in length, they fastened a great plug of concrete to the base of it, then positioned the entire thing, on its side, in the city square for all to see.

On the fifth night following the fall of the city, amidst an orgy of drinking and excess, the archgeneral's men forced the defeated officers and the town leaders one by one on to the spike's point. Impaled sideways like this, the male and female victims were drawn along its entire length, most dying in the process, until the spike was entirely filled by them. At its very tip, they placed Hano herself.

At a signal from the archgeneral, and with a shouted salutation to the defeated queen – at least, as Valores told it – the corpse-laden spike was hoisted vertically by three hundred enslaved townsfolk, there to be planted as a permanent monument to conquest.

It was a rousing tale and, years later, when Kirkus finally met Mokabi at a celebration for the birthday of the Holy Matriarch, Kirkus's own mother, he had found himself stuck for words in replying to the old man's kindly questions concerning his youthful studies – struck with awe at being in the presence of a living, breathing legend. But there had been something else too, something more subtle that had stilled his young tongue as he stood in front of the archgeneral and which took him several sleepless nights in his bed in the Temple of Whispers to fathom. For when young Kirkus had held the man's large hand in his own, something about that fleshy touch, cool and a little sweaty, had terrified him. Suddenly, all the stories of the general's exploits had become more than mere words on a page. This very man, his grip living and pulsing against his own, had commanded the slaughter of thousands; and not only defeated soldiers, but women and children, old men and babes. In that moment Kirkus had felt repelled by his touch, as though a mere handshake might infect him with something dreadful, something tainted. Afterwards, he imagined he could even smell blood on his hands. No matter how often he scrubbed at them, he could still smell it faintly, the metallic scent of it, when he lay alone at night with his own thoughts.

That sensation only diminished as his fourteenth birthday came and went, and he was allowed to share his bed with his temple friends at last: Brice and Asam sometimes but, after a while, mostly Lara. With such heady new experiences to explore, he allowed himself to forget about the imagined taint of blood on his hands. During the same period his lessons in the rituals of Mann intensified. He underwent his first purging. His mother, increasingly, allowed him to witness the intrigues and responsibilities of her newly seized position on the throne. Kirkus, over time, began to lose his inner sensitivities. He learned to appreciate the necessities of the ruthless act, and the basic selfishness of compassion. And when, on those rare occasions he again found himself seized by a sense of corruption – whether a greasy door handle or a glass of wine shared between friends, even a bathing pool already used by others – he would make sure to withdraw into the privacy of his chambers before he succumbed to the compulsion to scrub himself raw. After all, he was an initiate priest of Mann, and next in line for the throne. He could not afford to appear weak.

'Coming?' asked his grandmother, as she climbed down from the palanquin.

Kirkus tore his gaze from the mammoth spike, and in particular the patches of rust that stained it. He stared at her for several beats of his heart before her words sank in.

He shook his head, and watched as the old priestess wandered about the market, accompanied only by her personal slaves, freely sampling sweets and local wines. She declined an armed escort, staking her life on the intimidating power of her white robes alone, which parted the crowds everywhere as she went.

For some time Kirkus merely sat where he was and savoured the possibilities, playing fantasies in his head of those citizens that took his fancy. At last, when he was certain of who he wanted, he rose to his feet.

More quietly this time, he pointed out those who had caught his attention: two pretty sisters with manes of blonde hair sweeping down almost to the ground; a fat butcher who handled his cleaver like a veteran, and might offer some fight; a young man who reminded him of his boyhood friend Asam; an old fishwife with a body still lean and strong and interesting.

The Acolytes swept through the crowds, snatching those indicated where they stood. Shouts went up, only to be lost in the general clamour of the marketplace. Kirkus watched the ensuing commotion, following its stirs and eddies spreading throughout the square. He was mesmerized by it all, as distraught friends and relatives clung to those being taken away from them, crying out for help from others crowded around them. Each was apprehended in turn and the sounds of alarm rose higher, finally beginning to usurp even the din of the busy marketplace itself.

Kirkus knew, in that moment, that for the rest of his long life he could never grow bored of days such as this one.

As Kira returned accompanied by a hamper filled with choice goods, she left behind her a market square of depleted stalls and baskets still spinning where they had been dropped, their owners shouting as they fled the scene, intent on passing the alarm to adjacent streets. Behind the palanquin, the sense of shock felt by the newly acquired slaves emanated like a palpable force as in turn they were fixed to chains.

Several streets later, a man dressed in the faded leathers of a courier rode up to the head of the column, his striped zelback made jittery by the brooding atmosphere all around. The rider spoke briefly to the Acolyte captain, then handed down to him a scrap of folded paper, before he turned and kicked his mount into a canter, heading away.

Kira read the note with growing bemusement in her eyes.

'It would seem that word of our arrival has stirred more than just fear in this city. Listen to what it says: *This evening, when you meet with High Priest Belias, study closely the fit of his robes. You will find underneath only a charlatan.*'

'Is it signed?' asked Kirkus, only partly interested.

'*A loyal subject of Mann.*'

Kirkus shrugged. 'It is the same everywhere we go,' he remarked, disdainfully. 'The high priest doubtless has his enemies, and now they hope to jostle for position while you are here.'

'You have a fine mind when you put it to some use. You may well be right, but closely observe the man, anyway. It is a skill you must learn, to discern the true believers from the false, and yet another skill to know how to deal with them if they prove to be untrue.'

'We then dispose of them, what more is there to know?' he replied, while his attention returned to the surrounding street, searching still.

'Sometimes,' she crooned from behind her mask, 'your lack of imagination truly startles me. We must work on that fault.' She snapped her fingers, drawing the Acolyte captain to her. 'I think we will go to the high priest's mansion now,' she instructed him. 'I wish to rest there for a while, before we dine with this man who rules our city.'

'As you wish,' the captain replied, with a bow of his head.

The procession stamped onwards.

*

'I'm *bored*,' announced Kirkus to no one in particular.

The young priest was merely a guest at this meal, yet he sat at the very head of the table, where he had been downing the heady Seratian wine as though it was water.

'Ignore him,' recommended Kira to the family who played host to them this evening. 'He is merely drunk.'

Belias, the high priest of the city, and therefore its governor, acknowledged this statement with a brief if slightly nervous smile, whilst dabbing a handkerchief at the sweat gathering upon his bald pate. He felt oddly out of place here this evening, even though they were dining in the banqueting hall of his own mansion, where he was playing host to these two arrivals from far-off Q'os, the seat of the Holy Empire of Mann. Maybe it was the way the old priestess kept looking at him, something unspoken in her gaze.

Once more he wished they would finish eating and retire to their rooms for an early night. Belias needed to speak to his staff, find out if the city populace had heeded his hastily called curfew. Yet for the last two hours he had been trapped at the dining table with these guests, feigning interest in the old woman's talk while he eyed the rate at which they consumed their food and drank their wine, trying through simple prayer to hurry them up. Surely they must be sated soon?

By his elbow, his plump wife sat in silence. She was dressed in the finest of farlander silks, and sported jewels extravagant enough for a queen, or at least a minor, provincial queen. Again, she cast a demure glance towards the handsome young priest, sitting like a king at the head of the long table; again Kirkus pointedly ignored her attentions. Belias, too, pretended not to notice. He was hardly surprised by his wife's flirtations. She had always been drawn to power – it was why she had married him in the first place

He looked across at his daughter, Rianna. Belias often looked to his daughter when in need of a little support. She was whispering something to her fiancé, a man ten years her elder. He was an entrepreneur of the patrician class, who had finished his food long ago and watched all three priests seated at the table with barely concealed distrust.

They were a jolly group, for sure, as they dined silently in the draughty hall, listening to the rain gusting against the windows of stained glass, the munching of food and the tapping of cutlery against plates, the occasional civil comment; that and the cries of the slaves squatting out in the rain in the gravel driveway outside.

Belias had been informed by his chancellor of the occurrences in the streets of Skara-Brae earlier that day. That was partly why he was sweating so badly, and why he had to feign an appetite for the cold remnants of his food. The city folk were in an uproar, by all accounts.

They wanted their loved ones back; failing that, they wanted blood. It worried him greatly, these sudden public displays of anger, for Belias understood the Nathalese only too well, and how easy it would be to tip them into open revolt. After all, he was Nathalese himself.

'Are you quite all right, High Priest?' inquired Kira kindly, though he suspected that any kindness exhibited by this woman was more akin to a cat's toying with a mouse. Belias tried to compose himself. No, he was hardly all right. This old witch was the mother of the Holy Matriarch herself, and that lout, lolling in his chair at the head of his table was nothing less than the Matriarch's only son, likely next in line for the throne. It was enough to drive a simple priest from the provinces to distraction.

'I'm fine,' he heard himself reply to the old priestess. 'I was just wondering . . . you see . . . why you needed to acquire so many slaves today?'

The old woman sipped delicately at a glass of wine, fixing her gaze on him over its rim. She smacked her lips. 'My oaf of a grandson there is soon to undergo his initiation,' she explained, in a voice creaking like old stairs. 'We have been gathering what things we need for the ritual, stopping here and there along the river, at whichever towns take our fancy. I have brought him on the grand progress this last year, you see. I am sure, being a high priest, you have undertaken the pilgrimage yourself.' And for a moment she held up the crystal goblet to study it, as though looking for imperfections, and Belias saw her focus on him through its transparency.

Belias nodded, smiling like an idiot, not entirely offering an answer. No, he had never taken the grand tour himself, though he was not about to inform her of that fact. It was long, and hideously expensive if one wished to see it through in any comfort, and it involved all manner of orgies and ritual taboo-breaking along the way that would probably finish off his weakened heart for good. Somehow, Belias had just never quite got around to it.

'I see,' said Kira, whereupon Belias let the smile drop from his face. He didn't know what she saw, but his heart began to thump a little faster. He forced a slice of sweetroot into his mouth, a simple act of outward composure – though he spoiled the attempt when he tried to swallow, choking on the barely chewed morsel.

His daughter passed him a goblet of water, an expression of

concern creasing her forehead. He drained it dry and smiled at Rianna in thanks. She wore a dress of soft green cotton this evening, complementing her red hair and cut high enough to hide the seal she always wore about her neck, at his own fatherly insistence. Belias had snapped at her earlier, privately, for thus hiding the seal from sight, as she always did in company. It was of no use worn like that, he tried to tell her. It is not a deterrent if people do not see it. But Rianna had never fully understood the risks involved in being the daughter of the city's high priest. In a way, he hoped that she never would.

He now regretted those harsh words to her earlier as, across the table, his daughter returned his smile. He knew that she had already forgiven him. She always forgave him.

He was glad, at least, that these two priestly visitors had not turned the conversation to matters of doctrine and ritual tonight. He had always tried to shelter Rianna from the dark heart of this religion, its secrets and hidden rituals. He cherished her innocence; it was the only bright light in his otherwise mundane life.

'Look at him, there!' The old priestess now jabbed a finger at her grandson, though only half seriously, causing her host Belias to flinch. 'Drunk on wine and full to bursting and still he complains that he is bored. Would you believe he has seen an entire empire pass beneath his heels these last twelve moons, sights that only a privileged few will ever be fated to witness? No, he merely whines for more, like the spoiled child he is.'

Kirkus belched loudly at that.

There is no lord but thy own self, Belias silently recited, as though suddenly he was indeed a true devotee of Mann, while he covertly took in the intoxicated condition of the young priest sprawled in his chair. Could this truly be the next leader of both an empire and a faith that spanned two continents, and at least forty different races?

Unlike many of his fellow countrymen who would rather fight until independence or death if they could, Belias was by his own reckoning a realist. It was a trait he judged far superior to any other in his life, and which he found miserably lacking in his fellow Nathalese. Save, perhaps, for the merchant classes, who knew a good business opportunity when it came crashing through their doors boot-first.

All those years ago, when the imperial army had first rolled up to the Nathalese borders, and broken through almost without pause, he had recognized the future imperial occupation for what it truly was – *an inevitability*. And so, after the final stand of Queen Hano and her forces right here in this ill-fated city, which he had been fortunate enough to escape, through being far away with his wife and child on his family estate, and being the ambitious young politician that he was, Belias had switched sides accordingly. He became, of all things, a priest of Mann, seeing this as the only way to advance politically within the new order. It had been a simple enough business. All he needed to do was study for three years at the newly opened temple complex in Serat, where all manner of provincials were studying likewise to take on the robes of the order, and then to brave his way through the Cull, that mysterious ritual which would also signify his final initiation into the creed of Mann.

It had worked well, his change of allegiance – and Belias liked to remind himself of this, and of the subsequent success of that decision, during those darker nights when his conscience plagued him. He was now, after all, the governor of his very own city.

But, despite all such pragmatism, or perhaps because of it, Belias understood his less sophisticated countrymen only too well. An episode like today, a public press-ganging throughout his city, might well be enough to trigger a revolt, despite the threat of total retaliation that would be anticipated by all. If that uprising happened, High Priest Belias was undoubtedly a dead man. He would be the first to be strung up by the populace, seen as the traitorous figurehead that he was. And even if he somehow avoided such a lynching, the priesthood itself would finish him off for allowing such a revolt to occur in the first place. They would denounce him as weak, and no true priest of Mann at all, and he would be disrobed by their favoured method of disrobing one of the order – by sticking him on top of a burning pyre.

And all of this because of these fanatics from Q'os, sitting here at his dinner table, in his own home, in his city, gorging themselves on his food, while their stinking slaves cluttered up his driveway. It would be their fault if the citizens revolted, and their necks might even join his own in the noose. But that would not provide much by way of compensation. Dead was dead, after all.

Mann, the high priest reflected sourly. The divine flesh. Belias had made a point of learning everything he could about this all-consuming religion he had bought into. And he believed he understood it for what it truly was.

The Holy Order of Mann had not always been so holy. Once, it had been nothing more than a dark urban cult, a rumour whispered among the city states of the Lanstrada, where it was used as a threat by mothers to frighten their children into obedience. But that was before the same furtive cult had risen to dominance in the rich city state of Q'os – a populace gripped by fear and superstition induced by years of disease and failing crops – where the cult had seized power in a coup known as the Longest Night.

Driven by their victory and ambitions to consolidate their power as quickly as possible, the cult invested the vast reserves of wealth now under its control into reforming the city's army into a machine fit for conquest; their dream, to spread the Mannian philosophy throughout the known world. At first, their military endeavours did not go so well. But, eventually, armed with a new design of cannon – more accurate, less prone to exploding unexpectedly and requiring a smaller quantity of blackpowder – their fortunes on the battlefield finally turned. This led to an era of invasion and dominance that saw the brutal forging of an empire in little less than fifty years and, in the process, changed the very nature of warfare.

During those five decades in power, the cult had purposely wrapped itself in divinity. Over a relatively short period of time it had grown into a state religion, with many of its earliest customs hardening into tradition. The Cull was one such example. For the neophyte priests it was a ritual of initiation, in which they would lose the tips of their little fingers then proceed to murder an innocent with his bare hands, such a breaking of taboo being intended to hone the primal self into a point unstoppable.

Or so the faith went, though Belias thought it all so much fluff at the end of the day. He had merely felt sickened by his own long night of initiation. While more devout priests repeated the ceremony of the Cull many times during the course of their lives, supposedly honing the divine flesh further still, Belias had never repeated the experience, and tried hard never to dwell on that one and only time. Not once had he ever told his family what he had done to attain these white robes of his station.

Before now it had never seemed to matter that Belias did not believe in any of Mann's more fundamental nonsense. He was an ambitious turncoat priest in a religion that did not concern itself with selflessness or sacrifice, but only with power and self-divinity, and therefore Belias, a man of supreme self-worship in his younger years, had rarely ever felt himself a fake.

It was curious however, sitting at his own dinner table with these obvious fanatics from Q'os – *real* priests in every sense of the word, with their carefully shaven scalps and their abundance of facial piercings – that Belias was finally feeling himself to be the charlatan he really was. And it was this thought that lay at the forefront of his mind as he sat observing the scene before him, his sense of foreboding growing by the moment. He wondered just what they would do to him if they ever suspected.

*

Kirkus was feeling irritated. The wine was passable, the food at least filling, but it felt as though he had passed the last hour dining with corpses, so stiff and formal were the minor conversations conducted around the table. Not for the first time in the last six months, he wished he was back at the Temple of Whispers, along with his peers.

A sharp cry from outside broke his disgruntled train of thought. Likely, one of their newly acquired slaves was being coaxed into silence by the lashings of a whip.

'About time,' he commented, fumbling to refill his glass yet again. Such arrogance was partly for show, however, for Kirkus was not in every way the spoiled lout that he pretended to be: it simply entertained him to appear so at times such as now.

No one responded to his remark. The tinkle of cutlery and the crunching of food continued around the table.

Kirkus straightened the cutlery before him until each piece was again perfectly in its place. His teeth ground together. If he did not do something soon to relieve his boredom he would go mad.

A quiet conversation flurried for a moment between Kira and the high priest, something about the river, and how far along it the Lake of Birds must be from here. Belias was sweating even worse than before.

'I'm bored!' Kirkus cried out again, louder this time, though still not enough to scatter the polite conversation entirely from the table.

It was enough, however, to draw the attention of the high priest's daughter from her plate of fresh salmon. She turned round and fixed a smoky, indignant gaze on his own. It was the first time she had met his eyes since they had sat down for dinner. He leered back at her, making a show of it, and then he leered at her fiancé, too, that slick profiteer who looked up briefly to acknowledge him. As one, the couple returned their attention to their plates. Kirkus watched on, seeing the glances they passed between them after that. They shared something, these two: an unspoken connection.

He's probably riding her like a stallion whenever the parents are away, Kirkus mused broodingly. And, unwarranted, a memory forced itself into his mind: Lara and the last time they too had ridden together, her drugged and debauched hunger for sex driving him to a high he had never before known.

The memory lay like a leaden ball in his belly, and now it caused others to emerge. An evening spent with his grandmother in the cool shadowed room that was her personal chamber, her constant croaking reminding him of things he would rather not have to contemplate during those days in which all he wished to think about was when next he would see Lara. All that mattered to him was the scent of her skin, smooth and supple beneath his touch, or his bite; the sound of her laughter, clear and melodious, and provoked by things he could only guess at; the vision of her perfect face, flushed beneath him, or above him; her gifts of spontaneity and high spirit.

'Little Lara can never be your glammari, Kirkus,' his grandmother had told him bluntly, after spending an hour explaining yet again how only the women of Mann transmitted the power and wealth of their families, for only they could pass down an ancient bloodline with certainty.

'These things you must remain aware of more than merely who pleases your cock the most,' she had chided. 'Remember, Lara's kin are already allied to our own. You, my child, must chose your consort to the advantage of your position, from a powerful family we wish to bring over to our side. For you, Lara can be nothing more than what she already is, and you must be content with that, the pair of you.'

Kirkus had cursed at the old woman and told her to mind her own business. He had said nothing of it to Lara – not even knowing how to. Yet still she had come to hear of it, somehow.

Lara's behaviour had been skittish on the night that would prove to be their last together, though only she had known it as that. After their hours of love play, they had fallen into an argument over something of no importance, some vague misunderstanding that even now he could not recall. Lara had stormed off, shouting about how she never wanted to speak to him again, and he had laughed at her dramatics and thought it nothing more than one of their usual squabbles – not knowing he had lost her.

A few days after that, at the Ball da Pierce, Lara had arrived with a new lover, that ass Da-Ran strutting proudly in his dress armour with its ribbons, and a scar still healing on his cheek, having just returned that very week from putting down some tribes in the north.

Lara had not even looked at Kirkus that night.

Not once.

This girl at the table, Rianna, she had a way of glancing at her fiancé that made Kirkus feel uneasy; if he had been remotely inclined towards self-analysis he would have recognized it for the envy that it was. But instead, he merely sat with increasing ill humour and watched with darkening eyes.

One of her hands lay beneath the table as she ate, Kirkus observed. Peering closer, he saw how that same arm kept moving to a rhythm, though so delicately it was barely enough to notice. Kirkus grunted. With the showy subtlety of a drunk, he dropped his unused napkin to the floor, and ducked beneath the table to squint along its underside. There. Her fragile white hand gloved in lace, the tips of her fingers stroking lightly against her fiancé's crotch.

Kirkus retrieved the napkin and returned it the table. He was grinning now, and, as he looked upon the girl again, it was as though he suddenly saw a different person. His attention lingered on her skinny body beneath her green dress, the breasts pouting with youth, the long swan-like neck curving up to a face, that was soft-skinned, proud, both whitened and blushed with make-up, and framed with a great tumult of red hair.

'I want her,' he said to the room, and his quiet and fierce demand caught the attention of all.

'What, dear?' inquired his grandmother from the far end of the table, the old bitch pretending to be deaf.

He pointed a finger at Rianna.

'I want her,' he repeated.

The girl's plump mother broke her silence at last. She giggled into her fist as though she had suddenly found herself in the presence of the insane. The other diners, however, seemed far removed from laughter. They were still hooked on his words, their mouths open in shock, perfectly poised.

'Are you quite serious?' asked his grandmother, in a tone that implied he had better be sure of himself before he next spoke.

Kirkus knew what he was asking of her. Back in Q'os, she might well refuse such a thing; she had done so with Lara, when he had demanded her as his own after the night of the ball, too fearful of upsetting the delicate balances of power that his mother had contrived, as always, to maintain her position. But here? With this provincial fool of a high priest? The report she had been given earlier in the day was correct. Belias was obviously playing at his role of Mann, not fulfilling it.

'You know as well as I do what these people are. Yes, grandmother. I want her – for my Cull.'

The young redhead held a hand to her throat and turned to her father for reassurance. Her fiancé placed a hand against her arm and stood up in protest, though he said nothing. The mother continued to giggle.

The old priestess Kira sighed. What was passing through her mind in the next few moments no one in the room could guess at, not even Kirkus, but she stared long and hard at him down the length of the table, and he at her, till the silence grew into a hanging presence.

Turning to Belias, Kira studied him carefully, his face suddenly drawn tight and white with fear. It seemed to prompt her in her decision. Her smile, when it came, appeared merely for politeness.

'High Priest Belias,' she said deliberately, placing her cutlery down beside her plate, 'I would ask of you a question.'

The man cleared his throat. 'Mistress?'

'What is the greatest threat to our order, would you say?'

He opened and closed his mouth a few times before the words gained voice. 'I . . . I don't know. We rule most of the known world. We are dominant everywhere. I . . . see no threat to our order.'

Her eyes closed for a moment, as if the lids were heavy. 'The greatest threat,' she intoned, 'will always come from *within*. Always we must guard against our own weaknesses – of becoming soft, of allowing those into our order who are not truly of the faith. This is how religions become hollow in the end, and meaningless. You must surely appreciate this.'

'Mistress, I . . .'

She opened her eyes again, and the high priest fell silent. His hands, poised above the tablecloth, trembled visibly.

'Thank you for your hospitality this evening,' she told him, dabbing at her mouth with her napkin before setting it down.

The old priestess raised a skeletal hand into the air and snapped her fingers once, with a sound like the breaking of bone. As one, the four Acolytes stationed around the room began to move.

The girl shrieked as they fell upon her.

Her fiancé swung a fist, desperate and panicked enough for it to catch an approaching Acolyte on the jaw.

In the next instant another Acolyte drew his sword and raised it to strike – the fiancé, by instinct, raised his forearm to block the blow, and with a butcher's mindless simplicity the Acolyte hacked clean through it, then raised the sword again and hacked down through the wounded man's collarbone. The severed hand had already dropped to the floor. The arm flopped heavy and awkward next to it, where it rolled to settle on the open palm, while its owner fell screaming, blood spurting everywhere.

The mother stood up and vomited a shower of barely digested shrimps over her embroidered tablecloth.

The father mouthed words of inconsequence and stumbled around the table towards his daughter, his voice rising. But he slipped on the spreading pool of blood on the floor and, as he regained his footing, clutched at his chest, his face tightly pinched.

The doors at the far end of the room burst open and the mansion's guards tumbled in, weapons already drawn, anticipating trouble. They took in the scene: their master reeling as though drunk at the far end of the room, the bloody mess of a man still screaming on the floor, the daughter struggling in the arms of the Acolytes; and there, seated calmly at either end of the table and sipping wine, the two white-robed visitors from Q'os.

The men backed slowly from the room, closing the doors gently as they left.

The high priest groaned, then fell to his knees as Kira rose above him.

'Please,' he barely managed as he clutched at his chest. A small blade appeared in her hand. With the smallest of motions she swept it across his throat.

'Take the mother, too,' she commanded, as she stood over the dying man.

The Acolytes seized the mother and dragged both her and her shrieking daughter from the room. Kira paused to look down at Belias. She stared into his rolling eyes.

'Do not be bitter,' she told him, though it was doubtful if he even heard her words. 'You did well enough out of us – while it lasted.'

Kira stepped over the high priest, rather than around him, leaving a trail of dainty bloody footprints in her wake.

Kirkus finished his wine with one swallow and stood.

In the great hall of the mansion, the guards waited with expressions of poorly concealed fear. Egan, the high priest's chancellor, stood before them, his hands hidden within the sleeves of his white robe. His silver hair contrasted sharply with the flush of his face, and Kirkus assumed it to be anger until he observed an interested gleam in the man's eyes, which now followed both mother and daughter as they were pulled outside into the rain. He wondered if he was the one who had penned the note earlier that day.

'We have need of a new high priest, Chancellor Egan,' Kira announced.

'Indeed,' the man purred.

'I hope you prove a more dedicated follower of the faith than your predecessor ever was.'

Egan bowed his head. 'He was weak, Mistress. I am not.'

Kira appraised the man for a moment longer, then with a sniff she whirled about and swept through the front doorway.

Kirkus dutifully followed his grandmother outside.

CHAPTER FIVE

In Flight

The cabin stank of mould and dampness and vomit. Nothing moved in the room, yet the gentle motion of the skyship could be detected through the occasional creak of timbers, a rattle of the lantern hanging from the ceiling, a minute sense of lift or fall in the depths of the stomach. In his bunk, Nico lay wretched and pale-faced.

Almost as soon as the ship had lifted off from Bar-Khos and climbed into the cloudy sky, Nico had goggled at the unnatural sight of land diminishing far below him, and he had clutched at the rail with a sensation of lightness in his head, and a loose churning in his belly. For three days now he had lain in his bunk awash with fearful tension and nausea, leaning over occasionally to retch into a wooden bucket on the floor. It was now painful for him to speak, for his throat was burned raw from the bile. He ate little, consuming only what water or soup he could hold down long enough to digest. Every moment, awake or in restless sleep, he was aware of the thousands of feet of empty air gaping beneath him, and the constant tensions on the ropes and struts by which the hull dangled from the flimsy, gas-filled envelope overhead. Every sudden shout from a crewman on deck, every thump of feet or twist of motion within the ship, heralded for Nico impending disaster. It was a misery like he had never known before.

Most of the time he spent alone. Ash shared the cramped cabin, but the old farlander did not seem to appreciate Nico's prolonged bouts of retching; he would become impatient with it eventually, and set aside the little book of poetry he always seemed to be reading, and stomp out on to the deck, muttering under his breath. It was Berl the ship's boy, therefore, who tended to Nico and brought him food and water.

'You must eat,' the boy insisted as he held out a bowl of broth. 'There's nothing left of you but skin and bones.' But Nico grimaced, and pushed the bowl away.

Berl tutted at his stubbornness. 'Water, then,' he told him. 'You must drink some water, no matter if you hold it down or not.'

Nico shook his head.

'I'll have to fetch your master if you don't.'

Nico finally consented to take a mouthful of water, if only to placate the boy. He asked what time of day it was.

'Late afternoon. Not that you'd know the difference in here, with the shutters closed all of the time. You need some fresh air, it stinks in this place. No wonder your master stays up on deck more often than not.'

'I don't like the view,' Nico told him, and he thought back to his first morning on the ship when he had flung open the shutters, only to reel away from the sight that greeted him.

He groaned, a palm clasped against his ailing stomach. 'I think there's something truly wrong with me.'

Berl grinned. 'My first time out I was sick for a whole week. It's common. Some gain their wings faster than others.'

'Wings?'

'Yes. Don't worry, another few days and you should be fine.'

'It feels like I'm dying.'

The boy hefted the skin of water towards Nico's lips again.

Berl looked to be no more than fourteen, though he exuded a confidence of one older than that. As Nico wiped his mouth dry he studied the younger boy. There were scars, small ones, on his narrow face, concentrated around his brows and especially about his eyes, which themselves seemed hard like long-healed wounds.

'I used to work beneath the Shield,' Berl explained, noticing Nico's interest.

Ah, thought Nico. He had once been told by his father how boys were sometimes used in the tunnels beneath the walls of Bar-Khos, in spaces too small for men but large enough for boys and attack-dogs alike. He now said as much to Berl, how his father had been a Special himself, trying to make a connection with him perhaps. The boy simply nodded, and set the skinful of water on the floor next to the bucket.

'That's enough for now,' he said. 'But you need to keep drinking it, you hear?'

'I will,' Nico replied. 'Tell me, where are we?'

'Over Salina. We made its eastern coast this morning.'

'I thought we would already be heading for Cheem.'

'As soon as we find a favourable wind. The captain likes to conserve our whitepowder whenever he can. As soon as we do, we'll strike north through the blockade. Don't worry, the Mannians have as few airships as we, and the *Falcon* here is a fast ship. The crossing should be swift.'

He stood, saying, 'Come on deck later, if you're feeling up to it. The fresh air will help.' And then he walked with an easy gait across a floor that was sloping visibly upwards, the ship itself climbing. Nico could hear the hull drive tubes being fired, burning their precious fuel.

Before Berl left, he turned at the doorway, one hand gripped on the frame. 'Are you really training to be Rōshun?' he asked.

'I think that is supposed to be a secret,' replied Nico. The boy nodded and stuck out his lower lip, while considering it. Then he closed the flimsy door behind him.

Nico lay back and closed his eyes. It helped him with the sickness a little if he did not look at the sloping cabin.

Already his life in Bar-Khos seemed an awful long way away.

*

The next morning he felt better. It was as though his body had exhausted itself of its traumas, and had decided to relax in spite of his many anxieties. Nico sighed with relief and rolled free from the sweat-soaked bunk.

The cabin was located at the rear of the skyship. A ledge ran beneath the shuttered window at the back of the room, supporting a sink, and beside it, in the corner, was a lid concealing the privy. Taking a deep breath he fumbled with the shutter until it opened. He blinked at a clear blue sky, a few white clouds sailing past at eye level. A faint breeze brushed his face, fully waking him. Despite himself, he was drawn to peer over the sill. Far below lay a green and tan landscape – an island by the look of its curving coastline – with roads threading to and fro between a few hazy towns before converging on a sprawling, walled cityport. The sparkle of rivers running down from forested hills to a variety of lakes and then on to the sea was dizzying to look at. Nico gripped the window frame, and commanded himself to remain calm.

He tossed the contents of the bucket down the privy, just to clear the room of its stench, then stripped off his filthy garments. Ash had bought him a bag of travelling gear before they had departed, and from it he now took out a bar of soap and scrubbed himself from head to toe, soaking the wooden floor in his exertions. Then he dug out a new covestick, removed it from its waxed paper wrapping, and brushed his teeth long and hard.

As he was donning the clean change of clothes – a soft cotton undershirt, tunic and pants of tough canvas, boots of leather, a belt with a hardwood clasp – he realized how desperately he was in need of food.

Walking in short, careful steps, Nico left the cabin and followed the corridor, and the smell of chee, to reach a large, low-ceilinged common room. Crewmen sat in groups around the tables scattered around the room, muttering quietly as they broke their fasts for the morning, the dim air already filled with pipe-smoke. A few watched him darkly as he walked to the far end where the galley hatch lay open and where the cook, a skinny bald man with the swirls of a moustache tattooed to his face, served out warm mugs of chee and platters of cheese and biscuits. Berl was working in the galley, too, busy feeding wood into the fire that burned within a brick hearth. The boy nodded Nico a greeting, though he did not pause in his work. Nico contented himself by piling food on to a platter. The cook set a cup of chee in front of him before returning to his kitchen work, which seemed to consist of banging pans, flinging sodden clothes about, sweating and cursing to himself. Nico sat at an empty table and ate cautiously, testing his stomach. He gazed at the cannon sitting by the gun ports along both sides of this warm communal area and tried to ignore the occasional hooded glance cast his way. He wondered if the rest of the crew were always this friendly.

When he was finished, he thanked the cook and climbed the stairs that led to the upper deck. He took each step slowly, his hands sliding up the rails with each upward push of his legs. Near the top he paused, collecting himself.

He rose on to the weather deck of the ship, and for a moment he pretended he was standing on any normal sea-going vessel, afloat on fathoms of water rather than drifting on air. For the *Falcon*'s decks looked no different than those of any ship he had seen in the harbour: a high quarterdeck rose behind his back, a foredeck to the front. A group of crewmen sat nearby talking while braiding together lengths of rope. Another group on the far side of the deck played a game of bones; they were arguing amongst each other, while one man firmly held back another who seemed ready to pick a fight. In all, the crew seemed youthful to Nico: few of them being out of their twenties. They were notably thin, all sporting beards and wild hair.

It was strangely quiet save for the snapping of canvas, and he looked up to see the great gas-bag of white silk rippling in the wind, sheathed in a fine netting of rope and wooden struts. Its bulk cast a great shadow across the entire length of the deck. From the nose of the envelope an assortment of sails stretched taut between tiq spars; two great vanes of the same material projected like wings from its flanks. Men were up there, miraculously clambering over the lattice of rigging that confined the silk curvature. Their feet were bare, and their dirty pink soles skated along ropes that seemed too frayed to warrant such easy confidence. *Madmen*, thought Nico. *Bloody lunatics*.

At this great height, the air was cold. The breeze bit through his clothing and he felt the prickle of goosebumps rising on his flesh. For a moment he thought of returning to the cabin to fetch his travel cloak, but then he spotted Ash sitting cross-legged on the raised foredeck of the airship. The man seemed deep in meditation, and was wearing his usual black robe.

Nico found that he could negotiate the deck so long as he did not look over the rail, and therefore simply maintained the pretence of being aboard a normal ship at sea. Keeping his eyes fixed on the decking, he reached the steps to the foredeck and climbed up to join the old man.

Ash's eyes seemed to be closed, though a glint of pupil could be seen between his lashes, his half-lidded gaze focused on a point that could be near or far away. The old man sat like stone: not even his chest rose and fell with his breathing.

'How are you?' Ash inquired, without moving.

Nico folded his arms for warmth. 'Better,' he replied. 'Thank you for your concern, old man.'

A dry chuckle. 'I am not here to mother you, boy.' And Ash finally opened his eyes wide, looked up at him, held out a hand.

Nico stared at it for a moment, the fingernails bright against the pinkly black skin around them. Then he clasped it, rough as bark, and helped the old man to his feet.

'If you are walking, then you are well,' declared Ash. 'So it is time we began your training. Lesson one: you are my apprentice. Therefore you will call me master, or Master Ash, never *old man*.'

Nico felt the blood rush to his face. He did not like the other's tone. 'As you say.'

'Do not try me, boy. I will strike you down where you stand if you show me insolence.'

He sounded like Nico's father sometimes had after becoming a Special, or like one of the idiots his mother had taken in. 'Then strike me,' said Nico. 'That would be a lesson I already know well.'

Nothing changed in Ash's expression, but from the corner of his eye Nico could see the old man's right hand clenching into a fist, and he tensed.

Instead of hitting him though, Ash exhaled deeply and said, 'Come, let us sit together.'

He knelt again on the decking, this time facing Nico. After a moment's hesitation Nico followed his example.

'Take a deep breath,' Ash instructed. 'Good. And another one.'

Nico did so, and felt the anger draining away.

'Now,' began Ash. 'You are Mercian. Your people follow the Dao, or what they sometimes call Fate. You must know, then, the ways of the Great Fool.'

The question was an unexpected one. 'Of course,' Nico replied with some caution. The old man merely nodded: it was clearly a prompt for more. 'I have been to temples a few times, and listened to them reciting his words. And on every Foolsday my mother used to make me sit beside her during her invocations.'

Ash's eyebrows pinched together, as if unimpressed. 'And tell me, do you know where the Great Fool was born?'

'I was told he was born on one of the moons, and fell to Erēs on a burning rock.'

The old man shook his head. 'He was born in my homeland, Honshu, six hundred and forty-nine years ago. That is the birthplace of Daoism. The Great Fool never set foot away from Honshu, despite all your legends to the contrary. It was his Great Disciple who brought the Way to the Midèrēs, and it was because of her and her own disciples that it spread in its various forms across the southern lands, including your own. Now, tell me, do you meditate?'

'Like the monks?'

'Yes, like the monks.'

Nico shook his head.

'*Hoh*. Then you know nothing but religion, as I expected. In my order we are also Daoists, but we follow the teachings of the Great Fool without all this nonsense that has grown up around his words. If you are to follow his way, as you should do if you are to become a true Rōshun, then you must forget all those things and focus on only one thing. You must learn how to be *still*.'

Nico nodded slowly. 'I see.'

'No, you do not, but you will begin to. Now, do as I tell you. Place your left hand in your right. Yes, like that. Now straighten your back. More so, you are still slouching. Good. Keep your eyes partly open. Choose a point in front of you and stay focused on it. Breathe. Relax.'

Nico breathed, perplexed. He could not see how this had anything to do with the business of Rōshun.

'Observe the air as it enters your nostrils, moves through you, exits. Breathe deeply, into your belly. Yes, just so.'

'Now what?' Already his knees were beginning to ache.

'Simply sit. Allow your thoughts to settle. Let your mind become empty.'

'What is the point of all this?'

A slight rush of air from Ash's nostrils, but still a steady gaze.

'A mind that is forever busy is sick. A mind that is *still* flows with the Dao. When you flow with the Dao, you act in accordance with all things. This is what the Great Fool teaches us.'

Nico tried to do as the old man instructed. It was like trying to juggle three things at once: watch the movement of his breathing; keep his back erect; stay focused on a chip of wood on the rail in front of him. But he kept forgetting to pay attention to one or the other, and frustration began to build in him. Time stretched out till he was unable to tell if he had been sitting there for moments or hours.

It seemed that the more he tried to be still, the more his mind wanted to chatter to itself. His face itched, his straightened spine ached, and his knees throbbed with pain. It could easily have been a form of torture, and after a while he purposely set his mind to other things: where the ship was heading, and what was being served for dinner, anything that might take him away from his discomforts.

It felt like several hours had passed when a bell rang out to signal the end of the hour.

Ash rose with a soft rustle of his robe. This time it was the old man who helped Nico to his feet.

'How do you feel?'

He chose not to say the first thing that came to mind. 'Calm,' he lied, nodding. 'Very still.'

The old farlander's eyes lit up with humour.

*

Later that day the ship descended several hundred feet in the hope of finding a more favourable wind, and indeed she found herself in a stream of fast air bearing north-west. On the raised quarterdeck at the rear of the ship, his oiled black hair flapping over to one side of his head, the captain barked orders for the tailsculls to be trimmed and the mainsculls to be let out, his deep voice sending men scurrying into the rigging even before he was finished. Captain Trench was a tall man of perhaps thirty years of age, clean-shaven and gaunt in the extreme. His bony white hands rested in the pockets of a grey-blue navy overcoat of no visible rank; an affectation of sorts, or perhaps an indication of some earlier naval career, since his command now was of nothing more than a merchant vessel – though admittedly a rather remarkable one. His one good eye peered upwards at the envelope of gas keeping them aloft, which rippled ceaselessly along its windward side; while, on his shoulder, his pet kerido chattered in his ear as though in conversation, and shifted a leg for balance as he did the same beneath it. Like a fish, the *Falcon* turned, squirming, into the flow, her deck pitching over as she slewed around, still shedding height.

Nico gripped the rail with whitening fingers. He listened anxiously to the creaks of the wooden struts over his head that connected the envelope to the hull. The great curved mainsculls on either side of the envelope had caught the wind full now; next to the wheel, a crewman studying a spinning instrument called out the speed as the ship surged ahead.

They were leaving the Free Ports at last.

That evening they dined with the captain in his stately cabin beneath the quarterdeck, a low slab of a room that spanned the entire breadth of the ship. Windows lined the wall space, thick watery panes of glass divided into diamonds by crisscrossings of lead, some panes coloured in translucent green or yellow. Beyond them, the horizon merged with clouds lit by a falling ball of sun.

The meal was a wholesome affair of rice soup, roasted potatoes, green vegetables, smoked game of some kind, and wine. The courses were served on bone-white crockery ceramics, fine and expensive-looking stuff. Each piece was decorated with the central motif of a falcon in flight. A gift to the captain, Nico assumed.

There was little talk as they each fell upon the steaming food. Ash and the captain both ate with the concentration of men intent on savouring what they still could in life while the going was fair. Dalas, the captain's second-in-command – a big, dreadlocked Corician wearing an open leather jerkin with a curved hunting-horn slung from his neck – was a mute apparently from birth. Even the captain's pet kerido, excitable at first around the two guests present for dinner, now sat quietly on the table before his master's plate, softly clacking its beak and drooling in an attentive way as the man ate. The animal reminded Nico of Boon, back home in the cottage, when Nico had sat eating whatever half-heartedly prepared meal his mother had cooked for them, and surreptitiously passing morsels beneath the table. He had never seen a kerido before though had heard of them, from street performances of *The Tales of the Fish* recounting stories of merchants venturing to the forest-oasis in the shallow desert, and meeting with madness and death. *The Tales* always portrayed the kerido as a vicious creature despite its small size. With one of the creatures sitting before him now, Nico could imagine why. The colours of its tough hide invoked images of lush vegetation draped in shadow, and furtive movement, and the sudden pounces of a predator. He had not realized it was possible to make a pet of one.

Red wine had been produced from a locked cabinet fixed to the floor, and Ash and Dalas and the captain were now well into their second bottle, while Nico still sipped from his first glass. He suspected the pair of them were already a little drunk.

'It's good to see you on your feet at last,' Captain Trench observed quietly, as he used his handkerchief as a napkin to dab at his pale lips, and favoured Nico with a glance from his blind white eye, as though he could see more clearly with it. Even in the soft sunset hues that filled the cabin, his skin had a pallied complexion, like the slick greyness of rain.

Ash grunted at the remark, and Nico glanced towards the old man, but the farlander refused to return his gaze.

'A tricky business, adjusting to big sky,' Trench continued in his soft, clipped accent suggestive of a wealthy education. 'Worse than being at sea, most will inform you. Well, it's no shame on you, the reaction. Believe me, I am hardly any better myself when I make it back to land. It takes me – what – a full day in bed with a galloping whore before I feel steady again.' And he flashed Nico a good-natured smile, with a cock of an eyebrow, before looking quickly away again as though shy at having said too much.

Nico forced a smile in return, for it was hard not to like this man. Indeed, this evening he was gaining a sense that it was important to Trench to be liked by those sharing his company; which was surprising, remembering him earlier that day, as he screamed at one of his crew for fouling the rigging, his words flying incoherently with so much spittle that Nico had wondered if he wasn't in some way unhinged. Dalas had eventually stepped in to pull Trench into his cabin, out of sight of the crew, though not out of earshot.

Now, at dinner, the captain seemed calm. His smiles came easily and his sound red-rimmed eye held something of an apology in it: clearly whatever demons plagued him, they were restrained just now by this softer nature, which also seemed his truer nature, so that Nico felt reassured in his presence, despite his earlier loss of control.

From across the table, Dalas observed Nico coolly while he shovelled food into his mouth with a fork. The big Corician lifted his free hand and made a gesture in sign language, almost too fast to follow: a balled fist tilting from side to side, a waving motion, a flat chop, a palm soaring.

'Pay no heed to him,' advised Trench, dismissing the other man with a wave.

But Nico continued to stare at the Corician's hand, which now rested on the tablecloth, the forefinger rubbing restlessly against the end of its thumb. 'Why?' he inquired. 'What did he say?'

Trench raised his bunched handkerchief to his mouth, and murmured from behind it. 'He says, my young friend, that he doubts you have ever even sailed before, let alone flown.'

The Corician had stopped eating, his right cheek stuffed with food, as he awaited Nico's response.

'He would be right, then,' Nico admitted.

'Yes, but you may not have noticed *how* he said it. That gesture just now, with a loose wrist, it meant he intended it to be insulting.' Trench shook his head at Dalas reproachfully, and Dalas frowned back. 'Dalas was born on a ship. All his life, he has lived on one type of deck or another. He is often this dismissive with people who have never been to sea. He reckons, somehow, that their priorities are all wrong.'

Nico offered an awkward smile to them both. 'Once, when I was ten, and swimming in the sea, I found a log and used it for a boat.'

Trench withdrew the handkerchief from his mouth by a fraction. 'A log, you say?'

'A big one.'

Trench choked back a laugh, which in turn became a cough that he stifled with his handkerchief. Even Dalas's expression softened, enough at least to swallow his food.

'You are hardly drinking,' the captain observed, as he caught his breath. 'Berl, fill him up, if you please.'

Berl, standing by the table in attendance, dutifully stepped forward. He added more wine to Nico's glass, though it hardly needed topping up.

Nico studied the glass before him.

'I see you haven't acquired a true thirst for it yet,' Trench observed over the rim of his own goblet. 'You will, believe me. In lives such as ours it happens all too easily. Look at your master, there. When last he was aboard this ship, I had to keep all the stores under lock and key, his thirst was so limitless.'

'Nonsense,' said Ash, and downed the rest of his wine before holding out the empty glass for a refill.

Nico sat back in his chair, hoping to let their conversation drift by him. He picked up the glass, if only to have something to do with his hands. Everywhere around him, wood creaked to its own disjointed rhythms. It reminded him of the forested foothills back home, of standing alone deep amongst the pines as they swayed and groaned in the midday breeze. He tried another sip of the wine. Its aftertaste was a sweet one, not like the cheap, bitter stuff his mother sometimes drank. He could take to this, he thought, if ever he had the money to afford it.

An image of his father came to mind. His father raging drunk, breath hissing through his nostrils, tongue trying to push its way out through the obstruction of his lower lip. Nico found himself setting down the glass once more.

Trench leaned back in his chair, tilting it on to its two rear legs. His sigh only deepened the impression of weariness that hung about him.

'I have taken you from your land-leave,' Ash said by way of an apology.

'And the rest of the crew, too,' Trench muttered, then straightened his chair again, smiling with thin lips as his hooded eye surveyed the table without focus. 'They are somewhat displeased with their captain just now, and I can hardly blame them. We only just made it back from our last run. You saw the poor condition we were in, and that was after a full week of repairs. Now, they have to run the blockade again, with hardly more than a week on land for respite. It's hard on them – hard on us all.' And he dabbed his face again with his handkerchief.

Ash wiped his lips of wine. 'It is a short journey this time, at least.'

'Yes,' admitted the captain. 'Though with little profit in it, save for some cloth we might shift in return for grain, which will keep my investors happy at least. And of course in wiping my debt to you. I take it we are even?'

'You owed me nothing to begin with.'

'You hear that?' snapped Trench suddenly to the kerido, who aborted its reaching towards the scraps on his plate with a scaly claw, and instead looked up. 'He mocks his hold over me, even now.'

Absently, the captain picked up a half-eaten sweetroot, and the creature opened its beak as he offered the morsel towards it.

'Just promise me one thing,' Trench said to Ash, and then he paused as Nico shifted back from the table in alarm. Trench looked down at the creature perched between them. From its open beak it was brandishing its tongue at him, a long and stiff and hollow thing like a child's rattle, making a noise clearly intended to sound threatening. Trench tossed the morsel into the creature's mouth to shut it up, then continued.

'When next some old saltdog comes at my back in a taverna,' he said to Ash, 'do me the kindness of letting him have me. Friendship is one thing, but I'd rather a pierced liver than ever be in your debt again.'

Ash inclined his head in consent.

Nico watched the creature as it ate, both its claws holding the root as it tore off strips with quick jerks of its beak. He found himself holding his cutlery before him as though in defence.

A brilliant glow had permeated the cabin. The sun was now setting, throwing the last of its light through the stained-glass windows at the back of the room, printing diamonds of colour against the beams of wood not far above their heads, against the plank walls, the long desk with charts splayed out across its surface and kept flat with rounded stones. Nico peered over at the charts. He was close enough to discern a few oblique details: landmasses lost in symbols, notations, curving sweeps of arrows. Maps of the air, they seemed, as much as of the land surface.

That thought caused his eye to range beyond the desk. Through the lower portion of the rear windows was visible a sea made to look flat and featureless by height.

'If you don't mind me asking,' he ventured, dragging his gaze from the watery abyss, 'how long will the crossing take us?'

For a moment a shadow passed over the captain's features. Captain Trench sat forward and, with his goblet, gestured to Nico. Wine slopped out of the glass, and Berl frowned as red stains blotted the clean linen. 'It depends,' he said, in a voice more sober than before. 'Some time tonight we approach the imperial sea blockade. Maybe the wind will hold true. Maybe they don't have anything in the air here.'

'In the air?' Nico blurted. 'You mean, Mannian skyships?'

'There is always the chance, this far out.'

Again Nico glanced at Ash, but the old man was feigning interest in the bottom of his glass.

Trench registered his discomfort. 'It's unlikely, mind,' he said. 'Mostly their birds-o'-war are over in the east, preying on the Zanzahar run. That's where the main action is to be found, not here. Believe me, I know. Zanzahar's all we have left for foreign trade, so most longtraders are committed to it, the *Falcon* included. When the sea-fleets can't get through, or they take heavy losses, the longtraders pick up the slack. We've been flying the Zanzahar run close to four years now.' He paused to upend his goblet, draining it of the last drop. 'You have heard the stories, I'm sure.'

Indeed, Nico had heard the stories. How the Mannian skyships waited in packs like wolves along the route, ready to pounce on any longtraders that passed by. How every year the number of longtraders grew smaller and smaller. Trench hardly needed to explain as much, for it could be heard in the grim tone of his voice, a tone that had even caused the kerido to stop momentarily in its nibbling, to stare up at him.

Nico stared too. Trench no longer seemed to be present there in his chair; he was lost instead in the spots of wine on the tablecloth. For a moment, as the sun cast its final rays about him, Trench looked up, startled, as though returning from a great distance, and slowly inclined his head towards the dying light. In silhouette his nose was prominently hooked, a hint of some old Alhazii ancestry in his blood perhaps – though here, in this cabin, he was merely a ghost of the Alhazii desert, more a sick-looking Khosian, holding together his command with a sometimes trembling left hand and a slightly sturdier right, which seemed always to clutch a white, sweat-stained handkerchief of lace-bordered cotton within its fist.

Nico stabbed a potato from his plate and stuffed it into his mouth. It was cold, and his stomach was feeling queasy again, but he ate anyway. He did not like this talk. At least in Bar-Khos, the city walls still stood as a symbol of protection and life carried on. Here there was nothing but sky and, by the sounds of it, an absolute reliance on wind and good luck. It did not sound promising at all.

And, after this, what? Cheem, that notorious island of reavers and Beggar Kings where, according to Ash, they would travel into the mountainous interior to find the hidden Rōshun order, and where he would train to become an assassin. The more he thought of all that was to come, the more uneasy Nico became. It had all seemed easier when he had lived in Bar-Khos, simply struggling each day to survive. At least he'd had Boon by his side.

A shout, coming from outside.

Trench and Dalas looked to one another. The shout came again. The kerido clutched the remains of the sweetroot in its beak and clambered on to the captain's shoulder. Dalas rose and, even with his back bent, the Corician's scalp brushed against the roof beams. He stomped out.

'A little earlier than I was expecting,' Trench murmured, dabbing his lips one last time. His chair scraped back as he pushed himself to his feet. 'Excuse me, please.'

He took his goblet with him, Berl and the wine bottle trailing behind.

In the sudden silence, Nico and Ash were alone.

'A ship,' Ash explained at his side.

'Mannians?' Nico asked. His voice was subdued.

'Let us go and see.'

*

In the cool twilight, Nico could not make out anything at first. He stood close to Ash and peered in the direction that everyone else, including the kerido, was looking. He could see nothing but dull water beneath a faltering sky.

Then he spotted it. To the east on the surface of the sea – a white sail.

'Can we make their colours?' the captain asked Dalas. The Corician's waist-length dreadlocks writhed as he shook his head in the negative.

'We're too far out for it to be anything but an imperial – if not a merchanter, then a picket.' Trench seemed to be talking to himself at first, but, as he scratched his pale face, he glanced up at Dalas. The big man folded his tattooed arms and shrugged.

They had gathered on the quarterdeck, next to the wheel, the highest level on of the ship. Nico shivered, his eyes watering from the constant scrub of the wind. Captain Trench took a sup from his goblet, smacked his lips. With his other hand, still holding the hand-kerchief, he caressed the smooth wood of the rail as though he was cleaning it of dust. He had built this vessel, Ash had said earlier, from a wreck that had been sold to him as salvage. It had taken his entire family fortune, and more, to convert it.

Trench paced four steps towards the stern rail, four steps back, scuffing the deck with his boots as he stopped.

'The colours,' he bellowed across to the lookout by the foredeck rail, one hand cupping his mouth. 'Can you see the colours yet?'

'Still too far, Captain,' the lookout shouted back.

Trench tugged at his chin. He stared up at the envelope over their heads, the dying light painting it with intense luminosity. At this time of day, to a sharp set of eyes looking in their direction, it would stand out clearly for laqs.

'Have they seen *us*, that's the question we should be asking,' Trench muttered as he watched the far sail.

For an instant, on the distant ship, it seemed as though the sun was rising again. A blinding yellow brilliance rose into the sky, to hang there for some moments in the gathering darkness. Beneath it the sea reflected the Sun's light as a trembling, fiery disk. From the Mannian ship, a stark shadow fell long across the water.

Trench tossed the last of his wine into his mouth and flipped the empty goblet towards Berl. 'Well, that settles it,' he declared.

The flare descended slowly, the sea dimming in a shrinking circle as it fell. It landed in the water, burning up even as it sank: a strange, ghostly descent into the depths. Nico rubbed his eyes to clear away the after-images, then he opened them in time to see another flare climbing skywards on the eastern horizon. Meaning another ship was out there, still too distant to see.

'A formation must be nearby,' said Trench. 'If they have any birds in the area, we'll have the righteous bastards down on us before dawn.'

Nico shifted uneasily.

'Be calm,' Ash cautioned him, at his side. The old Rōshun stood motionless, hands buried in his sleeves, observing the fading flare.

'Orders, Captain?' asked the man at the wheel, an old ragged-ear sailor.

'Fire the tubes, Stones, and turn us west. Set us back on course when it's gone full dark.'

'Aye, Captain.'

Trench tilted his head back to take in the few evening stars appearing 'Dalas, make sure the blackout is well enforced tonight, with inspections every quarter-watch. Anyone found breaking it is to be thrown into the bilge.'

Trench turned his back to the sky, his teeth shining in the dimness.

'Thirsty work,' he said to Ash. 'Care to finish that bottle?'

*

Nico wasn't inclined to return to the cold remnants of his dinner. He returned instead to his cabin, alone and fretful. For a long time he tried to sleep. The bunk seemed harder tonight. Through the decking immediately overhead, voices murmured: Trench and Ash talking, still drinking. Try as he might, he could not calm his mind. He kept thinking of the future – tomorrow and the day after that, the weeks, the months, the years ahead. Sleep was to be a sanctuary denied him.

After some hours Ash stumbled into the blackness of the room, reeking of wine. He grunted as he collapsed over his bunk. Nico watched his vague outline as he rolled on to his back.

Through the gloom he saw the old man grip a hand to his forehead. Ash was breathing deeply, as though that helped in some way. He fumbled in the inside pockets of his robe. At last he located the pouch that he always seemed to carry with him, and lifted one of the dulce leaves it contained to his mouth.

The old man chewed, breathing noisily through his nostrils.

'Master Ash,' Nico whispered towards his dark form.

For a moment he thought the farlander had not heard him. But then Ash made a clicking noise with his tongue, and said, 'What?'

A dozen questions formed in Nico's mind. They had talked only briefly about the Rōshun order, of what he would be doing there, of the seals and how they worked. There was so much more that he desired to know.

Instead, he simply said, 'I just wondered if you were all right, that's all.'

There was no reply.

'It's just, I've noticed you using those dulce leaves a lot.'

When it came, the Rōshun's voice was stiff and restrained. 'Headaches, that is all.'

Nico nodded, as though the gesture could be seen in the dark. 'One of my grandfathers was the same,' he said. 'Not that he really was my grandfather. I just called him that. He died defending the Shield. I remember he took the leaves, too. When I asked him about it, he said it was because of his eyes. Because they were starting to fail him, and all the squinting made his head hurt.'

The bunk creaked, indicating that the old man had turned his back to him.

'My eyes work fine,' he muttered. 'Go to sleep now, boy.'

Nico sighed, rolled on to his back to stare up into blackness. He knew that sleep was still far away.

Somewhere over his head, in the captain's cabin, a pair of boots paced back and forth throughout the night.

CHAPTER SIX

The Birds of War

By sunrise there were no more signs of sails. They had passed the imperial naval formations some time in the night, while Nico had tossed and turned in his hammock, or slept in brief intervals that were filled with unpleasant dreams. Ash had already risen when Nico finally awoke to an empty cabin, the early light fattening the open window as the horizon dipped within its frame. The ship was climbing.

He listened to the men's talk in the busy gloom of the common room, as he held himself steady and bleary-eyed against the galley's serving counter and piled buttered keesh and seedcakes on to a platter. The crew were in better spirits at having crossed the Mannian blockade in the night, and at least were no longer scowling at him. Still, there was a sense that it was not over yet.

Nico ate his fill, his body still craving the nutrition it had been starved of for over a year. As he took his time over a tarred-leather cup of chee, he thought of beggar's broth, and wondered what Lena and the others he knew were doing back in the city. He even thought about his mother. Slowly, he began to properly waken.

He had barely finished his chee when he was startled by the most unexpected of sounds – a hunting horn calling out from the upper deck. The men froze and silence flooded the room.

The horn sounded again, with three high notes. Footfalls hammered across the planking overhead.

Instantly the men erupted into action with quick oaths and a general jostling towards the deck stairs or the cannon positioned along both sides of the wide room.

Sunlight flooded the low-ceilinged space as gun ports were opened up. Nico rose with panic in his chest. Amid the chaos, men outside shouted and heaved on ropes to pull the ends of the small guns out through the openings; a man shoved past him, not pausing to offer his pardon; others scurried for cartridges of blackpowder and cannon shot, or laboured with buckets of old nails, pebbles, coiled chains, forever cursing at people to get out of their way. A breeze played through the gun ports, dispersing the normally smoky atmosphere of the room, and carrying with it the sounds of snapping canvas and of the hull tubes burning fuel. Curiosity drew him towards one of the openings. With the ship still climbing, he shuffled across to the daylight, stopping himself with a palm laid against an overhead beam.

One of the sailors manning the gun poked his head out through the port. Nico leaned sideways until he could see past both man and gun.

A white speck, heading straight towards them.

'Bird-o'-war,' the sailor announced as he brought his head back inside and wiped his grim face.

Nico was possessed with a sudden urge to find Ash and to be at his side. He turned and hurried towards the steps. Berl was in front of him, loaded down with an armful of weapons.

'Take one,' the boy said, as they both climbed the steps.

Nico grabbed the first thing that came to hand, a stubby blade encased in a sheath six inches wide.

The weather deck was in bedlam. Sailors already armed with swords or axes were helping each other into tunics of leather armour. A group on the quarterdeck had set up three long-rifles on tripods by the starboard rail, next to the small swivel-mounted cannon. Others held bows, kneeling as they strung them. He could not see Ash anywhere.

Nico looked down to examine the weapon in his hand. Its handle was of simple wood, sanded smooth by use. He pulled it out of its sheath to reveal an ordinary meat cleaver. It felt ugly in his hand, weighted for a single brutal motion, and for a moment, when he thought of using this against another human being, he shuddered.

He kept it with him anyway as he made his way across to the other side of the deck, scurrying the last few feet as the ship leaned on its axis and tilted sideways. The starboard rail stopped him sliding further. A hard wind gathered his hair about his eyes.

To his right, up on the quarterdeck, Captain Trench peered through an eyeglass as he chatted to Dalas. His weariness seemed all but gone now, if not in the pallor of his skin or the soreness of his eyes, then at least in the way that he stood at ease, and how he spoke with decisiveness. The sun was rising behind the bird-of-war.

The skyship was approaching from starboard, but the *Falcon* was passing it on its north-westerly course. Nico shielded his eyes. Ahead of them, and further off to the east, another skyship was approaching on a course that would bring it across the *Falcon*'s path.

Like talons, he thought, *closing their grip on us*.

'Boy!'

He swung about. Through a parting in the scrum of men, he spotted Ash kneeling alone on the foredeck. The old Rōshun beckoned him with a flick of his head.

Nico walked the length of the ship by making careful use of the rail. The *Falcon* was levelling off, making it easier for him. He climbed the steps and approached the old man.

Ash nodded. 'You're late.'

'Late? For what?'

'Your morning session. Had you forgotten?'

'Ash, in case you hadn't noticed, we're in a bit of a fix here.'

'I told you before. It is master, or Master Ash. Now sit.'

'But we don't have time for this!'

The old man sighed.

'Nico, there is no better time for you to learn than when I am in the field and going about my work. This' – and he tossed a hand about, while a gust of wind tried to snatch it from him – 'is my work.'

Nico had no response to that. With a frown he took up the same kneeling position as the old man, setting the meat cleaver to one side.

'Now, remember, focus on your breathing. Follow it as it moves through you.'

This is absurd, said Nico's mind. For a moment he tried to focus as instructed, but through the struts supporting the rail he could see the second enemy ship growing steadily nearer. It was no longer just a dot but a bead of white.

'Relax,' the old man said.

It was odd, but as Nico inhaled and his heart began to slow

from its previous breakneck pace, the activity on the decks began to quieten too.

A hush descended upon the creaking ship. All ears listened to the drive tubes pushing them forwards.

There was nothing left for the men to do now but wait.

Nico closed his eyes and found that it helped. Within moments a vague sense of detachment came over him, so that he could tolerate the increasing pain in his legs and back. He observed himself inhaling cool air, then exhaling. A moment of emptiness; then the pain worsened and brought with it a return of his thoughts. Through his eyelashes he peered at the bird-of-war. It was closer still.

The ship's bell rang out the hour, sounding as though it was simply another routine day aboard ship. Save that there was none of the customary coarse laughter, and very little talk.

Ash exhaled a long breath. 'We must make ready now,' he said, unfolding himself from the deck.

Nico rose with him, wincing at the stiffness in his legs. He followed Ash to the rail.

The birds-of-war were close enough for Nico to make out the curving hulls hanging from beneath their envelopes. The approaching ships were twice as big as the *Falcon*, each hull lined with a double row of gun ports. The first was directly behind now, trailing them. The other was still ahead, angling on its intercept course, so that a great red palm could soon be seen stamped against the side of its envelope.

'Why aren't we turning away?' Nico exclaimed. He could see the imperial marines lining the rails of the approaching ship. 'We should turn west with the wind and make a run for it.'

'The captain is an astute man. Most likely there is another bird-o'-war lying to the west of us. They act in threes, in general. These two are trying to drive us towards the third.'

'So we're just going to let them run across us?'

'We lose speed every time we turn. The ship behind might gain range. Better to offer this one a parting shot, then race past as it makes its own turn.'

'It sounds like no plan at all.'

'It is the best plan available. It is what I would do, given the circumstances. The captain has speed on his side, for the *Falcon* is a fast ship. He will try to cut a path straight through.'

It was then that Trench finally broke the silence of the decks. 'Make ready,' he roared, as the leading bird-of-war flew across their course. Men squatted, seeking cover.

The imperial guns opened up, shattering the day with roiling eruptions of smoke along the ship's side.

'Down,' Ash growled, and the old man pulled him to the deck just as a nearby section of rail exploded into splinters. Something dark and spinning hurtled over their heads.

Nico gasped, deafened by the noise of the guns. Everything inside of him had turned to water. He covered his head with his arms. Shouts carried through the din, no obvious sense to them. There was a crash overhead, then a screech of wood and a muffled thump. He found himself buried by a heavy weight.

'Boy!'

Hands yanked at his clothing. He looked up to see Ash dragging him out from underneath the fallen rigging. Nico kicked his feet until he was clear of it.

The old man shouted something. 'My sword,' he was saying. 'Fetch my sword from the cabin. Quickly, now.'

Ash hauled him to his feet, and propelled Nico headlong towards the stairs. Nico slithered down them on his back. As he slipped at the bottom, he saw it was blood that slicked the hard deck. Right next to his right hand lay a dead sailor, his head mashed flat. Nico reeled away, but kept staring at the hideous sight. Matted hair and bone fragments smeared red amid tatters of skin. Grey matter that must be . . . *Sweet Erēs, that must be brains*. Nico's legs took over. He ran at a crouch along the deck, jumping over men who were lying prone for cover, dodging others who were rushing forwards to the fallen rigging. He glanced over his shoulder. The bird-of-war was turning to come along their port side.

'You filthy bastards!' Trench hollered from the quarterdeck, his hands clamped to the rails as he glared at the ship sweeping around them.

The *Falcon* bucked beneath Nico's feet. Smoke poured over the gunwales as she fired her own guns, pitifully few it seemed now, sending chains and debris hurling into the enemy envelope and rigging. He coughed, wiping his eyes clear. Gunfire crackled through the confusion. A sailor lurched in front of him, a look of wonder on his deathly white face as he pitched over the rail and into space. Another, a skinny youth, wept uncontrollably where he stood.

The top of the stairs came into view. Something hot brushed past his head. More chips of wood flew from the rail. He made a dive for the steps, rolled on his shoulder, fell and tumbled all the way down into the common room below.

He gasped at a sudden pain in his side. Fumes of blackpowder rolled through the cramped space, making him choke. This room was where he had earlier sat and eaten his breakfast in a quiet atmosphere of pipe smoke, but now men manhandled steaming guns and stepped without pause over their fallen comrades, ignoring their calls for aid. Nico was frozen where he lay: for a time he thought of nothing at all, entirely empty inside himself. It was easy when he did not try. He watched as though through a narrow tunnel, his own self far removed from what he was seeing. He glimpsed the bird-of-war sailing past the gun ports. It fired again, blackening the space between the ships. The room darkened. Trails of debris cut through the foul air – cannon shots, punching through the hull and filling the room with bright spinning shards of wood that clattered against beams and guns before finding purchase in men's flesh.

It was no safer here than above decks. Nico rolled over, panting. On all fours he crawled towards his cabin, muttering nonsense.

Berl passed him on the way. The boy was helping a wounded man to stagger clear. He glanced down at Nico, on all fours, but didn't stop.

In the cabin Nico swung the door shut, took a moment with his back against it to regain his wits. He was shaking all over.

Sweet Erēs, he thought as he gripped his stomach. His bowels were about to empty themselves.

He staggered to the privy hole at the back of the room and threw open its lid, revealing a chute stained with previous use and leading to a drop and the sea all that way below. He unbuckled his belt, dropped his pants, planted himself on the hole. Nico moaned with sudden relief.

He hadn't realized it would be like this. The rattle of gunfire against the hull made him want to crawl under the bunk and hide, as though he had become a young boy again. His father had told him once of how battle could turn a man's insides to liquid, or freeze him so badly he could not act at all. Somehow, at the time, Nico had assumed that his father was talking about the fainthearted, about men ill suited for war.

Perhaps he was, Nico thought now, and did not like the taste of it, a tangible bitterness in his mouth. *Perhaps he really was a coward, and I too am a coward, and we are both cowards, father and son.*

Nico spat, wiped his lips with the back of a trembling hand. Hastily, he cleaned himself with a graf leaf and fastened his pants.

Ash's sword hung above the old man's bunk. Nico would have forgotten why he had come here if he had not spotted it there. He took it with him as he stepped out into the fury of the common room, and then pounded up the stairs.

The second bird-of-war had passed them, and now was nosing across their tail. The first was still following. He joined Ash where he found him on the quarterdeck, keeping low as though the thin struts supporting the rail might protect him from incoming fire. 'Your sword,' he said, and Ash looked down at the offered blade for a moment, as though he had forgotten about it, too. He accepted the weapon.

'It is not safe up here,' Ash told him.

'It's not safe anywhere!'

Bolts ripped past him. Nico ducked lower. The kerido was cowering next to the wheel; it saw Nico crouching much in the same way as itself and, scrabbling across to him, leapt into his arms. Its hot breath stank of rotting food.

At the rear of the quarterdeck, Dalas directed the swivel-mounted cannon at the enemy ship crossing their stern. He aimed carefully as the vessel presented her broadside, tracking the gun to follow its envelope. Captain Trench stood by his side, taking a bearing along the gun's barrel. He slapped Dalas on the back.

Nico covered his ears just as the big Corician fired. The kerido flinched in his arms.

A tear sprouted near the nose of the envelope. Nothing happened for a moment, as the torn silk flapped just like all the other minor tears along its side. But then the prow of the envelope began to dip, and the ship went into a shallow dive.

'Good shot,' observed Ash.

As though in anger, the falling ship fired what guns it could still bring to bear. It was like being hit by a wave: the force of it threw Nico on to his back, and he coughed for air, winded, and swallowed dust. Splinters jabbed his legs; the kerido's arms dug into his neck; in a daze he saw Dalas sprawled on his back, with other sailors scattered around him. Half the wheel had been torn away, and Stones was nowhere to be seen. Through it all, Trench reeled about as though drunk.

Ash was still on his feet, by the remains of the rail, slightly hunched as though braced against a strong wind. He was looking at something, and Nico followed his gaze. A large object had just shot out from a cloud of smoke on the foredeck of the pursuing bird-of-war, trailing something as it raced in a shallow arc towards them.

A grappling iron crashed past Nico, and landed on the main deck of the *Falcon*. A chain was attached to it, whose heavy links crashed through the stern rail, its other end firmly fixed to the Mannian ship's prow.

'Quickly, over the side with it!' It was the thick voice of the captain, righting himself.

A few men leapt to the grapple, but they were already too late. The chain lost its slack and Nico stared in horror as the grapple dragged itself along the deck, caught on the lip of the quarterdeck, tore deep into the planking.

The *Falcon* lurched, losing speed. They were caught like a fish on a hook.

'All is lost!' cried Nico, frightened out of his wits. He didn't care that he sounded like some overripe actor exclaiming his woe to the crowd. This was madness.

Ash gazed down at his apprentice, as the pursuing ship closed the distance. Sailors began attacking the planking around the grapple with axes, trying to loosen its grip. For a spell, Ash said nothing, just stood there watching Nico, and gathering stillness about himself. Then he laughed, the sound of it rolling away with the wind, sharp mockery, yet with an underlying lightness.

'You youngsters,' he proclaimed, 'you despair so easily.'

Nico clutched the kerido's body close to him, both of them trembling.

'Captain,' snapped Ash, gaining Trench's attention. 'Turn us about.'

'Turn about? Are you mad?'

Yes, decided Nico, *he's flying with the fishes. Whatever he says, sweet Erēs, don't listen.*

'Turn us about,' Ash repeated.

Trench took position at the wheel, spinning what remained of it to turn the ship about.

The *Falcon* heaved around, losing a good portion of her port rails as the chain scudded along her gunwales. Their pursuer turned with them, though not as sharply. The chain slackened.

'Heave, you fellows!' shouted the captain to his men. Dalas had by now regained his feet. He strained to lift the grapple, then he and six other men rushed over to the side with it and pitched it into thin air.

Trench spun the wheel again, regaining their original course. They had lost height during the engagement, and at this lower level the wind was with them. The sculls snapped full with it and the *Falcon* surged forwards.

'Tend to the wounded,' Trench yelled. 'And get the stitchers up into the envelope. We're venting gas from the cells.'

The crew knew then that they were safely through. They didn't cheer like the heroes do in the sagas. Instead, as the imperial ships dropped behind, it was a stunned silence that fell across the decks.

'I hope you do not consider that another debt to be repaid,' Trench muttered over his shoulder to Ash.

The old Rōshun said nothing.

Nico stared about him. Even now he could hear the cries of wounded men who would likely not make it to the end of the day.

I'm much too young for this, he thought, with a sudden sobering clarity.

CHAPTER SEVEN

Congress

'We need those ships, Phrades,' announced First Minister Chonas, leaning forward in his chair as though to add some much needed emphasis to his words. He held up a fist to the dozen ministers assembled before him for this cabinet of war, and squeezed it until the knuckles turned white. 'Our people must eat.'

Phrades, Minister of Ship Building, glanced sidelong to his son, where the pair sat together at the great oval table of the assembly chamber, amid their fellow ministers. Most of the faces there were dusted white to mark them as members of the Michinè class born and bred, although there were a few notable exceptions. Phrades could not speak aloud these days, due to a cancer of the throat they said. Instead he whispered drily to his son, the young man's face in stark contrast to the pallid complexion of his father, being tanned and without make-up, as many of the Michinè youth favoured these days. The young man listened carefully with a tilt of his head, then cleared his throat and stood.

'We understand, First Minister, and you must believe us when we say we bend our wills to this task like no other. All resources that can be diverted from other projects have been appropriated so as to speed up the completion of the ships. We have even contributed a portion of our own family fortune to this task, in organizing the importation of raw materials. It pains me – us – to confess that we can do no more than we are doing now. It will take us one month more to finish the remaining merchanters under construction at the Al-Khos dockyards. In the meantime we must rely on the private longtraders to continue picking up the slack. The people, I fear, must tighten their belts further.'

A stomach gurgled loudly in the room just then, causing a few heads to turn in that direction.

First Minister Chonas was not the kind of man to acknowledge such a distraction, nor was he inclined to take no for an immediate answer.

'And what did the Pincho have to say to our requests?' he asked, referring to the main assembly on Minos, the seat of Mercian democracy.

'They, too, build as fast as they can, but they are still hard pressed to refit the fleets after the spring storms. The new vessels will not be with us until the beginning of autumn.'

'At least,' offered Minister Memès, sitting with his equally tanned face resting on his clasped hands, 'our food reserves should be restored to satisfactory levels in time for winter.' The voice of the wealthy gala exporter sounded restrained in the huge dimensions of the chamber, the speaker doubtless conscious of what he represented to these other men around him, his great wealth and political position having been gained despite being born of the lower classes – another reflection of the changing times.

'That is easy enough to say,' countered First Minister Chonas, 'since few of us here in this room look as though we have been going hungry.' Yet Chonas himself looked lean enough, as though he at times did indeed go hungry. The First Minister held up a palm to silence any protest at this accusation, before continuing in a voice flat with resignation. 'No, they are right to put the fleets first. It is better that our people tighten their belts a little further,' – he ranged around the room glaring from beneath enormous, bushy eyebrows – 'than we should lose our naval supremacy, and thus lose all.'

'General Creed, you have a request for us?'

At this, Bahn's hungry stomach grumbled loudly once again. He pulled his gaze away from the banquet of food waiting close to the main door of the chamber, and sat up in his chair next to the general. They sat at one end of the table, facing those opposite, and behind them the great sun-fattened windows of the south gallery. No reply came from his superior, nor did Bahn sense any shift in the man's posture.

Glancing sideways at the old warrior, he saw that General Creed, Lord Protector of Khos, was now staring out through the same windows at the pale blue sea of the Bay of Squalls. From here they could not see the cliffs on which the building of the Congress stood, let alone the slum-town of the Shoals, which sprawled along the foot of the cliffs, half submerged in seawater during storm tides. Instead the vista revealed was a pleasant one: the air was especially clear today, everything crisp in detail so hat landmarks appeared closer than they really were. A squadron of triple-masted men-of-war roamed the waters, bearing the Khosian flag. They ranged beyond reach of the heavy Mannian guns positioned on the far shore, seen from here as a coastline of russet hills made pale by the sunlight and dotted with grey fortifications. From here the forts could be seen to cluster most thickly around the dark smudge of the Pathian town of Nomarl where, within the harbour walls, the hulks of a Mannian fleet were reported to still lie abandoned in the water, charred and sea-rotted after being burned at anchor by a Khosian raid three years earlier – the last offensive action the Khosians had mounted with any success.

General Creed seemed to be eyeing the faint image of the fortress town. He looked like a man who wished to return to it.

Daydreaming again, Bahn reckoned, and he gently nudged the general's foot with his own.

'Yes, First Minister,' Creed replied smoothly, as though he had been listening attentively all along. His chair scraped as he stood up to address the room, his burnished armour reflecting the sunlight. The general pressed his palms against the polished tiq wood of the table, as his gaze took in the assembled ministers one by one. He did not look impressed by what he saw.

'My request is that we return to the issue of the coastal forts. And you may groan all you like, gentlemen, for I mean to have this issue decided upon here, this very day.'

'General Creed. We have been over this many times. We are aware that our eastern forts are undermanned. Yet what is it you believe we can do?'

'First Minister, the forts are not *under*manned, as this council is so fond of suggesting. They are barely manned at all. That is my point: they contain skeleton crews merely to service and repair them, no more – certainly not enough to offer solid resistance. They have little blackpowder, even fewer cannon, for instead all has been drawn to the defence of Bar-Khos and our southern coastline. Therefore we still have no answer for a surprise attack on our eastern shores.'

'That is to presume such a surprise attack would be possible, General. The third fleet has protected us thus far. We must pray it will continue to do so.'

Creed waved that comment away. 'First Minister, that is a lot of sea for the third fleet to patrol. We have been lucky so far, that is all. Now that the insurrection on Lagos has finally been quelled and its great harbour secured, the Mannians have the perfect anchorage from which to strike against us. We can no longer rely on the navy for our protection. First Minister, we must man those forts.'

First Minister Chonas, philosopher as well as politician, took this demand with his usual good grace. He nodded to his old friend and opponent. 'Truly, I understand, Marsalas. But we are overstretched as it is. You know as well as I, we have not the resources to equip and maintain more soldiery. Where can we find these extra fighters? You yourself have a solution, all of a sudden?'

'We divide our reserves in two, and use one half to man the forts.'

There was an outcry of protest from around the table at this suggestion.

'That is hardly a solution, General,' spoke up one voice. It was Sinese, Minister of Defence, third most powerful man in all of Khos, who sat back with his legs folded and white-gloved hands resting on the ivory head of his walking cane. 'This cabinet will not allow our reserves to be diminished any further than they already are. Even if we were to man the forts fully, it is doubtful they could hold off a full invasion. There is nothing new in what you propose here.' He paused to turn in his seat and address the man next to him. 'Minister Eliph, you have more pressing news from the diplomatic corps, I understand?'

'I do,' concurred Eliph, and avoided the general's sudden glare as he took a moment to gather his thoughts. 'Our ambassador in Zanzahar has arranged for further discussions with the Caliphate concerning their recent proposal. He believes they are sincere in their talk of extending the limit of their safe waters closer to us. There is real hope, it would seem.'

His words drew the scorn of half the chamber, evident in a general hiss of breath and the shaking of heads. Many believed that this recent proposal of the Caliphate was nothing more than empty words, amounting to simply another manoeuvre in the Caliphate's latest trade dispute with Mann.

'The Caliphate merely hopes to sustain this war for as long as it can,' said Chonas, as though speaking to a child. 'It profits too well in providing blackpowder to both sides.'

Some rapped their knuckles on the table in agreement with this. Others protested vocally and asked to be heard.

After that, the assembly broke down into a series of arguments. They could carry on this way for an hour or more, Bahn knew only too well.

It was hot in the huge room, with its windows facing the sun. Despite the hand-pulled ceiling fans and the cool sea breeze from those windows which stood open, a smell of sweat permeated the chamber, not quite concealed by the scents of sickly sweet perfumes. After a while Bahn's interest faded to mere observance, and then shifted to other matters entirely.

He had hoped today to hear of some resolution on their present food crisis, yet they could do nothing about that, it seemed. Food supplies to Khos had been reduced even further since they had lost a grain fleet on its return from Zanzahar. In theory Khos could sustain itself without these imports, being the breadbasket of Mercia after all. But with a steady influx of refugees into the Free Ports over the last decade, which the Mercians had finally welcomed, after heavy losses suffered in the first few years of the war – deciding they needed these desperate people after all – Khos had long ago ceased to produce enough to feed the other islands. With their summer harvest of wheat still in the fields, and a large proportion of their imports needed elsewhere, rations had become even more meagre than before.

Upon noticing the jutting bones on his son's body and even in his wife, Bahn had chosen to abstain from consuming any of his family's weekly rations, in the pretence that he could eat when he was serving at the walls or inside the Ministry. But even the soldiers there were suffering as everyone else, and received hardly enough to sustain a man.

A fist crashed against the tabletop next to his arm, jerking him from his thoughts. Bahn stared at it as though it had fallen from the sky.

'Enough of this,' the general rumbled to the gathered ministers, stopping their scattered debate in its tracks. He drew himself tall, not looking at the First Minister but at the others around the table instead, and with a firmness in his voice he said, 'We were discussing the forts, and I still have this to say on the matter. If you choose not to defend the forts, we must defend ourselves by other means. We must stop sitting here on our arses behind our high walls. We must attack, and take the fight to the enemy.'

Attack? Bahn was suddenly all attention.

A chair fell to the floor as old Phrades clambered to his feet, mouthing words no one could hear. Other ministers stood and added their own more substantial voices to his protests. Bahn pressed back in his chair, seeking anonymity from the suddenly angry Michinè. He blinked at the powder-white faces ranged around the great table. These men had been taught from youth to show emotion only when it was most required of them. It was said that they daubed their faces white so as to hide the merest hint of a blush. Now, in their hostile expressions, he saw the blood of their ancestors finally flooding to the surface, darkening the pallor of their dusted complexions. It was the same blood as ran through the veins of their great-great-grandfathers and uncles, those wealthy patricians who had deposed the first and only High King of all Mercia, and had done so backed only by a rabble army inflamed to action by the king's plans of foreign conquest – for such imperialistic ambitions had not sat well with the people of the Free Ports.

'Attack with what?' enquired Minister Sinese, shaking his walking stick in the air.

'With our reserves, damn it. Yes, that again. We have men enough to launch an offensive against Nomarl – there, you can see it right before your eyes, man, close enough you could almost reach out that stick of yours and touch it.' Creed gestured with one hand as he spoke, pointing to the windows at first, then further east so he was gesturing at a wall of the chamber instead – as though he could see through it to the entire coastline of the mainland. 'First we seize Nomarl. Then, with the reserves of Minos and the other islands, we can capture further harbour towns along the Pathian coast. We establish beachheads, gain a toehold on the mainland, and by this means we open up a new front. We give ourselves *options*. What good are reserves if all we do is shelter behind our walls with our hopes fading? While those men remain inactive, they are merely more mouths to feed, gaining us nothing but peace of mind. Well, gentlemen, I tell you now' – and his hard gaze roamed the room, taking the measure of them once more – 'we are long beyond peace of mind. It is time for us to act.'

The general had said nothing of such a proposal to Bahn before this meeting began, and yet Bahn was his closest aide. He knew, however, that the old veteran could be as calculating as he could be spontaneous. Perhaps he had broached the subject of the forts again, knowing full well they would dismiss it, merely with the intention of then demanding what he really desired: a renewed offensive against the Empire. Or perhaps, simply sitting here in this chamber, staring out across the narrow stretch of water to the enemy town, had invoked in him some passion or instinct for action, and now he was riding on the wings of it.

Sinese, Minister of Defence, quietened the room with a raised hand while he twisted the tip of his cane into the floor.

'General Creed, I have already stated our position on the reserves, both here today and in previous sessions of this cabinet. We will not leave ourselves exposed, without reinforcements, should another large-scale Mannian offensive take place against the Shield. And since, as you are so fond of reminding us, we are so vulnerable on our eastern coastline, as well, that gives even further reason for our reserves to remain intact, for at least then we do have something to respond with, should the Empire ever attempt such a manoeuvre. General, we are hardly in a position now to resume offensive operations against the Mannians. Across the Free Ports we produce modern cannon, rifles, ships as fast as we are able. More so now than ever before. We go hungry because we must give as much to Zanzahar for its blackpowder as we do for its grain. Yet still, we barely hold our own.'

'Hold our own, you say? For ten years now they have been slowly pushing us back. As I speak, Kharnost's Wall is ready to fall apart at the seams. This is not a stalemate, and you must dissuade yourself of that notion, if that is what you now believe. No, it is a slow but certain execution. If we do not change course, then all of us are dead already.'

The First Minister cleared his throat, and met Creed's eyes with an intelligent stare projected from beneath the overhang of his bushy eyebrows.

'You are the reformer as ever, General. All that matters to you is victory. You would change the world if that meant it would save us.

You would strip us of our only reserves of men in some mad dash for glory. Yet, for any gains we might make, think of all we could lose.'

And Bahn found himself agreeing with this sentiment, though he would never have admitted it in front of his superior. He thought: *Yes, we have lost too much already.*

'You are cuckolds to your caution,' Creed announced in a surprisingly quiet voice, again not addressing the First Minister but all the others in the room. 'Every one of you. What is this thing you harbour, this timidity? I understand it in boys, but not in grown men. We must be rid of it.'

'You have spoken, General, and we have listened. Do you now wish to call a vote?'

A snort of air from Creed's nostrils. The general's boots scuffed the floor as he turned and strode away from the table. Bahn stared after his superior for the length of a single shallow breath. *What's got into him?* he wondered.

Bahn remembered himself and started after the older man.

'Damned fools,' Creed said, loud enough for all to hear him. He stopped as he neared the door, turning to the table of rations and watered wines laid out for this session. It was simple food, and there was not so much of it, but to Bahn's eyes it held the glamour of a feast.

'Here,' the general snapped, and Bahn simply blinked as Creed shoved a wooden bowl of fruit into his arms, and dumped a roll of sweetmeat on top of that, and said, 'You look bloody starved, man,' and with that he swept out through the doors.

Bahn hesitated for a moment. He glanced back at the gathered assembly, all watching him now. It was the food that drew his attention, though. In particular a round of blue-veined white cheese that he could smell from several feet away. It might well keep until his daughter's naming ceremony, he thought, even as he inched forwards and gently lifted it into the cradle of his arms.

Before he left, he bowed as best he could to the assembly, holding the stance for the count of three.

Their pale faces turned away from him, as one.

CHAPTER EIGHT

Cheem

The Heart of the World was calm that morning, and as blue and empty as the sky that curved over it like a great vault of reflective sapphire, hemming it on all sides with the barest of horizons save to the west, where mountains hung amidst throngs of clouds. Sunlight fell upon the calm surface of the sea, bouncing back on itself in waves of heat. Birds wheeled ghostly and bright. From the south a lean breeze drew across the water's surface, ruffling the odd white-cap from the languid swell.

A chohpra, the crew of the *Falcon* called it. A perfect day.

The *Falcon* flew low above the peaceful waters of the Midèrēs, like a seabird skimming the waves, though perhaps a bird that had too long been subjected to the elements and was glad to be reaching journey's end. Ragged as its appearance might be, it had made good time on its crossing; though now, as it edged closer to its island destination, it was slowing as it approached the harbour of Cheem Port.

Gulls followed it in, catching lumps of keesh thrown into the air by the dark-skinned man standing at the prow of the ship. Ash was drawing the attention of a few bandaged crewmen currently at rest on the weather deck, shaking their heads as they watched and muttered words of mockery to each other. They thought of gulls as the rats of the sea, and why feed them, the old fool?

The old fool didn't seem to notice their scorn. Neither did Nico, who was standing beside him. He was half watching the attentive humour on Ash's face as he played with the swooping birds, half watching the nearing harbour and the many ships riding at anchor. Beyond them, the sprawling city rose into foothills, which in turn were dwarfed by black, snow-capped mountains as far as the eye could see.

This was the only city and deep-water anchorage on the entire mountainous island of Cheem. It was a large port, too, though not quite the size of Bar-Khos. It was also a place of infamy, and for once this infamy mirrored reality.

Nico had been raised, as were all Mercian children, on tales of the Cheem reavers. Amongst the Free Ports it was common practice for parents to warn ill-behaved children about how the reavers kidnapped young ones for their slaves. Parents painted them as monsters, crafting elaborate stories of how they would leave a wooden toy ship by the bed of a bad child they were planning on kidnapping soon. If that warning was not enough to inspire better behaviour, a toy ship would appear overnight beside the child's bed, to be seen with alarm when he or she awakened. Only the most unruly would fail to be chastened by such a portent.

Such fears only worsened when that child reached adulthood to discover that the reavers not only captured children as their slaves, but grown men and women too.

It was because of this that Nico's relief at having made the crossing intact was now diluted by a fresh apprehension. In fact he would have preferred that they were landing anywhere else but here.

Today's breeze was warm, laden with all the sharp scents of the sea and, whenever it paused for breath, a pungent aroma of melting tar rose from the decks of the ship. The wind blew in their favour, too, though the tubes were burning hot as they approached the port. They soared over the harbour's outer wall, and saw the narrow entrance channel leading through it: a passageway flanked by slimy stone walls, supporting squat forts of the new rounded design that was said to be effective in deflecting cannon shot. Looking down, Nico could see guns poking out from the forts, and older-style ballistae positioned on their flat rooftops, while soldiers in pale cloaks leant on their spears as they looked up at the skyship sailing over their heads, trailing black flags to indicate its neutrality.

Now that Ash had run out of keesh to throw them, the gulls screeched in protest. The ship turned, its crew scurrying to readjust the scull sails, and headed towards a beach on the southern edge of the harbour, where a windsock flew from a high tower mounted on the rocks. Mooring masts were fixed along the shore, and a rotting skyship lay on the sand, without its envelope.

'Stay close,' Ash instructed Nico. 'We will be stopping in the city for only a few hours, but the tales you may have heard of this place are not without truth. Cheem Port is a den of dogs. We will be safe enough in daylight, but even so, do not stray from my side.'

'And after that, how long will our journey into the mountains take us?'

'Long enough, but it is good country, if you know the trails. Peaceful, too. Few people live in the interior, save for religious orders in their hermitages.'

'And schools of assassins?'

Ash stiffened by his side. 'We are not entirely assassins, boy.'

Puffs of grey smoke erupted along the ship's right side. Anchors were dropped, dragging through the water and then up on to the beach, with clumps of seaweed now snared in them. Lines followed, and men on the beach grabbed hold of them and ran them to the mooring masts. Skittish in the vagrant breezes, the *Falcon* descended slowly.

Trench approached as his men vaulted overboard to secure the lines, his kerido hanging from his neck. The captain still walked with a limp gained in the battle.

'I got you home,' he said to Ash.

'Yes. My thanks.'

Trench shook Ash's hand, then Nico's. On his shoulder the kerido chattered its own farewell. Berl was not there to say goodbye, unfortunately. The boy was confined below, sweating feverishly in his bunk. He had lost a foot in the action.

Nico rocked as the flat-bottomed hull settled in the sand. He hoisted his pack onto his shoulder. Strange. Now that the *Falcon* was rested on land, he was almost sorry to be leaving it.

'Come,' said Ash, and stepped down the bouncing gangplank.

*

In the end, after all the warnings, Cheem Port was something of a disappointment.

Ash strode along with such speed and purpose that it was hard for Nico to take in much of the town at all. They stayed there only long enough to procure light provisions and two mules to carry them on their journey to the south of the island.

It was the stench of the place that initially appalled Nico the most. The streets were churned into mud after a recent rainfall, and sewage ran freely along their sides or down the middle, in fetid ditches, the overwhelming smell made even worse by the corpses of dogs and cats and at one point, ignored entirely by those who passed by, the body of a young woman stripped of her clothes.

Outside a store, Nico helped lash the newly bought provisions to the sides of each mule. Just as he was finishing this work, he was forced to jump out of the path of the city guards, a brigade of swarthy Alhazii mercenaries in harlequin armour, who moved quickly down the street, chanting something foreign and frightening. A short time later he and Ash passed the same guards in the process of breaking up a taverna riot. It was a mêlée, nothing less: men lay hollering in the mud outside while, within, steel clashed over the sound of numerous raised voices.

They hurried away from the scene, heading south through the city. Ash shouted in Trade at the grimy street urchins, scattering them from his path with the help of a few tossed coins. The children tugged at Nico's sleeves, pleading for food, for pennies, for tarweed, for dross. Prostitutes stood about everywhere; each was naked, and covered from head to toenails in golden paint. They flounced their breasts at Nico as he strained to look back at their bright nipples, the only parts not painted.

The slave markets were harder to bear. Through wooden gates he caught glimpses of men, women and children huddled together in rags while they were auctioned like so many cattle.

'Embrace the flesh!' shouted a street preacher, perched close by one such auction. 'Embrace the flesh or you shall be enslaved, as all the weak are justly enslaved!'

'What is he preaching?' asked Nico.

Ash spat at the preacher's feet as they rode by.

'Mann,' he eventually replied.

*

Unlike Bar-Khos, Cheem Port boasted no walls, and Nico was surprised when the dwellings either side of the road dwindled to outlying shacks and then to nothing, and then they were clear of the city entirely. He swayed rhythmically on the back of his mule, feeling his tension begin to fade.

The road wound its way between the foothills bordering the coast, never straying from sight of the sea and the ships that tacked across it. Cheem was an island composed of mountains and very little else, and most of its arable land was ranged along the coast or in the many narrow valleys that rose up towards the heavily forested peaks. For most of the day they followed the same road, passing a few hamlets and lonely cottages, where folk eyed them suspiciously and without greeting. By late afternoon they turned west into one such valley and rode upwards through sparse farmland until it gave way to heather and wild grasses suitable only for grazing hill sheep. On the slopes to either side, the trees began to cluster into silent forests of black pine.

A change came upon Ash as they rode into the high country, a softening of mood that went beyond even his usual calm countenance. His eyes mellowed. His lips pursed with satisfaction as he inhaled the fresh, still air.

'You seem happy to be back,' observed Nico.

A grunt was all that he got for his interest. The old man rode on in silence, and Nico had thought his comment forgotten when, ten or fifteen minutes later – as the setting sun ahead intensified the last of the day's colours, and all around them the cooling evening air hung with the scent of resin – the old farlander spoke.

'These mountains . . . they are home to me now.'

They made camp in a lofty clearing surrounded by aging jupes, their silvered leaves tinged red and golden by the setting sun. Nico's back was stiff after their long ride, his backside bruised. He watched Ash take one of the green leaves he always carried in a pouch and stuff it into his mouth; another headache. The old man set about spreading out blankets and some provisions for the night, then rubbed the mules down with handfuls of grass as they stood pulling wildberries from a bush. Nico cut some resinous bark from a nearby cicado tree to light a fire, and then gathered dead wood to feed it.

At last Ash settled himself down in a display of evident relief. He watched the darkening sky and drank from a wooden gourd as Nico prepared the fire. The boy used his flint and a piece of steel to strike sparks into the bark he had already ground into powder, then blew gently until flames took hold. The damp wood tossed white smoke into the air, contrasting vividly with the black mountain peaks that surrounded them.

'It's getting cold,' said Nico, rubbing his hands and holding them out to the newborn flames. He had regained some weight since setting out from Bar-Khos, but he was still thin enough to feel the cold keenly.

The old man barked a laugh. 'I will tell you about cold sometime.'

'Your vendetta that took you to the southern ice, you mean?'

Ash nodded, but said no more.

He had merely nodded the same way the last time it had been raised, before they left Bar-Khos, Nico asking one thing after another about the old man's previous vendetta, and receiving only the briefest answers. It had caused Nico to grind his teeth together in frustration, and he did so again now, desperate to hear more of these legendary far-off lands he had only ever heard of in stories and song.

'Is it true that they eat their own kind?' Nico tried.

'No, they only eat their enemies. They leave them to freeze overnight then pluck the meat from their corpses.'

Oddly, that awful image caused Nico's stomach to rumble. He was starving after their long ride. He tossed a fresh stick into the fire, then another.

'You still haven't told me how you ever made it back to the coast. You said you had already lost your dogs by then.'

A hiss of breath through clenched teeth. 'Another time, boy,' Ash said. 'For now let us just sit here a while and enjoy the silence.'

Nico sighed, rocking back on his haunches. He did not look at the old man.

'Here,' said Ash, holding the wooden gourd out to him.

Nico ignored it for the moment, instead watching as a soft gust fanned the flames so that they sparked into the night. 'I am not one for drink,' he declared at last.

Ash considered that. 'Your father . . . he was a drunk?'

Now it was Nico's turn to avoid the question. He rubbed his hands together again, blew into them. He could see from the corner of his eye that Ash was watching him.

'And what you feared in your father, you now fear most in yourself.'

'He could get angry on the drink,' Nico admitted. 'I do not wish to go the same way.'

'I understand that. But you are not your father, boy, just as he is

117

not you. Here, now, try a little. All things in moderation, even moderation itself. Besides, it will keep you warm.'

Nico sighed again, then took the gourd from the old man and sat studying it for a moment.

'Careful now. It is potent brew.'

Nico put it to his mouth and tried a sip. He gasped at its brackish sting against his throat, and coughed.

'What *is* this stuff?' he rasped, passing back the gourd.

'Barley water – and a few drops of sweat from the wild Ibos. They call it Cheem Fire.'

Nico did not like the sound of that. Warmth pulsed through his belly, but he knew enough to realize that it was an illusory heat. His father had once explained how falling asleep drunk in dropping temperatures could be fatal. 'You think it wise to get drunk tonight?' he asked.

The old man swatted at him as though he were a fly. 'Let your hair down, boy. Besides, a hangover will help us for what we have to do tomorrow.' Which of course made no sense at all to Nico, but he said nothing more.

They ate a supper of cured ham and a loaf of keesh shared between them, washed down with cups of chee brewed from the water of a nearby stream. They drank more Cheem Fire, and became merrier still as the light faded and the stars gathered overhead. The fire crackled and sparked against a darkness made blacker still by the light of the flames. They warmed their feet against it, their boots off.

'Is it far from here?' Nico managed, after some time gazing into the flames, that were hissing and dancing with life, almost lost in his thoughts.

'What?'

'The monastery. Is it far?'

The old man shrugged. He had picked up a stone, and was tossing it deftly into the air with one hand.

'Why do you shrug?'

'Because I do not know.'

He must be drunk, Nico thought. 'But if you live there,' he tried again, 'how can you not know how far we must travel?'

'Nico, trust me, will you? It will all make sense in the morning. For now, drink up, and enjoy. After tonight, when we finally reach Sato, you will have much hard work and tough training ahead of you.'

Reluctantly, Nico accepted the gourd once more. He took another fiery gulp and returned it, then lay on his back to watch the stars, one elbow crooked beneath his neck. It was getting colder.

From the corner of his eye he could see Ash still clutching the stone in his hand, as he studied the seal that hung about his own neck. Nico turned to study him: the man wore an expression of sombre self-reflection.

I might have known, thought Nico. *He's a maudlin drunk, just like my father.*

Ash looked up from the seal, to see Nico staring at him. He grunted and tucked it back beneath his robe. 'What?' he said.

'Nothing, Ash . . . Master Ash. I have a question.'

The old farlander sighed. 'Then ask it.'

'You said the seal you are wearing is dead now. But that it once belonged to a patron.'

'Yes.'

'If you use the seals as deterrents, why then do you not wear your own seal? Why do you not protect yourself with the threat of vendetta?'

Ash's teeth flashed in the firelight. 'At last,' he said, 'a question worthy of discussion,' and he again threw the stone up, spinning, and snatched it out of the air.

Ash leaned closer, as though to confide in him. 'I will tell you something, Nico, and you must remember it always.' His breath was hot, spicy. 'Revenge, my boy . . . revenge is a cycle that has no end. Its beginning is violence and its offspring is violence. In between, there is nothing but pain. That is why we Rōshun wear no seals to protect ourselves. In truth we hope always to provide a deterrent, and nothing more. For we know better than most that vengeance serves no positive value in this world. This is simply the profession which our life paths have led us to.'

'You make it sound as though what you do is wrong?'

'We do not see it in terms of either wrong or right. Our work is morally neutral, and this you must understand, for it lies at the heart of the Rōshun creed. It is like this: we are rocks on a slope, set into motion by the movement of other rocks. We simply follow the natural fall of events.

He paused for a moment's thought. 'But we must never make this business of ours personal. Otherwise, we become something more than a simple force of motion. We become part of the cycle itself. If I were to be killed in vendetta, another Rōshun would take my place, and then another, and another still, until the same vendetta was concluded for the patron and our obligations fulfilled. And then it would be finished. We wear no seal and we seek no revenge for ourselves. That way, we break the cycle.'

The old man finished with a long pull on the gourd. He wiped his lips, gave Nico a light shove. 'Understand?'

Nico's head was swimming, and not just from the drink. His thoughts were confused. Khosians understood vendetta; they felt it in their bones and knew its impulse like a fish knows to swim. Their sagas were full of bloody murder and revenge, and those characters who sought retribution were always the heroes of the story.

He nodded, even though he was a good deal uncertain.

'Good. Then you have learned the most valuable lesson of all.'

A burning ember spat clear of the fire. The sound caused Nico to jump. He watched the ember as it glowed on the grass between his bare feet, fading slowly to greyness. He accepted another pull of the gourd. Illusory or not, it was good to feel warm inside. He suspected he was already a little drunk, and decided that it was no terrible thing after all. In fact he felt cheered, and somewhat lightened of his many burdens. He settled back once more to take in the night sky.

The stars were bright up here in the mountains, the brightest of them almost pulsating in their brilliance. When Nico swung his head from far left all the way to far right, he could follow the milky sweep of the Great Wheel across the heavens; when he looked downwards from the Wheel, off to the right of the fire, he could see his two favourite constellations studding the blackness – the Mistress, with the stars composing her hand holding those of her broken mirror; and beside and above her the Great Fool, the Sage of the World, posturing with his faithful meerkat at his feet, four small glimmers in a jiggling line – his only companion at the end, when he gave up the celestial throne to wander the world and to bring the teachings of the Dao.

A meteor streaked overhead, followed almost instantly by another. To the east, a comet trailed a finger of light across the heavens. Nico breathed it all in, and felt at peace.

It was a peace interrupted, however, by the sound of Ash chuckling quietly to himself in the firelight.

Nico ignored him, thinking him drunk beyond sense. But the old man continued to chuckle.

'What amuses you?' Nico finally demanded, his words slurred.

Ash rocked back and forth, trying to contain himself, but a glance at Nico's expression only made him worse. He pointed the gourd in Nico's direction, tried to say something around his mirth, but had to try again.

'All is lost!' he cried in mocking mimicry of Nico's young voice.

Nico scowled, the blood rushing to his cheeks. The last thing he wished to be reminded of was the airship battle and the moment he had almost broken down. Such shame was something he needed to keep buried.

He opened his mouth to shut the old man up with some sharpened words of his own, but Ash pointed at him as he did so, and seemed to know what he was going to say, and it only made him laugh harder.

Perhaps it was the Cheem Fire, or perhaps it was the glint in the old man's eyes, without malice or condescension, for Nico suddenly found himself caught up in the man's humour, seeing the funny side of it without shame. Before he knew it he was laughing too, rocking back and forth like the old farlander, both of them howling like fools until the tears ran freely down their cheeks.

'All is lost!' Ash called out again, and they were beside themselves with their roars, holding their sides as the flames lit or shadowed their cackling faces, and the stars blazed within hand's reach just overhead.

'*All is lost!*' they cried out into the night.

CHAPTER NINE

Wilderness of Mind

'What is it?'

'A bush.'

'I can see that, but what's so special about it?'

'What do you mean?'

'Well, why are we just standing here staring at it?'

They were, too – just standing there staring down at a small green bush beside the gurgling of a mountain stream. It was early morning, the sun overly bright in their eyes. Nico had a horrible pounding in his head from the night before.

'Have you ever seen a bush like this before, Nico?'

'I'm not sure.'

'Then look closer. Look at its berries.'

Nico looked closer. The berries were small, oily black. They were patterned with curious white markings that looked a little like skulls. 'No, I don't think so.'

'No, you have not. There are only a few of these bushes on the entire island of Cheem. They were brought here from Zanzahar, and there all the way from the Isles of Sky.'

Nico listened without much patience. His stomach was dangerously afloat this morning, and he wanted only to lie down and curl up for the rest of the day. If this was how Cheem Fire felt the morning after, then he vowed never to drink the foul stuff again.

'My memory, Nico,' said Ash, as he dropped to his knees before the shrub. He plucked two berries from the same branch and dropped them into his battered leather cup. Nico watched him, in expectation of more. The old man sighed, paused in what he was doing.

'When we first came here to Cheem to found our order,' he began, 'we did so because there were many older sects already established in these mountains. Religious orders in remote places, where seekers would come to retreat from the world of men. Few other people live here. It is a wilderness, where it is easy to lose oneself.

'But that was not enough to hide our order from notice. We feared that if a Rōshun were ever caught, he might betray the whereabouts of our monastery, and put us all at risk. So our own memories of its location were . . . *altered*. Buried deep. The Seer at Sato knows the techniques for achieving that.' Ash began to pulp the berries with a broken twig, carefully and slowly, paying full attention to the task.

'When I use the juice of this berry, it will unlock the memories that have been hidden from me. It will show me the way.'

Ash spat into the leather cup, then held it out to Nico for him to do the same. Nico frowned, then leaned forward and spat into the cup. Ash stirred the pulped mess some more. 'If I fail to prepare it correctly,' he confessed cheerily, 'it can be fatal.'

He motioned for Nico to kneel at his side. At first Nico hesitated, wondering what the old man was getting him into now. He knelt anyway. The end of the twig emerged from the cup, and Ash lifted it towards Nico's forehead, whereupon he pulled back sharply.

'Stay fast, boy.'

'Why must *I* take it?'

'So *you* will not remember the way.'

Ash dabbed the concoction against Nico's forehead, humming something beneath his breath. He then applied the same ointment to his own skin.

'Now what?' asked Nico, as the old man was washing out his cup. Already, the blue stain on his forehead had dried to red.

'Relax. Take it easy. It comes on slow.'

So Nico relaxed. In fact, he curled up into a ball and promptly fell asleep.

*

The dreams came upon him like black tar oozing up through the ground. They enveloped him, slowly but inevitably, squeezing into his pores and up into his head until his mind was oozing like tar as well.

In these dreams he seemed to be fully awake, at times. It was twilight, his master leading them, seated on the mules, as they plodded through silvery forests where even the breeze could stir no sound or motion. The sky looked grey and washed-out above their heads, and it seemed lower than normal, almost crushing them. Clouds chased across it, tinged blue by the sister moons which swung across the sky much higher and faster than they should have done. Nico watched them for a time, the moons behind the clouds, one white and one blue, as some element of time pulsed through him, infinite and end-less and circular, and before he realized it, the clouds and the moons were gone and it was daylight, though a watery-thin daylight in which the night still hovered. They were walking their mules across a steep rocky valley, Ash singing something simple and foreign at the top of his lungs, the echoes of it bounding off the slopes of shale and coming back at them, creating a harmony like no other he had heard before.

Nico was crying, for some reason, as they huddled around a tiny fire of pitiful twigs in a cave that smelled of bat droppings and algae. Ash was crying too, sobbing about the family he had lost so many years before, his beloved wife and his young son; and at the sight of it Nico couldn't help himself, his own sobs turning suddenly to laughter, and Ash was growing angry at him, shouting in that alien tongue again, more like growling than words – but that only made Nico worse, and he was pointing at the old farlander's increasing wrath and shouting, '*All is lost! All is lost!*' at the old man, until Ash made a grab for him, but tipped forward instead and fell and rolled across the fire – so the flames were smothered dead – and did not get up.

But no, that wasn't right, for it was raining, and they were slip-ping in mud as they hauled the mules up a slope running with streams of icy water, and the clouds were so low and dark it was impossible to tell what time of day it was, and there ahead of them roared a great waterfall wreathed in mist, and they were soaked to the bone by the fine spray of it, drawing closer and closer to that crashing cascade of water by way of a terrible path that wound along a thousand-foot ravine. They walked straight through the falls, and emerged into a tunnel glowing eerily green with lichen furring its walls, the old man shouting something reassuring amid all the noise, though too loud to hear him, the constant crash of water shaking his stomach loose, and his mind, even.

And then he was dreaming for sure, for he was no longer in the mountains of Cheem at all, but on a great rolling grassland that seemed to go on forever beneath a sun that arched overhead shallow and pale. A solitary bird wheeled in the sky. Flies hovered in clouds just above the grasses, but no animals could be seen on the land, no sounds of life could be heard. In a blink night fell. The twin moons shone overhead. He was looking down upon a man curled up beneath a scrubby tree, wrapped in animal skins, sound asleep. The man wasn't alone. Shapes were moving silently towards him. What little Nico could see of them, they were shapes made from nightmares, for they looked like insects, spiders or ants perhaps – though huge in size. Each seemed the size of a mule, and scuttled rather than ran.

It was a dream, Nico realized, but unlike any he had ever experienced. He did not seem to be within this dream – rather, he was hovering in some disembodied form, witnessing the nightmare of another. Something else was strange about it, too, for he seemed to know this man, even though he could barely make out his face in the darkness.

Suddenly Nico was yelling at the familiar stranger to wake up, to gather his weapons and defend himself; but without effect, for no sound would come from his mouth. He yelled even louder, began screaming even, as the shadows converged on the sleeping shape. But the only thing to stir was a slight breeze, the rustling of a few leaves on the tree under which he slept.

A seed pod detached itself from an otherwise bare branch. Possibly it was the very last seed on the tree. Its wings caught the air and it spun slowly earthwards, before, it settled right on the sleeping man's cheek.

In an instant the man was up, and fighting for his life.

*

'Boy!'

Nico came awake with a start, gasping for air.

Ash was shaking him lightly, holding out a cup of steaming chee. Nico blinked at him dumbly. For some seconds he was unable to move; then, with an effort, he sat up.

He turned his head to see where they were. Yet another high valley, it seemed.

'Easy, boy,' said the old farlander, fixing Nico's hand around the mug. There was a wildness in his eyes this morning.

'Are we there yet?' Nico asked.

'Almost. How do you feel?'

Nico groaned in response. He felt particularly delicate, and a dull pain throbbed behind his eyes. His clothes were in a fine mess, too, torn and smeared with dirt and leaves. Ash looked no better, his robe in tatters, his face grubby and sprouting the beginnings of a grey beard. 'How long . . . ?' Nico began, not sure how to phrase the rest of his question.

'Five days, I think – maybe more. You did well. You held it together.'

Nico sipped the hot chee, though he could barely taste it. He badly needed to scrub his teeth. He studied his surroundings more closely now that his eyes had cleared of sleep. A high valley divided down its length by a broad stream that meandered calmly past their camp on the far side of the two mules grazing a few yards away.

His gaze followed the stream upwards, past the rushes that massed along its curving banks, towards the yellow grassland that spread beyond them across the whole of the valley floor, all of it rippling in a morning breeze that carried the scents of hot keesh and frying garlic, and occasionally a hint of distant laughter. At the very head of the valley sat a large building of red brick, with a tower rising at one corner. Around it huddled a small forest of low, gold-coloured trees.

They took their time striking camp that morning. Nico sat quietly and let the chee soothe his empty belly, idly observing the view as their small campfire kept the grassflies at bay. Ash shaved and washed himself in the stream, standing waist-deep and naked, occasionally whooping at the shock of the cold water. Nico pieced together what little he could recall of the previous five days . . . mere fragments of memory, vivid scenes framed by nothingness and, even more out of place, a strange dream of a man he had somehow known . . . None of it made sense to him.

He eventually decided that he really did need to wash himself and scrub his teeth. He cast away these futile recollections along with his clothes, drew from his pack a bar of soap and the little covestick, and went to join Ash in the slow, frigid flow of the mountain water. It was deep enough to swim in some parts, and he passed much of the morning like that, swimming or floating on his back, the sunrays bouncing down on him from high overhead, the occasional shy rainbow trout making dashes around his toes. His stiff, overstretched muscles gradually loosened in relaxation. His many cuts and grazes stung with the welcome freshness of the chilly current.

As Nico dried himself with his tunic, shivering in the cool breeze, he found himself staring down upon a small bush growing by the side of the stream. It was the same species that had sent them on their strange journey through the mountains for the last four or five days, with its oily black berries and white markings. Nico drew Ash's attention to it.

'Yes, we make use of its berries again when we leave,' explained the old man. 'Don't worry,' he said, on noticing Nico's obvious concern, 'we will be here for many moons yet.'

*

They were being watched, Nico sensed, as they began their ascent from the valley floor on muleback. Ash noticed his searching gaze, as he scanned nearby rises of rock. 'You waste your time,' was all Ash had to say, before spurring his own mule onwards.

It took longer than Nico had expected to work their way up to the monastery. Smoke rose lazily from the building's many chimneys, and the shutters of glassless windows stood open to the day. As they got closer to the small forest that surrounded it, they began passing walled gardens tended by figures in black robes; men of many races, sweating in the hot mountain sun, some laughing or chatting as they worked, others solitary and focused only on their tasks.

Many hailed Ash as he passed by, raising their fists in salute. Others bowed with palms pressed together in the traditional greeting of the Way, the sami, their mouths turning into soft smiles.

'Ash!' cried an old farlander, who flashed a gap-toothed smile as he pranced towards them on bare feet, his hands clutching the filthy hem of his robe. Of a similar age to Ash, he possessed the same unusual features, though stockier in size and sporting a top-knot of black and silver hair. 'By Dao, I thought you dead and buried in the ice by now,' panted the Rōshun.

'How are you, old friend?' inquired Ash.

'Better, now that you have returned to us safely. And not alone, I see.'

'This is my apprentice.' Ash jabbed a thumb over his shoulder towards Nico. 'Nico, greet this old fool, who goes by the name of Kosh.'

The man's eyes widened ever further as Nico offered him a weak smile. 'A quiet one,' observed Kosh with good humour.

'Hardly. He only speaks when it is least called for.'

'Well,' said Kosh, 'I will leave you both to get settled. But we must have a drink tonight, and some tales of your journey.' The man slapped the rear of Ash's mule to send it on its way. Nico followed, turning in his saddle to see the Rōshun pull himself erect and bow respectfully towards the departing back of Ash, while they moved on.

'These trees . . .' Nico began, as the mules crunched along a gravel path leading through the forest. Small trees, covered in a golden brown bark, with canopies of copper leaves and reddish blossoms shaped like stars. He had never seen their like before.

'Mali trees. They come from the Isles, too. From them we gain the seals.'

'From their seeds?'

'Yes.'

'The seeds grow into the seals?'

Ash sighed. 'The seeds *are* the seals, Nico. Although these particular trees you see around you . . . they are all barren, and they will bear no fruit themselves.' The old man tugged at the dead seal he still wore around his neck. 'I will find a suitable spot at the edge of the forest, and bury this one. In a short time, shorter than you might believe, it will grow into one of these same trees but, like the rest of them, it will yield no others, for it will have sprouted from a seal that no longer breathed.'

'So this forest . . . all of these trees . . .' Nico stared open-mouthed at the forest all around him, which was cast into silence by a momentary lull in the wind. 'They were all grown from seals of the dead?'

'Yes – every one of them.'

*

Men were practising archery in the open area in front of the monastery, on a wide swathe of grass kept short by a few wandering hill goats who seemed wholly unperturbed by the arrows flying through the air right above their heads.

Nico watched as the oldest of the archers, the only farlander amongst them, stepped up to take his turn. He might have been smiling, though it was difficult to be certain – for his skin was so ancient, and his back so stooped, that his face hung about itself as though in the process of falling off. The other men quietened as the farlander notched his bow. Without looking up, he inhaled deeply and held his breath. As he exhaled, he straightened his spine, before he drew the string and let loose the arrow in one single fluid motion, not moving from this final position until his arrow dropped out of the sky and struck the very centre of the distant target.

'Hah,' exclaimed Ash approvingly, as the mules carried them onwards.

They clopped through a narrow entrance to one side, and entered a square of dusty earth bordered on all four sides by the monastery building. At the centre of this courtyard stood another stand of mali trees, seven of them in all, surrounded by a picket fence painted white. A strange silence hung in this confined space. It centred on a dozen robed figures sitting cross-legged on the ground, each with his back to a tree. The men were deep in meditation, and paid no heed to the new arrivals, save for one, a bearded Alhazii dressed in a sleeveless cazok. He yawned at the sight of them, and stood and strode towards them through the morning light.

'You're back,' said the big man, as they dismounted from their mules.

'Baracha,' acknowledged Ash, by way of greeting, and the Alhazii bowed his head slightly.

'You look well for a man supposedly dead.'

The mule yanked the reins in Ash's hand, impatiently. 'It was close,' he confessed, hushing the restless animal. 'What news here since I have been gone?'

'Nothing much of interest.' Baracha shrugged his massive shoulders. 'We've all been praying for your safe return, of course.' He placed a hand on the nose of Ash's mule, as he spoke, and stared straight into the animal's eyes until it stiffened and became still.

'Who is this?' he asked, drawing Nico's attention back from the meditating Rōshun in the middle of the courtyard. This close, he could clearly see the many tattoos scrawled across the man's dark skin, tiny flowing Alhazii script, covering him entirely, even his bearded face. Holy verses, no doubt, as he'd heard these desert men liked to sport. The dark eyes slid carefully across Nico, before returning to Ash.

'My apprentice,' explained Ash, and Nico noticed the subtle change in Baracha's expression, his facial muscles tightening in surprise for the merest instant.

Baracha smiled as he again fixed his gaze on Nico. 'He has much to live up to, then.'

He smiles falsely, thought Nico, and decided this man was laughing at him. A spark of anger flared inside. It made him want to prove himself in some way.

Nico pointed to the stand of mali trees in the centre. 'Why do they stand alone like that?'

'Alone?' replied Baracha, turning to look.

'Master Ash told me earlier how you plant your lifeless seals in the forest outside. I was wondering why these seven grow here.'

'Can you not guess?' tested the Alhazii.

But Nico already had, and that was why he had asked. 'I would guess, then, that these trees were grown from seals that still . . . breathed. That means they bear seeds themselves.'

Baracha tilted his head sideways. 'I can't place your accent boy, Where are you from?'

'Bar-Khos,' Nico informed him, surprised by the pride he heard in his own voice.

'A Mercian? I might have known, from one so small and malnourished.' Again the Alhazii smiled, as if laughing at him.

'We Mercians have done well enough,' retorted Nico, 'in keeping the Mannians at bay these past ten years.'

'True,' Baracha acknowledged, placing a hand on the neck of Nico's mule. The animal flinched. 'But you should guard against talk like that while you are here. Perhaps your master has forgotten to explain these things to you. We include people here from every corner of the Midèrēs. We do not speak of politics.'

'Then I suggest you do not provoke such talk,' said Ash softly.

The Alhazii stared at the old farlander. Ash stared back.

Baracha snorted, then turned and strode off without another word.

'A hard man,' muttered Nico, watching Baracha walk away.

'The deep desert breeds hard men,' replied Ash. 'And its great emptiness gifts them with much imagination. I would caution you to provoke no one while you are here, Nico, especially that one. Now come. We have much to do before we may eat.'

*

They ate keesh and stew left over from lunch, since they had missed the noonday meal by the time they had rubbed down their mules and acquired fresh garments for themselves. Once they finished eating, Ash showed Nico to the door of the wardroom where he would be living with the other apprentices, and left him there to settle in.

Nico felt at a sudden loss, standing there alone in the corridor outside, after the old man so quickly departed. His new black robe hung stiff and heavy from his shoulders, smelling faintly of pine needles. He centred himself for a few moments, as the old man had been training him, then pushed open the door.

It was a large room with a stone floor and a roof of varnished wooden beams. A row of windows faced out on to the courtyard, with the bunks arranged along the opposite side. The room was empty save for two apprentices sitting on their beds. One of them was at work sewing a tear in his robe, his face screwed up in concentration. He seemed no more than fifteen years old, his white undergarments hanging loosely about his slight frame. The other apprentice, of a similar age to Nico, lay on his back reading a book, his long hair shining like straw in the light pouring through the windows. Both of them looked up as Nico stepped quietly into the room.

Nico nodded in their general direction, then looked around for a bunk not in use. He stopped at one with an empty chest standing at its foot.

'Hello,' said the young straw-haired man, as he put down his book and rose to his feet to amble across the room. When he offered his hand, Nico stared at it for several seconds before he took it and shook.

'You must be Master Ash's apprentice,' the young man said in a drawl, then caught Nico's puzzled expression. 'Word gets around rather fast here. Your arrival was the talk of the order during dinner.'

'I see,' said Nico.

'I am Aléas, and that is Florés over there. He is not rude. He simply has no tongue.'

The boy Florés opened his mouth wide to show them his vacant mouth. Nico smiled awkwardly and looked away, somewhat too quickly.

'Nico,' he told them both, as he transferred the few possessions of his pack into the chest.

'We know,' said Aléas. 'I have been warned by my master to keep away from you.'

'Your master?' Nico glanced up.

'Yes, Baracha. I understand you already met.'

'Your master judges others quickly, it seems.'

'He supposes we will likely fight, you being a Mercian and I being an Imperial,' explained Aléas, observing him with lazy, intelligent eyes. As Nico forced himself to return the young man's confident gaze, he found himself thinking: *An Imperial? I'm actually standing here face-to-face with the enemy. Strange that he does not seem so terrible.*

'So,' said the other, 'how does it feel?'

'I'm sorry?'

'Standing here, conversing with a foul Mannian?'

Nico considered the question. 'It feels fine,' he said at last. 'Though in truth I'm somewhat hungover just now, so it may be hard to discern any true discomfort.'

Aléas's smile was genuine. 'Then well met,' he said.

CHAPTER TEN

A Desertion

Nico tried to settle into his new environment, though at first it was not so easy.

There were nine other apprentices at the monastery, and all of them male. It was not that women were barred from the order – according to the other apprentices, they were simply never recruited, nor put themselves forth for recruitment.

Not surprisingly, all these young men spoke the common tongue that was Trade, their speech peppered with words and expressions from the older – and sometimes still native – languages of their home-lands. Nico was pleased that almost the first thing he learned at the monastery was a variety of swear words he had never heard before.

Each morning the young men awoke well before first light and washed themselves in the communal washroom alongside the other silent Rōshun of the order. Then they sat in the candle-lit dining hall, with the sun still not yet risen over the mountains to the east, and ate a simple breakfast of porridge and dried fruits accompanied by a choice of water or chee. The apprentices had to make the most of this fare, for their next and only other meal of the day would be dinner in the evening. Often they slept hungry, the food barely enough for their requirements. It was as though the Rōshun wished to encourage the theft of food-stuffs. For certain, they did not condemn such activity, only admonished the apprentice who was clumsy enough to get caught in the act.

Straight after breakfast, it was off to whatever lesson was sched-uled first for that morning, the young men's faces brightening along with the early light of dawn. For Nico, the rest of the day would comprise a confusing jumble of instructions quickly forgotten and lessons barely understood in terms of what purpose they might serve.

The evening meal, when it finally came round, was a relief like no other. He would sit and eat in numb exhaustion, thinking of nothing but his bunk.

The apprentices hailed from various corners of the Empire, though there was a surprising lack of tension for all the cultural differences between them. Still, Nico prepared himself for the worst, having never been overly sociable as a child. As a boy he had attended the local schoolhouse, and knew how his peers looked upon his solitary nature and his quick tongue when provoked.

But not so here, it seemed. Those few most likely to pick on him – big Sanse with strength on his side, fierce little Arados with the most to prove to the others – hung back for some reason. At first, Nico thought it was simply the strictness of monastery discipline. After a week or so, he realized it was something more than that. He realized they were somewhat in awe of Ash, and in return a portion of that respect rubbed off on to Nico himself, as the first apprentice Ash had ever taken on.

Those first early weeks of training were to be the most difficult. In a way the glamour that seemed to surround Ash, and therefore in a lesser form Nico, began to work against him. Nico felt as though he had a reputation to uphold, one that he had done nothing to gain – save for this assumption by the other apprentices that he must have something special about him for Ash to have chosen him in the first place. Yet he did not feel very special. He did not know why Ash had chosen him, though he suspected it had little to do with his abilities.

Nico would have told them as much, the truth of it, but each time he tried to, he found some inner resistance stopping him. He had begun to enjoy his minor celebrity. The others treated him with a respect he was barely familiar with after living rough on the streets of Bar-Khos and, before that, sharing a cottage with his mother's succession of indifferent lovers. He had found that he was standing up straighter than ever before in the presence of others. He would now meet their eyes and not so readily look away.

And so, in those early days, he tried too hard to impress, and because of this eagerness only made himself more inept in the trying.

He fumbled during his cali lessons – the style of sword-fighting practised by the Rōshun, and designed for confronting multiple opponents while always advancing, never moving backwards. He would wheeze to a dead halt during his fell running, vomiting from the sheer exertion of it; broke two fingers in unarmed combat and cried from the shock of seeing them bent out of shape; lost his temper with the frustrations of oni-oni, a test of the reflexes that involved the contenders trying to slap each other across the face every time a gong was struck. He even fell off while riding a zel, not once but twice – nearly snapping his neck in the process.

However, Nico distinguished himself in other activities, enough at least to preserve his reputation with the others. He flipped and jumped and climbed like a natural during the acrobatics classes; performed especially well in acting, requiring the use of subterfuge and disguise; grasped quickly the basics of breaching, in other words breaking and entry; remained undiscovered for hours in tests of stealth and concealment; excelled at archery, in which he did in fact have much ability, having both a natural eye and a great deal of experience from shooting birds for his mother back home. And, most especially, he shone in ali, the combined arts of evasion – otherwise known as running away – in which Nico found himself particularly talented.

Under different circumstances Nico might have expected to suffer from homesickness, longing for the familiar streets of Bar-Khos, or even for his mother's cottage. But for an apprenticing Rōshun there was, simply too much to learn and practise for his mind to dwell on such distracting thoughts. Only at night would a sense of isolation oppress his spirits, but even then not for long, since he was usually so weary that he fell asleep in minutes.

He saw very little of Ash during this time. It seemed the old man did not get involved in training the disciples. Neither did he offer personal instruction to his own apprentice, perhaps intending instead to train Nico only in the field, where it was said that the learning ceased and the knowing began.

Overall, the old farlander kept himself to himself, rarely seeking out his young protégé at all. It seemed almost as though he had discarded Nico at the first opportunity to present itself.

Nico was stung more than he would ever admit by this apparent desertion.

*

'Whet your knives!' Holt bawled over the heads of the ten apprentices gathered in the courtyard on a sunny day filled with wind. Instantly they bent their heads to the task.

135

Nico did not move, today. Instead he watched what the others were doing. Particularly he kept his eye on Aléas who he had already noticed tended to get things right first time. After a while, grasping a wooden practice knife in one hand and a steel carving knife in the other, he began to shave a fresh edge into the curved piece of wood that had been left blunt from its last usage. A guppy, they called this type of practice knife, perhaps because of the fish it resembled. The weapon lacked a point and was made from a piece of wintervine, a rare hardwood that normally grew on the sheerest of wind-exposed cliffs and, for some reason, only flowered in the depths of winter.

Suddenly Ash arrived by Nico's side, clasping a leather cup of chee in his hand. Haggard-faced, the old man stood and watched him work, one eye squinting against the stiff breeze snapping his robe around his ankles.

This was the day of the scenarios, mock situations intended to replicate, to some degree, the possible conditions in the actual field. The presence of their masters was compulsory at these fortnightly sessions, so today they were uncharacteristically tense and serious.

Nico had not spoken to Ash in six days. The old man had almost become a ghost to him, glimpsed only through windows, or occasionally in his sleep. Even the other youths had begun to notice this lack of attention, shown towards his apprentice. They had begun to mutter about it, fascinated by such behaviour from the order's most famous Rōshun, and they increasingly gave Nico strange looks whenever he chanced to walk in on them.

'Quickly, now, we haven't all week for this.' Holt, stood eyeballing them, with his chin held high.

Nico tested the edge of his wooden blade and found it sharp enough to draw blood. He sucked his thumb as he waited, and did not look at Ash.

Holt strode amongst them, testing the blades and retrieving the steel knives as he went. 'Now, my young squires,' said the blond-headed Pathian. 'The scenario today shall be cat and rat. Yes, Pantush, I know how much you adore this one. All of you now, choose a partner so we can begin.'

A partner? Nico mused, and cast a forlorn glance about him as the other youths quickly paired up with their friends. Within moments the press had parted to either side into pairs. Facing Nico, across a dozen feet of settling dust, Aléas stood alone, too skilled for anyone else to choose as his competitor on this of all days.

Nico's heart sank as the young man grinned at him. Towering behind Aléas, Baracha gave Ash a questioning glance.

'Cat, rat, west wing, ground floor . . .' Holt was saying, tapping one boy on the head and then the other, 'Cat, rat, west wing, first floor . . .'

He came to Nico and Aléas, and smiled. Everyone was smiling except for the two pairs facing each other. 'Cat,' he said, with emphasis, as he lay his palm on Nico's head. 'Rat,' he gestured to Aléas.

To their two masters he announced: 'West wing, attic. But be careful not to break anything up there, gentlemen.'

He then clapped his hands and marched onwards, hollering once more. 'You have until the next bell. One must hide, one must find. The first to draw blood wins. If you stay hidden until the bell sounds, you also win. That's it. Rats may go!'

Aléas was off, loping towards the door into the west wing. He ran like an athlete on the track, supremely confident in his own physicality.

First blood, reflected Nico, his hand already clammy around the hilt of his wooden knife. His mouth had gone dry. How much of a wound could this thing inflict? How bad was one allowed to make it? Typical of these Rōshun to tell you the bare minimum, then throw you in head first.

Baracha remained behind with arms folded, disdain in his eyes, confident of an easy victory.

'Better your boy had been the rat, eh? He hides well, I hear.'

Ash stiffened up at that, as if too world-weary to hold back what he would say next. 'Perhaps if you yourself were a little better at hiding, we might have spared ourselves much trouble in the past.'

A hoot from those of the Rōshun who stood close enough to hear him. Baracha hawked loudly and spat in the dirt.

It somewhat heartened Nico to hear the old man standing up for him. But then, he knew it was more than that. It was also this ongoing rivalry between the two – or, at least, sense of rivalry which seemed to emanate from Baracha.

A soft breath against his ear, almost lost in the breeze. 'Know that Aléas will not hide like a rat. He will position himself for an ambush, as the predator would. Tread with care, boy.'

'Cats may go!' came the order.

The remaining apprentices sprinted for the various doors of the monastery. Nico hesitated, and at last he met the old farlander's eyes. What he saw made him blink.

He thinks I will lose!

With the slightest of nods, the old man gestured for Nico to go.

Nico headed for the far door of the west wing. He was all at once focused on what he must accomplish, the urge almost overwhelming to prove them all wrong.

*

It was good, at least, to be out of the wind.

The monastery was even quieter than usual, its inhabitants having vacated much of the building for this afternoon devoted to scenarios. The west wing housed the library and study rooms, also the large chachen hall used for indoor meditation. Such spaces were brightly lit from their large windows, and smelled of polished wood and old dust.

A gust from outside as Baracha, and then Ash, entered the hallway, cup of chee still in the farlander's hand. Both wore white armbands, and were to follow him from a distance as supervisors only, since no instruction was to be the given during the coming trial. The object was to learn by *doing*, and thus nurture faith in following one's own instincts.

The attic, Holt had said, so Nico found the stairwell, and trod upwards to the first floor. A young Rōshun bustled past him. He acted as though Nico wasn't even there.

The wooden stairs leading to the attic were at the far end of a corridor lined with the doors to individual sleeping quarters. A window on the other side looked out over the rugged valley and towards an escarpment of dark rock beyond. A cloud mass drifted torn and tattered across a distant peak. Nico stopped and studied the open trapdoor at the top of the stairs. It was dark up there. Perhaps he should first find a lantern?

No, he thought, that was a stupid idea, he'd only make himself an easier target.

Ash and Baracha waited behind at the other end of the long corridor. They watched as he removed his sandals, laid them with care to one side.

Taking a deep breath Nico ascended as slowly as he could, staying to one side of the steps where it would make least noise under his weight. He ducked as he neared the opening. This would be as good a place as any for Aléas to launch an ambush, just after Nico poked his head though, momentarily blinded by the gloom.

Moments of reflection passed, and no ideas came to him.

There was only one thing for it, then.

He scrambled upwards, vaulted through the opening and tumbled across the creaking floor of the attic. He lay there on his back with the knife held before him, waiting for an attack.

When nothing happened, Nico lay where he was, trying to subdue his breathing. He'd already made enough racket by his entrance. He remained like that, until his vision adjusted to the lack of light, and gradually he could see about him the shadows of dark objects.

Without sound, Nico stood and inched away from the dim light of the opening. The attic was warm, and larger than he had expected. It ran for ten or so feet in all directions before becoming veiled in blackness, but he could sense the scale of the place from its faint motions of air. Items in storage stood everywhere: crates and boxes, piles of cloth, discarded furniture, even stands of arms. To hide in here successfully was just to pick a spot, any spot, and simply not move.

Nico took a step forwards, testing his weight on the floorboards for creaking, then another step . . . The wind outside pulled at the wooden roof tiles above his head. Some had worked loose enough to clatter, and now a chorus of them provided an eerie accompaniment to the keening of the wind itself.

He stopped at the very edge of the light infiltrating up through the trapdoor. Here too was a likely place for the ambush. Nico was still visible here, while the ambusher could remain in darkness.

Aléas was close by. He could sense him.

Nico squinted and peered into the dark spaces beyond. To the right of him, a cobweb hung from the sloping roof, glowing a ghostly white. Beneath it lay a jumble of shapes he could barely discern. To his left was an even deeper gloom, the light obstructed by something large. Nico took a step backwards. By inches he eased to one side at a crouch, continually scanning from left to right. He opened his mouth to hear better. He waited, almost without breathing.

It suddenly struck Nico how absurd this situation was: like play-ing a children's game of hide-and-go-seek, armed only with wooden knives. But then he thought of the knife in Aléas's hand, doubtless somewhere close, sharp as his own, and as capable of drawing blood. Nico's heartbeat began to pump in his ears.

For a moment the light diminished behind him, enveloping all in deeper blackness. He swung his head around to see the silhouettes of Ash and Baracha stepping through the opening. They made no sound either.

Nico waved them out of the way, until they had crouched either side of the opening and the meagre light was restored.

Now, he urged himself, *think*.

The cobweb nearby stirred. Nico had only time to lean back sharply as a vague form loosed itself at him from his right. He felt the air brush past his face, detected a blur of motion . . . then lunged forward, with his own knife. But it slashed through empty space, and then he felt the sting of pain across his left cheek, and again, across his right.

He was stunned enough to fall back upon his haunches. Crouching there, he clasped a hand to his face, blood leaking through his fingers.

'Owhh,' he moaned.

Aléas stepped before him into the dim light. The young man had streaked his face with grime, so that only the skin immediately under his hairline was still white. A chuckle sounded elsewhere in the attic, before Baracha clomped heavily back down the stairs.

Ash still waited, as Nico gained his feet and turned to him. He could not read the old man's expression.

Ash took a drink of chee and smacked his lips.

'Keep trying,' Ash murmured. 'You must be ready when I take you into the field.' And, with a swirl of his robes, he departed too.

Aléas nodded to Nico's facial wounds. 'Coat them with beeswax,' he suggested. 'It will keep the scars small. Come, I'll help you.'

For a moment, Nico found himself alone in the clammy darkness of the attic. Through his fingers blood dripped in a slowing rhythm. His right hand, shaking, sought the cool hard assurance of the wooden floor, and he sank down with it, his legs dangling over the edge of the trapdoor. He let out a long breath, and waited for his heart to stop pounding.

CHAPTER ELEVEN

The Cull

The night lay brooding in its own heat.

At the centre of the Lake of Birds, the imperial barge rocked gently, far from the distant lights of the towns that glittered around its shoreline. A jangle of music could be heard from those towns across the still water, and shouts and laughter, and the barking of dogs.

On the barge itself the only sound was the whispering of the slaves and the steady, heartbeat rhythm of a single drum. The atmosphere was unreal, heavy. The Nathalese slaves could sense it, huddling terrified together in their cages at the near end of the barge. They knew at last why they had been abducted so roughly from their everyday lives along the Toin. Tonight was to be their last night of captivity.

Above the rank stench of the slaves themselves, the air was pungent with musky incense wafting from the prow of the vessel, where the two priests, naked, stood, attended by their personal servants. Their bare flesh shone in the glow of several burning braziers, glistening with the oil that had been lavishly applied by their attendants. Two of the Nathalese slaves already lay prone at that end of the barge. A third had finally stopped screaming, and even now was crumpling to the deck, whether alive or dead they could not tell.

An Acolyte motioned quickly for another slave to be dragged forward. Most of the Nathalese captives protested, cowering at the rear of the cage as the guards kicked their way through to snatch one of them with rough hands. This time they seized a middle-aged woman, whose fine silk dress was stained and torn from her long captivity. She did not resist. She did not even appear to be aware of them. By her side, a young red-haired woman cried out and clung to her companion's arm.

An Acolyte kicked the younger woman aside so that she shrank back, whimpering. Before they pulled the older woman out of the cage, they tore the expensive jewellery from her neck and cast it at her feet, where it sparkled next to the length of chain shackled around her ankles. The other slaves watched with varying degrees of empathy, though primarily with relief that they too had not been chosen. Shame hung heavy within the cage: they could barely meet each other's eyes.

But the woman was not as helpless as she had first appeared. As the Acolytes began to lead her away, she stumbled and broke free from their grasp, making a sudden shuffling sprint for the rail at the near side of the barge. One of the Acolytes tried to restrain her, but a fraction too late. She pitched over the side, crashing into the water with a terrific splash, then vanished instantly as she was pulled down to her death by the shackles fixed around her ankles.

The red-headed girl whimpered as she watched her mother disappear over the rail. It was a pitiful, animal sound that came from Rianna's throat, but it was all the emotion she had left in her.

She failed even to notice as her quaking hands tugged fistfuls of hair from her bleeding scalp. Her mind had detached itself from the physical, though it was still capable of thought, in a way. It was thinking: *now my mother is dead, and my father is dead, my dear beloved Marth is dead, and I am dead, and everything everything everything is dead.*

'Oh Erēs!' she cried out in her head, seized by the sudden image of her mother struggling for breath down there in the freezing black depths of the lake. *Oh mother, oh dear mother . . .*

To stop thinking of that awful thing, she began to crack her skull against the bars of the cage, over and over again. A woman by her side tried to offer comfort by wrapping her arm around the girl's shoulders. Making soothing sounds, she squeezed tighter and tighter, as though to stop both of them from rattling apart with fear.

Do the same with yourself, some residual part of Rianna's mind spoke to her. *Throw yourself into the water as soon as they release you.*

No, said another voice, *you don't deserve such a clean death. They're all dead because of you . . . because you caught that young priest's eye with your look of defiance, and made him want you.*

'Mother,' she croaked aloud, and everything cracked loose inside of her. She needed to get away from this nightmare. She needed to wake up from it all, and flee back to the world she knew as her own.

In a way her wish was granted her. She passed out, and descended into a sweet blackness.

*

When she came to, apparently not much later, she was still huddled against the bars amid her fellow prisoners. Rianna choked as the horror returned to her. She tried to breathe, spluttering for air.

She might have broken then, lost her mind entirely, had she not noticed how her hand was clutching something slung around her neck.

Without thinking, she used her other hand to pry open her bone-white fingers, gazing down at the object in her grip. The seal, she realized, staring dumbfounded, an item all but overlooked until now. It was the seal her father had bought for her on her sixteenth birthday, worrying as always over the safety of his family.

Rianna had been appalled when her father had first forced her to wear it. The thing was just as hideous to look at as it was to touch. She had been even more horrified to awaken that first night to find it breathing and alive against her chest.

But her father was adamant. *I am High Priest of this city, my daughter,* he had reminded her. *Many would like to see me dead, and if they cannot get to me personally, they may still get to my family. You must wear this always, if only for your own protection.*

She had argued with him, complaining how awful it looked, and then howled that it wasn't fair, because *he* didn't have to wear one – nor did mother, so why should she? But still he would not be swayed. *Your mother follows my example,* he had explained. *The order of Mann does not allow me to wear such a thing. It would be seen as a weakness,* and he waited on her bed until her tears had run their course.

Look after it, he had cautioned her. *It is bonded to you now – and if it perishes then so shall you.*

She had been petrified at that thought of being linked so inseparably to this ugly thing. With ill grace she agreed to wear it always, though always she had tried to hide it beneath her clothing. That had made her father angry, claiming it was no deterrent if she kept it hidden from sight.

But would such a talisman stop these priests from Q'os? Rianna wondered now, as the seal pumped in her hand like a living thing. A seal was a seal, was it not? Surely even these priests of Mann would be made to pay for her death like anyone else?

It was a chance at life, she realized, and she felt wretchedly guilty as she thought this.

But then, what if she tore the thing off and let it fall unnoticed to the deck? The seal did not have to actually be worn to be aware of her death; it was connected to her now, no matter how far away it found itself. What if she hid it from sight, and just let them have their way with her? What if she had the strength to do such a thing as that? If they took her life, a vendetta might be declared. Revenge for her loved ones would surely be exacted on these animals.

Rianna moaned aloud, doubting she would have the courage for such a sacrifice.

Suddenly the choices before her were almost worse than the hopelessness she had faced before. Rianna was frozen with indecision, and on the verge of losing her mind.

But then they came for her.

*

'Quiet!' the masked Acolyte shouted, dragging her on her back to the far end of the deck.

'Wait!' she cried out. 'I'm protected, you see?'

But the Acolyte could not see, for it was too dark and he was too fevered with the rising excitement in the air. He threw her to the planking alongside one of the large braziers, and she saw a glint of steel as a knife came out.

The man ran it along her back, cutting her dress open from neck to waist. He pinned her struggling to the deck with a knee pressed painfully between her shoulder blades. Another Acolyte approached, bearing something in a clear-glass jar. He bent down to her face, showing her that it held some kind of worm: a fat and sickly-white atrocity wriggling for release from its glass prison.

'Wait!' she tried again, as the Acolyte tilted the jar and pressed its open end against her bare spine.

She cursed her father then, cursed him with all the passion she had left in her, for ever getting his family involved with these people, this obscene religion. What had he been thinking of? What crimes such as this had he himself committed in the name of Mann?

Rianna screamed: the pain was beyond bearing. But what was worse, much worse, was the sensation of the worm burying its way into her flesh.

The Acolytes released their pressure, and Rianna tried to fling herself upright, her hands scrabbling at the open wound in her back. A finger worked its way into it, seeking out the intruder.

Then something unexpected happened: all strength in her limbs deserted her. She collapsed back on to the deck, beside the three other slaves already lying there, panting helplessly, only the whites of their eyes showing. Rianna found herself unable to move or speak. All she could do was watch what happened next.

More slaves were fetched forward, and a worm was given to each one in turn. Soon, a dozen of them lay sprawled and paralysed on the deck. An atmosphere of panic increased with the slowly rising tempo of the single drum. The two priests watched the gathering number of victims with lustful excitement in their eyes. They exchanged words with each other as they stroked their own bodies, and occasionally inhaled deeply from a steaming bowl of some kind of liquid narcotic, the fine-linked golden chains of their facial piercings dangling just above its surface.

It began with the killing of a single slave, an elderly man with cataracts in his eyes; the priest woman, naked, her empty, sagging breasts swinging low as she bent over and took a knife to him.

Immediately, the atmosphere intensified to a higher pitch. It was as though the priestess had pierced more than a mere physical barrier by the work of her knife, but breached an abstract one too: a skin of the world that stretched over all life, shielding normal eyes from an outer reality devoid of humanity, boundless and alien. The dying man's squeals pierced the night air. The paralysed slaves saw the fate in store for them, as he lay on the deck quivering and gurgling his last breath, bubbles of blood forming on his lips. This slaying, though, was purely the opening act.

The old woman turned and spoke to the younger priest, Kirkus, who stood trembling and staring at the knife in her bloody hands. The priestess snapped her gaze towards a young girl to Rianna's left, pinning her with a glare. 'Up,' said the old woman, with a flick of her head.

Suddenly the girl was able to move. She clambered to her feet – then without warning, she sprinted for the rail.

'Stop!' snapped the old witch. The girl collapsed to her knees, her legs suddenly gone from under her.

'Now, you try,' the old priestess instructed her grandson.

Kirkus fixed his attention on a fat man still clad in the blood-stained apron of a butcher. 'Come here!' he commanded.

The butcher grunted as he sat upright. He looked to the far rail, then to Kirkus before he rose unsteadily to his feet. Growling deep in his throat, he suddenly leapt at the young priest, moving fast despite the bulk of him. 'Stop!' commanded Kirkus, but the man already had a grasp around his neck as his legs collapsed, and he dragged Kirkus down with him.

'Focus, you idiot,' chided the old woman by his side.

Kirkus choked and struggled harder to break free.

'Cease,' snapped the priestess.

The fat butcher released his grip and fell to his knees, palms pressed against the deck, roaring his defiance at the planking in front of his nose.

'I suspect this one was once a soldier,' observed the old woman.

'I know,' replied Kirkus with irritation, massaging his bruised neck. 'He has a tattoo there, on his upper arm.'

'Ah,' she observed. 'A Nathalese marine.'

She stepped lightly behind the old veteran. She fixed her claws against the sides of his head, yanking it back so that he straightened up on to his knees. 'Your eyes,' she suggested into his ear. 'Pluck out your eyes.'

The man spat words of outrage. Still, his hands lifted involuntarily from his sides and rose towards his face. They trembled under an inner struggle of will, but he could not stop them as his fingers curled deep into the sockets of his eyes, and wrenched.

He made a rasping sound but, incredibly, did not scream as his eyeballs popped out like small boiled eggs from their sockets, and fell dangling against his cheeks.

'More like a fat pig for the slaughter,' she said, letting him drop back to the deck.

Kirkus indulged in another loud inhalation from the bowl of narcotics. The old woman moved to his side, stroked his stomach.

Rianna watched with eyes wide. Inside her head she was screaming.

'Do as you please,' said the witch to the young man, her voice husky. 'Tonight you must shed all qualms of conscience still lingering within you.'

The young priest hesitated. He studied the slaves arrayed upon the deck, then turned away again to draw in another breath from the steaming bowl.

'Work yourself up to it,' the old crone suggested. 'We have all night. As I said, do as you please.'

His eyes fell on Rianna, and she tried to look away. But her body was not hers any longer: her eyes would not close for more than a blink.

He passed the bowl to the priestess, then stepped towards Rianna. No sound would come from her throat.

Eager hands ripped away the remnants of her dress. His face was a mask as he stared at the rise and fall of her white breasts, at her nipples stiffened by fear. The seal still rested between her breasts, pulsating as it always did. He fixed his gaze on it, puzzled at first, and then a cool understanding followed.

He bared his teeth, and snapped them at her. At first, she thought he was trying to bite her, but instead he ripped the seal away with an angry jerk. He spat it into the flames of the brazier.

'The flesh is strong,' breathed the young priest foully upon her face.

But by then, Rianna was already dying.

CHAPTER TWELVE

Vendetta

'Where are we going?' demanded Nico as he hurried after Ash into the west wing of the monastery, along the main tiq-panelled corridor, down steps into a dim basement that held casks and boxes and various assortments of stock. Ash moved quietly to the centre of the wooden floor, his form casting a long shadow from the solitary lantern hanging above. Nico stopped by his side. He followed Ash's gaze towards their feet.

The old man took a key from his robe. It was as thin as a carpentry nail, and fine-toothed at one end. He bent to insert it into a hole in the floor that Nico was unable to see. A twist and a click, and suddenly Ash was tugging open a trapdoor that uncovered a stone stairwell and a release of stale air. They descended in silence.

Twelve steps down, they reached a low, damp tunnel, and they followed it to a source of light at its very end.

'We call it the watching-house,' Ash explained softly, as he nodded a greeting to the two long-haired Rōshun who knelt, back to back, in the centre of the brightly lit vault they now stood within. A ceiling of white plaster arched high over their heads, an occasional root poking through it to dangle as if lost in the smoky atmosphere. The ceiling curved down to meet a circular periphery of walls plastered in the same sad, damp white.

The walls were lit by countless lanterns, and punctuated by rows of identically tiny alcoves, hundreds upon hundreds of them. Inside many of these alcoves Nico could see the familiar dark shapes of seals hanging from hooks. There were thousands all around.

What might ordinarily have been a solemn experience, standing deep beneath the ground surrounded by their sheer multitude, was instead something creepy and surreal, owing to the fact that all the seals were moving. Nico peered closer at them. It took several moments, as though his mind refused to see things for what they really were, but suddenly the scene snapped into clearer focus and he could see that steadily, perhaps five times in a minute, these thousands of seals were breathing in and out like tiny leathery lungs.

All of them, except for one.

They moved to stand before it, Nico's breath sounding loud in his ears, while Ash explained in a low drone about how it had died during the night, and how he hoped it was merely an accidental or natural death, and not murder and thus requiring vendetta. And, with that, Ash plucked it from its hook and swept out of the watching-house with Nico scurrying in his wake.

They left the monastery at a fast trot.

'Where are we going?' asked Nico, as they turned to hike a path up the valley floor.

'To see a man,' Ash replied over his shoulder. 'A man I should have taken you to visit long before now.'

'So why didn't you?'

The farlander leapt over a small slope of stones, and kept walking without reply. Nico scrabbled up after him, increasing his pace to catch up as the dry grasses clutched at his legs.

'Who is this man?' he called out.

'A Seer. He will read the seal for us, and then tell us what occurred in the night.'

'It's true, then?' panted Nico. 'What the other apprentices say, that he's a miracle-man?'

'No. The Seer merely understands subtle wisdom. With technique, and great stillness, he can do things that others can achieve only by chance, if at all.'

'I don't understand.'

'I know.'

They followed the stream for a short time, then angled away from it, treading across marshy ground that sucked at their sandalled feet. Ash continued walking without effort, as though he was taking an afternoon stroll. Nico, by his side, was now sweating.

'The Seer is our order's most valued member, boy. Remember this when you meet him. Our lore, our history, all of it has been passed down through the line of Seers. Without a Seer we would become blind, without direction. He alone can look into the heart of a seal and tell us what we must know from it. He can look equally into the heart of a novice, and judge if he is worthy. In a way, he will do so with you.'

'I am to be judged?'

'You will not know it. Mostly he will concentrate on the seal.'

'I still think he sounds like a miracle-man.'

'Boy, there are no miracles. What the Seer does is wholly natural.'

'In the bazaar of Bar-Khos, I once saw a man who could stand upside-down balanced on his lips. He could do press-ups of a kind when he pursed his lips against the ground. If that's not a miracle, I don't know what is.'

Ash gave a dismissive toss of his head. 'The Seer is what you Mercians call a . . . prodigy. They have not always been so, our Seers, but this one . . . this one is a man of learning as well as of intuition. When we first came here, to the Midèrēs, he heard of Zanzahar and the many things they imported there from the Isles of Sky. He travelled to the city to study them, though it was not always clear what those things had been designed for. The seeds of the mali tree, for instance. They are sold in that city as rare charms capable of bonding to their wearer. They store a person's life in some way, so the wearers, if they practise certain techniques, can relive those events in dreams of their own choosing. The Seer – it was he who discovered how to bisect those seeds and twin them, so we could use them for our own purposes. In that way he invented the seals.'

'So how did you conduct vendetta before then?'

'With great difficulty.' Ash cast a backward glance at his apprentice. There was a sparkle to his dark features, a vitality that seemed to have been absent for some time. 'Your wounds have healed well,' he observed to his apprentice.

'Yes,' Nico agreed.

It was true. The wounds caused by Aléas had been small enough cuts, as it turned out. They had not even require stitching. Nico had simply applied beeswax to them, as Aléas himself had suggested, whereupon the wounds had not bruised but stayed red and raw for some days, before scabbing over, causing the discomfort of constant itching more than anything else. When Nico had later caught his reflection, backlit by candle flame, in the glass of one of the kitchen windows, he was even somewhat taken with what he saw. The small scars made him look older, he decided.

The Seer lived alone in a little hermitage further up the valley. His hermitage sat on a hump of grass in the bend formed by a small, frothy brook that ran between rocks turned green with algae. Trees protected it on the windward side, gnarly jupes in full bloom and a large weeping willow whose leaves trailed in the current of water and sparred with its passing. The hermitage itself was nothing more than a shack, with a rectangular hole cut in one wall to overlook the brook, and which served as both window and door.

'Remember what I have told you,' said Ash as they approached.

Nico followed him inside. For a moment, in the dusty sunlight filtering past him though the doorway, he wondered if they had come to the wrong place.

In the centre of the tiny hut, the Seer sat cross-legged on a mat of woven rushes, facing the door with his eyes half closed. He was a skinny, ancient man, with a milky film covering his hooded eyes, and skin like that of fruit left too long in the sun. He was a farlander, obviously, and his dark skin contrasted sharply with the great puffs of white hair sprouting from his nostrils and ears. His scalp was bald. His earlobes, ritually mutilated, hung obscenely down to his shoulders in a manner Nico had never seen before.

Nico turned with open mouth to Ash to find him kneeling on the ground. With a jerk of his head, he indicated for Nico to kneel beside him.

The ancient farlander stared at Nico silently, in a way that reminded him of one his mother's cats, as if gazing at something that was not even there. The old man blinked slowly, then spread his lips into a grin that exposed his toothless gums. He nodded once, as though in greeting, seeming pleased at the sight of the young man before him, or amused at the very least.

He became serious as he turned to Ash who, without comment, passed the dead seal into the old man's shaking hands.

They waited expectantly. A chant filled the air as the old Seer whined something in the farlander tongue, and scratched at the lice infesting his robe. Eventually he fell silent, sitting entirely motionless with his eyes closed, the occasional grassfly settling on his bald, liver-spotted head. It was like those initial sessions of practising meditation on the *Falcon*, in which Nico had been unable to settle, and the aches of his body had eventually turned to agony. Indeed, he tried to settle into meditation, but it was useless, for he was too impatient to find out what would happen next. Absently, he chewed at his lip and stared at the damp-stained planks lining the opposite wall.

It was a blessed relief when the old Seer finally broke his meditative silence, smacking his dry lips and leaning away from the lifeless seal cradled in both hands.

'*Shinshō ta-kana* . . .' he croaked in a high-pitched voice. '*Yoshi, linaga!*' And then he nodded his head and frowned quite sadly.

'Murder,' Ash translated for the boy, his voice hard.

*

That evening, as the Rōshun finished their supper around the tables in the large dining hall that occupied much of the north wing of the monastery building, and the candles brightened against the fading light coming through its many windows, a sudden ringing of cutlery against glass silenced the quiet chatter.

Nico looked up from the table where he sat with the other apprentices, still chewing on the last of his rice cake. Aléas stopped talking to him, and did the same. From the back of the room, a wizened farlander rose slowly from his wooden chair. He was older than Ash, though not as ancient and withered as the Seer. Nico knew him to be Oshō, the head of the order, the man who had founded this very monastery here in the mountains of Cheem. He had several times seen him limping around the place, but never before had he heard him speak.

The old Rōshun's voice echoed with a clear resonance around the hushed room.

'My friends,' he declared to the multitude of faces now turned towards him. 'We have, on this night, a task incumbent upon us of an exceptional nature. One of our patrons has taken to the High Road. The Seer informs us that it was murder. He has also told us, through his wisdom, of the culprit responsible for this act.' Oshō paused and studied each face in turn, measuring them for attention, or perhaps some other quality only he could perceive.

'Tonight we must declare vendetta on a priest of Mann. Not merely any priest, take mind. No, as always, life refuses to be as straightforward as that. Tonight, we declare vendetta on Kirkus dul Dubois – that is, the son of Sasheen dul Dubois, the Holy Matriarch of Mann.'

Murmurs broke out around the room. Nico stole a glance towards Ash, who sat at the same high table as the old leader. Ash merely sipped from his goblet of water, his expression neutral.

'We have declared vendetta many times upon citizens of the Empire, but never against one of such standing. To do so tonight will be a hazardous venture for our order. Kirkus was aware that his victim wore a seal and was thus under our protection. Therefore, the Empire must know that we will seek vendetta against him. No doubt, they will do all in their power to stop us, including, I suspect, engineering our total destruction. He is, after all, the only child of the Matriarch herself.

'I believe their first response will be to target our agents scattered around the Midèrēs ports, in the false belief that our people there in the cities will know the whereabouts of our location here. Since we have no other contact with our patrons save through our agents, that is all the Mannians can do for now. Tonight, I have already instructed that carrier birds be sent out to all of them, warning them to be vigilant.

'Being of consequence to all of us, I have chosen to speak here at a time and place where we come together to share in simple nourishment. We must be, every one of us, aware of what we undertake tonight. In such a spirit, I select no one to be sent on this vendetta. Instead, I ask for three volunteers.'

A pause, and then in the centre of the dining hall a man stood with a scrape of his chair and clasped his hands before him. Almost as quickly, a dozen more Rōshun rose from their seats.

'Thank you.' Oshō smiled. 'Now, let me see, who do we have? Ah, Anton, you shall go. And Kylos of the little islands. And you – yes, Baso, I see you – you shall go also. Good, three of our finest.' The others returned to their seats, leaving those three standing alone above a sea of heads. 'You must leave tonight, I am afraid. We may already be too late to intercept Kirkus dul Dubois before he is able to return to Q'os, but we must still make haste before the Empire has sufficient chance to prepare for our retaliation. For retaliate we must, despite the obvious threat to our own order.

'Remember, an innocent woman lies dead tonight. Her life ill-taken by this young priest. For once, and we all know this for the rarity that it is, the righteousness of our task is clear. This time, we are not merely hunting the killer of a wealthy thug, or a patrician who has caught his brother sleeping with his wife, or a woman cornered into actions in which she had no reasonable alternative. There is no greyness here, as there so often is, and for which we so often seek forgiveness in our hours of quietness.'

Heads nodded in agreement, but there was a notable exception, Nico noticed. Baracha, sitting beside Ash, looked troubled and obviously wished to speak.

'We hunt a monster of the very real kind. And we have a pledge to keep, which we shall fulfil regardless of the cost. For truly, if we Rōshun are to be of any worth to the world, then we must prove it now. This is it.'

He bowed his head. 'That is all.'

*

'It is a bad business,' announced the head of the Rōshun order, the next morning, from the padded chair in his study at the top of the monastery tower. He spoke in their native Honshu, its syllables harsh and short-lived, as he always did when they were alone together.

Ash, sitting on the window seat at the other side of the room, did not respond.

'We take on an entire empire by pursuing this one vendetta,' continued Oshō. 'I pray it will not prove our undoing.'

'We have stood against powerful enemies before, master,' Ash reminded him softly.

'Aye, and lost all.'

A muscle in Ash's jaw flinched at that remark.

'Perhaps we had no other choice then,' he replied. 'As we have none now. What else can we do but honour our pledge, and act from our Cha?'

It was an interesting word, Cha. In the common language of Trade, many words would be needed to describe it, like 'centre', or 'stillness', or 'clear heart'.

'Cha? . . .' mused Oshō, irony evident in his vague smile. 'My Cha seems always clear to me, my friend, when I slice cheese or drink chee or fart in my old pine bed. But when I sit and ponder such things as this, affecting the future of the monastery itself, and the many hazards I must be aware of for the sake of *all* our futures, my Cha muddies itself with uncertainty. And then I wonder if perhaps I have not lost my way.'

'Nonsense,' snapped Ash. 'Last night you stood and explained to us why we must pursue this vendetta, regardless of the consequences. Your actions decided the issue. What more certainty can you expect?'

Oshō sighed. He responded quietly, as though talking only to himself. 'And all the time, I wondered if my words were not leading us to yet another massacre, or at the very least, another exile from our home.'

Ash returned his gaze to the window. He felt tired today, like on every other day since his return to the monastery, for his head pains had grown more common, and he had been sleeping poorly. Ash had been expecting this to happen. Often, when intent on a vendetta, his body would wait until it had reached a safe haven again before allowing any sickness or injury to run its natural course.

He had always tended to keep his own company while living here in the monastery. Since returning, though, he had become even more secluded than before. When he felt well enough, he trained outside the monastery walls, or undertook long walks through the mountains, avoiding others he spotted on their own hikes, his young apprentice amongst them. Mostly, though, he stayed alone in his cell, sleeping when he could manage it, or reading poetry from the old country, or just meditating. He did not wish the other members of the order to perceive that he was ill.

'It is not that kind of certainty I ask for,' Oshō pressed. 'I have been more in my life than merely Rōshun. I have led armies in the field, you recall? I have commanded a fleet across the great ocean of storms. My dear Ash, I once slew an overlord in a chance encounter that lasted for the entirety of three seconds. 'No, it is not certainty in my actions that I am lacking, or have ever lacked. I think perhaps it is Chan that I have lost, and I fear it makes my decisions weak.'

Another interesting word, Chan. Like Cha, in Trade it could mean many things: *passion, faith, love, hope, art, blind courage*. Sometimes, it could mean the mysteriously clever ways of the Fool. It was, in actuality, the outer manifestation of Cha in action.

'I grow tired of this business, that is all. Too much of my life have

I spent as Rōshun; soldier, general, nothing more. It has become a life hardly worthy of breath. When the time is right I will hand over the reins to Baracha. He is much more the scheming politician than I, even if his Cha is unclear.'

'*Phff*, if he were in charge now, he would have us parlaying with the Mannians and discussing a pay-off in return for the young priest's life.'

'Then perhaps Baracha is wise beyond his years. Who is to say he would be wrong, if it resulted in our survival?'

Ash felt the blood rush to his face, but kept silent.

'You were never Rōshun; back in the old country, Ash, as I was,' continued Oshō. 'You do not know how it was – not truly. Our patrons there wore a simple medallion for all to see and if they were slain, we gathered what information we could that might lead us to the killer. It was a messy business, I assure you. Sometimes we killed the wrong person. Often we were never able to track down the true culprit at all. Even today, here in the Midèrēs, with our seals and our mali trees imported all the way from the Isles of Sky, we have some-times failed to finish vendetta.'

'Yes, but we have always *tried*. It is the promise that we make.'

'Our promise, yes,' Oshō agreed. 'But in the old country, our prom-ise was always a practical one. I doubt that we would have ever risked our entire order in such a way as this.'

Ash shook his head. 'That may be. But we are a different thing here, in this land, than the old assassins. We have remained detached from the politics of the world, and neither do we manoeuvre for our own gain. We simply offer justice for those that are in need of it. If we do not risk ourselves now, then our promise to all those people means nothing, and *we* mean nothing, and all we have ever lived for is merely a sham.'

Oshō considered his words. It seemed he could not find fault with them.

Ash continued: 'What did you yourself always say to me when I was most anxiously facing a decision?'

'Many things, most of them nonsense.'

'Yes, but what was the same thing you said to me, time after time?'

'Ah,' growled the old general. '*Grin, and roll the dice.*'

'A worthy sentiment, I always thought.'

Oshō's sigh was audible. It was an expression of release, though, not exasperation, and he relaxed further into his deep chair, his eyes regarding something on the chee-table set in the middle of the room, perhaps the play of sunlight across its surface. The table itself was of wild tiq, carved from the planking of one of those ships that had brought them both here all the way from Honshu thirty years before.

Ash studied this old man he had known for so much of his life. His master seemed unaware of his own hand scratching idly at his left leg. Ash noticed it, though, and he smiled to himself, without commenting.

It appeared that, in some way, the debate was settled for now. They fell into one of their comfortable silences, the kind that could last for hours without any need for talk. A clatter sounded somewhere beneath the floorboards, distant enough to be subdued, probably someone dropping an armful of training weaponry, or perhaps a stack of platters from the nearby kitchen. Nearly lunchtime, Ash thought, so more likely platters. Friendly smells wafted in though the open window: keesh baking, and spicy stew.

Oshō stirred in his chair, glanced down at his hand, saw it scratching his leg. He snatched it away, bemused. 'Over twenty years I've been with this wooden leg of mine, and still I scratch at phantom itches as though they really existed.'

Ash barely heard him though. The dull ache in his head was worsening, and he clasped a hand to his forehead.

'Are you all right, old friend?'

Oshō arose into continuing silence, adjusted his false leg and limped across the room to where Ash perched on the deep, sunlit window seat.

'Yes,' replied Ash, but with his voice shaking. He pressed both temples with his fingers, trying to squeeze away the pain.

'The headaches again?' inquired Oshō, resting a hand on his shoulder.

'Yes.'

'They grow worse, then?'

Ash fumbled deep inside his robe, then produced his pouch. His fingers shook as he opened it and drew out a dried dulce leaf. He placed it in his mouth, settling it between tongue and cheek.

'They have grown so bad recently, sometimes I cannot see at all.'

Oshō's hand squeezed his shoulder. It was not like him, to offer a gesture of comfort.

Ash drew out another leaf and placed it inside his mouth, against the other cheek.

'Is there anything I can do for you? Ch'eng, perhaps?'

'No, master. He cannot help me.'

'Please, enough of the *master*. You ceased to be my apprentice a long, long time ago.'

The pain slowly subsided. Enough at least for Ash to smile back at him – though he avoided his master's eyes, which had grown watery and dark all of a sudden.

'We grow older than we think,' he said in an attempt at lightening the mood.

'No,' said Oshō, as he shuffled back to his padded chair. '*You* grow older than you think. *I* am already aware of my decrepitude, and plan to retire as soon as possible with what little dignity remains to me.'

'I have been pondering the same thing,' admitted Ash.

The old general settled back in his chair and fixed Ash with a look that was familiar after these long years – his head tilted back, his sharp features drawn in concentration, his hooded eyes appraising whoever was before them. 'I had hoped as much, when I saw you with an apprentice after all these years. What prompted your change of mind?'

'I have not changed my mind. But we had a conversation, you and I, some months ago. In my head.'

'When you were on the ice?'

He nodded.

'Perhaps, then, it was more than that. I had a dream some months back. It was very cold. You did not think you were going to make it.'

'No, I did not. But you offered me a bargain, and a promise that I would make it home alive if I agreed. So I took it.'

'I see. And what was this bargain?'

'That you would not stop me from my work, so long as I was training an apprentice.'

Oshō chuckled. 'Ah, that would explain it. Yes, a fair bargain – one that I will stand by.'

'Good.'

'Tell me, then. How did you choose him?'

Ash was unsure of how to answer that. For a moment he was back in Bar-Khos, drifting in dreams during the long hot siesta, as a young man sneaked into his room to steal his purse.

Ash had been dreaming of home then: the little village of Asa, snuggling deep into a twist of the high valley floor – the view pitching sharply downwards past the many terraces of rice and barley to an endless stretch of blue sea that reached as far as the horizon.

Butai, his young wife, had been there, too. She was standing in the doorway of their cottage, a basket of wild flowers in her arms. She had a gift for making them into subtle perfumes, forever surprising him with new fragrances, and she was watching their son for a moment as he chopped wood in an easy, practised way; a boy of perhaps fourteen.

Ash had waved to them, but they did not see him – they were laughing instead at something the boy had said. Beautiful in her laughter, his wife looked as girlish as she ever had.

And then Ash had awakened in a strange room, in a strange city, in a strange land, in a strange life that was not in any way his own . . . his eyes wet with grief, the sense of loss within him as raw as though it had happened only yesterday. Pain washed through his head so sharply it was enough to blind him. He had called out to someone nearby, thinking for a moment that it was his son – yet, even as he did so, he knew that it could never be his son. In that same moment he had felt an isolation so all-consuming that he could not move for it. *I will die alone*, he had thought. *Like this, blind, with no one by my side.*

'It seems', he heard himself say to Oshō, 'as though he was chosen for me.'

Oshō accepted this, at least partly. 'For what purpose, do you wonder?'

'I do not know, but it is as though we both have need of each other in some way. I cannot say how.'

Oshō nodded, with a knowing smile, but whatever it was that he suspected he chose not to voice it. Instead, he said, 'So you have not changed your mind about taking over the reins from me? I thought perhaps that you might, if I goaded you enough with Baracha's name.'

Ash could no longer meet his master's eyes.

'What would be the point? The illness is growing worse, and I do not think I have much time left to me. You know of my father, and his father before him. After their blindness struck, they went with great speed in the end.'

The smile on Oshō's face faded, as a soberness came over him. He inhaled a sharp breath. 'I feared as much,' he admitted. 'But I hoped otherwise. I am deeply sorry, Ash. You are one of the few true friends I have left.'

A bluebird was singing outside in the courtyard. Ash turned his attention to it, away from his friend's untypical display of emotion.

The young Oshō would never have been so open-hearted – not that Oshō who had trained as Rōshun back in the old country and in the old ways where only a few ever survived the ordeal. The same Oshō who had left the original Rōshun order after they had sided with the overlords, and who later became a soldier and fought at Hakk and Aga-sa, and somehow survived them both too; who had gone on to win honour after honour in the long war against the over-lords, creating a name for himself, earning a high command in the ultimately doomed People's Army. Back then, it would have been unimaginable to hear the general lamenting so openly over the fate of a comrade. Even less so as he subsequently led them into exile, the only general able to fight his way out with his body of men intact after surviving the final, fateful trap that had destroyed the People's Revolution once and for all.

Oshō had been lean and strong and tough in those days, a hard bastard in truth. His firm command had held them together on their long voyage to the Midèrēs, when most of those in the fleet, includ-ing a grief-stricken Ash, had simply wished for death after their defeat and the loss of their loved ones either fallen in battle or left behind. When they had finally made it here to the Midèrēs, and others in the fugitive fleet had taken up arms to serve as mercenaries for the Empire of Mann, or else turn against it, Oshō had struck out on a different and much more uncertain path. The path of Rōshun.

Yet here he was a withered old man on a withered old chair, both he and the chair sprouting tufts of hair and creaking every time their age-worn bodies shifted their weight; allowing his regrets to flow freely from his heart, as he finally looked towards the end.

Ash peered out from the high turret window over to the mali trees that clustered in the centre of the courtyard. The singing bluebird could be seen perching down there, its sky-blue plumage distinct against the bronze leaves.

'To be sad at passing is to be sad at life,' Ash quipped.

'I know,' said the old general, with a shake of his head.

The two veterans sat there in the dusty sunlight, listening for a time to the brief, fresh song of the late-summer bird. Calling out for a mate, Ash thought. A partner lost to it.

'I only wish . . .' Oshō managed at last, but he faltered, and let the rest of his words hang there without being voiced.

'*To see once more the Diamond Mountain,*' Ash finished for him, reciting the old poem. '*And lay my lips on those I love.*'

'Yes,' said Oshō.

'I know, old friend.'

CHAPTER THIRTEEN

Serèse

A strange hush fell upon the monastery after Oshō's announce-ment of vendetta, and the departure of the three Rōshun set upon fulfilling it, inspiring a new sense of purpose that had been lacking before then. Even the older men, who had been spending more time cultivating their gardens than engaged in practice, began to re-hone their skills. Rōshun huddled together, talking in serious tones, and laughter became altogether less common.

The apprentices remained largely unaffected by all this earnest-ness. They were still too ignorant of the gravity of the situation, and their punishing training regime was sufficient to keep their youthful minds focused on their own daily concerns.

*

Nico had never been able to make friends easily, and he discovered that had not changed much, even here in this high place of isolation. The constant company of others tended to drain him after a while, to the point where he often withdrew into himself for escape. At times, Nico knew, this made him appear aloof.

He had found, in the past, that this reticence had attracted its fair share of trouble, but here he found the opposite to be true. The other apprentices appeared to like Nico well enough, and joked and con-versed with him easily. But they also sensed his distance and, knowing him at least a little better by then, took it not as arrogance but solely a desire to be left alone. They respected that desire, and in doing so often excluded him from those moments of true camaraderie that they shared amongst themselves, so that even when he genuinely wanted their company, he could never quite manage to breach the gap that had grown between himself and the others.

It was ironic, therefore, to discover, that another of the apprentices was afflicted by a similar condition and that one should turn out to be Aléas.

They all liked Aléas, too, but he was the apprentice of Baracha, who they roundly despised. More than that though was Aléas's manner. The young man was humble in his way, and naturally so, yet all the rest could see how brilliant he truly was. This unsettled his peers. Such talent and modesty combined suggested to them, in their own private thoughts, that Aléas was somehow superior to them, and they in turn his inferiors. Such personal dynamics do not offer a sound basis for friendship.

Yet it was because Nico and Aléas were both outsiders that inevitably their shared condition each spoke to the other. It suggested something of similar ways. At times, the two young men would both laugh at something only they considered worthy of humour, or one would find his words supporting the other's in some heated group debate. Often they would find themselves paired together for want of anyone else. Still, that distance remained between them as it did with the others – Nico somewhat intimidated by this confident young man, while Aléas felt restrained by his master's wish that they stay apart.

For Nico, a natural loner, life here was not at all as he had imagined it, though it was hardly as if he'd had any clear notions of what to expect upon his arrival. But whatever dim expectation he may have entertained of this strange place where men trained as assassins, it was not this.

For hours each day he hacked at the air in the practice square, stabbed and garrotted straw-stuffed mannequins, concealed himself from imagined foes, poured arrows on distant targets painted as men. Yet so engrossed was he in doing well, in maintaining his reputation, in surmounting the challenges of each new exhausting day, that rarely did he pause to connect these actions with the reality of what they meant, or the path that he was now set upon. For he was carefully being trained to cross a threshold without thought or hesitation. Some day, he would be expected to commit murder in cold blood.

Still, that was not on any day soon, and meanwhile the practice eventually made him insensitive to such a prospect, and hard effort obscured his contemplation of what it was all leading to. After a while, Nico did not dwell on it further.

It was a pleasant surprise for him to find how much he began to look forward to his daily sessions of meditation. They took place twice a day, for a full hour each time. Some of the apprentices struggled with these sessions, mostly those who still held to religious beliefs other than Daoism, which was odd, Nico thought, since all that was required of the apprentices was a commitment to the Daoist practices of stillness.

Nico was hardly much of a believer himself, having rarely connected with the rituals his mother had forced him to sit through, performed by those droning monks in their smoky temple whenever he had been unfortunate enough to be dragged along. Yet now he began to look forward to these hourly sessions in the quiet polished-wood confines of the chachen hall, or outdoors in the courtyard whenever the weather was fine. There was little religion involved, he found, for the Rōshun did not concern themselves with doctrine. They merely knelt there, with hands in laps, and concentrated on the soft inrush and outrush of their breaths until a chime sounded the end of the session.

In time, Nico found that stillness was increasingly attainable once he learned how to relax while still maintaining his focus. Afterwards, he would feel refreshed and centred; altogether more comfortable in his own skin.

Weeks passed before he remembered to write a letter home. Nico felt somewhat chastened that he had forgotten about his mother so easily. In his untidy handwriting he let her know that he was well, and filled the rest of the page with an account of the more mundane aspects of his new life. He carefully left out anything that might suggest how desperate certain situations had been.

Ash's old friend Kosh was happy enough to arrange for its delivery, and had it taken down to Cheem Port along with some of the Rōshun who were travelling down to purchase supplies. From there it was passed on to a smuggler who made his living by running the Mannian blockade of the Free Ports. Nico hoped that it eventually reached her. In truth though, after that, he did not think of his mother often.

Every Foolsday they were given a day off, and were free to do as they pleased. On such days, when the others would team up in groups of two or three, Nico would leave them to their bantering and their small complicities and take himself off for a hike into the surrounding mountains, to spend some cherished hours by himself in their high clean splendour. It was like nourishment to him, to be this alone with his thoughts, which on those particular days, after a long enough walk, were mostly a form of no-thought, the same as when he had been a boy, and he had ventured into the foothills near their cottage for an afternoon just with Boon; times of peace, a way of finding quietness.

The routine of it all carved its own particular grooves in him. For a time, Nico looked neither backwards nor ahead.

*

One morning, before breakfast, Nico spotted a girl crossing the courtyard, and was startled enough to drop his pail of water to the ground. It was not simply that she was female that gave Nico such a start and set his heart hammering. Neither was it her appearance: a simple black robe which matched the hair that swept long and straight down her back, framing a sun-kissed face of sharp angles and large eyes. Rather, it was the way she walked, long-limbed and confident, with a swinging grace evident beneath her robe that captivated his male eyes starved of such a sight for so long. Nico forgot his bucket as he darted after her, watching her enter the door leading into the north wing. He thought quickly of some excuse to follow and discover who she might be.

Nico hurried through the door, and glanced to his left and right. She was gone. He even wondered for a moment if he had imagined her.

*

Over the next few days he saw her several times again. But each time it was merely a passing glimpse, and always he was engaged in training or on his way to training, and could not linger. It was frustrating, and he soon found that his eyes kept darting constantly from here to there, looking out for her.

'Who is she?' he demanded of Aléas, one evening at supper.

'Who?' inquired Aléas, betraying himself with a feigned tone of innocence.

'You know who! The girl I keep seeing about the place.'

Aléas flashed him a wolfish grin. 'That is not just a *girl*, Nico. That is my master's daughter, and you would be best to keep your eyes off her – let alone your hands. My master is fearfully protective.'

'Baracha's daughter?' Nico was stunned at such a thought.

'Nico, your liking or disliking of a fellow hardly affects his abilities to sire children.'

'Well, what is her name?'

'Serèse.'

It was a Mercian name, and he said as much.

'Yes,' agreed Aléas. 'Her mother was Mercian. Why all these questions, or need I ask?'

'What questions?' he said, glancing away. But then he asked, 'How long is she staying?'

Aléas sighed. 'You sly, sly dog. Let me repeat myself, at the risk of sounding a bore. She is the daughter of Baracha and she is here for a few weeks visiting her father. When she is done, she will return to Q'os, since she works for us there. If, during her stay, she has been molested or accosted in any way – and by molested, I mean talked to, looked at, thought about while fumbling with yourself beneath the blankets – if any of these things have occurred between you and she in that time, then be assured, my master will take a knife to your balls. Look at him yonder. He watches us even now. He will have words with me later for even talking to you.'

Nico leaned back warily in his chair. He did not doubt Aléas's warning.

Even so, after Aléas had returned his attention to his broth, Nico scanned the dining hall to catch another glimpse of her, and felt disappointment when he did not gain one.

*

The next morning their paths finally crossed, and he instantly knew they were fated to have met. Nico believed in such things.

It was a Foolsday, therefore his day off, and he was entering the laundry room to wash some clothes before setting off on his customary hike across the valley.

There, in the steamy atmosphere of the cavernous room, she stood wringing out the last of her own washing. Nico halted in the doorway, unsure of whether to enter or leave.

'Hello,' she said casually, after a glance over her shoulder.

Her tone drew him into the room. He closed the door behind him, and crossed the floor. He dumped his clothes next to the metal tub of water bubbling over the fire, then nodded again to her, and smiled.

She finished folding a wet tunic and placed it on the pile of clothes already in her basket. The sleeves of her robe were rolled up, and her black hair tied back from her face, which was flushed pink from the heat and exertion. He realized that she was around the same age as himself.

'What?' she asked with a quick smile, aware of his scrutiny.

He shook his head. 'Nothing. I'm Nico, Master Ash's apprentice.'

He saw the swift change in her at that information – a reappraisal of who she spoke to. Her dark eyes took in his features, seeming to linger. It was the kind of glance, he realized, that always made him look away with a blush – and turned him into a quivering idiot inside.

Nico kept his mouth shut, fearing that whatever came out of it next would be stammered or stupid or, even worse, both.

'I'm Serèse,' she told him, in a voice that was deep and husky. It sent a thrill up his thighs.

'I know,' he replied, and instantly regretted it.

She seemed pleased by that – the fact that he knew her name or his sudden condition of embarrassment, he didn't know which.

'You must be Mercian then,' he ventured, trying to recover his composure. 'Serèse. It means "sharp" in the old tongue.'

'Ah, I thought I recognized your accent.'

'Yes. I'm from Bar-Khos.'

'Ah.' Impressed again.

A bell rang outside, calling the hour.

'Well, it's all yours,' she said, gesturing to the bubbling water as she arranged the last of the clean garments.

'Wait,' he blurted, even as he recalled the stark warning of Aléas. But his pulse had quickened at the sudden thought of asking this girl to spend his free day with him. He pictured them hiking across the valley together, talking, laughing, getting to know one another. 'It's my day off,' he explained. 'I'm going on a hike after I've finished this. Why don't you join me?'

She seemed to consider it, at least for a few heartbeats. But then she shook her head. 'My father will be waiting for me, I'm afraid.'

'Oh,' Nico said, defeated; though a small part of him was relieved.

'But another time,' she said, brightening up. As she stooped to pick up her basket, he could not help but admire her shape from behind.

'Here,' he said suddenly. 'Let me help you with that.'

'It's fine. I can manage.'

He pretended not to hear and snatched the load up anyway. It was heavier than he was expecting, and he barely suppressed a groan.

Serèse followed him outside where, in the brighter light of the corridor their faces shone with perspiration, and their hair clung in rat tails from the steam. They stopped, exchanged looks. His heart was still racing.

He wanted to touch her.

'Serèse?'

Baracha stood in the open doorway that lead out into the court-yard.

The girl rolled her eyes. 'Goodbye,' she murmured smiling an apology. She went to join her father, looking back just the once.

Baracha glowered at Nico, his expression dark.

*

It was a slow Firstday afternoon, and Nico and the other apprentices were sweating through their cali manoeuvres as usual. The training ground was crowded with assembled Rōshun all working their skills to a finer degree, the open space barely large enough to hold them all, while up in his tower, Oshō could be seen watching from the window overlooking the courtyard.

The apprentices were confined to a far corner, panting heavily from the drawing strokes they had already been rehearsing, and now moving through some simple in-stroke, out-stroke combinations, as Baracha barked them through the drills.

He seemed his usual short-tempered self that day, no better or worse than normal, and his hand had clapped more than a few of them moving too sluggishly for his mood. At one point he yelled into the face of Aléas, for not paying attention to what he was doing, not unusual that, for he always pushed his young apprentice harder than the rest of them, but it disturbed Nico to see it, and the others too. They knew Aléas to be the best of them, and that he did not deserve such treatment.

It was in the midst of this tirade that a sudden hush fell upon the training ground. Baracha stopped in mid-flow, his angry eyes flashing about to locate the source of this new distraction.

There, striding on to the dust, Ash had appeared, with a sheathed sword in his hand, coming out to train with the others for once, rather than performing dawn exercises on his own.

The assembled Rōshun quickly got back to business, but the apprentices now found their concentration less focused. Many watched from the corners of their eyes as the old man in his black robe practised along with the rest of them, his naked blade flashing and glittering in the sunlight, through a series of moves too fast for most of them to follow. The distraction only served to worsen Baracha's mood, and he slapped a few of them back into order, until they returned in proper earnest to their exercises.

After a while he allowed them to break for water and to take a breath.

'I see the old man plays with the rest of us today,' he called out to Ash, loud enough for all nearby to hear. Ash met his eyes for the briefest moment, then continued with his routine. He henceforth ignored the big Alhazii, and Nico could see how this lack of response stung the big man's pride.

During the break several of the other apprentices gathered around and asked Nico what his master was like in action. Nico waited for their eager questioning to descend into an expectant silence, then proclaimed in a hush: 'He is like the calm centre of a storm,' and the other boys nodded, seeing it in their own imaginations. And Aléas chuckled.

*

The next morning, Nico encountered Baracha again on his way to archery practice. The Alhazii was just leaving the armoury, and stopped dead in his tracks as he spotted Nico walking towards him.

'You!' he barked.

'Me?'

'Yes, you. Come with me.'

'I have a lesson to get to. I'll be late.'

'Come!' Baracha barked impatiently.

Nico swallowed as the Alhazii strode off along the corridor. For a moment he considered making a dash for it, but that would look stupid and childish. Instead, he propelled himself along in his wake.

They marched through the kitchen area, steamily hot. The two cooks paid little heed to them, engrossed in a tug-of-war over use of an empty pot. Towards the back of the kitchen Baracha bent and opened a trapdoor in the floor. He stepped down into darkness.

Nico peered down at the stone steps, and the massive form of Baracha vanishing into the gloom. He wondered what this was about. But then, he already knew what it was about.

An angry, over-protective father.

'Down here,' echoed Baracha's voice, and it tugged Nico forward so that he placed a foot on the first step. He descended the rest as though in a dream.

It was a storage room, stone-clad and cold. The only light came from the stairwell behind him. In the dimness, Nico could discern shapes hanging from iron hooks fixed to the wooden ceiling: joints of wild game, smoked and salted, next to sacks of flour, spices, or dried vegetables. Something swung on its hook just to the right of him. A bird ready plucked and gutted.

He stepped that way, stilling the bird with one hand as he passed by. It felt cool and fleshy beneath his fingertips.

Ahead, a shape shifted in the darkness. He saw a sudden flash of whiteness: Baracha's grinning teeth.

I did nothing wrong, Nico reminded himself. *We merely talked for a moment.*

It hardly reassured him, and sweat began to prickle his forehead. 'Over here, boy.'

Nico swallowed nervously. In a daft moment of fantasy he wished he was carrying a blade on him.

The silence was heavy like that of a tomb. Baracha leant back against something, arms crossed. As he drew nearer, Nico saw it was the raised lip of a stone well, perhaps six feet across, covered by a rusty iron grille. Within it, deep down, he could hear the echo of fast-flowing water.

Without a further word, Baracha turned and laid his hands upon the grille. With a grunt of exertion and a squeal of hinges he pulled it open.

Nico stared down into darkness. Water rushed down there, unseen but frightening. He felt the coolness of it against his face. It was an underground stream running right beneath the grounds of the monastery.

Nico took a quick, involuntary step away. 'What do you want of me?' he demanded.

Baracha bent to lift something from the floor. It was a bucket, green with algae, fixed to a rotten rope. The end of the rope was tied to the iron grille.

The Alhazii lowered the bucket down into blackness.

'My daughter may have lost something yesterday,' he explained. 'I want you to climb down there and find it.'

Nico took another step away from the well. 'I'm fairly certain I will not.'

The rope almost yanked itself from Baracha's hand, suddenly caught by the flow. He tightened his grip on it. Nico could hear the bucket bouncing against stone, the sound of water even louder as it rushed past the obstruction.

'You will,' said Baracha. 'One way or another, you *will* climb down there.'

Nico stared dumbfounded at the man's shadowed face. He couldn't tell if he was being serious.

If he's trying to frighten me, he is succeeding!

Nico wanted to run but his feet seemed rooted to the stone floor. Baracha took a step towards him, dragging the rope with him. Still, Nico could not move.

The young man opened his mouth – to shout for help, to plead his innocence, he wasn't sure – as a large hand fell on his shoulder. Baracha's fingers grabbed a fistful of his robe. The cloth tightened against Nico's throat. Without any visible effort, the big Alhazii pulled him back towards the well.

'Get off me!' Nico shouted, as he felt his feet dragging across the floor. He struggled then, trying to break loose of the man's grip. 'No!' he yelled in anger, as the dark opening of the well reared towards him. He tried to get a hand up to Baracha's face, fingers groping wildly for his eyes. The man lifted his face out of reach. His strength was staggering as he shoved Nico's head down into the well, tried to get the rest of him inside too. Nico's hands flailed for a grip against the slimy rim, while the unseen waters crashed deep and cold through the earth below him.

And then, mercifully, Baracha's grip loosened and with a surge Nico broke free. He staggered away from his tormentor, catching the amused look on the man's face. 'Bastard,' spat Nico, retreating in a rush, batting aside the hanging obstructions, as Baracha's laughter flayed his back with mockery.

Nico did not stop until he was outside in the fresh air, gulping deeply, squinting in the sunlight and cursing himself for the fool that he was.

Serèse, he later heard, was sent away from there that same day.

CHAPTER FOURTEEN

Divine Assurances

In the windowless antechamber of the arena known as the Shay Madi, Kirkus watched his mother holding court before the priests gathered about her.

Her two years as Holy Matriarch of the Empire had begun to take their toll on her, in spite of the Royal Milk she paid for so handsomely to sup each morning. The noticeable lines across her forehead could only come from frowns generated by worry, though here today, in public, his mother preferred to smile, and smile often.

This visible aging had been the first thing Kirkus had noticed upon his return from the state progress with his grandmother, when laying eyes on his mother for the first time in many months. It had been the first thing he had commented on, bringing a laugh to her lips and a gentle kiss to his forehead.

Save for the priestly fine-link chains of gold that dangled from the lobes of her ears to her nostrils, and the light-reflecting sheen of her shaven skull, his mother might have been the madam of some bawdy city brothel at the high point of a comfortably busy night. Sasheen's plain face was flushed from the heat of so many bodies crammed together in close proximity, the many gas-lights in sooty alcoves along the walls, and the lack of any breeze coming through the sunlit portal in the wall behind her that led out to the imperial stand. She stood with one hip aslant, a bent wrist resting on her pelvis. Beneath a chin held high her heavy breasts thrust through the white cloth of her robe.

Alluring but dangerous, was the first thought that came to the minds of most men. She was, perhaps, the only thing Kirkus knew about his father – in as much as she indicated this man's taste in bedfellows.

The male and female priests thronging the room talked amongst themselves, except for those gathered closest to the Holy Matriarch herself. These listened respectfully to Sasheen but spoke in their turn with a lack of formality common to the High Priests of Q'os, and which had surprised Kirkus on the first occasion he had attended the court of the previous leader, Patriarch Nihilis. Kirkus had expected a greater degree of pomp and ceremony, as was shown during official ceremonies of state.

Instead, the high priests of Q'os acted like uneasy comrades involved in a grand and impossibly ambitious conspiracy: the ruling of the entire known world no less. What deference they chose to show to their Holy Matriarch arose not simply from their respect for her position, having risen as she had to the leadership of Mann as though from nowhere, but from awe at her readiness to snuff out any least sign of disloyalty, as manifested in the deaths of so many of their former colleagues.

A threat they remained close to even now, in the form of her two massive bodyguards, their eyes masked by goggles of smoky glass so none could tell where they looked, and their hands sheathed in poisonous scratch-gloves.

Kirkus only half-listened to what his mother or the others had to say. This wasn't an official gathering of court today, only an after-noon of leisure here at the Shay Madi, in which members of the higher caste took the opportunity to socialize while watching entertain-ments in the public arena. Still, they were men and women of lofty positions and they could not help but continue manoeuvring for advantage amongst themselves.

Kirkus allowed such petty concerns to wash over him as he chomped the soft flesh of a parmadio fruit, quivering at each spike of narcotic pleasure as he crunched down on its bitter pips. Occa-sionally his eyes would rove the room, and study its occupants as they inhaled from steaming bowls or imbibed cooling liqueurs. But always, his gaze would end up watching the large double doors at the far end.

Lara would not be appearing today, he suspected. Indeed her latest lover, General Romano, had arrived by himself, and was now stand-ing in a corner in deep discussion with General Alero. Even as Kirkus studied the young general, the man turned his head and locked eyes with him across the distance of the room.

Something of hatred passed in the look between them.

Romano was nephew to the last Patriarch, and considered the leading prodigy among one of the oldest and most powerful families within the order. Young Romano was the foremost rival to Sasheen's position, though it was understood he would wait for her reign to come to an end before making his own attempt at the leadership, a time when Kirkus himself would be expected by many to assume the position of Patriarch; in her own way, Lara could not have chosen herself a new lover placed more firmly against Kirkus than this one.

Across the chamber Romano inclined his head towards Kirkus. Kirkus bowed in response, his eyes guarded.

Lara would have come with Romano, if she was coming at all. Obviously she was still avoiding Kirkus. His latest public outburst, in the upper baths of the Temple of Whispers on the day after his return, had been an embarrassment for them both.

He had hoped that, upon seeing Lara again, he could be calm and mature about their situation. He felt he had developed that much, at least, during his ventures abroad. Instead, as soon as he laid eyes on her, his body had suffered some overwhelming reaction of shock, so that, standing there in his tower, stunned as she walked by him without the merest glance in his direction, Kirkus had found himself shouting at her departing back, his voice so shaken with rage that it took long moments for him to decipher exactly what he had said.

'I will require your consent soon, Matriarch,' the priestess Sool was murmuring to his mother. 'It is little more than a month now before the anniversary of the Augere el Mann.'

Kirkus swallowed around a painful lump in his throat. He dragged his gaze from the closed doors at the rear of the chamber, and refocused his attention on the general conversation around him.

The priestess Sool had her head bent low, playing the loyal subservient, as always, though Kirkus sometimes suspected otherwise. 'I will need to know if our plans for the commemoration are suitable. After all, this *is* the year in which we commemorate the fiftieth anniversary of Mannian rule. Perhaps you have some ideas yourself.'

'Oh, don't hark on so,' replied his mother with a throw of her hand, the other holding her robes hitched over one extended thigh, cooling off. 'I leave all such decisions to you and your people, you know that. Believe me, I have other things to concern myself with just now.'

'Yes,' said Sool submissively, her head dipping a fraction lower. 'I suspect I may have heard of them. This new petition of Mokabi's: another invasion plan for the Free Ports. The old warrior grows restless in his retirement, no doubt.'

'As always, your ears hear only whispers borne on the wings of boredom.' There was impatience in his mother's tone, and a weariness that Kirkus noticed ever more often these days.

'Still. Even so . . .' Sool continued, then checked abruptly.

Kirkus was laughing at her. 'It is just as well you and my mother are the closest of friends,' he quipped. 'Who else would listen to both your nagging?'

Sool smiled, though it may have been a grimace. 'Your mother gave birth to you in her time,' she said. 'You might show some respect, young pup.'

His reply was another crunch of seeds between his teeth. He did not say what he might have said next.

Kirkus had watched this interchange with interest. In her own subtle way, Sool had been like a maternal aunt to Kirkus as he was growing up, or at least as much as any woman could be maternal within the order, where such bonds were nurtured by loyalty and necessity – certainly not love and seldom kindness. As a boy, Kirkus had lived in the Temple of Whispers, in the extensive apartments of his mother and grandmother, one of them the latest glammari, or chosen consort, to Patriarch Anslan, the other a long-trusted advisor in the ways of the faith. Sool had often visited the women there, sometimes accompanied by her daughter Lara. On summer evenings, Sool would tell them stories from the past, he and Lara, as they sat together on the balcony of his personal chamber, with the many animals he had collected over the years squawking and clattering in their cages, while evening light hung like a shroud over the city of Q'os below them.

From that high vantage point perched on the flank of the Temple of Whispers, the full shape of the island-city was visible to the eye. On the coastline to the east, a natural protrusion of land stabbed diagonally into the sea; to the north could be seen the four manmade landfills that so closely resembled fingers: all the Five Cities, as they were known collectively, each teeming to the water's edge with buildings. As a child, Kirkus had scanned the landscape from east to west: it was possible to see the island as shaped in the form of a great open hand, its palm facing skywards, its end-digit of land truncated to represent the shortened little finger of the followers of Mann. He had never bored of this sight, as a boy, perched there at the city's very heart.

On those long-ago warm evenings, Sool had recounted her tales in a harsh whisper, as though her words were precious things that needed guarding. She had told him of the time when her own mother and his grandmother had been young women working secretly for the cult during that time of famine and pestilence known as the Great Trial, each of them wild at heart, kindred in spirit, their recruitment into the order the result of having a lover they both shared without contention.

Both had taken part in the Longest Night, that evening which had followed the destruction of the city by fire. Acting as a pair, they had murdered one of the city's highest-placed officials, living in opulent splendour in his palace while the city lay in ruins and starvation all around it. They had both witnessed the frenzied execution of the girl-queen, indeed had taken their own small part in it. They had knelt prostrate and panting at the feet of High Priest Nihilis himself, as he was anointed first Holy Patriarch of Mann.

Sool had told him and Lara these things, and many others, proud it seemed of the closeness of her family and his, of their rise to power together. It was only when he was older that Kirkus learned of other sides to these stories. He recalled his grandmother, half broken after a purging, lying on her bed speaking out in some kind of delirium, grasping Kirkus's arm to detain him as she told him of the murder of her oldest friend, Sool's mother, for falling from the ways of Mann.

It had now been over a year since Kirkus had last seen Sool in the flesh. As he faced her in the close press of the antechamber he saw her as though through the eyes of his own boyhood self, and wondered when they had lost that special connection that he had cherished secretly as a child. He assumed, perhaps, it had been since he and Lara had parted ways, but on deeper reflection he knew it to be much longer than that. Since he had grown up, he realized – when he no longer needed such people in his life as this kindly matron.

I cast this women aside, Kirkus thought, as he gazed into her blue eyes, and she into his. *And all the kindnesses she ever showed me.*

Kirkus raised his hands up to his chest and then held them

outwards, in an acknowledgement of concession. The woman blinked in surprise.

Beside him a clearing of a throat. It was Cinimon, high priest of the Monbarri sect – that cult within a cult who declared themselves inquisitors and defenders of the faith so fervently that they frightened all others. The man spoke in a voice like the shifting gravels of a flood stream, his expression all but unreadable behind the sagging burden of the many piercings that adorned his face.

'It is true, then?' he asked of Sasheen. 'Mokabi thinks he can crack the Free Ports at last?'

Sasheen tilted her head to consider the question. 'So he believes, though we have barely found time to look into his proposals yet. I meet with my generals soon to discuss the matter. You will, of course, be the first to hear of our findings.'

'We have also the Zanzahar question to decide upon,' muttered little Bushrali from behind the rim of his goblet, High Priest of the Regulators, and clearly drunk already. 'This quibbling over grain and salt prices can lead to no advantage for us. If we do not lower our prices, and the Caliphate extends its safe waters two hundred laqs towards the Free Ports, as they threaten to do, then this war of attrition may become a war without end.'

Cinimon shook his head, his heavy facial piercings clinking together as his black eyes shone from amongst within. The priest's arms and legs remained bare under his plain white cassock; they rippled with slivers of precious metals buried beneath the skin, slivers that ran like a host of snakes all the way down to his ankles and into his sandaled feet – as though, at any moment, they would break through the skin, and wriggle free on to the ground as living things. 'We should make our own demands of the Caliphate,' the priest grumbled. 'We should insist that they cease selling to the Free Ports the very grains we sell to them. It is altogether obscene. They no longer even try to hide the practice.'

'Make such a demand and we risk an embargo,' whined Bushrali, pausing to place a hand over his wine-stained lips to cover a belch. 'And where would we be then, without a steady supply of black-powder?'

'So be it, then,' interrupted Kirkus, intrigued enough at last to contribute to the discussion. 'Perhaps it is time we tested this monopoly of Zanzahar, and saw how long they survive without our grain. I have studied the figures as much as anyone has. I am not so certain they speak of only one outcome.'

'Well spoken,' agreed Cinimon, and his mother too eyed him with interest, though said nothing.

Bushrali showed his irritation by waving his goblet about, a slosh of red wine arcing across the marble floor like pearls of blood. 'The figures are accurate, young master. Our stockpiles of blackpowder would run dry long before Zanzahar would be forced to seek grain, salt and rice from elsewhere. You think they would allow things to be any other way? You think they ration us our supplies of blackpowder simply because they do not like to trade it? They know to the nearest garan how much we have stockpiled throughout the Empire. They know how much we use each month against Bar-Khos and elsewhere. They even know when a store of our powder has become aged beyond use.

'Who is it, do you think, my Regulators are working so hard to thwart? Rebels and heretics maybe? Aye, indeed so, for each week we pass hundreds of such traitors into the hands of Cinimon's Monbarri after we ourselves have finished with them. But I say this to you: at least half the reports I read concern the El-mud alone. The Night Wing has eyes and ears everywhere, and we have yet to find a way to neutralize them.'

The man stopped as he noticed the glow of anger in Kirkus's eyes. He seemed at last to remember who he was addressing, for he suddenly flushed, his bald scalp deathly pale in contrast to his burning face, and glanced towards Sasheen and the two bodyguards that flanked her. The man bowed low. 'Forgive me,' he said to Kirkus. 'I seem to have drunk too much, and lecture a man as though he was still a boy.'

Kirkus, continued to glare, enjoying watching the little man squirm. It was Cinimon who finally broke the silence amongst them.

'I would think, Bushrali, you should be the last to admit to such a deficit in your capacities.'

'I do not water the truth like some,' he retorted. In a more measured voice, he addressed Kirkus once more. 'These desert men of Zanzahar have been making an art out of shadow-play and intelligence for a thousand years now. You cannot hope to dupe them for long. The agents of the El-mud are the true reason for Zanzahar's monopoly. We could not even commit to an invasion of the Caliphate without their knowing it. To talk of such things, even here in this room full of only the most loyal, is to say too much.'

'Which is why it is merely talk,' interrupted Sasheen herself, smoothly. 'We have no intentions for Zanzahar, either now or ever.' And she sounded sincere in her words, though even then Kirkus could see that his mother was not entirely telling the whole truth. His grunt of disbelief drew a flash of warning from her eyes. He quickly hid his smile by taking another bite of the parmadio.

'Maybe you forget the history lessons I was so ardent in having schooled into you?' she reproached him. 'How Markesh fell when they brought an embargo down on their heads, for seeking out the Isles of Sky and its sources of blackpowder for themselves?'

He knew the history well, but he would not rise to the bait. He continued chewing, and watched his mother as she watched him.

'Without cannon, their enemies devoured them over the course of a decade. You should remember this, my son. Markesh was hardly weak. Their merchant empire was so influential that even now all of the Midèrēs shares their common tongue of Trade. If not for them, we would all still be using iron tubs for cannon, and hollow sticks for rifles. And still, they fell. You really think we are so immune from such a fate?'

'We are Mann. They were not.'

'We are Mann, yes. But we are not invulnerable. Perhaps, during your recent cull, you should have remembered that also, hmm?'

She said no more, not in front of the others, at least.

Kirkus tossed the core of the parmadio to a passing slave, wiped his hands on his robe. He said nothing more as the conversation turned to different topics.

His mother had been livid upon his return, angry to the point of striking him, when she had found out how he had slain the wearer of a seal during his cull.

'You think they will not try to reach him, even here?' Sasheen had yelled at his grandmother.

'We have contingencies against that, if they do,' he had heard his grandmother reply through the heavy door he listened at. 'Calm yourself, child. We did not rise so high by fearing the likes of the Rōshun. Such worrying is a weakness. You must purge yourself of it.'

Kirkus himself had experienced no such worries at first. The Cull had transformed him, in some way. His normal everyday arrogance had settled into something deeper instead, so that he had felt a rightness in every action he performed, whether small or consequential. He knew, with every touch of his fingers, that he had taken life with these same hands. He had bent his will to the task, and it had not been so difficult after all. At long last, Kirkus had experienced a brief taste of the divine flesh.

On his arrival home at the Temple after their grand progress, he had half expected Lara to be waiting there to see this new-grown man standing before her, and for her to come rushing into his open arms in a deeply satisfying display of regret and tears. The very last thing he had expected had been a continuation of their old hostility.

After this freshest blow of rejection, Kirkus had found himself becoming increasingly reclusive in his personal chambers, turning his other friends away more times than not. He began to dwell on the image of the seal hanging about the dead girl's neck. Stories came unbidden of the Rōshun, of the impossible myths that surrounded them. He found eddies of fear often rippling in his stomach, till his new-found sense of power began to diminish.

There would be other culls, and purges too. He would feel that power again, and practise the wearing of it until he became it entirely. But still, he felt that gnawing worry as he lay awake at nights, listening to the closing of distant doors, the silences that were not silences at all but a cacophony of sounds too subtle for him to hear.

Kirkus looked down at his hands and felt the tacky sweat of them. His nostrils seemed clogged with the dust of the arena outside, borne within.

I must wash, he thought.

He turned to make his excuses to leave, but saw the priest Heelas approach from the entrance leading to the imperial stand, the man shrouded in the lace hangings for a moment as he passed through a haze of sunlight into the antechamber within. 'Holy Lady,' announced his mother's caretaker with a bow. 'The people call for you.'

The chatter in the room fell silent. Indeed, the sound of the crowd had now risen to a percussive chant that Kirkus could feel in his stomach.

'Then let us go and please them,' said Sasheen, her smile brightening in an instant.

Kirkus wiped his hands against his robe again, and sighed as he followed her outside, the high priests trailing behind them.

At the appearance of Sasheen, a hundred thousand voices roared approval from the stands of the vast arena. She raised a hand aloft to acknowledge them, and for a moment Kirkus forgot his personal grumbles as he felt a rush of excitement rising within him.

It was cooler in the imperial stand reserved for the Holy Matriarch and her high priests, the sky above it cloudless and bright. On the sandy floor of the Shay Madi arena, a host of naked men and women huddled together in chains, looking like the refugees from some natural devastation. They were heretics from around the Empire, caught in the act of practising the old religions – a furtive sign made to one of the spirit gods, a prayer to the Great Fool – and informed on by a neighbour or even by their kin.

Their ranks included the poor, too; the homeless and the crippled, those who could barely fend for themselves let alone thrive. These were people seen as failures in the eyes of Mann, parasites and carrion all, as far from the divine flesh as they could be.

One by one, they were being branded by white-cassocked members of the Monbarri, Cinimon's dour inquisitors, their heavy piercings hanging darkly in the sunlight. Some would be sent from here to the salt pans of the High Char, to serve out the rest of their short lives in heavy labour. But most would become slaves within the Empire's cities, as manual labourers or even sex workers. The useless would serve as sport for the crowd's entertainment here on the arena floor.

The work of branding quickly ceased, now that Sasheen stood with both arms held aloft. The Monbarri stood ready with their loops of rope and smoking irons, sweating from their exertions, and waiting for her spoken words. The crowds fell to silence around them.

Sasheen called out in a high clear voice that rebounded around the other stands of the arena. She told the crowds what they wished to hear most from their Holy Matriarch: how, in their devotions, they were all of Mann together; how in their loyalty they had built this great empire as one. They were the victors in life, she declared, for they had helped spread the true faith, and when death came to take them they would all be victors still.

All of it nonsense, Kirkus knew, as he gazed out over the herded masses; though still he swelled with pride in the force of the moment. His gaze dropped to the arena floor, and hungered after the white flanks of the naked women huddled in a flock at its centre, each stood facing inwards as though to hide her shame and to shield her eyes from their surroundings. Kirkus could hear their exhausted sobbing, and in the distance, the shrill cry of gulls in the bay of the First Harbour.

His mother suddenly gripped his wrist, startling him as she jerked it into the air and shouted his name out to the crowds. Another roar sounded.

Kirkus felt a moistness in his eyes. The soft sting of goosebumps upon his flesh. He was filled once more with Mann, with a sense of his own self-importance.

His divinity.

CHAPTER FIFTEEN

Inshasha

'Have you informed Master Ash of this?' Aléas asked him.

Nico, a pitchfork in his hand, tipped a scattering of dung into a bucket and shook his head. 'I have not seen him since.'

'Perhaps it's better he does not know,' responded Aléas, with a pitchfork in his own hand, as he stood in a spear of sunlight cast through the open doors of the stable where they had both been sent by Olson, the monastery disciplinarian, due to a poor performance of their kitchen cleaning duties the previous evening.

Around them the stalls were empty, the mules and the few zel owned by the monastery out grazing in the lower slopes. Their task here was to gather dung for use as fuel. Aléas yawned, as tired as Nico from their previous night spent out in the open, while the apprentices served their regular turns at sentinel duty. 'It would only antagonize the two of them even further. My master was playing with you, Nico, but I did warn you what might happen. It could have been worse.'

'But I only talked with her . . . and for a moment.'

Aléas stretched his back, the bones of his spine cracking. 'Of course you did,' he said. 'And let me guess. When my master came across you both, just *talking*, you were likely standing close to her, with your tongue hanging loose, your eyes fixed on her pumps, and your prick as stiff as my little finger beneath your robe. A man like Baracha, where his daughter is concerned . . . he will notice these things.' And Aléas feigned a solemn raising of his eyebrows, and turned to find more fodder for his pitchfork.

Nico lent him a hand, in the form of a scoopful of dung tipped over his head.

'What did you to that for? I'll have to wash this shit off now!'

'Sorry, my little finger must have slipped.'

The young man scowled, wiping at the fresh smears on his robe. He in turn, swung a load of dung at Nico, but Nico blocked most of it with his pitchfork.

At that, they were suddenly duelling.

It was hardly serious: a pretend fight almost, having switched their weapons around so as to aim them shaft first. They were grinning to begin with but, as they hacked and stabbed at each other, pressing forward or falling back, the in-overturn of it grew into something more competitive.

Even when using a simple pitchfork, Aleás was a finer swordsman than Nico by a factor of at least ten. Nico improvised, however, as he had learned to do while living rough on the streets of Bar-Khos. He threw a wet lump of dung at Aleás, so that the young Mannian tried to dodge it, and since Nico had been anticipating this response, and Aleás merely reacting, Nico was able to follow it up with a strike aimed at his rival's head. Except, in his enthusiasm and lack of ability, Nico swung his weapon much too hard and much too wildly, catching Aleás on the mouth and splitting his top lip open, so that blood swelled from the gash.

'I'm sorry!' Nico held up his free hand.

'Sorry?' Aleás spun and ducked and, out of this blurring motion, launched a sweeping one-handed lunge at Nico, cracking him smartly across the side of his skull.

Nico staggered back, his head ringing.

Now it was Aleás who held up a hand, before he cast his pitchfork to the straw-covered floor and flopped down next to it. He dabbed a finger to his wounded lip, his wry smile only increasing the flow of blood 'Not too hard, I hope?' he inquired, with a double tap to the side of his head.

Nico collapsed to the floor too, out of breath. Dust motes danced in the sunlight between them, settling slowly as the two apprentices regained their breath.

'Have they always been this way?' Nico asked.

'Who?'

'Master Ash and Baracha, of course'

Aleás sucked on his lower lip for a moment. 'The older hands would say so. But, myself, I believe it got worse after Masheen. It is mostly my master's fault. He cannot tolerate being bested by anyone.'

'Ash bested him?' The surprise was clear in Nico's voice. He thought of Ash with his thin frame and ageing skin, his frequent headaches; he thought of Baracha practicing with his blade, the man massive and quick.

'Not in that sense.' Aléas shrugged, leaned to one side, and spat blood. 'Ash had the temerity to rescue my master, when he could not rescue himself.'

'What? Well, tell me more!'

'Make yourself comfortable. It's a long story.'

*

Six years ago, shortly before Aléas had arrived here to begin his train-ing, Baracha had run into the kind of trouble that every Rōshun in the field dreads most of all. He had been caught.

Baracha had been committed to a vendetta in Masheen. Or, more precisely, in the mountainous country known as Greater Masheen, which surrounded that great eastern city on the delta of the Aral river, where the ice-melts from the High Pash ranges drained themselves, languid and wide, into the Midèrēs.

Baracha had been there to kill the 'Sun King', a man claiming to be the living incarnation of Ras, their sun deity and, incredibly, had gained credence among the mountain people there, who were as devoutly superstitious as all eastern peoples, if not more so.

They held to a prophecy in those parts: that when the mountain should fall, and crush the World Serpent coiled in its lair within the mountain's rocky heart, a god would appear in human form from the lands of the rising sun, and walk amongst them to herald a new age of enlightenment. Even with the subjugation of their native religion by the Mannian Empire – which had, several decades ago, annexed Masheen as the furthest province of their eastern conquests – the local people's belief in this prophecy remained prevalent.

They did not even know which mountain the legend spoke of. To them, all mountains held evil at their core, and were to be trodden with care. Still, when an earthquake shook long and hard enough for a certain peak to collapse in its entirety, save for one free-standing column rooted in a colossal mound of rubble, like a marker for a grave . . . and when out of the east came a man with gold skin leading a train of disciples celebrating his divinity ... the peoples of Masheen knelt at his feet and offered him all.

This Sun King reigned from a sprawling palace perched on the highest shoulder of a mountain overlooking the port city of Masheen. The Cloud City, they called it. The Sun King was old and in his decline by then, from what Baracha had been able to discern during his first week within the port city. It seemed this new age of enlightenment had changed little for the people, save for imposing an even higher burden of taxation. Some had inevitably become cynical about this deity of theirs, who squatted high over their labours and demanded tributes equal to any tyrant. The Sun King now lived as a recluse, seeing only those few he trusted most completely. Once a year he would release a pronouncement of his Most Glorious Wisdom, offered to the population in the form of thousands of parchments each lovingly transcribed by hand. Always, they tended merely to rant, to threaten.

Within the Cloud City, it was said not a week went by without some official or priest being put to death by scalding alive for reasons of treachery. The Sun King had banned all weaponry within the walls of his palace complex, save for those in the hands of his hitees, the Glorious Virgins – female bodyguards chosen young from among his harem for their love of him. In his paranoia he had outlawed the wearing of hats, and even garments with sleeves. At nights, from the depths of his inner sanctum, his howls could be heard on the far reaches of the Midèrēs sea, so mad was he become, they said.

Baracha was caught just as he breached the inner sanctuary itself, which was a palace within a palace, secluded from the rest of the Cloud City on its own promontory of rock, and known as the Forbidden Sanctuary. It seemed he had underestimated the vigilance of the hitees. Even so, he was armed substantially, and they lost no small percentage of their sisterhood before Baracha was overwhelmed by sheer numbers and beaten to the floor unconscious.

He was thrown into a stone cell in the bowels of the Forbidden Sanctum, where for some days they tortured him without the least degree of mercy. They wanted to know who he was, where he came from – and, of course, why he had come to slay their god.

By his own account, Baracha gave them nothing. It was evident that they were unaware of their Sun King's guilty secret – that this so-called god had recently murdered his own twelve-year-old son – a seal-wearer whose life was wrenched from him in a fit of delusion. The Sun King had since passed it off as a mysterious accident, though the Rōshun knew otherwise.

On the fifth day of his captivity, they dragged him to a wood-panelled room with a lace-work screen at its far end, and secured him by the hands and throat with leather bindings to one of the wooden columns, before tearing the remaining tatters of cloth from his body. They then hauled in one of the wild mountain dogs of the region, stinking from its own filth, and crazed with hunger, its claws scraping reluctantly across the polished floor. They left him alone with it. The dog eyed him warily from across the room. Then dipped its head and growled.

He knew what animals in the wild went for first, the soft genitalia of their prey. All of a sudden, Baracha became acutely conscious of his own exposed nakedness.

The animal padded towards him, swinging its head low across the floor, sniffing. It came close enough that he could see the muck caked in its fur, hardening it into tufts, the white lice crawling through them. The hound paused a few feet away and growled with bared teeth.

Baracha growled back at it.

When the beast started forward, already snapping for his groin, he found himself, without transition, rolling on the floor with the animal, his thumbs crushing its throat while its feet scrabbled at him for purchase. He did not let go despite the savage wounds it was causing him. It took long grim moments before the dog died in his grasp.

As its reflexes stilled, and his own vision cleared, he saw the broken twines about his wrists and the torn skin underneath them, realizing that he had somehow broken free of them in his moment of greatest terror. Though he did not call it that, instead he called it his *moment of distress*.

A strange whimper sounded from behind the lace screen. Baracha knew then that the Sun King was observing him – and that the man was fearful of the Rōshun.

Bloody and staggering, Baracha was surrounded once more by the hitees, who hurried him away from the scene, down steps and ladders until he was thrown once again into the hole in the rock that had been his cell. They told him they would have another dog for him tomorrow; that they would ensure his bonds were stronger next time.

By then, the monastery of Sato had become alerted to Baracha's plight. The Seer had had a vision in his sleep: Baracha was in torment prolonged and unspeakable. They informed Ash – who happened to be on the island of Lagos at the time – via a carrier bird sent to their agent there. He made haste to the mainland, to Masheen, and from there to the Cloud City, disguising himself as one of the many devotees who travelled to the palace to give praise to their god. His plan was hatched only after several days of reconnoitre.

A feast was to be held in the Forbidden Sanctuary to celebrate the birthday of the deity's favoured mistress. Only the most trusted of his disciples would be allowed access to this event. On the night of the feast, these privileged guests dined on only the most exotic of fare: baked firemoths and honeyed sandshrimps, rare flightless birds still with their feathers, poached muala eggs, grotesque specimens of fish so large they could not be cooked in the kitchens of the Forbidden Sanctuary, but were instead prepared elsewhere within the palace complex, and borne under guard to the banquet hall. Central to this experience of culinary discovery was a murmur worm. The creature was carried inside by forty palace attendants, and stretched along the full length of a sixteen-foot table. It was as wide as a barrel and as white as a maggot, having never been exposed to daylight in its long life amid the crevasses and caverns of the deep earth. The guests had not yet sampled this delicacy when the Sun King himself entered the room, flanked by his ever-watchful hitees. Silence descended as all threw themselves prostrate to the floor.

They did not notice at first the thing emerging from the flank of the great worm.

It appeared from one of the great incisions made in the creature's flesh for the cooks to fill its innards with delicate stuffings. But then someone cried out – the Sun King's fêted mistress no less – and a rustle of heads turned in time to see an arm pushing its way out into the air. It was followed by a head, then another arm, and finally the entire body of a man, who flopped to the floor gasping. He climbed to his feet without hindrance, his clothes sodden from the worm's internal juices.

On the far side of the hall shone the Sun King, his naked form coated in glittering gold, even his hair and his eyelashes. The intruding stranger, on the other hand, was unadorned, his hands empty.

As he strode towards the Sun King the disciples cleared a path before him, many gasping in shock as at the sight of his coal-black skin. It was as though the World Serpent had come back in the form of a man.

So stunned were they by this apparition of darkness – even the hitee guards staring wild-eyed at the approaching figure – that all froze to the spot as the stranger stepped upon to the dais where the Sun King stood, and bent forwards as though to offer him a kiss.

It was the knife that broke the spell at last, emerging as though from nowhere, to be pressed against the throat of the golden-skinned god.

'Back!' Ash hollered, stopping them even as they began to rush to their master's aid. It seemed they did not did consider their Sun King to be invincible, after all.

They watched the blade at his throat; watched the face of the stranger, his dazzling white eyes and white teeth.

Ash ordered that his comrade be freed and brought before him. When no one moved he repeated his words – this time addressing the Sun King himself. 'Do it', he urged, 'and I will not kill you.'

Whether he believed him or not, Sun King responded with a trembling gesture to his followers.

They remained long moments standing there waiting for Baracha to be brought up from his hole. Eventually enough time passed for the disciples to begin shifting uneasily and to whisper amongst themselves. A stink of fear-sweat rose from the skin of the Sun King. The situation might have become farcical, if not for the hitees getting restless as their patience diminished. Ash was fully aware that, despite the risk to their god, one of them might break rank at any moment and try to rush him.

Finally the doors clattered open, and Ash barely recognised Baracha as they dragged him into the hall. When the prisoner looked up through his one sound eye to see the old farlander standing there in their midst, he reasoned that Ash must have come to finish vendetta and then die by his side. There would be no way out for them once the Sun King was slain. 'Now tell me,' Ash instructed the god. 'Tell me who you really are.'

The Sun King looked close to breaking, the sweat running off him in sheets. An actual puddle of it had formed around the soles of his bare feet.

At the first bubble of blood from the prick of the knife, the false deity began to babble in terror.

He told them all who he really was: how he had been born into a clan of travelling hedge-rogues, who made their living from one petty deception after another. He rambled on about how they had heard of the fallen mountain, about the ancient prophecy and how the idea had struck him fully-formed of masquerading himself as a god, with his family of chancers acting as his first disciples. Hushing to barely a whisper, he confessed to their murders and betrayals committed over the following years – no longer trusting them once his pre-eminence was established, removing them in one way or the other until only he himself remained.

By now the looks of alarm around Ash and the Sun King had turned to uncertainty and then anger.

'Please,' he pleaded. 'Surely a god's hand did indeed truly guide me here. Who could have done so without a spark of divine aid, I ask you? If I am not a god, then know at least that I am a god's chosen intermediary.'

'Then go to your god,' said Ash, and finally stepped away from him.

The assembled crowd did not try to stop the old Rōshun from leaving. Instead they turned to the naked, golden man quivering before them . . . and fell on him as wild animals fall on their prey.

*

'And so you know all this from Baracha and Ash, that talkative pair?' inquired Nico, squinting in the sunlight of the stable.

'Well, I may have embellished the gaps a little, I confess. And I've heard other variations of the story told. But what counts is that my master was hardly grateful for Ash's intervention. No, he actually felt slighted by it, and from then onwards has never missed an opportunity to match himself against his rescuer, or to pass derogatory comments within the earshot of others. He most of all wishes for a reckoning between them both, to prove he is not second best after all.'

'But you think Ash would win such a contest?'

'Of course he would win. Haven't you been listening?'

Aléas had been digging around inside his robe as they spoke. He produced two dried preens, and tossed one to Nico.

'I'll tell you this much,' he continued. 'Consider a hundred vendettas conducted by this order – ninety-nine of those will involve the killing of greedy merchants or jealous lovers. Not for Ash, though: the Rōshun have a name for him here. They call him *inshasha*, which means killer of kings.'

Nico bit into the dried fruit, relishing its smoky sharpness on his tongue. He swallowed some, considering all he had heard.

'And what is it they call Baracha?' he asked.

Before Aléas could reply a shadow fell across their laps. Olson stood in the doorway, hands planted on hips.

'What's this idling?' he sneered, taking in the two apprentices lazing on the stable floor. He squinted at Aléas's bloody lip. 'And you've been fighting, too!' He bustled towards them in his loose robes, grabbing each by the ear and pulling hard.

'Up! Up!' he commanded, yanking them simultaneously to their feet.

The sudden pain was sharp enough to blur Nico's vision. 'What do they call Baracha?' he nevertheless hissed, half bent-over in the grip of Olson's fingers.

Choking on a mixture of laughter and pain, Aléas managed to reply, 'Alhazii.'

*

'What's going on here?' bellowed a voice from across the courtyard as Olson hauled them, stumbling, from the stable. It belonged to Baracha, breaking off from his practice session with a great broadsword.

Both young men straightened up instantly, as Olson released them. 'I caught them lounging about, eating stolen food. They've clearly been fighting too.'

'Is that true, Aléas?' the Alhazii demanded of his apprentice. 'You squabble now in the dirt like a child?'

'Not at all,' Aléas replied as he wiped the remaining blood from his chin. 'We were merely practising our short-staff skills. I fear I was a little slow in defending myself.'

'Just practising?' The big man took Aléas by the chin, inspecting his wound. Displeased at the sight, he released it. 'I told you to stay away from this one, and now you see why. Remember, you are training to be Rōshun. We do not settle our differences like dogs fighting in the street. If you have a problem with each other, then we must settle it in the proper way.'

Aléas and Nico exchanged apprehensive looks.

'But we have no problem between us,' Aléas said with care.

'What? You have been bled, boy.'

'Yes – and it was but an accident.'

'It is still an insult!'

'Master,' said Aléas, 'I have hardly been insulted. It was merely sport.'

'Be quiet, Aléas.'

His apprentice looked to the ground glumly.

'We must settle this properly,' repeated Baracha, exchanging a knowing glance with Olson. 'And we will do it in the old way – you understand, the pair of you?'

Oh no, thought Nico, not liking the sound of that.

'A fine idea,' said Olson with a renewed sparkle in his eyes. 'I will fetch what they need.' And he hurried off towards the north wing.

'What we need?' echoed Nico, asking of no one in particular.

'We are going fishing,' said Aléas with a sigh, his gaze still fixed firmly on the ground.

Fishing? marvelled Nico, but he knew better than to open his mouth again. Instead he wondered, with a rising panic, what terrible ordeal could lurk behind such an innocent phrase.

CHAPTER SIXTEEN

Fishing

'You keep your distance from him, I see,' Kosh remarked in their native Honshu.

'I keep my distance from everyone,' replied Ash, passing his old friend the gourd of Cheem Fire.

Kosh took a drink and returned it. 'Aye. But particularly from the boy, is what I mean.'

'It's best for him that way.'

'Really? Best for him, or best for you?'

Ash leaned his back against the tree they sat beneath at the edge of the mali forest. He took another mouthful and felt the liquid searing down his throat and into the depths of his stomach. It was an unusually hot day for the mountains of Cheem, so the shade here beneath the leaves of this mali tree was a pleasant relief to the two farlanders. The everyday sounds of the nearby monastery fell into the silence of the valley floor extending before them. The valley itself was reduced to something small and precious by the stark mountains rising all around it: high snow-caps soaring in the distance, the lower slopes closer by speckled with wild goats, and above them the intense blue of the sky, the clouds sailing across it looking flimsier than paper.

Kosh belched. 'I sent off a letter to his mother, you know,' he said tightly.

'Did you read it first?'

A shake of the head. 'That boy seems a sensitive soul. I hear he keeps himself to himself most of the time.'

'Perhaps he prefers it that way.'

'Aye, like his master. I wonder, though. I wonder if he is ready for all of this.'

Ash snorted. 'Who is ever ready for this?'

'We were,' said Kosh.

'We were soldiers. We had butchered already.'

'Soldiers or not, we were both cast for this life. When I look at your boy, though, I do not see it in his eyes. He could be a fighter, yes . . . but a hunter, a slayer?'

'You speak nonsense, Kosh, as you have always spoken nonsense. There is only one thing that counts in this work, in this world even. And it's that which he has most of all.'

'A handsome mother in need of stiff action?'

Ash raised his chin. 'He has heart,' he replied.

For a time they sat and gazed out over the bright valley, without speaking. The sunlight was catching itself in the ripples of the river, producing a long, twisting ribbon of silver with reflections of gold. Kosh still had questions on his mind, Ash could tell. The man had been holding them back ever since Ash had first returned to the monastery of Sato with an apprentice in tow.

'I'm just surprised, that's all,' said Kosh at last. 'I didn't think to see you with an apprentice after all this time. And they say you can't teach an old dog new tricks.' His tone changed, became softer. 'Has time healed, at last?'

Ash looked sidelong at him, the answer in his eyes.

Kosh nodded. His own eyes turned away and squinted into the distance – perhaps seeing his own memories of that day neither of them wished to speak of.

Long ago, Ash had found that he could not bring to mind his son's face unless he recalled it in those last moments of the boy's life. It was the irony of memory, he thought: to see clearly only those moments most painful of all.

He could see his son's features now, more like his mother's than his own. His son, his battle-squire in training, just fourteen years old, and awkward in his heavy leather half-armour, carrying the spare spears and with the water bags hanging from him. The boy struggling towards him over the dying men and corpses scattered on their position, on a small hill to the far left of the main battle line, tripping in blind fear. Ash's words were lost in the deafening tumult of the fighting that raged around them. His son's young face suddenly gone white as he turned back towards the steaming cavalry thundering into the rear of their tattered ranks without warning. Men of General Tu's, their own men of the People's Army, gone over to the side of the overlords in exchange for a fortune in gold.

Ash had realized in that moment that the battle was lost to them. He had known too that his son was dead even before a rider swept low in his saddle and hacked his blade against the boy's neck, taking his head clean off in one blow . . . so that one moment the boy was there, the next only a horror to be relived in the mind forever afterwards, a thing falling lifeless, to be lost amongst the other dead on the field.

Ash would have gone berserk if Kosh, and his own squire, had not clubbed the strength from him and dragged him away from the boy's body and out of the fray, their entire left flank already scattering like seedsails on the wind. From Oshō's position the signal for retreat waved unnoticed, for it was already a full rout. As they fell back through one of the ravines cutting across the field of action, the general had placed himself and his bodyguard in the path of the main body of zels pursuing them, and there fought a stubborn retreat while the rest of his men, three thousand or so, ran without heed for anything else but their skins.

At the time, most had thought themselves lucky to escape alive. But Ash had never considered it so.

A bell was now ringing. It might have been ringing for some minutes before either of them paid heed to it.

Ash and Kosh stirred and looked back towards the monastery.

'Is it breakfast?'

'We had breakfast two hours ago.'

'So what is it, I wonder?'

But Ash had already risen, beckoning Kosh after him with a jerk of his head.

*

Nico stood with a growing self-consciousness as the bell continued clamouring, while the assorted men of the monastery gathered in the courtyard around them. No one had asked for the bell to be rung – neither Olson nor Baracha – but another Rōshun, his name unknown to Nico, upon seeing what was about to take place, had grinned and set himself the task of beckoning everyone to witness the afternoon's sport.

Every Rōshun in the monastery seemed to have turned out in the open space. Since it was a Foolsday, and was their day off, they stood chattering and laughing, the warmth of the late-summer sun drawing easy smiles.

Aléas stood ten steps away, with Baracha hissing in his ear. The young man appeared no happier about their present circumstances than was Nico.

Just then, Ash came striding through the gateway with Kosh by his side, the two walking with the careful gait of men who were already somewhat drunk. *Wonderful*, thought Nico. *Now I get to make a fool of myself in front of the old man too.*

Ash stopped and surveyed the scene before him. The swollen lip of Aléas, his chin still stained with dried blood; Baracha hovering over him; Olson's expression sombre but his eyes amused; the open ground between the two apprentices, and the collection of items lying there – two rolls of fishing twine, each fitted with a hook and silver twists of foil, and beside them two large weighted nets.

Ash said nothing as he joined his apprentice, and Nico resolved not to address the old farlander until the man spoke first. Thus they stood side by side like a pair of mutes, the Rōshun muttering amongst themselves all around. Aléas was shaking his head, but Baracha scowled, then hissed in his face. He pulled his apprentice towards the equipment strewn on the ground, the blood flowing again down Aléas's chin.

'It's all a nonsense,' Nico blurted out at last to his master.

From the corner of his eye, he could see the old man nod his head. 'See it through,' he said.

Olson raised his hands to quieten the gathered audience. 'Step forward,' he commanded the two apprentices.

Both young men stepped up to the fishing items; Aléas studied them or the ground they lay upon. Nico studied Aléas instead, but the other wouldn't meet his eye.

'We have a way of dealing with feuds here at Sato,' announced Olson. 'You will settle your differences, both of you, in this the old way, for it was inspired by wisdom.'

Olson gestured to the equipment. 'You will each choose one of these items. Armed with that, you will make your way to the chain of pools at the very top of the valley. There you will keep fishing until noon, catching as many as you can, of whatever size you can, and then you will return promptly. You have three hours. If you are not back by the ringing of the bell, then you will be disqualified. He who brings with him the most fish to display in this courtyard at that time will be declared the winner. Your dispute will then be settled. Do you both understand?'

Aléas nodded grudgingly. Nico followed his example a moment later.

'Good. Now make your choices.'

Nico looked to the old farlander for guidance. Ash blinked, giving nothing away.

Fishing? he thought. *Maybe they really do just mean fishing.*

But, at the same time, it had to be more than that, and the interest of the other Rōshun made this clearly so. The apprentice was the mark of the master. A public contest between these two was a public contest between Baracha and Ash.

Nico wished he could say as much, to tell the two grown men to go and settle their differences between them, and to leave him out of it. Instead, he remained silent. After all, he considered, I may actually have a chance at besting Aléas here.

With a sudden renewed focus of mind, Nico found his gaze roaming over the items before his feet. *Fishing twine or net?* he pondered. He would catch more fish with the net, but it would be heavy, by the looks of it, weighed down by a number of stone weights attached around its edges. He would first have to run all the way to the top of the valley carrying that load across his back, and then set out on his return early in order to make it back in time for the ringing of the bell. No, he was hardly strong enough for that. He would waste too much time. Besides, Nico knew how to fish. A net like that would scare away all the fish after the first haul. So instead, he knelt and scooped up the small ball of twine.

He glanced to Ash again. Almost imperceptibly the old farlander nodded.

Aléas made his choice, too. Nico felt a brief feeling of satisfaction, for the other youth had chosen the heavy net.

'Remember,' said Olson, 'he who returns here with the most fish, within the given time, is the winner. Now go.'

A chorus of jeers and yells rose among the Rōshun, as Aléas tossed the net across his shoulders and sprinted for the gateway. After a moment of hesitation, Nico set off in pursuit.

*

It was a hot, sweaty climb. Nico jogged until his legs ached but still he maintained his pace, gaining some encouragement early on as he overtook Aléas on the stony track, the young man already slowing under the weight of the net slung on his back.

'I'll keep some fish for you!' he shouted over his shoulder, but Aléas didn't answer, just kept his head down, his legs pumping.

Nico pulled off his heavy robe as he ran, so that he wore only his thin grey undergarments. He cast the robe far into the tall grasses so as not to give Aléas the same idea.

Staying focused on the ground before each footfall, Nico fell himself into a stride he felt confident of maintaining. On his right the course of the stream wound upwards, but Nico stayed clear of it, so as to avoid the marshy ground along its edges. The sun rose ever higher, though denser clouds came drifting into the valley from further up, to obscure its heat, and after them came a wind that whipped at his hair and set the grasses surging in steady currents all around him.

Nico passed the Seer's hut, and nodded briefly to the ancient monk who sat outside, painting something on a square of parchment. The old man nodded back.

Stopping for the briefest of moments to gulp a mouthful of water from the narrowing stream, he chanced a look behind him and could just make out the shape of Aléas hauling himself laboriously along the same trail. It was a gratifying sight.

Half an hour later he had reached the top of the valley, where Nico veered towards the stream again, and a series of bubbling springs. He could see trout darting within the pools they formed, and he quickly chose the likeliest spot, a large pond with overhanging vegetation, which he approached at a crouch.

With haste he unwound the twine, as he studied the pool and the fish swimming in its clear waters. Then he shook out the hook and foil, until they were both fully untangled. He would need a float, he realized, so he wrenched off a twig from one of the windswept bushes and secured it to the twine. With a final deep breath, he cast the assembled line across the water, and hunkered down to wait.

The fish were hungry. Almost as soon as the silver foil flashed in the water, a trout darted out, gulping both foil and hook in one go. Nico yelped in excitement and quickly drew it in. It was a small fish, but size didn't matter. He felt the slight weight of it as he pulled it free of the water, proceeding carefully now, the fish flapping at the end of the line. Up it came into his hands, wet and slippery and real as it tried to struggle from his grasp. With his childhood practice, he unhooked the fish and clobbered it to death against a rock.

Quickly, he cast the hook back into the water, his heart pounding. He could not quite believe how easy this was going to be, and his face grinned with the joy of it. 'For once, my little friends,' he said to the fish still uncaught, 'fortune chances to look on me.'

*

The hours passed slowly. Nico worked with hook and twine, waiting until the pool seemed fished enough, then he would move on to a lower pool and continue trying his luck there.

It was a pure and satisfying task. His mood was as warm and mellow as the sun's heat against his bare arms. A breeze played down the gulley carved by the passage of the river, just cool enough to be refreshing. The occasional bird sang somewhere out of sight. Water tinkled. Grassflies buzzed in lazy arcs, sometimes came close enough to trumpet in his ear.

He had not caught sight of Aléas again, which he thought odd. At first he worried that his companion might be up to something devious. But, as time passed and the sun rose slowly towards the point of midday, he allowed himself to believe that Aléas had come undone somehow. Perhaps a twisted ankle, or perhaps he had simply opted to try fishing lower down the valley, after deciding his net was too much of a burden.

Twenty-two small trout now lay on the grass beside him, strung along a spare length of twine. By the angle of the sun he reckoned he had perhaps another half hour before he would need to start making his way back. He was determined to leave himself with plenty of time.

So lost was he in his calculations, Nico failed to notice the subtle sound of movement approaching from behind.

A bird fell silent in mid-song. A tuft of grass rustled as though trodden underfoot. Nico noticed neither. Instead, with a brief twist of the wind, a smell came to his nostrils. He sniffed at it, barely aware of doing so: his mind, back where it was watchful and wary, tried to place the sudden scent in the air – and then it did so. It was the reek of human sweat.

Nico swung around in alarm.

But much too late.

*

'I hate to do this to you, I really do, but my master leaves me little choice in this matter. So, here we are.'

Impressive words, thought Nico, if only because they were spoken with barely a hint of breathlessness, as though Aléas was merely taking in the fresh air of the day when, in reality, he was labouring downhill with a catch of fish fastened to a long twine draped over one shoulder, and a fishing net filled with a bundled Nico slung from the other.

Nico blinked the sweat from his left eye. The other one had already swollen shut from a blow he could not remember. All he recalled was turning around and seeing a flash of motion, then he was here – in the most embarrassing position he could have ever imagined.

'Your words,' Nico muttered through clenched teeth, and through the sharp press of the net criss-crossing his face, 'do very little to reassure me just now, Aléas.'

The other man grunted, as though to confirm it was an ungrateful world they lived in, and he, most of all, must suffer it.

'Why do you do this?' asked Nico, a strand of the net between his teeth. 'Are you so much in fear of your master?'

Aléas stopped for moment. He swung around to speak as though Nico was standing just behind him. 'It isn't fear, Nico. I could best the man with any weapon he might choose for me, though he doesn't know it.'

'Oh?' said Nico, buying time.

'I owe him my life, Nico. What choice do you have when you owe someone as much as that?'

Aléas set off once more, and Nico winced at the pain in his cramped limbs with each bouncing step, already going numb save for the one arm he had managed to poke out through the net.

'I'll make it up to you,' came the other man's voice again, though quieter than before. 'I promise it.'

Nico felt the twine of the net give way between his teeth. His free hand yanked hard and pulled another strand wide apart . . . and then another until, all at once, he tumbled out through the hole he had just made, and fell on his shoulder to the ground.

Aléas immediately turned and watched him rise unsteadily to his feet, a look of amused interest on his face rather than of surprise. His hands still clutched the empty net draped over his shoulder.

Nico knocked the smile from his face with a sudden right hook. As Aléas staggered for balance Nico's foot caught him so precisely in the crotch that he himself winced from the sudden impact.

Aléas turned white.

He sat down in a delicate descent with the breath hissing out of him and his hands clutching at his lap. 'Sweet mercy,' he breathed. 'Was that entirely necessary?'

'Such are the choices we are forced to make in this sorry world. So, here we are.'

*

'Should be any time now,' Kosh decided, as he passed the gourd to Ash.

'You really think he can win?' Oshō asked, still watching the entrance to the courtyard.

Kosh shrugged. 'You always said no victory was ever certain, not even after it was achieved.'

Oshō chuckled at this response, and it lifted Ash's heart to hear it.

'If your boy wins,' commented Baracha, also peering at the entranceway as one hand tapped restlessly against his leg, 'I'll eat my own tongue right where it lies in my mouth.'

'Please,' said Kosh, 'I would really prefer it if you did not.'

In a corner of the yard, the waterclock trickled noisily as it counted down the hour. Ash was surprised to feel a flutter of anticipation in his belly. Perhaps it was only Baracha's tension rubbing off on him a little. Perhaps, though, he did really care about beating the Alhazii in his petty games.

If nothing else it would be good for the boy. A victory in front of all of them would help to settle him, and nurture his own self-belief.

'They are coming,' said Kosh, a moment before the two apprentices appeared through the archway of the courtyard. A shout went up from some of the Rōshun, as they rose to their feet or emerged from indoors.

'Hah!' exclaimed Kosh. 'They walk side by side. And, look, they carry the fish between them!'

What's this? thought Ash, his face breaking into a grin.

Baracha crossed his arms. His jaw clenched tightly from side to side, as though indeed he was biting through his own tongue.

Both boys were stained with sweat and dirt and, as they stopped before the assembly of Rōshun, their eyes said they were finished with this business, regardless of what anyone else had to say about it. As one gesture, they tossed the net and the dead trout in a heap before their masters.

'Enough of this,' Aléas muttered to Baracha, and the big man inclined his head.

The Rōshun gathered closer around the two apprentices, and Kosh slapped each on the back, while Aléas put an arm around Nico's shoulders with a quiet grin.

It was Oshō who first spotted the arrival of the Seer. He drew Ash's attention by taking a few steps forwards, casting his gaze towards the entranceway where the old man stood, waiting in the heat.

A hush descended as the rest of the Rōshun began to take notice. Breaking away from their ranks, Oshō and Ash approached the ancient man.

'Something's wrong,' observed Aléas, drawing Nico with him.

'*Ken-dai,*' the Seer proclaimed to Oshō, his voice loud in the sudden silence.

'*Ken-dai,*' replied Oshō.

'What is it?' Nico whispered, but then the Seer went on to say: '*Ramaji kana su.*'

Aléas leaned close to his ear. 'He has had a dream,' he translated. '*San-ari san-re, su shidō matasha.*'

'He thinks we should know of it, before the world turns any further.'

'*An Rōshun tan-su . . . Anton, Kylos shi-Baso . . . li an-yilichō. Naga-su!*'

Aléas drew a deep breath, as did all those around him. In the quietness of the moment, he whispered: 'Our three Rōshun, those we sent against the son of the Matriarch . . . they have all been killed in Q'os.'

'*An Baso li naga-san, noji an-yilichō.*'

'Baso took his own life, in the old way, rather than fall into the hands of the priests.'

Nothing stirred now in the large open space. They waited for something more, but seemingly he had nothing further to tell them. '*Hirakana. San-sri Dao, su budos,*' the Seer said finally, brushing his hands together once. Then he spun on his heels and headed off, his extended ears flapping from side to side as he disappeared back through the courtyard gate.

'That is all. Be with the Dao, my brothers.'

All eyes turned to Oshō. Nico noticed how the farlander's fists were clenched tight, though his expression remained one of perfect calmness.

The silence stretched on as the assembled Rōshun waited for a word from their leader – perhaps a speech of some kind, or a few words honouring their dead comrades. Nothing came from him, though. Slowly, the silence expanded into an emptiness needing to be filled.

Nico's attention stayed on Oshō's hands, the fingers clenched white with tension. As the awkwardness of the moment increased, some of the younger Rōshun shifted with unease.

Ash began to take a step forward. At the sight of it, Baracha did the same. They both tried to speak at once.

'I will go,' declared Ash.

'As will I,' said Baracha, and he and Ash eyed each other with visible surprise.

Behind them, Nico and Aléas did the same.

CHAPTER SEVENTEEN

The War Below

Bahn spent most of the day underground.

He had been sent by General Creed into the warren of tunnels and chambers that cut through the earth and rubble foundations of the outer wall – Kharnost's Wall – where the sappers and the Specials worked endlessly to stop the Shield being undermined by the enemy. His instructions were simple: assess, through independent eyes, the present condition of the men below.

Like ghosts, Bahn concluded, in his first hour of being underground in those cold dark spaces where they toiled and sometimes fought.

The sappers were ragged and filthy. Many were criminals pardoned only on condition of working here, though some had volunteered, ex-miners and skilled labourers mostly. Any patch of their skin still free of grime shone sickly white in the pale swing of the lanterns. They dug dirt and carried dirt and shored up roofs with tarred timber in abject silence like that of a coffin. Working days for the sappers were merciless and exhausting, leaving little time for sleep. They worked in shifts of eleven hours, a half day, which in the tunnels felt more like twice that length of time, then rotated back to the surface where they drank the fresh air and rubbed their eyes in the burning daylight like men restored from the dead.

The Specials were a different breed entirely. Lean and wild-looking in their creaking, compact casings of black-leather armour and with their bare faces heavily scarred, they sat around in squads in small rooms barely large enough to hold them all, playing cards or fixing kit or simply waiting, eyes dulled by boredom, for some sudden signal of alarm. They had dogs with them, strong blunt-faced animals specially bred for underground baiting, just as scarred as their handlers. These lay with their leashes tied to posts, their bodies similarly encased in a simpler form of leather armour; occasionally their ears would twitch at the distant barking of other dogs below ground.

The air was foul and tasted spent. The low light strained eyes. The silence became a pressure on the ears, like the prelude to something terrible.

This was the first time Bahn had ever visited the tunnels. Like most ordinary soldiers he was glad to avoid them, and would listen to stories of the underground fighting with a mixture of horror at what those men went through and relief that he was not down there himself. He could not help but think of his own brother once living in these tunnels, passing each shift in tedium as a volunteer Special, knowing that at any moment an alarm might ring out, calling him to a desperate squalid fight in some pitch-black passageway no taller or wider than himself. His brother Cole had lasted two years in these tunnels before he had cracked under the strain of it, and had deserted the army and abandoned his family and everything else that he knew. He had never once spoken of his experiences below ground, not even to Bahn.

Coming to the end of a tunnel so low that Bahn had to stoop to avoid the sagging roof beams half-eaten with rot – a tunnel which zigzagged for hundreds of yards lit by lanterns strung too far apart for their light to meet, and sealed at every juncture by a heavy door that was opened and closed behind them by a Special, and with a hard-packed earth floor that dipped and then rose up again, heading beneath Kharnost's Wall then out beyond it, out beneath no man's land. At the end of the great tunnel, with that sense of weight pressing above his head like a sky of earth, Bahn found himself guided to a wooden stool set in the eerie confines of a listening post, a room just large enough to contain a pair of bunks, a desk, a bucket for crapping in, and two sweating Specials. He sat down with some uncertainty and pressed his ear to the opening of a conical device that resembled a bullhorn, itself in turn pressed against a wall of solid dirt.

In the silent depths of this place, Bahn listened to the dim and frantic howls of a man.

'Enemy sapper, I imagine,' one of the Specials explained. 'Trapped in a collapse somewhere.'

Bahn looked up and saw that he was grinning.

'Must be new at this, too, otherwise he wouldn't be shouting like that.'

The other Special looked up from where he sat whittling a length of wood. 'They always carry a bell with them, so, if they get trapped, they can untie the clapper and ring it for help. Uses up less air that way, than shouting.' He jerked his head towards the wall. 'He's panicked, though.'

Bahn eventually left them in their dingy cell of a room. On his way back, riding in the same small-wheeled cart drawn along two metal rails by a dwarf mule, an alarm sounded out. They had reached a crossing of tunnels where, from a passage on the left, came the clanging sound of a bell loud enough to spook the draught mule.

'Come on, now,' said the driver, attempting to sooth the frightened animal, just as a detachment of Specials ran across the junction before them, moving at a crouch and armed with punch-knives.

The mule shied up in alarm and kicked its hooves at the air. Failing to jump free of its harness, it only grew worse in its panic.

With hands held out, the driver went forward to calm his mule, clucking his tongue and speaking soft words to it. The mule snapped at him with its teeth, eyes rolling, then it began to shoulder-charge the wall, harness and all, colliding against it with dull thuds like a great fist smacking the ground. Bahn climbed out and stepped forward to lend a hand. It was clear they would have to restrain the animal before it broke its own neck.

Bahn could approach no closer, with the driver in his way. He retreated around the back of the little cart and squeezed along the other side of the tunnel until he had cleared it. He paused, a hand held up to protect his face, the mule's back legs kicking out next to him, splintering the wood of the rig and its own hooves along with it. *No good this way*, he thought. *Need to get round to the front.*

He leapt forward just as the animal dropped its legs again. But the mule sensed him coming and lashed out a hoof that caught him a breathtaking kick to his side. Bahn rolled to the ground, felt the iron rails biting into his back. He lay there desperately trying to find breath.

There was no calming the creature. In the end, the driver had to put an end to its life with his knife drawn across its throat, a grim determination on his face.

Merciful Fool, Bahn thought, some time later, his hand still clutching his throbbing side, his legs striding ever faster towards the beams of sunlight that blasted down the entrance-shaft like the welcoming hand of some benign god . . .

This is where my brother lost his mind.

*

Bahn felt too rattled to climb the hill to the Ministry and make his report immediately. His shift was over for the day, regardless, so he decided to leave the report until the morning, and instead stopped a passing rickshaw and gave the man his address as he climbed into the narrow seat, and took in the glory of the clear open sky overhead.

The streets were crammed with the usual bustle of traffic and commerce. The rickshaw wove through the throng with some difficulty, as its owner pulled Bahn along at a slow jog, shouting out when he needed a clear path. Heading through the Barber Quarter, they passed streets where Bahn had grown up as a youth, a poor but close-knit district of hairdressers and small-trades shops and crumbling tenement buildings, though lined now mostly with beggar carts and gossiping prostitutes, a sight he would never have witnessed during daylight hours before the war began. He watched the street-girls as the cart trotted past them, their flimsy garments concealing little from his roving eyes.

It was late in the afternoon when he arrived at their home in the northern quarter of the city, located as far from the Shield as one could get. With relief that his work was done for the day, he stepped off the rickshaw in the street in front of their townhouse just as his sister-in-law Reese was pulling up in her own cart.

How strange these occurrences are, Bahn thought, sensing something of Fate, of the Dao, in this coincidence, his brother still lingering so strongly in his thoughts.

Reese embraced him with a kiss to the cheek as he led her into their small two-storey dwelling. It was somewhat more spacious than the first home he and Marlee had shared above the public baths together, though it was still cramped. The house was empty, which surprised him for a moment, until he recalled that she and the children were visiting her own sister today.

He and Reese drank chee and chatted on the first-floor balcony, having not met since her last visit to the city.

'Where's Los today?' he enquired politely, thinking he should ask about her latest partner, at least for form's sake.

Reese merely shrugged. Bahn knew that Los could disappear for days without any word of his whereabouts. Gambling and whoring, Bahn supposed, from his vague impressions of the man. Los was of enlistment age, which meant he was either avoiding the draft or he had succeeded in buying his way out of it.

It was a shame, Bahn reflected, since the man would no doubt return to her when he was again out of money and with nowhere else to go.

'It will be time for your daughter's naming ceremony soon,' Reese observed with a forced smile.

'Aye,' said Bahn, trying to keep his breathing shallow. He had found that his bruised side did not hurt so badly that way.

'I'm keeping some foodstuffs aside for it. Some potatoes for pies, some peppers preserved in oil. It's all I can manage, I'm afraid.'

'That's kind of you,' sighed Bahn. 'Marlee doesn't seem to believe me when I tell her there is no extra food to be found anywhere.'

Reese nodded thoughtfully, staring into her cup.

'Something's bothering you,' he said. 'I can always tell.'

She didn't speak, so he continued and as he tried to think of what he should say next, it suddenly came to him what was troubling her.

'It's Nico, isn't it?'

Her eyes flinched and she looked away. 'He's gone,' she confessed.

'Gone? Gone where, exactly?'

Again that shrug, as though everything was hopeless.

'He's left the city to take up some . . . apprenticeship.'

'What?'

The pain in his side suddenly worsened. He deliberately slowed his breathing as he waited for her to answer. It was clear that Reese wanted to say more, but she hesitated in her response, then seemed to give up on the effort, as though it was too ridiculous to voice aloud.

'Have you heard from him? Is he well?'

She didn't seem to know.

Normally, Reese could talk easily with Bahn. They had a closeness of sorts, an openness that had intensified after his brother Cole had left her, Nico's father, as though this shared loss allowed them to share other things of intimacy and worry. They often spoke of Cole, sharing what little rumour they had heard of him from old veterans they had run across, or who had visited on purpose with some news. Cole's last-known trail had led to Pathia, where, it was rumoured he had been hanged for a highway robbery, though others claimed he was now a longhunter, crossing the mountains into the world of the Great Hush, to live wild there for months on end. How unhinged he must have become, Bahn often considered, to have abandoned a woman such as this to go and live in the wilderness by himself.

The pain in Bahn's side had now spread into his bladder. He needed to relieve himself. Cursing his body for its poor timing, he excused himself and stood up.

'Are you all right?' Reese asked him.

'Yes. Just a few sore ribs, I reckon.' He did not wish to mention the tunnels, with their inevitable reminders of Cole.

Bahn made his way down to the backyard privy and found that he was pissing blood. With his tunic hauled up and clenched in his teeth, he probed the ugly bruises on his side, and checked once more for any fractured ribs. Contenting himself that they were all still intact, Bahn swept back his hair, smoothed down his tunic, and turned to go.

As soon as he returned to the balcony he wondered if it had been a mistake to leave his sister-in-law on her own. Reese still sat with one arm resting on the wooden rail, and the other holding the cup in her lap, but was now surveying the tree-lined street with a brooding stare.

She didn't seem to notice as he sat himself down again gingerly. In anyone else he might have suspected this behaviour as some sort of self-indulgent drama – but not in Reese.

'What are you thinking?' he asked her, softly.

She turned back to face him, her brief smile holding something of an apology. The cup of chee now seemed forgotten in her hand.

'I was just thinking . . . I was thinking how Nico and Cole are both gone now.'

Her voice was quiet, restrained. Bahn was reminded of the faint yelling of a man trapped in the earth, with nothing to see or feel or hear but the darkness all around him.

CHAPTER EIGHTEEN

The Sisters of Loss
and Longing

The sister moons shone overhead in a dark, star-spattered sky. They rose with a fullness that narrowed the eyes – one dusty white, the other blue – and they climbed together on a course that took them partially along the Great Wheel, the visible galactic core, obscuring that vast stain of starlight. Only once in a year did the two moons rise together in all their fullness and, in doing so, they heralded the coming days of autumn. Perhaps it was the reason they had been given their names: the Sisters of Loss and Longing.

The two figures hiking up the hill were small and insignificant beneath this vista of galactic sky. The night was bright enough to see the ground in front of them, and they walked with their heads down, watching their footfalls, thoughtful. Because of this, it was almost a surprise to them when they drew up before the tiny shack at last, noticing it squatting there in the dimness all of a sudden, set against a sound of coursing water that was reminiscent of flames snapping on a distant fire. There was no fire lit in the tiny hut tonight, but a single lantern burned within, spilling a tongue of welcoming yellow light through the mouth of the open doorway. Without hesitation they followed it inside.

The Seer sat cross-legged upon a mat on the floor, a book lying open on his lap. He was squinting down at it through a pair of exceedingly thick-glassed spectacles, as one hand scratched idly at his lice.

It was some time before he acknowledged his visitors, and Nico stood there with dwindling patience, willing Ash to at least clear his throat and announce their presence.

When the Seer looked up at them at last, he smiled and set the book carefully to one side amongst a stack of others. He beckoned them to sit.

Ash began to speak. The older man nodded, listening closely, occasionally exchanging a question for an answer. Their words were soft, respectful of the night hush around them. The old Seer did not seem to be bothered by this late-night intrusion; rather, he seemed to welcome the company. It was as though he had been expecting such a visit from one of the Rōshun tonight.

As he and Ash finished their conversation, the Seer gathered up a varnished featherwood box from one corner of the shack, and settled it on the floor beside him. Items appeared from the box in his trembling fingers, and Nico examined them closely as they were arrayed upon the mat.

A square of black slate lay with a lump of chalk resting upon it. Beside these, a bundle of what looked liked dried reeds, each about a foot long. They were left untouched for some minutes as the Seer composed himself with a series of carefully focused breaths. Then he announced his readiness to proceed by a swift clap of his hands.

As he set to work, his hands moved fast for one of his age. He began by tossing the bundle of reeds against the mat, and quickly sweeping a hand across them to divide the resulting pile in two. He then gathered up the right pile and, in a blur of motion, flicked reed after reed from one hand into the other, stopping each time he was left with four or less in his right hand. As he did so, he would lodge the reed or reeds between two of his fingers, and he would begin the whole process once more, minus those ones already singled out.

Once all five fingers held reeds between them, he stopped to count how many there were. The resulting number seemed meaningful in some way. He chalked a mark on the slate – just a single line – and threw down the reeds to begin all over again.

It was a lengthy process, during which the Seer would occasionally scratch another line of chalk on the slate, either a solid line or a dash, which gradually built up into a series. Nico lost track of time and his eyes were already drooping when the Seer finally appeared to reach the end of his task, with six lines in all now scratched on the slate.

The old man squinted down at the results, muttering to himself. 'Ken-yoma no-shidō,' he offered Ash. The Rōshun nodded earnestly in response.

The Seer rambled on, outlining what he foresaw. When he paused again to study the slate, Nico whispered to Ash for a translation.

Ash was annoyed at this interruption, but a look into Nico's tired eyes seemed to soften him, enough to offer a brief explanation.

'I ask how we will fare on this vendetta. He tells me of thunder, *shock* – how some shocking event will lead to a great course of action. Now hush, he comes to the crucial part.'

'After shock, you will have two paths facing you,' the Seer announced in sudden, perfect Trade, his eyes glancing at Nico before returning to meet the intense gaze of Ash.

'By taking one path, you will fail in your task, though with no blame and much still to do . . . On the other, you will win through in the end with great blame, and nothing that would further you.'

Ash considered this divination. He cleared his throat. 'Is that all?'

The Seer smiled kindly, but did not reply.

They left soon after that, bowing and scraping their way towards the doorway. As Nico turned away from the Seer, he shouted after him, 'Boy!'

His call drew Nico back. The old man smacked his gums and squinted up at him.

'You did not ask me for a divination. It is your right, on this night.'

'I would not know what to ask you.'

The ancient farlander tilted his head. 'You do not wish to go off on this crazy venture of theirs.'

Nico glanced back to see if Ash was listening, but his master had already stepped outside. He looked again at the Seer, his mouth open but no words coming forth.

'You fear you are not ready for this vendetta your master takes you on. You suspect that you are out of your depth.'

It was true. All day, Nico had been struggling to face the thought that in the morning he would be leaving this hidden refuge in the mountains, this place that had begun to feel a little like home. And for what? To cross the sea to the city of Q'os, the very heart of the Empire, in order to kill the son of the Holy Matriarch no less, and with Nico himself still barely able to wield a blade. Sweet Erēs, it set his blood racing just to think of it.

'Will you listen to my guidance, then?' inquired the Seer.

Nico cleared his throat. 'In truth, I'm not yet sure if I believe in all these things ... divination and such. Your guidance may be somewhat wasted on me.'

'Know this, my young friend: the seeds of things show what fruits will come of them.'

Nico nodded, out of politeness rather than anything else.

'When the time comes to leave him, you must follow your heart.'

'What?'

The old man smiled, began packing away the paraphernalia before him.

Nico backed quickly to the doorway and stepped outside.

All around them lay the night's stillness; even the flow of the stream seemed more subdued to his ears. Master Ash stood in silence next to it, watching the water gathering and unfolding amongst the rocks.

Together they walked home through the semi-darkness.

'A strange fellow,' Nico commented.

Ash rounded instantly on his apprentice. 'You owe that old man more respect,' he snapped. But then he seemed to regret his outburst, and tried to say something else – an apology perhaps. He could not find the words though. Instead, he turned and continued onwards.

As the moons of Loss and Longing shone down to light their way, the two figures descended slowly, each lost in his own thoughts. Below them, the warm and welcoming lights of the monastery windows stood out clearly amidst a forest of silvery leaves.

CHAPTER NINETEEN

The Diplomat

On the first day of autumn, in what would soon be the fiftieth year of Mann, in a deafening rainstorm that slashed through the air to burst against every surface like a torrent of glass shots, a man hurried from the dark and hooded entranceway of the Temple of Whispers, and threw his own hood about his shaven skull, and set off at a brisk stride across the planking of the wooden bridge, his priestly white robes whipping behind him with their own wind, the stamp of his footsteps falling lost in the thrashing waters of the moat below.

The man did not pause as he passed the masked Acolytes standing on duty in the shelter of the guard house at the far end of the bridge. His gaze remained fixed to the ground as his pace bore him through the empty streets of the surrounding Temple District, his skin constantly itching so that he kept scratching at his arms and face. A few fellow priests scurried past, their similarly hooded heads bowed low in submission to the elements. Puddles boiled without reflections. A white cat huddled in a doorway, silent and watching.

Behind him, ever further behind him, the Temple of Whispers loomed amid curtains of rain like a living thing; its flanks bristling with spikes in such numbers that they looked like a covering of fur; a tower that was not one tower but a great twisting column of fluted pillars and turrets wrapped and warped by bands of stone. With every step, the young priest could feel it at his back, a massive sentinel watching him. It was a presence that flattened his mood even further – this sense of confusion he had awakened with on the morning of his twenty-fourth birthday.

The further he went, the busier the streets grew. Ahead rose a clamour of voices, and wild cries as though from some exotic menagerie.

The rain had settled into a steady drizzle as the priest entered the great plaza called Freedom Square, where distant marble buildings lined three sides of the open space, and behind them, in turn, were visible lesser skysteeples – pale spikes partly obscured by the shroud of rain.

The bad weather had barely diminished the vast crowd of devotees already gathered in the square in anticipation of the forthcoming festival of Augere el Mann, which was still almost a month away. The majority were pilgrims from across the Empire, drawn in ever greater numbers than usual by this Augere marking the fiftieth anniversary of Mannian rule: men and women alike, foreigners who had fervently embraced the religion of Mann even though many of their compatriots still grumbled bitterly and called for insurrection. All wore the common garb of the lay devotee, a vivid red robe hanging almost down to their bare feet. The front of their sodden garments bore the testimony of their past conversions: white open-palmed handprints flaking with age so that many were now a mottled pink.

After several years living in this city, the young priest Ché was still barely inured to the sights and sounds of these mass devotions. As he splashed his way across the flagstones paving the square, he eyed his surroundings from within the reassuring folds of his hood.

The pilgrims called out in tongues whilst thrashing about wildly on the spot. Or they listened with bright eyes to the inflammatory sermons of priests perched on canopied podiums, firebrands who shouted and gesticulated with fervour at their nodding heads and calls of concordance. They skewered their bleeding faces with spikes, or paraded with scalps afire, or copulated on the ground, or simply wandered about like dazed sightseers, with mouths agape at everything going on around them.

Ché skirted a great block of conformity that stretched from one side of the square almost to the other, ten thousand converts who stood facing the rain-shrouded Temple of Whispers, all dressed in unmarked red robes, their arms raised above them, mouths chanting constantly, faces aglow with the same fervour that had drawn them all the way to Holy Q'os for the ritual of conversion.

As one, they knelt on the flagstones, ten thousand robes rustling like a murmur of the wind. They bowed prostrate on the ground then stood up again, only to repeat the ritual. The young priest continued past lines of such dripping converts as they waited in turn to step forward and receive the press of a painted hand upon their chests from an ordained priest of Q'os. Ché did not slow in his stride even here, the pilgrims clearing a path for him, as soon as they recognized his white robes. He walked between the legs of a dripping statue of Sasheen, the Holy Matriarch, sitting astride a rearing white zel, and another of Nihilis, founding Patriarch of the new order, his bronze face grim and ancient.

Towards the eastern end of the square, the press began to thin, pilgrims mixing with ordinary citizens going about their daily business. The usual vendors' carts had been set up, with their simple, sagging awnings, from beneath which their owners sold paper cups of hot chee, bowls of food, bundled rainslicks. Others stood in the rain hawking souvenirs: cheap tin figurines of Sasheen, Mokabi, Nihilis. They observed the practices around them without fondness in their eyes, and cast furtive looks at the plain-clothed Regulators who stood in pairs around the edges of the crowd, watching over all.

A pair of guards mounted on zelback halted to give way to him, their unstrung crossbows resting on their laps. Ché did not bother to acknowledge them, but marched on out of the square through Dubusi street on the eastern side. He took a quick left and then a right through some smaller side streets, the noise of the crowds fading behind him with every step. His senses grew alert for any indication that he was being followed.

By the time he approached one of the smaller skysteeples, the constant rain had soaked his white robes grey. The cloth clung to his arms and legs, showing the hard wiry muscles beneath. His face still itched abominably, so that he paused before the bridge accessing the smaller tower, threw back his hood and stared up at the dark sky, then twisted his neck back and forth in the soothing rain. After a minute of such self-indulgence, he spat out a mouthful of the acrid water and wiped his eyes clear.

A flight of bat-wings were circling up there in a slow descent. They were larger than the type he had become accustomed to seeing above the city, which were used for surveillance or as couriers dispatched from one temple to another. He assumed these must be the new Warbirds that the Empire had been developing over recent years, purportedly strong enough to carry ordinance in the field and he knew it was so when they suddenly turned and swept towards Freedom Square: a fly-over, intended to dazzle the pilgrims with the endless innovations of Mann.

Ché set foot on the bridge, treading slowly. Reaching the entrance, he stopped by a stout metal door. A grille was embedded within it at head height, though it was too dark to see the eyes he knew were watching him from behind. A hatch slid open at waist level, to acknowledge his presence. Ché scratched at his neck one more time, before sliding both hands into the black space now revealed.

As a series of clunks announced the manipulation of the door's many locks, the young priest withdrew his hands, and a smaller door opened within the larger one. It was narrow and low, intended to force any visitor to stoop and turn sideways in order to step through. Being short, Ché was able to enter without having to duck.

Every hindrance a blessing, he thought drily; and even here, in the heart of the Holy Empire of Mann, he did not find it odd to be recalling that old saying of the Rōshun.

*

The Sentiate Temple was quiet at that early hour. Its circular ground floor was as dim as it always would be, windowless and lit only by a few gaslights sputtering along the curving wall. The two Acolytes on duty watched from behind their masks as Ché shook his shaven head dry, as a dog would, and then his dripping robes too.

'It's raining,' he explained, as though in apology.

The guards wondered if he was an idiot, one of those privileged young priests that sometimes slipped through the examiners' nets by way of money and parentage.

The taller loomed over his head; like another tower watching him. 'We serve only the high caste here,' the guard said. 'State your business.'

Ché frowned. 'Mostly this, I'm afraid.'

They had time enough only to widen their eyes before the two punch-knives drove up through their throats.

The two Acolytes convulsed where they stood. Ché withdrew both blades simultaneously and at the same instant stepped aside to avoid the discharges of blood he knew exactly where and how would follow. He walked a tight circle around the spreading pool of gore as he glanced around for any witnesses, and returned in time to see the two guards only then crumple from the knees up, one man folding sideways to the stone floor, the other on to his backside, and then on to his back.

Ché felt nothing.

He was quick to drag the corpses out of sight, behind a statue of an imperial celebrity; Archgeneral Mokabi – retired – he noticed when he paused long enough to inspect the alcove it stood in. The pools of blood would eventually give the game away, but in this gloom only if someone chanced to pass them directly.

It would do, for all the time his work here would take him.

He crouched in the shadows, using a knife to cut free one of the men's robes. He bundled the garment beneath his arm.

The north stairwell was merely a spiral of steps fixed around a central pillar. Ché followed it upwards for seven floors, proceeding casually as though he rightly belonged there. No one he encountered cared to challenge him.

He halted at the seventh floor of the skysteeple, where the stairwell opened on to a lush and spacious room of pink marble with a water fountain playing at its centre surrounded by potted plants. The air within this space tingled with the heady fragrance of pleasure narcotics. Three bald and slightly plump eunuchs lolled on the edge of the fountain, wearing loose-fitting robes, yet armed with dirks. They occasionally tossed water at each other, throwing giggling glances at the two priests who sat on the opposite rim of the fountain, one wearing an expression of eagerness, the other of acute boredom. From beyond them, through an archway of sensual mosaics and flowing red silks, emerged the sound of laughter, both male and female, mingled with the music of flutes and light drums beating like a steady pulse.

Ché, still hesitating in the stairwell, ducked his head back below floor level. He scratched unthinkingly at his arm while he quickly calculated his options.

He retreated to the floor below, seemingly empty except for the steady resonance of mass snoring.

A window shone pale light into the darkened space before him. It drew Ché to it, and he opened it inwards and poked his head out into the rain.

Looking up, he found it was just as he had known it would be. A concrete facade, nearly vertical, dotted with decorative protrusions too widely spaced to aid climbing. It was windowless for another four floors up.

Ché worked fast. First he donned gloves of the thinnest leather, then withdrew a clay jar from the equipment webbing slung beneath his priestly robes. The jar was sealed with a thick wax plug, and had a shoulder strap fixed to a wire wrapped several times about its neck. As he pulled out the wax stopper, a stench of animal fat and seaweed assailed his nostrils; he checked that the creamy white contents had not hardened inside. Satisfied, he pulled the strap over his head so that the jar hung against his hip, then shook open the bundled robe he had taken from the guard. He began to cut the material into strips using a knife drawn from his boot. Only once did he cast a glance backwards to check his surroundings; even then he did not pause in his task.

With the shreds of cloak stuffed into another pocket, Ché jumped on to the windowsill and turned so that his back faced out into the rain. His balance was precise, like that of a rope walker. Still, the empty air sucked at him.

He pulled out one strip of cloth, rolling it into a ball, then dabbed it into the jar before fixing the sodden ball to the outside wall next to the window frame, where it stuck against the concrete surface.

He proceeded to do the same with further strips, sticking a total of six rolled-up rags upon the surface within easy reach of his hands. By the time he had finished the last one, the first and lowest had dried into a hardened footrest.

Ché removed his boots. He tied them together by the laces and slung them around his neck. Tentatively, he stretched a leg to the side and tried the first foothold with a bare sole. It held firm.

'World Mother preserve the foolish,' he muttered, and stepped out on to it with all his weight. Ché did not dare look down. With a fierce grimace, he began to climb.

*

Despite his relative youth, Ché was experienced at such work. He had discovered a natural aptitude for it, which was surprising, considering he had never been given any say in the matter.

It was this he reflected upon as he forced himself to climb the near-vertical wall of a tower in the freezing rain a few hundred feet above the ground, his fingers trembling with the effort, the sting of water in his eyes. A life without choices.

For instance; his childhood.

Ché had been lucky at conception. He had been born into a family of great wealth – the Dolcci-Feda merchant clan, with warehouses covering half the northern docklands. At thirteen, he had been living happily enough in an affluent suburb to the east of the city. Like any other boy of that age, he had been easy with laughter, and daring, though at times overly wild. But life had changed dramatically when he had fallen into trouble of his own making – the worst kind of trouble, involving the daughter of a family that were commercial rivals to his own. In short, Ché had got their fondest treasure with child.

One sultry afternoon, with dark thunderclouds pressing down upon the city, Ché had been forced to watch a duel with blades, fought between his own father and hers, as was the custom of settling disputes of honour in Q'os. Though both men were wounded, they survived, and without a death it settled nothing. A few days later, a cannon shot exploded through the outer wall of Ché's bedroom. Thankfully, he was not in the room at the time.

The shot had been launched from an artillery piece set up furtively on the roof of a neighbouring household, whose occupants were away summering at their vineyards in Exanse. Initially, Ché's father was enraged by the act. Later as the dust slowly settled throughout the great house, his mood turned quiet and nervous.

Even within the military, blackpowder was the rarest of commodities. Yet this had not dissuaded their enemies. Neither, for that matter, had they been deterred by the seal which Ché had worn around his neck since the age of ten, thus protecting him by means of the threat of vendetta. It was now clear that their enemies would stop at nothing to settle this dispute.

Ché was the only son of the family, and some day he would take over the reins of their business empire. It was quickly announced to him that he must leave for his own safety. His father could think of no other way to guarantee it.

The very next morning, Ché was smuggled by a covered carriage to the local agent of the Rōshun order. Once safely inside the building, with the doors locked, the windows shuttered, the lamps turned low, his father offered the woman a small fortune in gold, trying to persuade her to send Ché away somewhere to train as a Rōshun apprentice. She was reluctant at first, but Ché's father pleaded and begged, claiming that the boy's life depended on her.

Ché left there a week later, after hiding out in the agent's cellar. Someone had turned up to collect him, a middle-aged Rōshun with the sharp cheekbones and hard, violet eyes that signified a native of the High Pash. The man growled his name, Shebec, and after that hardly spoke again. Without any chance of saying farewell to his family, Ché was smuggled on to a ship which set sail the moment they were aboard. In just over a week, it had crossed to Cheem, and from there began a strange and frightening journey through the island's mountainous interior.

And so it was that pampered Ché spent the rest of his boyhood learning how to kill without mercy, and with whatever means came to hand. As the weeks passed into months, and the months passed into years, it surprised him to find that he did not miss his family at all, nor the life of luxury he had left behind.

Ché had always been a fast learner, so as an apprentice assassin his progress was swift. He made friends readily, and he was careful not to make any enemies. Yet for all that, he was a youth troubled within his own skin.

At night, lying in his bunk in the dormitory that housed all the apprentices, Ché would dream another's dreams.

He would dream of having lived another life entirely – a life in which his mother and father were not his real parents, nor their home his true home. So real were these sleeping visions, so founded in fact and minutiae of detail, that he would awake in the morning feeling a stranger to himself, floundering to grasp what was real and what was merely sham. Sometimes, secretly, Ché suspected he was losing his mind.

As the years advanced, he did his best to hold himself together. He kept those dreams of another existence to himself.

Eventually he grew into a man. He became Rōshun.

*

At the time it had seemed like any other day, save that it was the eve of his twenty-first birthday, which in fact meant very little to Ché.

His master, Shebec, had got his days mixed up as always, thinking it was already Ché's birthday. Shebec made a bit of a fuss by preparing a honeycake crammed with nuts, then sat down and shared some wine with him. Ché did not have the heart to correct his master's mistake, but when he retired to his room it was with a growing, indefinable sense of unease.

That night, for the very first time since arriving at the monastery, Ché dreamed of nothing at all. He slept deeply, without constant shifting, without muttering into the darkness, and awoke on the morning of his real birthday to find that he was no longer himself.

Suddenly, like seeing through a window thrown open upon a vista that had always been there but never acknowledged, he knew the truth about his life. And in the privacy of his small, neat cell, in the early light filtering through the gaps in the shutters, Ché shook with bitter laughter and tears welling out of relief, desperation, and all that he had lost.

He did not say goodbye to his master. He fought down the urge to seek Shebec out, to offer him even a subtle farewell, a smile perhaps. He feared the older man would catch wind of his intentions. Ché walked out of the monastery gates as the rest of the order slowly awoke to the new day, leaving everything that he possessed behind him, save for a travel bag stuffed with dried foods.

He didn't descend the valley but headed across it instead. A stout, grey-sloped mountain, which they called the Old Man, reared above a twisting side-valley cut deep by a rushing torrent. In the dawn light Ché began to climb the Old Man's steep pitch of shale. He knew where the closest Rōshun sentinel was hidden in his lookout, watching out over the path below, and he made sure to cut a course leading behind him. When Ché reached the top of the peak, he looked back at the monastery of Sato with his heart in confusion.

Ché then turned and descended the other side.

He was to climb many high passes in the days that followed. He hiked in the tracks of mountain goats, picking his way along trails that ran along sheer cliff faces, with great airy drops yawning below him. Always Ché sought routes that would lead him gradually downwards. His meandering became purposeful like water seeking the sea as he steadily left the heart of the mountain range behind him.

He was ragged and starving by the time he came down from the foothills to the coast, twelve days having passed since he had first set off from Sato. He purchased food from the occasional dour home-steaders he passed, and a mule at the first harbour town he reached, and so made his way along the coast road to Cheem Port.

From Cheem Port, he caught a fast sloop straight to Q'os.

Ché never returned.

*

Now, many floors up, three years later, Ché perched within a finger-tip's reach of an open window. If he had chanced to look down just then, he would have spotted a diminishing sequence of solidified rags spiralling down around the curvature of the tower – for he had climbed not simply up but around it as well, fixing new handholds and footholds as he went. However, Ché did not look down.

The sound of love play tumbled from the open window above him. It was loud and reckless, and he waited without thought until it was finished. It did not take long.

A daring glance into the room revealed a man's fat backside, pale and dimpled, before it was covered by a hastily donned robe. 'My grat-itude,' the fat priest breathed to the woman sprawled naked on the tussled bed, before hurrying out without a further glance.

Ché failed to gain a proper look at the woman's face, but some-thing about her, unconsciously, sent a thrill of warning along his spine. He waited out of sight, and listened to the whisper of silk as she too threw on some clothing.

Ché placed the garrotte between his teeth.

Then, fighting his body's resistance, he sprang.

He was into the room, and stretching the length of wire between his fists, even as she turned and put a hand to her mouth as if to stifle a scream.

With a sigh, Ché sagged back against the windowsill. He rested the garrotte in his lap as the woman dropped her hand.

'Can you not use the door like everybody else?' she demanded, scowling now.

'Hello, mother,' he said.

The woman busied herself for a moment with tidying up. She dragged the sheet from the bed, sprayed a mist of cloying perfume into the air, which smelled of wild lotus and scratched at the back of his throat. Finally she paused and, with a questioning frown disturbing her fine features, turned back to him.

'Are you here to kill me?' she inquired, with a nod towards the garrotte wire.

'Of course not,' he protested 'I was instructed to count coup, then return to the Temple immediately.'

'So you are here on an exercise then. But what possessed them, I wonder, to send you after your own mother?'

Ché remained calm on the surface, as always, though within him a quiet rage was building. 'I don't know,' he admitted. 'You normally live on the floor above this one, surely?'

'Ah,' she purred, as though realizing a sudden truth. 'Yes, of course. They had me moved here just this morning.'

As she stepped closer, he could smell a musky after-scent. She smiled at him, almost seductively, the only smile that she seemed to know.

'I wonder,' she mused, 'what you would have done if they *had* ordered you to throttle the life from your own mother?'

Ché frowned. He tucked the garrotte away among the folds of his robe, unable to meet her eyes. 'I wonder, too, if you would have enjoyed your lovemaking quite so much had you known your only son was dangling just outside the window.'

She turned away at that remark, pulling her thin robe tighter about herself.

'You shouldn't goad me, then,' he said to her stiffened back.

She crossed to a table, poured water from a jug into a crystal glass, several slices of orange peel bobbing upon the surface.

His mother – though that term still came to Ché with some difficulty – remained beautiful for all her years. She was forty-one now he reckoned, despite any vain lies to the contrary. She was also in no way the same woman he had remembered being his mother when he was a youth, living in Q'os's most affluent suburb, without a care in the world.

In fact, that mother of his childhood memory had never existed at all. Nor had that life.

What Ché had suddenly discovered in the monastery, on the morning of his twenty-first birthday, was this: every memory he retained of life before his exile to Cheem had been fake. They had all been implanted within his head for the younger Ché to assume as real.

Upon awakening that morning he had realized this quite clearly; and that his mind had, in some way been instructed to remember it on the precise day of his twenty-first birthday. Like a surging tide his real memories had washed through the previous foundations of his life, carrying them away like so much useless flotsam. In their place, Ché had suddenly known that he was no son of a rich merchant family at all. Instead he was a simple bastard, his father unknown, and his real mother a devoted Sentiate in one of the many love cults found within the Mannian order, in which Ché had originally been raised as an Acolyte, a warrior priest in the making.

When the tide of recall had swamped him, Ché had been left floundering and breathless and with only a single purpose in which to hold on to: leave Cheem, return to Q'os.

It wasn't until his eventual return to the capital that he discovered precisely what had been done to him. Ché had been used for the Empire's own purposes. They feared the Rōshun, it seemed, and years before, they had deemed it prudent to send one of their own novices to train as one of these secretive assassins, in the hope of gaining information on them not only of their ways and methods but more importantly their location, in case the Empire ever had need to combat the order.

They had chosen Ché for this particular task by a selection process unknown to him. Perhaps it had been a random choice. Perhaps he had shown some aptitude for such work. For several moons they had subjected his thirteen-year-old self to an intensive regime of mental manipulation, drugged beyond stupefaction as they talked him clear out of his young mind, repressing crucial memories, planting and reinforcing others.

Of course it had shocked Ché to the core, these revelations. Without time to find his feet again after his return, even to be certain of his own identity again, the imperial Regulators had questioned Ché for a full moon by using truth drugs and hypnosis to strip the smallest of details from him. Satisfied that he had been plucked clean, they ordered the tip of each little finger to be chopped off as part of his initiation into Mann. And let it be known how pleased they would be if he continued in his vocation as an assassin – not as Rōshun, of course, but as one of their own.

They had left him no choice in the matter.

'Water?' asked his mother, crossing the room with the glass held out to him.

Ché accepted. He drank it in one swallow, and for a moment he simply sat there, savouring the taste of it in his mouth.

The world intrudes, though, on all moments of quietness.

I must know why they sent me here today, to feign the murder of my own mother. Sweet Erēs! Look at her, the empty-headed bitch. In her devotion to them, she believes they are merely playing games with us.

For a moment he wanted to seize and shake her slender body in his grip, then slap her hard across the face, again and again, until she woke up to all of *this* – these lives that he and she were both living.

Instead, Ché cleared his throat. 'How are you?' he asked.

'Mm? Oh, I am well, thank you.' She was seated in front of her mirror now, untangling her long golden curls with a fine-toothed comb carved from bone, her hair a luxury of her Sentiate calling. She paused to glance at his reflection. 'Really, I am well. It has been a good season, what with the festival and all.' As her comb encountered a stubborn knot, she held out a fist of blonde hair and tugged the comb lightly to tease it through. 'In fact I am better than well – I feel wonderful, as though I was a young girl again. I have become the main object of desire for one of Sasheen's high priests. Me! Can you believe it?'

'Yes, I think I caught sight of his bare arse just now.'

'Rainee? Oh no, my dear, oh no, the very thought of it. No, he is merely one of my regulars. Farando is of a different mould entirely. Alas he is indeed a little ugly, but he has strength, power, position, and he plies me with gifts and fine nights out in the city. I could not ask for more.

'And you,' she asked, twisting to face her son. 'How are you?'

Ché was scratching at his elbow; not absently, but with a will. 'I am fine,' he said, and inside he thought: *She does not recall it is my birthday.*

'Your skin looks better today. Is the ointment working?'

Yes, she had given him another new ointment to try out, in the hope that it might soothe the scaly rashes that forever afflicted him. He shrugged – a measured, careful gesture, like all his movements.

'If only I could remember what I used on you when you were young.'

She shook her head, exasperated. 'It's lost to me. Am I getting old, do you think? Mm?' She studied her reflection in the mirror. 'Has my face begun to turn away from the sun at last – along with my memory?'

'You're old enough for melodrama, I'll give you that. I'm glad that you are well, mother, but I must leave you now.'

'So soon?'

'I'm being timed on this exercise. And I must find out what this is about.'

Ché climbed on to the windowsill, but turned back for a final remark. 'Something is wrong in this,' he said. 'Be careful.'

He was gone even as she opened her mouth to say farewell. 'Oh,' she said, instead.

She returned to her reflection, humming softly as she raked her golden curls, taking care not to notice the rhythm of a heaving bed resounding through the floor just above her head.

*

'You counted coup as instructed?'

'I did,' replied Ché.

'Excellent. Any collaterals?'

'Two Acolytes. Their deaths were . . . necessary.'

'Two? You could not have found some way around them?'

'It would have taken more time. I chose the most direct course of action.'

'You always do. It is the Rōshun in you, I fear. Fine. And how, please tell me, was your mother?'

Ché drew back a fraction from the wooden panel facing him. He sat in an alcove within a shadowy chamber, somewhere within the intricate maze comprising the lower floors of the Temple of Whispers. The alcove itself was pannelled in darkly varnished teak. At its rear, at head level when sitting, was a small lattice-work screen, the vacant spaces in between dark with the mystery of who and what might lie behind. A cool and spicy draught wafted through the gaps, though the absence of sound suggested that the space beyond was small, and private.

'My mother seems well enough,' the replied flatly to the unseen inquirer.

'I am pleased by that. She's fine woman.'

The voice was pitched annoyingly high, making the speaker sound perpetually on the verge of hysteria. Ché knew of four different voices that would speak to him from this alcove – all four of them acting as his handler, though he had no idea who they might be. Neither, for that matter, had he any idea who his fellow assassins were, for they were all trained separately and so rarely allowed to meet.

Again Ché leaned closer to the panel as he waited for more.

'Will you not question me, Ché, as to why you were sent there today?'

'Would you tell me?'

A soft chuckle. 'No, I would not. But I do know of someone who will, in her own, roundabout way. She would like to talk with you now, young Diplomat.'

'Who do you speak of?' he kept his voice steady, though his heart had skipped into a faster rhythm.

'Report to the Storm Chamber immediately. She awaits you there.'

*

Ché rode in a noisy climbing box, flanked by two masked Acolytes gripping naked daggers; smeared in poison, he knew, for a scent of the stuff was evident in that confined space. The climbing box creaked and cranked alarmingly as its massive counterweight pulled it slowly towards the very peak of the steeple. When it stopped, with a lurch that caused all three of the men to wobble, the doors were pulled open by another guard already waiting on the other side.

The rooms at the top of the tower were large but windowless, and their footsteps echoed as they strode beneath high ceilings adorned with friezes of ornate plaster, depicting faces frozen in every conceivable emotion. The gleaming floors underfoot were of polished wood laid with the furs of exotic animals, their fierce heads still attached and snarling silently at the passers-by. The furniture, though sparse, was elaborately plush and stoutly crafted. The air was stuffy, the light dim.

Acolytes stood guard at the occasional closed door, through which voices could be heard, distant and muffled. Everywhere drifted smoke, carrying the reek of narcotics; it seemed to gather around the yellow orbs of the gaslights hanging along the panelled walls.

The Storm Chamber itself was approached by a broad flight of steps carved from pink-veined marble. On either side of each step stood an Acolyte with a naked blade held ceremonially across the crook of his left arm. Here Ché's escorts came to a halt, motioning for him to continue alone. Ché did as instructed, and climbed.

Through their masks, he noticed the guards' eyes were glazed as though drugged. They stood like statues, breathing so shallowly that even their chests failed to visibly rise. Boredom washed off them like heat.

At the very top of the steps, a huge embossed door of cast iron barred his progress. At that point, the female guard standing next to it turned and pounded it with a gauntleted fist. After a brief delay, the mighty door creaked and swung inwards. A torrent of sounds burst forth: the twittering of birds, the cascading of water, music and laughter. An old priest appeared at the threshold and bowed.

Ché entered, uncertain what to expect.

Windows ran from floor to ceiling for the entire circumference of the circular chamber. They sloped inwards as they rose, giving a clearer view of the sky. Right now they showed a wrapping of white clouds and showers of early autumn rain as it gusted against their transparency.

Ché squinted about, taking in every detail possible of the Storm Chamber with a single sweeping glance – just as he had been meticulously trained to do. In truth, he had been expecting something different from this; perhaps something darker, less inviting. More holy. Instead it was a warm and open space. A fire crackled in a stone fireplace in the very centre of the room, hooded by a metal chimney which ran up through the middle of the floor of a platform built above it; an upper storey, reached by steps, and enclosed by thin wooden walls. Retiring rooms he supposed; private areas of relaxation where the caged birds could still be heard.

In the cosy space around the hearth itself, plush leather armchairs were arranged so as to face towards an easel, on which was displayed a detailed map of the Empire. A group of priests slouched upon the armchairs, with their feet propped upon padded stools, drinking spirits, smoking hazii sticks, or just talking amongst themselves. Servants moved among them, bearing platters of fruits, and seafood, or else bowls of narcotics, and Ché knew their tongues would be missing and their eardrums punctured. As for the priests themselves, he recognized each and every one of them gathered around the fireplace.

Ché was a Diplomat, an imperial assassin. A great deal of his so-called negotiations involved powerful movers within the Empire itself. It was his business to get to know these people, for some day he might be ordered to kill any one of them.

They had the rank of general, mostly, so they kept their faces free of the usual ornate jewellery worn by priests of Mann. The exception was a single spiked cone of silver pierced through the left eyebrow in military fashion, as Ché himself wore. Their clothes, too, were the plain ceremonial robes of the Acolyte order, though there was nothing otherwise plain about these men.

He scanned each countenance in turn. There was Archgeneral Sparus, 'the Little Eagle', small and quiet and intense, not long returned from putting an end to the insurrection in Lagos and minus his left eye, which he had covered for good taste with a black patch. Then General Ricktus with his badly burnt face and hands, ugly to look at, and his black hair sprouting in patches above ears that were little more than ragged flaps. Beside him, General Romano, still young, boyish even, though the most dangerous man in this gathering, and the one most covetous of the throne itself. And, finally, General Alero, the old veteran of the Ghazni campaigns, who had gained the Empire more territory than anyone save for Archgeneral Mokabi himself – and had been damned for it, for stopping when he did.

All of these men were possible contenders for the throne, key players in that subtle yet deadly game of political manoeuvring that was the backdrop to all that occurred within the Empire. Each had their own factions at hand. In relative terms, the Empire of Mann was still young, and it had been proved that anyone could claw their way to the throne if they were determined enough to do so. The Matriarch herself stood as living testament to this fact.

Three other figures occupied the room. One was young Kirkus, the only son to the Matriarch. He slouched in a chair, his eyes hooded from intoxication, though becoming lively for some reason whenever they glared towards Romano. The second was the young man's grandmother, mother to Sasheen herself, fast asleep in her chair or so it seemed. Around her sandaled feet padded a few scaly lizards wearing collars of gold chain. The last of them was Matriarch Sasheen herself, who stood before the map with a sparkling goblet in one hand, dressed in a long, green chiffon gown that hung loosely open from throat to ankles, save for the waist where it was cinched by a belt of the same material, and which showed her nakedness underneath. As she moved, flashes of soft belly, or pubic hair, or full swinging breasts caught the eye, drawing attention from her face, which was plain and without beauty; the dark eyes were a little too close together, the hooked nose too long, but still, there was something attractive about the woman. Perhaps it was the manner in which she flaunted herself, as though this world was all hers and she could do with it as she pleased. Or perhaps it was due to her smile, which she used often.

'But can it be achieved before winter?' she inquired of old Alero, as she studied the details of the map.

General Alero shrugged in his chair. 'Only if we commit to it now and stop wrangling over the finer points.' The aged veteran appraised the younger men around him, causing a pause in their discussions.

'And you still maintain it can succeed?'

The general chose his next words with care, as one might pluck the exact coinage from a palm where precious few remained. 'Yes, I believe so, though only with some good fortune. There are many things that could go wrong with the plan, and too little room to improvise. If it works, well, it will lead to a resounding and decisive victory. The Free Ports will be ours. If it fails . . .' he shook his head '. . . it will be Coros all over again.'

The rain could be heard against the group's overwhelming silence. Ché stood motionless. He saw, from the corner of his eye, bright birds swooping high across the room. A servant padded after them, dabbing up their droppings with a cloth.

'I still say it is madness,' broke in Sparus, the Little Eagle. Leather squeaked as men turned to face him. He drew a long breath from his hazii stick, letting them wait for him to continue.

'Two separate naval actions against the Free Ports, not to mention the most important component, a sea invasion of Khos itself – and, by that time, with winter closing in fast. That's presuming the land force even succeeds in reaching Khos intact, and that's a huge gamble in itself, that our diversions will work, that the invasion fleet will avoid interception. Even then, if our land campaign falters in any way in the field, it will be mired helplessly until spring. The Mercians will have time to rally, while our First Expeditionary Force will be trapped with no way out. It would be *worse* than Coros.' He looked straight at the Matriarch, his one eye glittering. 'For I will say this. If the campaign fails, you will lose your throne along with it.'

'Is that a threat?' quipped young Romano, but Sparus ignored the remark and kept his eye fixed on Sasheen. What he said was true. The Mannian order despised leaders who failed in battle or betrayed signs of weakness. They tended to be disposed of rather swiftly.

The Matriarch glided across the floor between herself and Sparus. She placed a manicured hand lightly upon the Little Eagle's arm, and gave him a brief smile. She turned towards the others, the motion sudden enough to cause one of her breasts to leer from her thin gown.

'Well?' she demanded, directing a scowl at the assorted generals.

The scarred mouth of Ricktus opened to speak. 'Sparus is right,' he declared, in a voice as coarse as his burnt skin. 'The plan is a reckless one, and I cannot believe we are yet this desperate. Let us maintain our siege of the Free Ports. They will fall eventually, so long as we continue to strangle their trade.'

'No,' replied the Matriarch with her palm held up. 'I had good reasons for requesting solutions to the Mercian problem, and they are still valid. For ten years now, we have strangled their trade and battered at their doors. Yet still the Free Ports stand. Others are meanwhile beginning to gain courage from their defiance. We must defeat these Mercians, and do so decisively, if our Empire is to avoid appearing weak. Khos must therefore be taken. Without it, the rest of the Free Ports will either surrender or starve.'

She returned to the map again, which Ché had been studying even as she spoke. Pencil strokes had been drawn across it, quite roughly, denoting fleet movements and land actions. He could discern the symbols of two fleets encroaching along the western isles of the Free Ports, one ranging along the archipelago, the other concentrating upon Minos. A third fleet could be seen far to the east, denoted by a heavily pencilled arrow sweeping from Lagos down to Khos. The Matriarch jabbed at this now.

'The Sixth Army remains in Lagos at Mokabi's suggestion. They are sharp from their recent work quelling the insurrection. It would be the perfect surprise, and Mokabi sees it, as he has always seen these things. We create this First Expeditionary Force from the Sixth and what other remnants we can put together, and from Lagos ship them straight down to Khos.'

'But Matriarch,' rasped Ricktus, 'even if their Eastern Fleet were to be drawn away by our two diversionary campaigns in the west, the Mercian squadrons defending the Zanzahar convoys would still remain active in the region. Our ships at Lagos are mostly transports and merchant vessels, along with two squadrons of men-of-war. The Expeditionary Fleet would be poorly protected, as Sparus has already noted. It would take only a handful of squadrons to send the entire force to the bottom of the Midèrēs.'

Young Romano, a smile tugging at the corner of his mouth, sat forward now as though to pounce. 'Remember though, these diversionary fleets will be the largest yet seen in the course of this war. Mercia will be hard pressed to match their numbers even with the full extent of their navy. They will *have* to draw the Eastern Fleet away to defend the west.'

'So speaks the expert on naval tactics,' declared Kirkus unexpectedly, and received a glare from Romano in return for his own.

'The Expeditionary Fleet will not be tarrying to engage in any sea battles, gentlemen,' declared Sasheen. 'It will punch straight through any squadrons it encounters, and its men-of-war will sacrifice themselves, if they have to, in order for the transports to make it through. All that ultimately matters is that the Army reaches land.'

Sparus interjected, 'It is fine for Mokabi to sit there in his villa in Palermo, and sketch great campaigns of daring on parchment as though he was still the archgeneral. It is another thing entirely to see such a venture through.'

'He has agreed to come out of retirement, if we sanction it,' declared Sasheen.

'Aye, to lead his beloved Fourth Army while it's safely encamped beyond range of the walls of Bar-Khos. If the Expeditionary Force takes the city from behind, then they merely open the door for him, and he gets to parade through in triumph. If not, well, he can blame someone else for the failures, and assure himself of a safe return to his estate.'

'Mokabi is committed to this venture,' protested Alero, an old comrade of the absent general. 'He will risk his neck like the rest of us.'

'Aye, well, it's telling that he does not volunteer to lead the Expeditionary Force either. And I understand his reasons for that, unspoken or not. I would not wish to lead such a reckless campaign either.'

Sasheen finished her drink and thrust the empty goblet at a passing servant. 'That is a pity, Sparus, for I was hoping you might like to come along with me.'

'Matriarch?'

'I will be accompanying the Expeditionary Force myself.'

Surprise rippled through the gathering. Ché's breath caught in his throat, where he still stood to one side, entirely ignored.

'As you so rightly put it,' continued Sasheen, and for an instant her eyes flickered between young Romano and fat Alero, 'my throne will depend upon its outcome. It is fitting therefore that I should be there – shaking the spear so to speak.'

'This is madness, Matriarch. You cannot risk yourself in such a way.'

'All life is a venture in risk, Sparus. And you will go, if you wish to see your Matriarch safely through this endeavour in one piece.'

Romano was enjoying this, till Sasheen chose that moment to offer the young general a smile.

'And you too, Romano. Sparus will lead the Expeditionary Force, and you will be his second-in-command.' The young man sat up abruptly, causing a trickle of ash to fall from his hazii stick and scatter over his lap. 'Alero, Ricktus, you will each take command of one of the diversionary fleets, and cause such a storm down there that we may find enough space to slip through. This is how it shall be.'

The youth, Kirkus, leaned forward, his eyes bright. 'And I, mother . . . I would like to go with you also.'

'But you will not', she replied firmly. 'You are to stay here, within the Temple, until we have dealt with our other problem.'

At this she glanced at Ché for the first time. He found himself standing to attention as he held her gaze.

'But who knows how long that might take?' demanded Kirkus.

'You should have thought of that, my fine son, when you were performing your cull, and so rashly flaunted the privileges of your position.'

The boy's sullen response was stifled by a sudden loud croak from one side of the room. All heads turned to it, including Ché's. He expected to see a pet kerido perhaps, squatting on the floor and tearing at a lump of flesh. Instead it was the grandmother, her eyes still tightly closed.

'The boy acted rightly,' rasped the ancient priestess. 'He acted dutifully in accordance with Mann. Do not fault him for that, my daughter.'

The Matriarch blew out a prolonged mouthful of air. 'Be that as it may,' she said, 'but for now he is not to set foot from here for any reason.' And she chopped her flattened hand through the air, cutting off Kirkus from further protest. She was displeased at this public discussion, and even Kirkus knew to remain silent, though his face burned.

'Now,' continued Sasheen. 'If you will all excuse me.'

Matriarch Sasheen departed from the group and strode deliberately past Ché. 'Come with me,' she snapped in her wake.

He followed her perfumed scent to the windows, where they stepped through a set of sliding glass doors onto a terrace that encircled the tower. Potted plants stood around its periphery, straining against the wind. As Sasheen slid the doors closed behind them, the rain spattered their faces, cold as the gusts that drove it.

'You are wondering why I allowed you to witness the workings of my Storm Council.'

'No, Holy Matriarch,' Ché lied, instinctively. He knew better than to openly acknowledge a lack of trust in him from his superiors. It might indicate a guilty frame of mind, a dangerous condition in an order where treachery was almost a doctrine.

Sasheen appraised him for truth. 'Very well,' she said at last, still staring at him without blinking. 'Your handlers all agree upon your loyalty. Perhaps they are even right in their judgement.'

He bowed his head, but said nothing.

'You wonder, then, why I sent for you?'

'Yes, Matriarch,' he replied, head still inclined, and this time he told only the truth.

'I will speak plainly, then.' With her chin she pointed to the Storm Chamber within. 'My son, young Kirkus there, has killed one who bore a seal.'

Ché at last looked up at her. Sasheen was taller than he, as most people were.

'In her *wisdom*, my mother made no effort to stop him. She has always considered the Rōshun to be of little threat to Mann. I myself am not so certain.' Her gown blew open in the wind; water trickled between her breasts, over her belly, down into the wispy hairs of her pelvis.

'Several days ago we intercepted three of their number as they tried to gain access to my son. Two were intended as a diversion, but another almost succeeded – though we cornered him in time. I'm told he took his own life. Regardless, they will send others.'

'I see,' he murmured. Ché's heart was beating faster now. He could feel the blood throbbing in his fingertips, his toes.

'Do you, I wonder?'

'Yes. You must know I was trained as Rōshun – as a future safe-guard against a situation such as this.'

'Then you know why I sent for you.'

Ché wanted to scratch his neck again, but he fought against the compulsion. Instead he turned his face into the rain. It stung his eyes, but at least it helped soothe the itching. 'You wish me to lead you to the place of the Rōshun order,' Ché spoke into the wind, 'so that you may destroy them before they destroy your son.'

'Indeed,' she replied, and he could hear the smile in her voice. 'I have a company of my finest commandos readying themselves even now for your arrival. You are to lead them to Cheem, and make use of this plant of theirs that I hear will guide you to their monastery.'

'They are prepared to follow a guide through the mountains even while he is deranged?'

'They know of the knowledge buried in your head. And they are prepared for anything. Once they find this monastery, they will kill all they find there and burn it to the ground, so that none shall survive.'

Ché exhaled a soft breath through his nostrils, seeking a state of emptiness.

Her eyes narrowed as she leaned closer 'Does this mission trouble you, perhaps?'

'I do not believe so.'

'You do not, perhaps, feel some remnants of loyalty to your Rōshun friends?'

Ah. Now it all begins to make sense. 'Holy Matriarch, I am loyal only to Mann.'

She gazed into the depths of his eyes. He became aware then that he was scratching his arm – though he dared not stop for fear it might give something of himself away.

Sasheen rose above him again. 'I see. And tell me – your mother and you, are you close?'

Abruptly, Ché ceased scratching. He bought himself a few moments of time by wiping the sheen of moisture from his face.

'We are not particularly close, no. We were parted for eight years while I was in Cheem, studying to be Rōshun.'

'I am told that she is rather fond of you, despite that.'

'Then you know more than I.'

'Of course I do. I *am* the Holy Matriarch, after all.' She smiled. 'But I am also a mother,' she added more sincerely. 'You can be certain that she holds much affection for her only child.'

Sasheen glanced into the room, at her own son. When she turned back to Ché, her eyes were hard and devoid of humour.

'I would take great care over that relationship, if I were you. Such bonds are precious in this world. Sometimes, our loyalties are all that can maintain them.'

Her thinly veiled threat prompted him to look away. Ché turned instead to the potted plants lining the terrace, whipping noisily against the window glass, and fixed his sight on them as though for steadiness.

Sasheen followed his gaze and reached out with a drifting hand. Roughly, as though it were a pet, she stroked the leaf on one of the bedraggled specimens.

'Do we have an understanding, you and I?'

Ché dipped his head in acknowledgement, a sharp lump in his throat.

'Good, then, let us delay no longer. Return to your handler. He will already have a full brief for you.'

Ché watched her from between his eyelashes, as she turned her back on him and slid open the glass doors.

In mid-step, she paused and looked back at him with a languid stare.

'And Diplomat . . .'

'Yes, Matriarch.'

'Never lie to me again.'

CHAPTER TWENTY

Impressions of Q'os

The last thing anyone was expecting to hear in the hurried press of disembarkation was a rifle shot. It silenced the passengers once the sound cracked over their heads, and drew them in a mass towards the port rail of the fast sloop *Mother Rosa*, as though the ship's deck had suddenly pitched to one side during heavy weather.

People pushed and peered over shoulders for a better look at the sluggish waters of the harbour below. A figure was down there close to the hull, splashing with all the grim determination of a soul alerted to the imminent prospect of drowning.

'There's a man down there,' observed Nico over the rail, and he glanced towards the dockside, where he noticed a puff of smoke still trickling from the end of a rifle held by a soldier in a white cuirass.

'Yes,' said Ash by his side, 'I see that.'

Another soldier hurried to the side of the first marksman, as he broke his weapon in two to replace the spent cartridge. The newcomer carried a crossbow, and was still loading it as his comrade raised the rifle once more.

Nico saw the splash of water before he heard the second shot. It erupted right next to the swimmer's head, though the target seemed not to notice it.

'What's he doing?' inquired Nico, fascinated.

'The man is a slave,' explained Ash. 'Here in Q'os, they have more slaves than free citizens – over a million of them, or so they say. It would seem that this one was hoping to escape the island as a stowaway on board one of the ships.'

'Well, if that was his intention, he's made a poor job of it.'

Ash studied his young apprentice for a moment. 'Perhaps you should jump in, and show him how it is done correctly.'

Another shot. For a second, Nico looked for a splash that would show where to hit the water. He did not see one, though, and then the man caught his eye, a pool of bright crimson spilling from the side of his skull as he turned slowly in the water. The man settled with his face wholly submerged, unmoving.

'They killed him,' exclaimed Nico.

'That was their intention.'

'But . . .'

'He took his chance,' Ash told him softly. 'He was unlucky. Come, let us leave the ship quickly before the other passengers grow bored of staring at his corpse.' Ash tugged at his sleeve pulling him towards the gangway.

They descended on to the dockside with their packs heavy on their backs, Nico stumbling along in something of a daze.

It had been eight days since they had departed Cheem, and as the ship had approached the First Harbour of the great island city he had been stunned by the sheer scale of the skyline that spread out before him. Q'os was the largest city in the known world, more populous even than ancient Zanzahar on the far side of the Midèrēs. Never before had Nico seen buildings so tall. They rose in great blocks towards the sky as dense as undergrowth in a forest, their armies of windows dark against the dim light of the day. Amongst them, clustering most thickly at the city's heart, the skysteeples of the temples rose like needles piercing the underside of low-lying cloud. To the eye they did not seem physically possible, not even after Ash's accounts of steel skeletons and some strange form of liquid stone. Nor could he quite take in the figures that swooped between their peaks – people slung from artificial wings, Ash had told him with a straight face. But then, nothing had seemed possible about that alien landscape as it slowly approached the bobbing prow of their ship.

Now, a man dead in the water, a paddling dog dragging his corpse in with its teeth, and hundreds of yammering people mixing together in the chaos of a dockside that was only one of many on the island of Q'os, Nico wondered exactly what, in the name of the Great Fool, he was doing here.

He felt like an ant amid the hurried press of so many. Buildings reared high behind the rows of warehouses facing the eastern harbour front. In the distance, stacks of chimneys belched black smoke into the air. With Ash's guiding hand on his shoulder Nico pushed ahead, no idea where he was going. They headed past a group of soldiers lounging on some covered crates, then approached a vast open-sided building, and found themselves stepping into a great space with a high sloping roof of sooty glass and metal girders. The noise there was tremendous, too loud almost for them to talk. Nico stared mutely as he was halted at a high desk now barring their way.

'Next!' shouted a bored official from behind it, and flapped a tired arm which he supported on the padded elbow of his white robe. In his other hand he gripped a cloth rag, and as Ash stepped up to the desk, he proceeded to blow his reddened nose into it.

The desk was so high that the official was looking down at them. 'Any goods to declare?' inquired the priest in a nasal tone.

'No, I am a blade instructor,' explained Ash, adopting a smooth patter, while tugging the heavy tunic beneath his cloak to smooth out its travel creases. 'I am here to work at the Academy of Ul Sun Juan, and this is my apprentice.'

Nico forced a smile of verification.

'You carry weapons with you?'

Ash held up the canvas roll he was carrying.

'Fine, fine,' the official decided at last. He looked as though the only thing on his mind currently was his bed and a bowl of hot soup. 'A surcharge of one marvel is to be paid by anyone carrying weapons on to the island. Two more – that's one each – for entrance into the city for the pair of you. Plus one for administration. That makes it a total of four.' The man held out his palm.

Ash dropped the coins into it, and the priest made a show of biting each coin between his teeth to test it. He placed one into his pocket, dropped the others through a slot in the desk, then scratched something on a piece of paper and half-tossed it to Ash.

'Welcome to Q'os,' he said as he pulled a lever and a grille clanked open beneath the level of the desk to allow them through. '*Next!*'

*

It was cold in Q'os, with the sun hidden behind a heavy layer of cloud. Ash and Nico stayed close to the docks, losing themselves in the crowds as they pushed on through one cobbled street after another.

The buildings towering on either side were constructed of brick rather than cut stone. Cranes could be seen wherever he looked, new constructions being built on demolished sites or superimposed upon older structures still standing. Everywhere along the streets flew flags of the red hand of Mann, while above them streamers trailed high in the wind, as though the area was preparing itself for a festa of some kind. A canvas painting of Matriarch Sasheen hung across the entire side of one building, while banners stretched from block to block with the word *Rejoice* emblazoned across them.

Nico had always thought Bar-Khos a busy city, but it was nothing compared to this metropolis. The streets were so packed that people barely had room enough to move in them. Every conceivable fashion was on display: flowing silks from farland, furs from the north, suits made from the black and white striped skins of zels, rainslicks of oiled canvas, feather cloaks with massive bobbing hoods, ubiquitous robes of red. Most prominent of all, though, was the tan garb of collared slaves, walking alone or in work-gangs, often burdened with bundles and parcels. At the sides of the roads, children rolled steaming lumps of zel manure into buckets. Priests shouted from the high balconies of temple towers, through bullhorns to amplify their hoarse cries. In a cage hanging from a post in the middle of a crossroads, a naked criminal sat with his legs dangling, slinging his own excrement at anyone unlucky enough to venture too close.

It was the wet season in Q'os and, as though to remind them of that fact, a heavy rain began to fall. At least the downpour helped to clear their way as people hurried to find shelter.

'It feels like we're walking in circles,' complained Nico, wiping his face in vain.

'We are. If we are being followed by anyone we should lose them, given time.'

'Followed?'

'Yes. Q'os is a city rife with paranoia. The priesthood here has its own secret police force – Regulators they call them. Anyone suspected of disloyalty or heresy is arrested, imprisoned. People are paid to inform on their neighbours. With the threat of vendetta hanging over Kirkus, which they now know to be real after our first attempt on his life, the Regulators will be doubly vigilant. They may be keeping tabs on everyone new entering the city.'

'We are in danger, even now?'

'We are in danger every moment we remain here, Nico. Now listen to me. As long as we are here you will do as I say, without argument or hesitation. If we fall into trouble, your only concern should be your own safety. If anything happens to me, get out. *Leave.*'

These words did nothing for Nico's confidence. As they walked on, he could not help the occasional glance over his shoulder, until Ash told him to stop being so obvious. They grew wetter by the moment.

'This rain stings my eyes,' complained Nico, catching up with Ash again, after swerving out of the way of a passing cart. 'And it tastes foul on the tongue.'

'The sky itself here is polluted. It is all the coal they burn. When it is not raining foulness, the city is usually covered in a reeking fog. Baal's Mist they call it, in memory of an old king famous for his flatulence. I have heard it said you get used to it, given time.'

Nico doubted that. For an hour he dogged the old man, taking in the strange city sights while trying, with increasing effort, to ignore the gnawing in his empty stomach, for they had missed breakfast.

At last they stopped at a hostalio, a squat building of tired grey brickwork, its windows dull with grime, the paintwork flaking from their rotten frames. The building sported an oversized sign some thirty feet above the street. It read 'Hostalio el Paradisio' in Trade, above a picture of a bed.

It would do, Ash declared. One such place was as bad as any other in this district.

Inside, they gave false names at the desk, as they stood dripping on to the tiled floor. The attendant barely looked up from his newspaper as Ash signed the register. He only interrupted his reading long enough to recite: 'Rooms still available on the fourth floor. Try there. No visitors after nine. No food to be cooked in the room. Absolutely no fires, not even candles. Oh,' he added, looking up at last, 'and no disposing of waste from the window. There's a privy hole on every floor for such purposes. This is a respectable establishment and we'd like to keep it that way, understand?'

'Then I will show it the respect it deserves,' remarked Ash, and squeezed his fist until water dripped on to the open register, staining the paper with spots of sooty grey. With a snap the attendant closed the book from further harm, and announced their transaction finished with a loud sniff. He returned to reading the newspaper, as Ash and Nico carried their bags up the stairs. All the same, the attendant watched them from the corners of his eyes.

Finding an empty room was a matter of finding a door, any door, with the key still protruding from the keyhole. They located one on the fourth floor as they had been told they would. Nico, being in front, took hold of the key and turned it. The key refused to move.

'Move aside,' instructed Ash.

The keyhole wasn't fitted to the door itself. Rather, it was located in a stout metal box that in turn was fitted to the doorframe. Before the key would function, Ash had to deposit a coin into a slot in this box, an entire marvel of silver it turned out, since the smaller quarters merely popped out again from below.

With his ear, Nico tracked the heavy marvel rattling away inside it, the coin sounding as though it was tumbling downwards through the wall itself. Then something clicked inside the box, the key turned in Ash's hand, and he plucked it out and shoved open the door.

The room was an irony of the word, having barely the space to lie down in. It contained two beds which folded down from the wall, one on top of the other. At present they were both folded away. Ash deposited another coin into another coinslot fitted against the hinging of one of the beds and swung it down. He sat heavily, leather pack in his lap. He sighed like the old man that he was.

Nico closed the door and crossed the few strides to the window opposite, where he set down his pack against the stained plaster beneath it. The room smelled of tarweed, old sweat, dampness, and was in bad need of an airing. He tried to open the shutters covering the tiny window, but they refused to budge.

'Nico,' interrupted Ash, gloomily handing him a quarter. Nico noticed the coinslot fixed to the window frame. Incredulous, he dropped the coin into it, heard an interior click as the coin tumbled away. Finally he pulled open the shutters, only to cast his eyes upon a brick wall, sooty and guano-stained, not more than seven feet away on the other side of an alley.

The windows opposite were mostly open, framing the backs of people resting in chairs, pale faces looking out, dim flashes of movement, an argument. The air pervading the alley was worse than the air inside the room. Sounds of the city tumbled in, and Nico leaned out to examine the alley far below, filled with rubbish and puddles of water; when he looked left he could see along a whole series of similar alleys leading all the way to the bay forming the First Harbour.

He again surveyed the windows opposite as his companion unpacked behind him. Through the window directly across, he could see an old man sitting on a stool, building something out of a heap of matchsticks.

Nico turned away from the view and leaned back against the sill. He noticed how the weak daylight only made the room's disgrace more apparent.

'When do we meet with Baracha and Aléas?'

'Tomorrow,' said Ash, as he carefully lay his wrapped covestick and soap next to the washbasin. 'Though first we must meet with the agent to make certain they have arrived safely.'

'We could go now.'

'No. Better to wait for dark.'

Wonderful, thought Nico. He did not cherish the prospect of sitting in this room all afternoon with nothing to do.

'You've been to Q'os before. May be you could show me some of the sights?'

'Here,' said Ash, handing him one of the tiny books he carried in his pack. 'You can read this to fill your time. It is written in Trade. As for myself, I will take a nap.'

Nico looked at the book being offered to him, but did not reach for it. Poetry, he presumed. Ash was always reading the stuff.

'I'd rather spend the day pulling out all my fingernails, to be honest.'

Ash shrugged a single eyebrow, set the book on the bed. He had displayed the same neutral reaction during the voyage, each time he had offered Nico something to read and Nico had declined. This time though, he added: 'You cannot read, can you, boy?'

Nico straightened. 'Of course I can read. I just choose not to.'

'No. Perhaps you can read single words, but I do not believe you can read properly.'

Nico snatched the book from the bed. 'You want me to read something? Here, it says . . .' He squinted again at the words on the binding. '*The – Heron's – Call*,' he recited, and opened the book to look down at a page of fine black print. '*A coll – ection of mus – ings from – from . . .*' the words began to swirl before his eyes, as they always did. He lost focus, blinked trying to regain it. But it was no good.

Disgusted, he tossed the book on to the bed.

'It isn't as though I've never tried,' he said. 'The words lose themselves in each other. They jump around, change when I'm looking at them. At least with plays I can follow what's happening. But not books.'

'I understand,' said Ash. 'I have the same problem.'

'But you read all the time!'

'I do now, yes. But as a boy I had difficulties, and it made me fearful of words. Some of us are born that way, Nico. It does not have to stop us from reading. It just makes it harder. You need to practise, and take it at your own pace. Come, sit with me and I will show you.'

Nico would have backed away if he could. Instead he felt the windowsill press against him. Ash sat on the bed, opened the book on his lap. He noticed Nico's resistance.

'Trust me, Nico. To be able to read is a worthy thing in this life.'

'But all you have is poetry. Poetry bores me.'

'Nonsense, poetry is what we live, what we breathe.' The old farlander opened the book at random. He studied one page for a moment, then licked his thumb and flicked to another. 'Listen,' he said. 'This is how we sometimes write poetry in Honshu. This is Issea, writing of sitting alone at night.' Softly, he read:

> 'Mountain pool,
> Drinking the moon
> Drinking me.'

He looked to Nico. 'Do you sense it? The solitude?'

'I think you'd better read it again. It's so short I hadn't realized it had begun.' But even as Nico said the words he was drawn to sit beside Ash, and to look down at the printed words.

Ash lay the book on Nico's lap. 'Try reading something – at your own pace.'

Nico read each word carefully, mouthing their sounds as he did so. As soon as they began to change and shift, he forced himself to relax. He could read when he wanted to. It was the draining effort of the process that he hated, and the frustration at his own ineptitude. It was easier with these short poems, the language simple, bordered amply with white space. He flicked through the pages, choosing poems as they came to his eyes. He found himself reading one aloud:

'In the doorway,
The space
Of a startled bird.'

'You see?' said Ash. 'You read fine. It is hard, but not impossible.'

'These poems – they either come to you in a flash, or they don't at all.'

Ash nodded. 'Here, you may keep this book. Consider it part of your education.'

'Thank you,' said Nico. 'I have never owned a book before.' He stared at it. Brushed the leather cover with his fingers.

Nico stood up, the book in his hand.

'Now please,' he said, 'for the love of mercy, can we go out and do something?'

CHAPTER TWENTY-ONE

Paradise City

It was almost three in the afternoon, according to the clock mounted on the pinkish façade of the local Mannian temple. Nico and Ash ate at a side-street eatery, perched on tall stools by an opening in the wall where the customers' orders were taken, and through which the sweaty cooks could be seen at work in the tiny, steamy kitchen. They ate in silence, working eagerly at noodles in a spicy sauce, as they watched people scuttle past through the drizzle falling from a low sky, water dripping constantly from the corners of the canvas awning extending above their heads. Ash remained alert despite his obvious weariness. Nico knew him well enough by now. He could tell that the old man was observing those around them from the periphery of his vision, no doubt looking for any sign that they were being watched. If he noticed anything, he did not share the fact.

The temple across the street attracted Nico's attention. It was not just the people going in and out of it but the structure itself. It was unlike any temple he had ever seen before, being basically a stone spike that thrust up from the squat surroundings of the neighbourhood; a smaller version of the skysteeples found elsewhere in the city. He wondered again how steel and liquid stone could be impressed to stand in such a way, so tall and thin.

Quietly, he mused: 'I sit here, eating soft noodles in Q'os itself, and I realize I know nothing of these people at all, save that as a Mercian they are my enemy, and therefore to be feared.'

Ash chewed slowly. Swallowed. 'They are just ordinary people,' he said, 'save that their ways have become extreme, and likewise their hearts, so that they are ill in a way – ill of spirit.' Ash slurped another strand of noodle into his mouth, as he glanced over his shoulder towards the temple. 'If you knew their priests, you would fear them more.'

Nico wondered if that was true. The stories of human sacrifice by the priests of Mann and the lesser depravities of its followers – sitting here now on a street corner in the very heart of the Empire – began to seem like so much myth and nonsense. He was quiet for a time. Then once more, he found himself thinking out loud. 'Perhaps we would have less to fight over,' he ventured, 'if we did not have all these differing faiths in the first place.'

'Perhaps,' replied Ash, licking his fingers clean. 'But think further on that. Do you really suppose we would wage war on each other any less if we all shared the same faith, or even had none at all?' Ash shook his head, a curiously sad gesture. 'It is our way in this world, Nico, to pretend that our beliefs mean everything to us. But wars are seldom fought over beliefs. Wars are fought for land and spoils, for prestige, for foolishness. They are fought because one side wishes dominion over another. If there is a difference in faiths between opposing nations, all the better for concealing the very things they share in common. Only rarely does genuine belief come into it. The Manni-ans are no different, despite appearances. Dominion is their deepest creed. At heart, they desire to rule all things.'

Across the street, the temple clock chimed out the hour. A priest emerged on the tower's high balcony and called out through his bull-horn to the people below as other similar calls sounded across the city. At his muffled words the strangest of sights confronted Nico. The entire population of the street ceased what they were doing and knelt on the ground as one, holding their faces and arms up towards the distant Temple of Whispers.

Nico felt his arm being tugged, and he was drawn down on to his own knees as Ash did the same. Looking around he could see he was not the only one to have been slow at genuflections to Mann, nor the only one who seemed unhappy about it.

'The daily call,' Ash said with a hint of contempt in his tone, and thrust his arms into the air, exposing them bare to the rain, as the sleeves of his cloak slid to his elbows.

Reluctantly, Nico followed his example, feeling like an idiot as he did so.

*

At six they caught a tram, a large carriage drawn by a team of twelve zels, their black-and-white striped coats steaming from their exertions. The sign over the door read: *Paradisio City*.

Ash slotted a half-marvel into the turnstile at the rear of the tram to gain access to board. Behind him, Nico did the same. There were no seats left, so Nico followed Ash's example and gripped hold of the luggage rack running the entire length of the vehicle. The rack itself was stuffed with sacks of vegetables, rolls of cloth, even a crate of live chickens that watched Nico with their small, glassy eyes. He and Ash stood rocking to and fro as the tram worked its way through the heavy traffic of early evening, their swords carefully hidden beneath their rain cloaks. The passengers were subdued and the carriage strangely quiet save for the steady drum of rain against the windows and roof.

'No one talks to anyone else,' whispered Nico. 'They don't even look at each other.'

Master Ash smiled thinly.

The carriage gradually emptied as the tram made one stop after another. At last some seats became available, and Ash and Nico made themselves comfortable. The old farlander immediately closed his eyes.

Nico noticed his forehead furrow in pain. With trembling fingers, Ash pressed his temple as though relieving a sudden pressure. He took out one of his leaves and placed it in his mouth.

'You don't look well,' Nico observed.

In a weary voice, and with eyes still closed, his master replied: 'This place does me no good at all, Nico. Wake me when we reach the last stop.' And with that he wrapped his damp cloak tighter around himself, and was still.

*

The island of Q'os had four harbour bays, each created by the spaces between the 'fingers and thumb' known as the Five Cities. The First Harbour was a bay bounded on one side by the protrusion of land known as the thumb, and on the other side by that resembling the index finger.

Paradisio City, also known as the First City, was the largest entertainment district of Q'os, and occupied most of the land forming the island's thumb. Its main thoroughfare ran along the coastline and looked out over the First Harbour and the eastern docks where Nico and Ash had rented their room. Crossing into this district, they could now clearly see the cluster of skysteeples surrounding the vast structure of the Shay Madi, the island's newest and largest coliseum, whose flanks sprouted like a small hill rising above the suburbs around it. It was there the tram stopped for the final time, right in the shadow of the mammoth stadium itself.

Nico could only gape at the soaring bulk of arches and columns, as they stepped out into the drizzle with the last remaining passengers. The tram drew away, the zels looking tired but picking up speed with the lighter load and the lure of home. The journey had taken them the better part of an hour, if the public clock nearby was correct. They set off quickly, seeking refuge from the elements under the hoods of their cloaks.

Crowds of revellers pressed through the streets of Paradisio on their way to the stadium. This slowed progress for Ash and Nico, heading as they were in the opposite direction to this excited current. At last they came to a halt in a quiet side street. It had grown noticeably darker by the time a man on clacking stilts came into view, igniting each street light as he went.

'Gas lights,' Ash explained, just as Nico opened his mouth to ask. 'The city sits on a reservoir of the stuff, so they utilize it wherever it comes up to the surface.'

Nico tried to imagine what the old man might mean by that.

'Think of the fumes,' Ash pre-empted him again, 'that come from the back end of a pig. You can bottle that smell, or channel it, and so it will burn whenever you need it to.'

'They bottle the gas coming from the arses of pigs?'

The old man sighed. 'No, Nico, I was providing you with an example. But it makes use of the same principle.'

'I had wondered why Q'os smelled so terrible.'

Ash turned to survey him. The old man stuck out his lower lip, then slid it slowly back again.

A group of women passed by, chattering in some dialect that sounded like Trade, though a strangled form of it, and entered the public bathhouse that he and Ash now stood facing. Hanging next to the entrance, a sign caught Nico's eye. It was painted with what looked like a Rōshun seal.

Ash ignored it as they entered the bathhouse behind the women.

Inside, he fed coins into a slot and gained them two clean towels, before moving on into the humid atmosphere of the changing room. It was empty save for a few men and women talking under the dim glow of the ceiling lights.

Nico stepped into an empty cubicle at Ash's instruction. He waited there on his own while Ash himself ventured off out of sight. Nico listened to the conversations in the room outside, but they sounded dull, made little sense to him.

A sudden sound above his head caused him to look up. There was Ash, blinking down from the ceiling through a space made by the removal of a large wooden tile. Ash lowered a hand; Nico clasped it and was pulled up into the dark, dusty roof space.

'These buildings share the same attics,' Ash whispered into his ear. 'We can reach our agent from here without being seen entering the house itself. No doubt it is being watched.'

Ash led the way through the gloom, treading with care along the beams rather than on the flimsy wooden tiles themselves. He held his sheathed sword out to one side for balance. Nico struggled not to sneeze from all the dust, and concentrated on keeping his own footing. He could see himself all too easily toppling off the beam, and crashing through the ceiling straight into some poor bather's lap.

After a time Ash halted. He tugged loose another tile and laid it to one side, then shoved his head through, checking below. Satisfied, he lowered himself through the gap, then Nico clambered after him, agilely.

They stood in a small study, their damp backs warming against a fire of coals that provided the only source of light in the room. In a deep leather chair sat a woman, a book lying open upon her lap, though it was neither her shadowy figure nor the book which seized Nico's attention. Rather it was the large pistol held in one hand, aimed unwaveringly at Ash's chest.

For a moment everything in the room was still, save for the shadows flickering over the walls and the simple wooden furniture. Then a spark spat in the fireplace, and Nico jerked. The woman raised her free hand. Carefully, she placed a forefinger to her lips.

She lay the pistol down on a small table beside her chair, immediately followed by the book. Smoothly, she rose and stepped over to the fireplace, then motioned for Ash to come closer.

Nico followed after him, and noticed the seal hanging openly from the young woman's neck as she crouched there and waited. He watched as she gestured to the chimney. Ash set down his sword and knelt on the floor, peering as best he could up the flame-lit chimney. He nodded, gathering up his sword, and rose to his feet just as she did.

She motioned silently again. Nico glanced back at the fireplace briefly, then followed them out of the room.

*

In a short, unlit hallway they turned aside from the kitchen area and entered the privy instead. It was a confined space, barely large enough for the three of them, and once the woman closed the sliding door, it was thrown into total darkness.

A match flared and guided itself towards the wall. It lit a wick standing in a bowl of oil nestled in a sooty alcove. As the flame slowly grew, the oil cast off the scent of honeysuckle. At least it helped to mask the foul smell of the room.

Once they could see each other again, the woman turned a spigot in another alcove housing a hand basin. The sound of running water filled the room.

'We're in trouble,' she began in a low, husky voice, as she manoeuvred around Ash to sit herself on the privy, in an attempt to give them more room.

Then the wick caught properly and, light blossomed between them. Nico looked down upon a face he had dreamed about.

'Serèse,' he blurted.

The young woman held a finger to her lips. 'You're not safe here,' she whispered. 'The building is being watched.'

Ash nodded, unsurprised. 'You look well,' he observed.

She did look well, Nico thought, her hair hanging in plaits, her trim body encased in brown leather.

'Well, *you* certainly don't,' she replied. 'What have you been doing with yourself? You look awful.'

'Thank you. Now tell me, how long have they been listening?'

Serèse shrugged. 'I found the device in the chimney when I first returned to the city. They'd left a fingermark of soot where none should have been, for I'd cleaned carefully before I left.' She shook her head. 'Please listen to me, though. That's hardly the problem just now. My father made a sweep of the surrounding area last night – you know how careful he likes to be – and there are Regulators, watching the agency from every side.'

'Baracha made it to the city, then?'

'Yes, but you're still not listening. My father sent a note to me rather than visiting in person, saying how I should leave right away. I thought it best to stay until you arrived, though. He thinks the Regulators are watching the bathhouse as well as this place. Don't ask me how, but they seem to know of the access route from there. They will have seen you go inside.'

Nico shot a glance at the old man. *Sweet Erēs*, he thought. *They might know that we're here right now.*

Ash considered this news, stroking a thumb against the sheath of his sword.

In the silence, Serèse looked up at Nico and attempted a brief smile. *She's afraid*, he realized, and was glad to find that he was not the only one. For a moment, gazing at her, he was reminded of their brief encounter in the laundry room of Sato, her hair bedraggled by the steam. He could hardly connect that young woman with the one before him now.

'The rendezvous?' probed Ash. 'Did your father mention it?'

'Yes, he said he would meet you tomorrow as planned.'

'Good. Then we leave now.'

'Of course,' said Nico. 'We simply walk out of here, casual as you like, and they wave us on our way. I can't think of a single thing wrong with that idea. Not a thing.'

'We leave by the bathhouse when some others are leaving too. That will spread them thin, at least. It is the best we can do.'

Serèse agreed. She stood up and squirmed her way out into the hallway, her leather-clad back momentarily pressing up against Nico. He and Ash followed as she wrapped a dark red cloak about herself and grabbed a canvas rucksack she had already packed.

They gathered in the study. Ash chanced a peek through a slat in the shutters. Nico took the initiative, pulling the leather chair beneath the space in the ceiling and hauling himself up. He held his hand out for Serèse to take hold of, but she ignored it, and tossed her pack to him instead. She scrambled up next, and Ash came last, carefully setting the tile back in place.

The changing room was quiet as they climbed down into an empty cubicle. For some minutes they sat waiting, crammed together on the wooden bench. Nico could feel the heat of Serèse's leg pressing against his own. He tried his best to ignore it.

Ash raised a hand to his forehead and began to massage it. 'The Temple?' he said, as though to take his mind off the pain. 'Did you have a chance to gain any information?'

'I watched its perimeter for a few days,' she whispered. 'Then I told Baso and the others what I'd seen. The truth is, it can't be done.'

'Baso managed it.'

'Yes,' she hissed. 'And how far did he get?'

Ash said nothing to that.

'We don't even know if Kirkus is still inside.'

'The Seer believed so, before we left Sato. So we can only assume Kirkus remains there.'

They fell silent as a bather entered the main changing room outside, whistling loudly and seemingly by himself. More soon followed him, arguing about the choice of brothel to visit next. Ash stooped to peer beneath the cubicle door.

'Listen to me,' he whispered as he sat up again. 'We leave when they do. If we are attacked outside, you must both make a run for it, and I will do my best to hold them off. Nico knows where to go.'

'I do?'

'The hostalio, Nico. Get to the east docklands, and anyone there can direct you to it.'

They waited for a few heartbeats, till Ash nodded, then all three pulled up their hoods and slipped out of the cubicle, following the group of men out into the street. The twilight had thickened into night but at least it had stopped raining. Instantly they turned in the opposite direction to the one the party of men was taking, and casually strolled away.

Nico could sense hidden eyes watching their progress; whether it was down to actual intuition, he could not tell. Serèse began to chatter, either out of nervousness or as a ploy to make them appear more ordinary. Her words sounded odd against the backdrop of that dark street poorly lit by gaslights.

'Your name,' she said to him, 'It's Nico?'

'Yes. You remembered.'

'It means *canny* in the old tongue, does it not?'

Nico swallowed a dryness in his throat, scrutinizing a shadowed doorway to their left. He muttered that it did.

'And are you?'

'Am I what?' He could have sworn he had seen a shadow shift just then.

'Canny, I mean. Do you see into people's motives?'

'So my mother would have me believe.' Nico continued to watch their surroundings from under his hood, and fought hard not to look back along the street.

Ash seemed to sense his struggle. 'Do not look back,' he hissed. 'Keep prattling.'

Nico did his best to resume the conversation.

A puddle splashed behind them, even as Serèse opened her mouth to say something.

'We're being followed,' she whispered instead.

As Nico fought the urge to run, Serèse began to hum something beneath her breath. It sounded like an old nursery rhyme Nico had heard as a child.

'Take my arm,' Ash ordered by his side.

'Why?' Nico asked.

'Because I can barely see.'

Ash didn't wait for a response, but took Nico's hand and placed it on his own arm. The old man was squinting as though trying to peer through a dazzling light.

A zel-drawn tram clattered by over to their right, casting a sickly yellow light on to the street. Its carriage was far from full, the windows framing the occasional face that peered out into the darkness without expression, lost in its own world . . . As soon as it was gone two cloaked figures were there in its place, walking directly to cut them off.

'What?' snapped Ash, feeling Nico's grip tighten.

'Two more, in front of us.'

'Then change our course,' growled the old man.

Nico guided them left into a side street. Serèse was silent now. Ash loosened his cloak, brought his scabbard ready to hand. Nico did the same, wondering at himself as he did so. His whole body was trembling. He remembered to focus on his breathing.

The side street ran along the rear of a broad marble building, its grand façade adorned with gargoyles with faces fixed in grotesque grimaces. Music could be heard through the glowing windows, some form of opera not unlike something Nico might have heard back in Khos. Above the sound, barely audible, came the clacking of iron-shod footfalls from behind. Nico cast a glance over his shoulder to see five figures striding after them.

'Master,' hissed Nico, as further shapes stepped directly into their path only ten paces ahead. Regulators, undoubtedly.

A rasp of steel in the night air. Blades glimmered. 'Halt,' instructed a voice. 'You're to be placed under arrest, all of you.'

'Keep walking,' instructed Ash as he cast his cloak from his shoulders. They advanced towards the Regulators in front, even as those behind closed the distance. 'You will have to fight, both of you. Remember your breathing, and once you see a clear space, make a break for it, understood?'

It was no plan at all, as far as Nico was concerned. He gripped the leather-wrapped hilt of his sword for some vague reassurance, ready to draw it as he was trained to. Nothing any longer seemed real to him.

One of the figures raised a pistol in his hand. A pistol. 'Halt!' he shouted again.

Ash: 'How close are they?'

'Six paces.'

Nico jumped in shock as something exploded next to his head. In front of them, the pistoleer cried out and tumbled backwards to the ground.

Serèse tossed her own smoking pistol away and drew a long hunting knife without breaking stride. Nico paused, marvelling at the sight of her – and then Ash sprang into action too.

In one seamless movement the old man drew his blade and ducked, with foreleg bent and hindleg stretched back, and raked his sword across a man's belly; still following through the same motion, he deflected a down-coming blow from another Regulator, turned away the blade, stabbed out.

Nico missed what happened next. By then he was in the thick of it himself. He swerved from a slash as he had been endlessly drilled to do, felt the cool breath of the blade as it passed his face. *This is real,* his mind suggested. *These men are trying to kill me.*

His body took over. He drew his sword and with his next step thrust it forwards. He felt resistance and then he was through it – a face grimacing inches away from his own. It was a man, a human, impaled on his blade. The man struggled. Nico could feel his desperate movements through the hilt of his sword. He would have let go out of disgust if he hadn't felt a sudden lightness in his grip as the man pulled himself clear of the blade, gasped as though in relief, then sat himself down on the ground.

Nico backed away from him.

He felt arms lock around his neck, pulling him backwards and downwards as his sword was knocked from his grasp. He hit the cobbles, a weight pressing on him, a man's stinking breath in his face as someone else held his legs. Cursing and struggling, Serèse was thrown to the ground next to him.

Nico wrenched his head free and lifted it enough to catch sight of Ash.

The farlander was still on his feet, cutting a dance through the cloaked men gathered round him. Nico watched him in awe as did the Regulators pinning him down. For a moment it looked as though the old man couldn't be stopped, his movements so fast there was no chance to react to them, his own actions seeming to pre-empt all others that occurred around him.

But there were too many Regulators, and anyway, Ash could barely see. He missed with one strike and suffered a cut across his left arm, a sudden slash that would have taken off the limb entirely had the old man not somehow known to swerve aside in time. He took the wound with a grunt and a defensive sweep of his blade. A blackness dripped in the dim light from the sudden rent in his sleeve.

'Run!' the old farlander hollered, unaware that both his companions had been brought down. Another sword struck Ash, the flat of the blade crashing into the side of his head. He reeled, bounced off the wall, came off it with a snarl and his blade already lashing out. The Regulators jumped back beyond his range.

One drew a pistol, took careful aim at Ash's kneecap.

'Master Ash!' shouted Nico in warning, trying to fight free as the Regulator squinted and pulled the trigger.

There was the slightest of delays before the blackpowder charge ignited . . . and then something wholly unexpected happened.

A giant of a man crashed on to the scene. With a single swipe he took the top of the pistoleer's skull off, so it flapped against his cheek on a vivid hinge of raw scalp. The weapon fired even as the pistoleer toppled to the ground. The shot flew high. The giant charged onwards into those pinning holding down Nico and Serèse.

It was Baracha, and behind him came a wild-eyed Aléas. As though felling wood, Baracha heaved and chopped with his oversized blade. Aléas followed him, covering his back, jabbing and cutting left and right. Ash pressed the attack.

On his back, still numbed by shock, Nico watched the three Rōshun cut down their opponents in a grimly indifferent silence. Within moments, every Regulator was down.

A roar of applause erupted from inside the opera house. The perfomance drawing to a close.

Nico kept shaking, and his stomach heaved as he looked across the bodies bleeding out on to the cobbles, unable to stop gagging at the copper stench of it. His man was there somewhere, he knew, the one he had struck down. He could not even tell which one it had been.

He heard retching and turned to see Serèse vomiting against a wall. It surprised him to witness that.

Ash was cleaning his blade on a cloak of one of the fallen. Baracha just stood there, breathing heavily, and looked at his daughter with obvious relief. Around them, on the wet cobbles, the fallen men coughed, wheezed, struggled to move.

'A fine mess,' the Alhazii growled at Ash. 'It's as well we've been keeping our own watch on the house. I feared this might happen when you finally arrived. You did not take adequate precautions, old man.'

Ash sheathed his sword with a firm shove. 'It is good to see you too, Baracha.'

A shrill whistle sounded in the distance.

'Perhaps we should leave our chit-chat for a later time?' This from Aléas.

Nico picked up his fallen sword. It took him several attempts to grasp it then he noticed the blood on his hands, and wiped his palms against his tunic. It would not all come off. He tried to sheathe the blade but he could not seem to manage it.

Ash settled a hand on his arm. 'Just breathe,' said the old man.

'Yes, master,' Nico said, and slid the blade home.

'Tomorrow then?' Ash said to Baracha.

'Aye, tomorrow – and be sure you take proper precautions this time.'

With quiet words, Ash instructed Nico to lead the way.

*

Ash's wound continued to bleed badly on the way back. He and Nico tried to stem the flow, but still the blood ran down to his hand, dripped from his glistening fingers. Ash refused to catch a tram back to the hostalio, considering his wound too conspicuous for that. He clenched a torn-off piece of his tunic against the wound for the entire journey back, making no complaint on the way. They stopped twice at deep puddles at Nico's insistence, where he tried to wash the gore from his own hands as best he could.

'Can you see again yet?' asked Nico, as he shook his hands dry.

'Yes, my sight clears.'

'I don't understand. What's wrong with you exactly?'

'*Nothing* is wrong with me. I told you, I suffer from head pains. If they get bad enough they can make it difficult to see.'

Nico did not press him further, not while his master was still in obvious pain.

When they at last reached the hostalio almost an hour later, they were bone-weary and beyond. They made it past the dozing night attendant without trouble, clambering up the four flights of stairs with thoughts of nothing but collapsing on their beds.

They first locked the door of their dark room with a quarter taken from the pile of loose change Ash had left in the washbowl for their purposes. They then fed another quarter into the slot beneath the gaslight, and lit it with a match. Another coin was necessary to unfold Nico's bed.

Before they could sleep, though, they needed to attend to Ash's wound. Nico used yet another quarter to run the spigot and fill the washbowl with water, the remaining coins still lying at its bottom. Meanwhile Ash took out the medico pack and rummaged through it for sterilized bandages, a vial of pure alcohol, also a needle and thread.

The old man dripped some alcohol into the wound, hissing through his teeth as he did so. The gash was not overly deep, but gaped open and pink. The flesh around it, for the entire span of his upper arm, was now bruised a dark purple. Some more of the alcohol he poured on to the bandages. He used a match to heat the end of the needle red-hot, then threaded it with precision, though his fingers shook as the blood coursed freely down his arm. Once it was threaded, he held the needle up to Nico, and said, 'Stitch me up, boy.'

Nico rocked back on his feet. He blinked, barely able to keep his eyelids apart. His body trembled with exhaustion, and he was close to falling down. There was no getting out of it though, so he took the needle and sat down beside the old man. He tried to pretend to himself that he knew what he was doing, that he had been listening during the field surgery lessons back at the monastery, that he had not been fooling around with Aléas at all.

Carefully, he stitched the ugly lips of the wound together, while Ash sat impassively and observed his work. In a way, Nico's exhaustion was a blessing just then; his brain was too far gone to become squeamish at what he saw.

At last Ash nodded with a sigh: 'That will do.'

Nico cut the thread with a knife and fixed a bandage, as best he could, around the arm. He then took off the old man's boots and helped lift his feet on to the bed, making sure his head was properly propped on the pillow.

Ash closed his eyes. His breathing grew shallower.

Nico thought of this old man dancing through the armed Regulators while near-blind, wielding his blade as though it was weightless, all the glamour and myth surrounding him suddenly bearing truth.

'I think I killed a man tonight,' Nico said quietly over his master's still form.

Ash inclined his head by the smallest degree to look up at him. 'And how do you feel, now it is done?'

'Like a criminal. As though I took something I had no right to take. As though I have become someone else, someone tainted.'

'Good, may it always be that way. Only worry if after the act is done and your blood cooled, you feel nothing at all.'

But that was what Nico wished for most of all, just to feel nothing.

How could he ever return home to his mother and meet her eye, knowing what he had done?

'He might have had children,' Nico said. 'A son, like me.'

Ash shut his eyes, let his head straighten back on the pillow.

'You did well, Nico,' the farlander croaked.

The words barely registered on Nico. He kept his own boots on as he made the hardest climb of his life up on to the top bunk. He had barely sprawled on the thin mattress before his body gave up on him. He fell into a deep unconsciousness.

Both of them lay dead to the world, each covered in a sheen of sweat and dried blood, oblivious to the pounding of a fight in the room overhead, the coins falling and clattering endlessly behind other walls.

*

It was quiet in the dark streets surrounding the opera house. The great building itself lay in silence, the perfomance finished for the night. Its patrons had long departed for home or gone on to further late-night engagements.

The cart rocked on its wheels as another corpse was thrown on to it. The clean-up squad worked in silence, save for the occasional grunt of exertion from behind the kerchiefs wrapped around their faces or the odd curse in response to the reeking evacuations of the bodies they trod amongst. Two figures stood apart from the scene, a man and a woman. He puffed on a hazii stick; she leaned against a wall, wrapped tightly in her cloak.

'He comes at last,' the man declared.

Another zel-drawn cart creaked into the side street, a stout wooden box on wheels. Its driver clucked the zel on as quietly as he could, and pulled in the reins as he drew parallel with the two figures.

'You took your time,' the woman reproached him, pushing herself off the wall.

The driver shrugged. 'How long?' he asked, before dismounting.

'An hour – no more.'

The driver clucked his tongue, strode to the back of the cart. He tugged open the doors and a pair of bloodhounds stared out at him from a wire cage, their tails wagging furiously.

'Come my darlings,' he said to them. 'Time to earn your supper.'

After opening the cage he fastened thick leashes to their collars, then allowed them to jump down.

The hounds pulled hard against his bodyweight, keen to begin the hunt. They remained quiet save for their open-mouthed panting, as they had been trained. 'The trail of blood leads that way,' the woman pointed out helpfully.

But dogs were already on to it, and they scurried after the scent with their handler barely able to restrain them. 'We move fast,' he warned over his shoulder, not waiting to see if anyone came after him.

The two Regulators exchanged a glance, then followed.

CHAPTER TWENTY-TWO

Fishing With Pebbles

In any other city port on the Midèrēs, alarms might have rung out at the unexpected arrival of a war galleon flying no colours save for a neutral black, and carrying a force of men clearly fitted out for war.

But this was Cheem, and sights like that were as common as fish. As the vessel moored by the wharf side and the men disembarked with military discipline, a few of the local beggars – ex-sailors mostly, crippled or burned out – turned to see if it might be worth their while asking for spare change, and quickly decided against it. Only one of these beggars allowed his gaze to linger for any length of time: a man in his forties, his left arm ending abruptly in a leather-bound stump. Once, he had been a soldier in the Imperial Legion, and he was not so far gone with age and drugs to miss noticing the imperial military tattoos on the bare wrists and arms of the men disembarking, nor the camouflage attire they wore under their plain cloaks, nor their obvious self-regard.

Commandos, the old addict decided, and slid further back into the shadow of the doorway. He watched carefully as one of their officers approached a city guard. Arrangements were made. More guards were summoned upon and mules soon brought forth. Sailors from the same ship offloaded caskets heavy enough to be holding gold, and strapped them on to the mules. That done, the officer, a few of his men and an escort of guards set off into the city along with their loads.

The remaining men, perhaps seventy in all, were told to stand down. They relaxed nearby in the early morning sun, grumbling whenever they were picked out for duties. Small groups filtered out into the streets occasionally, given heavy purses and instructions to procure riding zels, mules, supplies.

From his doorway, the old addict, his cravings forgotten for a grateful moment, watched with a frown and a curious pang of nostalgia, and wondered which poor fools had provoked the Empire's wrath now.

*

A bitter wind blew through the open window of the tower, carrying with it the scent of rain. Oshō, looking out at the darkening sky, drew the heavy blanket tighter about himself, and shuddered.

A storm comes, he thought, as he gazed across the mountains to the black clouds that crowded the far distance. *So soon after the last one too. Winter comes early this year.*

It was not a pleasing thought. Oshō did not look forward to the winters here in the high mountains. The constant damp chill in the air made his bones ache, so that every movement cost him strength. The simple act of rising from his warm bed each morning was a battle of will that seemed to require ever more effort as the years went by. The winters made him feel his age, and in a way he resented them for it.

I grow weak in my old age, Oshō thought. *Once, I would not have been plagued with so many doubts as I am now.*

Below him, Baso hurried across the courtyard with his thin robe flapping in the wind. Oshō followed him with his gaze, thinking to call out to his old friend. But then he frowned.

It could not be Baso. Baso was dead.

He looked harder and saw, instead, that it was Kosh, red-eared and hunched against the chill wind. He disappeared into the kitchen, no doubt seeking an early breakfast for his ever-needy stomach.

It had been hard news, hearing of Baso's passing. It had stunned Oshō to the core as he stood there in the courtyard, with the rest of the assembled Rōshun, while the Seer told them of the loss of their men in Q'os. Oshō's body had frozen with the shock of it, his chest tightening so that he could barely breathe. For a moment he'd thought he might be experiencing a heart attack, even though the bad turn had not lasted long. For the first time in his life, surrounded by men under his command, Oshō had been unable to take the lead.

Only Ash had saved him face, and then Baracha. They had taken on the demands of reaffirming vendetta, allowing Oshō to return to his room and close the door firmly behind him, there to grieve in his own private way.

Standing before the window now, an image came to Oshō's mind of Baso laughing as a fork of lightning split the sky above his head. Oshō smiled at the recollection. He had not thought of it in many years.

It was a memory from the second day of their flight from the old country, following the final defeat of the People's Army at the battle of Hung. Oshō had been the only general to escape from that fateful trap. In a fighting retreat, he and the tattered remnants of his command had made it to the surviving ships of the fleet, harboured thirty laqs up the coast. Without adequate provisions, in disarray, they had set sail towards the silk winds, knowing that their homeland was now lost to them, and exile their only remaining hope; and a slim hope, at that, as the overlords' navy heaved into sight under full sail.

Unable to outrun them, the ships of his fleet found themselves trapped between the rocky coastline to the west and a storm front approaching from the deep ocean to the south, a sinker of ships if ever there was one; and, right behind, the closing ships of the enemy, outnumbering them at least three to one.

In a last throw of the dice, the fugitives in the fleet turned towards the approaching storm like the desperate men they were.

Baso had been merely a boy then, no more than sixteen, still clad proudly in his battered, oversized armour when most of the other survivors of the defeated People's Army had removed theirs for fear of drowning. All had seemed lost in those dark hours at sea. Prayers to ancestors tumbled from quivering lips. Amid the screaming gales, rigging and masts broke loose, waves swamped decks and carried men away, capsized vessels entirely. No one expected to make it through alive. Even Oshō thought they were dead men, if not by the hands of their pursuers then by the ferocity of the storm; though he had kept his fears to himself as he ordered the fleet to push onwards, making a show of bravado for the sake of his men, though in reality, within his heart, he felt as broken as the rest of them.

But seeing Baso laugh out loud like that as the ship heaved under his feet and the sky raged above his head, so alive in the madness of the moment and without fear or worry for past or future, or even now . . . The sight had straightened Oshō's spine a little, and lent him courage when he needed it most.

And now Baso was gone, like so many others, and precious few of

Oshō's original people remained. Kosh, Shiki, Ch'eng, Shin the Seer, Ash ... he could count those left from the old country on a single hand now. Those few were all that linked Oshō to the distant past in his homeland. It seemed that as each one passed away he grew ever more vulnerable to their loss, and fretted ever more deeply about who might be next.

It would be Ash, he knew. Ash would go next, and his former apprentice would prove to be the bitterest loss of them all.

Ash was still out there somewhere, no doubt in Q'os in the midst of vendetta – at his age, by Dao! Oshō should never have let him go, he knew. Not a man in his condition. But, in his own grief, it hadn't crossed Oshō's mind to try and dissuade Ash from his decision, at least not until later, after he had already departed, when Oshō had paused to realize that his old friend was most likely not coming back from this one – just as Baso had not.

He didn't know why he felt such an intense premonition, for he had experienced no tragic dreams or heard morbid readings from the Seer. He simply felt a great heaviness whenever he thought of his old friend, as though certain he would never see him again.

The whole sorry business of this vendetta made him feel like that. Oshō did not think it could end in any way but badly for all of them.

At the open window, he braced his body against another gust of wind. Somewhere out of sight, a shutter banged once, twice, and then fell silent.

I have grown melancholic in my old age, he reflected, but then he chuckled at his own folly. He knew that his age had nothing to do with it.

Oshō pulled closed the shutters, sealing out the storm that approached across the mountains. He shivered once more, then returned to his books and his padded chair by the welcoming warmth of the fire.

*

It was late afternoon in Q'os. The Five Cities taverna was as busy as always at that hour, with the local dockworkers and street merchants knocking off for the day, and the customary mix of outlanders staying in the area's many hostalios drawn by the taverna's fine foods and wines.

In a corner, beneath the little hissing flame of a gaslight fitted to the smoke-stained plaster of the wall, six individuals sat huddled in private conversation. The local patrons paid them little notice, save for the occasional glance at the young woman in her brown leathers, for she was a sight for sore eyes to working men who had sweated for their wages since dawn, and likely to return to wives aged beyond their years by regular childbirth and hard, daily graft.

'It's impossible,' Serèse kept her voice low, though the noise in the taverna was enough to easily mask her words. She seemed not to notice the occasional lingering attentions of the male patrons elsewhere in the taproom. Perhaps she was simply used to such scrutiny, and had learned to ignore it. 'I'd doubt if there's anywhere in the Midèrēs more heavily guarded than the Temple of Whispers just now. I can't see any way it could be breached.'

Baracha, musing over his shot glass of rhulika, raised a single eyebrow in disbelief.

'I tell you it's true, father. Even the moat around the tower has been filled with some kind of fish, tiny things with a craving for flesh. They draw crowds every day, for the city watch has begun to dangle criminals into the water just for the sport of it. I saw it only three days ago. There was a great feeding frenzy, and when they drew the man from the water, the flesh on his legs was stripped to the bone. How do you reckon on getting past such an obstacle?'

Nico, sitting in glum silence next to his master, looked up at that revelation. He had never heard of flesh-eating fish before.

'I'll tell you this,' Baracha said, still unconvinced. 'In all my life I've never known a place that could not be breached, given enough time and inspiration. If we cannot swim the moat, we can raft across it.'

Serèse sighed in exasperation. 'Only if you can get past the boat patrols – and evade the watchers on the steeple itself. And the regular patrols along the shore.'

'Then we disguise ourselves as one of the boat patrols, row across to the tower itself, climb it.'

'Even at night you'd stand out. They've positioned lights all around the lower floors. You wouldn't get ten feet before a patrol or one of their flyers spotted you.'

'So we forget the moat. We steal ourselves some priests' robes, cross the bridge, enter the main gates in disguise.'

It seemed easy, the way Baracha put it.

'Yes, except no one is allowed through the gates until they've placed their hands through a grill. They're checked, to see if the tips of their little fingers are missing or not. In fact, no one is allowed to even set foot on the bridge until they've been checked for that proof of identification.'

'Well then, the answer's obvious,' said Aléas, and all eyes turned to him. He grinned handsomely. 'Each of us chops the tips from our little fingers, waits some moons for them to fully heal, then walks inside unmolested.'

'Shut up, Aléas,' warned Baracha.

Aléas raised his eyebrows and glanced at Nico. A look passed between them, though Nico didn't match his friend's easy smile. He was tired today. He had slept poorly, haunted by nightmares in which he had relived, over and over again, his actions of the previous night.

'If you are to find a way inside,' Serèse continued, 'it must be by some method they have not foreseen.'

Aléas was bored of this. 'He can't stay in the tower for the rest of his life. If we can't breach the place, we can wait for him to come out. Maybe during the Augere. Maybe he will come out then.'

'And what if he does not?' demanded Baracha. 'They almost had us last night. Even now, as we speak, they're likely combing the city for us. All of us are outlanders here, save for you. It's only a matter of time before they find us out. This is hardly a friendly city in which to linger, in case you hadn't noticed.'

His words silenced the group. Nico found himself observing the rest of the taproom to see if they were being watched.

There: a man turning away too quickly from Nico's glance. Nico studied him for a moment, waiting to see what he did next. The man ordered himself another drink, and continued the conversation with his companions.

Nico breathed again, trying to relax. The fellow had likely been staring at Serèse, nothing else. *I'm seeing phantoms*, he told himself. *This foul city is getting to me. I wish we could leave now and never return to it.*

Baracha sat back and exhaled loudly enough to show his displeasure. 'We should take it as a compliment,' he consoled. 'They show us a great deal of respect.' But it was no answer to their problems, and Baracha was clearly troubled as he smoothed the long sweep of his beard.

For the length of their conversation, Ash had been sitting quietly with his gaze lost in his drink and the hand of his wounded arm resting in his lap. As the silence lengthened, he raised his glass of wine with his good arm, took a sip, and set the glass back down.

'We are all forgetting the obvious,' he said unexpectedly, without looking up.

Baracha folded his arms and sighed. 'And what is that, oh wise one?'

'They are expecting stealth. Not attack.'

Aléas stared, eyes wide. 'Storm the gates, you mean?'

Ash nodded, faint humour pulling at the corners of his mouth.

'A wonderful thought,' said Baracha, 'except of course that it would need an army.'

Ash studied each of their expressions in turn. He took another sip of the wine, set the empty cup back on the table with a thump of decision.

'Then, my troubled friends, we must find ourselves an army.'

*

It was bright outside, the sun shining in a rare clear sky. It was not a particularly complimentary light however, for it merely showed up the city's drab, lacklustre character even more clearly than usual. As it filtered its way down into the canyon-like streets Nico watched as it transformed itself into something thin and muted instead.

'Meaning no offence here,' Aléas said, 'but I fear Master Ash might have lost his wits at last.' He was standing outside the taverna, along with Nico and Serèse, as their two masters discussed something beyond earshot.

'I suspect he had few to begin with,' replied Nico drily. 'Do you think they will really go through with this? Truly?'

Aléas considered this question while he studied his master. 'They're both of the same cut,' he said, with a curt nod. 'Now that one has suggested it, the other will feel that he cannot back down. They will do this, even if they risk all in the trying.'

It was enough to set Nico's stomach afloat. He looked up at the distant heights of the Temple of Whispers, visible even from here in the eastern docks. He could not believe they were truly considering an attack on such a stronghold. Surely it was just talk, despite what

Aléas might think. Their plans would amount to nothing in the end, and they would be forced to leave the city without finishing their vendetta. It wouldn't be the first time, or so he had heard.

But Nico understood Ash only too well now, and knew himself to be cradling a false hope. He turned away from the sight of the tower, tried to turn his thoughts to other things.

Serèse studied him carefully. 'How are you this morning?' she asked.

'A little tired,' he confessed. 'I didn't sleep well. I think I will be glad to leave this place.'

'You do not like it here.'

'No, I don't. There are too many people and too few places to be alone.'

Aléas slapped his shoulder. 'Spoken like a true farmer.'

'When, in all the world, did I ever claim to be a farmer?'

'You didn't. It's the smell, mostly.'

Nico was in no mood for their usual banter, and would have said something short-tempered in return if he had not seen Baracha departing just then. The Alhazii jerked his head at Aléas and his daughter, beckoning them to follow.

Aléas nodded goodbye to Nico. 'Stay safe,' said Serèse as they hurried to catch up.

Ash approached, his head bowed in thought.

'I must make some inquiries,' he informed Nico. 'Come.'

'Wait a moment.'

Ash turned back, impatient.

'This thing you're proposing – to attack the tower, I mean. It sounds like madness to me.'

The farlander's dark skin looked thinner in the afternoon sunlight. He had lost a good deal of blood the night before. 'I know,' he said, and his voice sounded tired. 'But not concern yourself with it. I made a promise to your mother to keep you safe, remember?'

'I think my mother's notion of safety and your own are two different things entirely.'

Ash nodded. 'Still, I mean to keep my promise. When we breach the tower, you will not come with me. It is too dangerous. You are hardly experienced enough for such a venture. I agree, Nico, there is a touch of madness to this plan, but I fear that a little madness is necessary if we are to see through our vendetta. When we are inside, you will stay with Serèse and help us to escape the immediate area if we make it back out.'

'It isn't only myself that I'm concerned about.'

A little colour returned to the old man's face. 'I understand. But this is our business, Nico. These are the risks we must take.' He cast further debate aside with a shrug.

'Enough talk. Come.'

*

The house was on a street of many houses, all of them empty shells of former dwellings, their windows smashed or boarded up, their interiors strewn with wreckage, a few burnt black and gutted. Only the house itself was still lived in, neighboured on each side by a derelict in a terraced row of derelicts. Even then it looked barely more habitable than the rest of them. Its windows were grimy with soot and blanked from within by dark curtains. Paint that may once have been an optimistic yellow hung peeling from the brick walls. A weather-vane – depicting a naked man holding a bolt of lightning – dangled from the guttering of the roof and swung, creaking, in the soft breeze.

Nico stared up, feeling exposed beneath this swinging vane that looked as though it might topple at any moment, though probably it had hung loose like that for months before now, years even. Through the front door, the heavy knocking of the clapper still echoed within as Ash lowered his hand and stepped back to wait.

Behind them, the fringes of what was once an expansive block of buildings lay in collapsed ruins, destroyed by fire long ago. A great midden heap rose from the ruins to block out much of the sky. Rats worked across its flanks without shyness, scampering through scraps of rubbish that flapped like hands waving for help. The stench of rot was overwhelming. It was so prevalent that even the odd gust of wind could not shift it, but instead stirred it around in sudden, unexpected concoctions that made the throat gag and the eyes water.

Nico tried not to breathe as he turned back to face the heavily scratched wooden door of the house they were visiting. By his side, Ash hummed something under his breath. It didn't sound like music to Nico's ears; more a series of words spoken without actually opening the mouth.

'The art of melody was never discovered by your people then?'

The humming stopped, as Ash stared at him. The old farlander was about to speak when they heard from within a chair crashing over, or something equally as heavy. Someone swore. A chain rattled, then a bolt was withdrawn, and another. The door scraped against the floor as it was tugged inwards.

'Yes?' The woman was short, stooping almost to the waist. She clutched a lantern in one hand, a stick in the other to support her weight, as she craned her neck to squint upwards at the two strangers standing before her. Nico blinked down at her filthy face; her hair so scraggy it resembled fur; a moustache better developed than any he might have grown for himself.

'We are here to see Gamorrel,' said Ash. 'Tell him it is the farlander.'

'What?' she said.

Ash sighed. He leaned closer to her ear.

'Your husband,' he said more loudly. 'Tell him an old farlander wishes to see him.'

'I'm not deaf,' she said. 'Come in. Come in.'

Inside, the house was much the same as on the outside. They followed the old woman as she shuffled slowly along the hallway, Nico and Ash stepping side by side as though in a processional march into the heart of some hidden temple – though a temple whose walls were built from brick coated with flaking plaster, and adorned with pictures hanging in frames too dim to see in the stuttering light of the lantern – held by the woman at the height of their waists – and a wooden floor illuminated before them, deeply coated in white dust and with grit that scratched the soles of their boots. Around them the air was filled with unholy stench, like cabbage boiled solidly for a day and a night. A rat scurried past their feet; others wormed along the edges of the hallway.

They ascended stairs that creaked beneath their weight in a manner suggestive of imminent collapse. They could only take one stair at a time, waiting for the woman to move on before taking another. Nico and Ash glanced at one another, saying nothing. Then another door: a sigil painted in red paint, or blood, depicting a seven-pointed star.

They entered a parlour: a room lit by a few smoky lanterns sitting

273

on a table already covered with figurines, charms, stone mortars and pestles, knives, pins, other items unknowable. Sheets of cloth sagged across the ceiling, like the roof of a tent. Beneath them, on a chair positioned near the curtained window, sat an old man in a waistcoat with his hands resting upon his stomach, his eyes closed, snoring loudly. His lap was filled with a mound of rats, who lay there with tails entwined and watched the newcomers enter.

The man stirred at the sound of the door closing behind Nico and Ash. A lock of lank, black hair fell across his face and he scratched himself, then continued to snore.

'Gamorrel,' Ash said loudly, as he nudged the old fellow's foot, scattering the rats from his lap in the process.

The man did not jerk awake but instead opened the lids of a single eye just wide enough to peer out through them, as though to spy the lie of the land before emerging any further from the safety of sleep. At the sight of Ash his face twitched. He roused himself.

'I might have known,' emerged his time roughened voice. 'Only a Rōshun would dare awaken a sleeping sharti.'

'Up. We have business to discuss.'

'Oh? What kind of business?'

A leather coin-purse dropped into his lap, the weight of it enough to jerk him upright. A grin stretched across his whiskered face, revealing teeth as brown as ale.

'Interesting,' he crooned, and rose smoothly without effort. 'Please, step into my chamber.' And he led just Ash into another room, and closed the door firmly behind them.

'Have a seat,' said the old woman, guiding Nico to one of the chairs by the window. 'Chee, yes? Some chee?'

Nico smiled and shook his head. He thought of the rats scurrying over everything, the grime and filth of the whole place, the dirt embedded in the old woman's yellowed fingernails.

'Yes?' she insisted and, before he could say no, she had shuffled off into another room, the suddenly open door releasing a cloud of steam that carried in it the humid whiff of cabbage. He heard her shoo something out of the way, and then the clinking of cups.

A mechanical clock was ticking somewhere in the parlour, though he could not see it amid all the mess and clutter crowded about the walls. The chair was uncomfortable, as though he was sitting on gravel, so he rose, and brushed a scattering of rat droppings to the floor. He sat down again gingerly. He was about to place his hands on the arm-rests, but changed his mind and settled them in his lap instead.

The old woman emerged precariously bearing a tray with a pot of steaming chee and two cups of white porcelain. 'Let me help with that,' Nico said, as he rose and took the tray from her, carrying it back to set on a small side table. She smiled and settled herself with care in the chair opposite him, remaining stooped even as she sat, her hand still resting on her stick. She watched him clearly as he poured the chee.

'Thank you,' Nico said, with a tight smile, and sat back with his own cup – though he did not drink from it. The old woman nodded, still studying him deeply. He wondered what it was that she saw.

'Tell me,' she said. 'Do you dream much?'

He thought for a moment. 'A little too much, of late,' he confessed.

'Some dream more than others, you know. Some see more than others, too. I can tell that you are one of those. You are fortunate. My husband, he is the same.'

Nico stared down into the cup in his hands. The chee looked pleasant enough, and the porcelain was clean. He glanced up and smiled and then looked elsewhere, and saw the clock at last standing on a pedestal against the far wall, next to a coat-stand, where a single flap-coat hung alongside a black top hat. He felt uncomfortable under her gaze, and the smell of the steam still pouring through the open doorway was starting to make him feel ill.

Nico forced himself to look at the old woman. She was the colour of burnt stove grease. He met her soapy eyes and saw something vulnerable within them, a sensitivity scarred by old wounds. He saw boredom too, in the guise of her present attentiveness.

She nodded as though he had just returned to her. 'That is why he is a sharti you know. My husband, he is very powerful in the old ways. Many people still come to him – the poor, the desperate. Many call on his services.'

'You are not Mannians, then?'

'Eh? Mannians? No boy. The Mannians would seize us for slaves, or worse, if they knew what we were. We practise the old ways here, the first ways. Heretics they call us. We and the poor are who they despise most of all.'

She paused to lift her cup from the table and drew it to her puckered lips. She slurped noisily, twice, then returned the cup to the table.

'You do not know what I speak of . . . the old ways?'

Nico considered the question. He thought of his mother making the sign of protection each time she saw a single pica bird, a habit she had infected even him with. He thought too of how she always left a burning candle on an open windowsill every night of the winter solstice.

'Perhaps.' He shrugged. 'These old ways, they are still practised elsewhere?'

'Oh, they are practised *everywhere*, but only in the shadows. In traditions long hidden from meaning. By those old enough to remember our lives before Mann, mm? Only in the High Pash will you find the old ways lived by all and still with meaning. And further a-reach than that even – in the Isles of Sky, even there. That is how they live forever, you know. When they die, they use the old knowledge to return them to life. Yes, these are the things the Mannians would have us forget.'

Nico listened to her words with a glaze of apparent interest fixed to his face. He fought the urge to scratch at his ankles, where he could feel the fleas leaping and biting. He glanced at the closed door and wondered how long Master Ash was going to be. What were they doing in there, for mercy's sake?

The woman inhaled and wobbled the top of the stick from side to side in her withered hand. 'You are a kind boy,' she said. 'You listen to an old woman when you would rather be anywhere but here. Now then, I believe they are finished with their business.'

Nico set the chee down the instant he heard the door being tugged open. He was on his feet even as Ash emerged, with the other man following behind.

' . . . closer to the time then,' Ash was saying.

The farlander glanced at the cup of chee sitting on the table and stopped to pick it up. He took a large gulp, then smiled at the old woman as he set down the empty cup. He jerked his head for Nico to follow as he strode to the stairs.

'Thank you for the chee,' Nico said quickly, and followed after him.

*

They caught a tram back to the district of the east docks, sitting in one of the seats at the back. For a time, Ash sat looking behind him through the rear window.

'You think we are being followed?'

Ash faced forwards once more. 'Hard to say,' he muttered. He did not seem very concerned.

The tram was clattering past a great square fronted on three sides by buildings of white marble, filled in its entirety with milling figures in red robes, thousands upon thousands of them.

'Pilgrims,' said Ash before his apprentice could ask.

'I had another question in mind,' Nico said, loud enough to be heard over the noise of the crowds. 'Back at that house, did you get what you went there for?'

'I hope so.'

'And you're not going to tell me any more than that?'

'Not yet, no.'

Nico exhaled in exasperation. 'This is a great way to teach your apprentice. Tell him as little as possible, even when he asks.'

'In the field, it is always best if you work things out for yourself.'

Nico snorted. 'A convenient theory, in that it saves you having to answer any questions.'

'There is that, too.'

A bump in the road shook the windows of the tram. Ash twisted to look behind again. Once he straightened, he sat stroking a thumb against a forefinger in contemplation.

A few moments later he stood up, grasping for the luggage rack overhead for balance. 'Go back and wait for me in our room. Stay inside until I return.'

Without waiting for a response, he moved to the open exit and hopped down into the street, walking off quickly even as the tram passed him by, oblivious to Nico's face pressed against the glass of the window.

Some time later the tram entered the district of the east docks, and Nico began to recognize where he was at last. He gazed out the window at the passing streets, their vague familiarity an equally vague comfort to him. On the pavement a girl strode past. He caught sight of her dark hair.

Nico jumped up, made his way to the exit, and stepped out.

'Serèse!' he shouted, but the girl was too far away to hear him.

He lost sight of her on reaching the end of the next block. It had been her, he was sure of it. Nico kept walking in the same direction, looking one way and then the other. The streets were busy with late-afternoon traffic. Pedestrians hurried along the pavements, trams and carts trundled along the roadway. A nearby temple rang out the hour, two bells and then silence.

He headed along a street of identical buildings, the windows tall and standing open to the city air, leaking sounds of industry from within. He stopped at one of the ground-floor windows to chance a look inside. It looked like a workshop, though a massive one, spacious and dusty. Hundreds of people, mostly women and young children, sat on rows of mats on the floor and worked at simple repetitive tasks that made no immediate sense to his eyes. Other children swept loose debris from the floor and the few grown men sweated as they pushed handcarts filled with material along the aisles. Those sitting on the mats tossed finished items into the carts as they passed by, while others grabbed things out. A few supervisors stalked between the workers, shouting at one every so often. After a minute, Nico passed on, seeing no sign of Serèse. He had clearly lost her.

For a moment he considered returning to the hostalio, but the mere thought of sitting there all on his own, dwelling on what he had done last night, was a depressing one. He might as well take a stroll, even if the city streets were barely more welcoming than his room.

He walked on into a prettier district, where trees lined the avenues and small plazas offered space for chee houses or fountains of clear running water, the mood of the area less hectic than the eastern docks. Still, Nico could feel in his blood how he did not belong in this city. It had little for him to relate to, little he could settle his eyes upon in welcome recognition. It was all so daunting to him, not simply the scale of the architecture but the manner of the people themselves.

At least in Bar-Khos strangers still spoke to strangers. Smiles appeared readily on the faces of shopkeepers; if there was a sudden fight or argument, others would always be quick to calm things down. As war-weary as Bar-Khos might be, or perhaps even because of that, there was still a spirit of community amongst its beleaguered populace, a sense of lives shared in a common purpose that transcended creed or religion or acquaintanceship. Here, though, there was something sour and self-contained about the people. It was as though they had been promised much in their lives – yes, and had gained it all too – and yet here they were, even more harried and discontented than before.

Perhaps what Nico needed most was to see something green and spacious as opposed to this endless oppressiveness of concrete and brick. On a whim, he stopped a boy in the street and asked him where the nearest park could be found, hoping the youth would not squint at him in confusion and say there were no such things.

But the boy gave him simple enough directions, a mere block away it turned out. As he turned a corner, Nico's eyes lit up, for there, directly ahead of him, was indeed a small green park surrounded by a black iron railing. He quickened his pace and hurried through a gateway, his shoes crunching on a pathway of gravel. He slowed, gradually, to take in the scenery. It was attractive in its own way, and largely empty, save for the occasional figure squatting in the bushes to relieve itself, and a few drunks lying sprawled in the overgrown grass as though someone had staked them out under the sun.

Nico chose a spot as far away from these park denizens as he could find, and sat himself down beneath a tall cicado tree. With his face to the weakening sun, he almost began to relax.

Eventually, Nico closed his eyes and imagined he was elsewhere. He imagined he was back home in Khos, sitting in the forested hills that rose up behind his mother's smallholding.

On days like this one, back home, he had often gone hiking with Boon by his side, the pack on his back holding a loaf of keesh freshly baked by his mother, also some cheese, a flask for water, his bird whistle, some hooks and twine. He would climb away from the mundane problems of his life, sweating and panting his way into the crisp air of the higher valleys, his mood lightening with every footstep as Boon ranged to one side or the other, sniffing for rabbits, mice, anything he might chase.

Sometimes, after Boon had calmed enough to lie down and be still, Nico would fish in the cold mountain pools, catching one small rainbow trout after another, fish which he would proudly bring back to his mother for supper. At other times, in a more contemplative mood, he would find a slab of ancient rock overlooking some deeper pool, and would fish with pebbles instead, tossing in a small stone so that it plopped gently into the water. He would watch it keenly as it sank beneath the surface. If he was lucky, a young trout would dart for the sinking pebble from some hiding place by the edge of the pool, only to dart away again when it realized it was not potential food. In this way Nico would fish not for the meat of the animals, but for the sight of them. He would spend hours at this, hours.

If it was still early enough, Nico would choose the nearest mountain and climb to the very top of it, regardless of how tired or hungry or footsore he became, wondering if his father had ever come this way when he had hunted for game, or on one of his own solitary hikes. Once he reached the summit he would collapse to the ground next to Boon, his breath ragged in his throat, his eyes absorbing the vast spread of the land below and the blue-green press of the sea beyond. Salt would lace this high air that he sipped. His skin would cool against the soft ruffle of the wind. He would feel at peace with the world, his life placed in a truer context, his problems petty, without meaning; nothing really mattered, he would realise, not his fears and insecurities and hopes and desires, shifting and transitory, only the permanence of the moment, this presence of being. He would look into Boon's soft eyes and realize that the dog already knew this state of mind, and he would envy him his simple existence.

'Hello, you.'

The voice was of the present, and Nico returned to it simply by opening his eyes. Colours returned to his vision slowly, so at first all he could see was a green silhouette framed against the sky, looming above him. He craned his neck and shaded his eyes.

Serèse, her hands on hips, frowning.

'You're on my spot,' she announced before he could say a thing.

'What?' he asked, sitting up.

'*You*, you're on my spot,' she repeated, and Nico smiled it her, puzzled, and cast a look around at the drunks and the addicts scattered about the little park.

'I see. You come here a lot, do you?'

She sat down next to him, and nudged him aside to gain more room against the tree. He felt her heat against his own; it sent a physical shock reverberating up and down his spine.

'Our hostalio is nearby,' she explained. 'My father refused to let me stay in the squalor he and Aléas have been putting up with down at the docks, so he had us all move to better quarters. They have returned to our rooms to lie low and discuss plans. I can't think of anything more tedious. I thought I'd take a walk, find somewhere to sit in the sun.' She looked about her, wrinkling her nose. 'And, I am afraid, this is it.'

Serèse took a brown roll-up from her pocket and struck a match to light its tip. The smell of hazii weed filled Nico's nostrils as she inhaled life into the stick and exhaled.

'Smoke?' she ventured, passing it over to him.

His mother had claimed hazii was bad for the lungs, worse even than tarweed. True enough, she herself often coughed fit for dying after a heavy night of smoking it. Nico almost waved her offer away, but then he thought, why not, and took it warily. He drew a trickle of smoke into his lungs. With a cough he passed it back to her.

'Am I interrupting something?' Serèse asked at his silence, for Nico was still partly back in the hills of Khos.

'No. Only a few memories.'

'Well, in that case I'll leave you to them.' She stood up in one single graceful movement, like a big cat.

'Don't go on my account,' said Nico quickly.

She held out a hand. 'I'm only playing with you. If we're going to spend some time together, I'd rather it wasn't here.'

Nico couldn't help but agree, so took her hand and allowed himself to be pulled to his feet. 'Where do you suggest, then?' he asked, their hands still clasped.

She shrugged. 'Let's walk a while.'

She released his hand, and instead slid an arm through the crook of his own. The air was growing cooler as the sun dipped behind the surrounding buildings. On all sides, pedestrians hurried to and fro; and iron-collared slaves carrying heavy burdens balanced on their heads. They passed several restaurants with the scents of cooking wafting from their open doorways.

'Are you hungry?' asked Nico, though he himself did not feel any need to eat.

Serèse shook her head, her dark hair rippling around her shoulders. 'I need some fresh air. Don't you like to just walk sometimes?'

'Of course,' he replied quickly.

She passed him the hazii stick again, and he took a deeper pull this time.

'You and Aléas,' she said, 'you seem to have become friends after all.'

'I suppose so. Not that Baracha . . . I mean, not that your father approves very much.'

'No, he wouldn't. You are Ash's apprentice.'

Nico looked at her with questions in his eyes.

She shrugged. 'Master Ash is the best the order has, and all know it. That is something that displeases my father, for he has always had a consuming desire to be only the best. He can't stand it when he's not. But you mustn't hold it against him. My mother told me of his childhood, about his father, who was fierce and overbearing, but also small, in his own mind. He put down his son at every chance he could, and showed him nothing but contempt, till the day that he died. It has shaped my father's spirit in some way, and he can do nothing to change it.'

Nico considered this, and tried to match it with the overbearing Alhazii that he had come to know.

They strolled past side-street cafés, the chatter of the patrons becoming loud and raucous. The shadows began to stretch further.

'My mother is like that, too, in a way,' he said after a time. 'Something in her past still shapes her now.'

'Her parents?'

'No. My father.'

Serèse said something in return, but he didn't hear it. His steps faltering, he came to a stop.

Straight ahead of them something was spinning quickly to the ground. As it landed, he squinted down at it.

A cicado seed, its fresh greenness contrasting with the dull greyness of the cobbles. Around it, all across the street, fallen leaves lay trodden and torn, and amongst them were similar winged seeds, though smaller than he was used to, not as large as they should be. Nico looked up, his eye travelling past floor after floor of the building they were walking alongside. Over the edge of its lofty roof hung the branches of a tree.

Serèse followed his gaze. 'A roof garden,' she explained. 'The wealthy like to keep them.' Her lips pursed briefly. 'Come on,' she said as she ducked into an alley running to one side of the same building.

With Nico following her, Serèse stopped beneath a ladder fixed to the brickwork over their heads: a fire escape running beside a window on each floor all the way to the top. He realized what she was thinking.

He felt distinctly light-headed as he gave her a boost up on to his shoulders; himself grinning, wobbling under her weight, as she flexed her knees and made a leap and a grab for the lowest rung of the wooden ladder. She hauled herself suddenly upwards, and Nico admired her lithe figure as she tugged on the latch securing it.

The sliding ladder clattered down, with her aboard, and came to a stop right beside him.

'What are you gaping at?' she breathed.

*

It was a small roof garden, though beautifully arranged. A careful hand had allowed it to grow naturally, without appearing overly wild. Around its edges stood undersized trees in clay pots, and bushy shrubs in troughs of soil covered in wood chippings; wild grass grew over most of the space between, dotted with blue and yellow flowers. At the very centre were a small fountain and water course constructed from smooth but irregular stones to give the appearance of a miniature mountain stream.

The artful combinations of growth screened off the surrounding buildings, giving Nico and Serèse the impression of standing anywhere but in the midst of the largest city in the world. A shack with a doorway stood at the rear of the flat roof, obviously leading to some internal stairs. It was locked, when Serèse tried it, which was only to her satisfaction. Together they sat on a bench beside the flowing water, both appreciating the secret garden in silence. From here the constant buzz of the city could only dimly be heard.

Serèse lit another hazii stick, blew smoke into the fading light.

'You did well,' she said 'Last night, I mean.'

It was the one subject neither had yet mentioned.

'You think so? I was so gripped by fear I was numb with it.'

'So? You were hardly the only one. But you did what you had to do. You showed courage.'

Nico looked long and hard at the girl by his side eyeing her properly, without shyness or agenda. At once he noticed something else behind the mask of spark and beauty. Serèse was on edge, and badly in need of company.

She took another deep puff of the stick, then passed it to him.

'Courage?' Nico repeated, as though trying out the word for the first time. For an instant the face of the one he had slain rose before him; the man's determined glare even as Nico stabbed him, changing first to wonder and then, by degrees, to a terrible awareness of everything lost to him. 'No, it wasn't *courage* that prompted me to stick my blade into that man's belly last night. It was fear. I didn't want to die there. I didn't want him to kill me. So I killed him first.'

He felt surprised at how he could speak so plainly about his deepest feelings. He wondered if something had changed in him, if he had grown a little older since last night. Perhaps it was simply the liberating effects of the hazii smoke.

'It's funny,' he said, still thinking out aloud. 'Since leaving Khos, I've come to realize a few things. My father for instance. He was the bravest man that I knew, though at the time I hardly understood it. I think, deep down, I always feared that he was a coward after all – for running away from everything like he did. I had such notions, when I was younger, of bravery, courage under fire and all that. The stuff of stories, of course. But now I've caught a glimpse of what my father must have gone through every day there under the walls. I wonder now how he was able to live that way for so long, to rise each morning knowing what faced him. I can see now why he chose a different life, away from it all, wherever that may be. I only wish I possessed half his strength.'

Nico looked again at the hazii stick in his hand: all but forgotten, it had gone out. He passed it back to her, his head swimming. 'Courage isn't something I know much about, Serèse – not when it comes down to it. Whenever there's trouble, mostly all I feel is frightened.'

Serèse relit the roll-up, sat with a fist supporting her chin.

'I understand,' she said quietly, exhaling. 'Last night was my first time, too. I don't think I'm taking it very well either.'

Her eyes seemed suddenly wary. A passing shadow drew their attention to the sky. They both looked up in time to catch sight of a passing flyer, its black bat-like wing carrying it upwards on the thermals above the city. Serèse shivered.

'Are you all right?'

'Yes,' she assured him, though her voice betrayed her.

Take her mind off these things, his mind suggested.

'Tell me something about yourself, Serèse.'

'What would you like to know?'

'I'm not sure. Your mother – tell me of her.'

It was a mistake, that question. He saw it instantly in her eyes.

All the same, she tried to answer him. 'My mother passed away some years ago. That's how I met my father; it was only after she fell ill. He came to us in Minos, and when she had gone he took me back to Cheem. I stayed there until I was sixteen, up in the mountains among all those men training to kill.'

'You never thought of following in your father's footsteps?'

'Me a Rōshun? No, I would hate such a life.'

'How did you come here then?'

She smiled, though it was a twisted smile without humour. 'I went a little crazy with the boredom of it all. Twice I tried to run away. Once, I fell in love and caused a great commotion. Then old Oshō suggested I move to Q'os. The agent here had begun to lose her health, and needed someone to help her. I snatched up the chance. Mistress Sar passed away ealier this year, from the coughing sickness. I agreed to stay on here until they could find someone else to replace her.'

Serèse looked at the roll-up in her fingers, lifeless once more. She cast it away from her. 'And you, my inquisitor, how did *you* end up here, mixed up in all of this?'

'Lately, I've been wondering that myself.'

'You sound as though you regret it.'

Nico stood up and wandered over to the running fountain, feigning to study its miniature relief close up. In truth, he saw nothing.

'I didn't mean to pry,' she said to his back, reading something in his posture. 'I've just smoked too much weed.' She hesitated, seeking a better explanation. 'You have a way about you, Nico. It draws out words.'

The fountain really did look like a miniature mountain pool. Nico almost expected to see miniature trout swimming around beneath its surface. 'You're right, though, I do have regrets. Since last night

I've been wishing I'd never left Bar-Khos. I know now that *this*,' and he looked about him, without focus, 'this is hardly any way to live. As a killer in the making. You know, I'd almost forgotten what I was learning to be, back at the monastery. I was so occupied with doing well. Today though, it stares me right in the face.'

Serèse joined him, by his side. He could see her reflection in the water.

Nico wiped a hand across his face, exhaled into his palm. 'Perhaps I'll be fine once we leave this city,' he said, looking at her, forcing lightness into his tone. 'Tell me. Will you stay here in Q'os, after this is done?'

'No,' she responded. 'I'll have to move on, for my own safety.'

'Where will you go?'

'I was thinking, with the money I've saved . . . I think I'll travel for a while, and see Mercia again while it's still free. It's been some years since I left the islands and I hear it's safe enough for a woman to travel alone.' Her voice held a smile in it now. 'And I'll relax, and take life as it comes, and carry only those things that will fit into my pack. Simple and carefree. That sounds like a fine plan to me, just now.'

'It does,' agreed Nico, and in his voice there was a tone of longing that surprised even himself. Yes, it sounded a wondrous thing to do, to hitch a pack and travel across the islands of the Free Ports.

For a moment he enjoyed a fantasy of undertaking such a venture with this girl as his companion, living each fresh day without fear or threat to his life. He glowed with inner warmth at the thought of it, as unreal as it might be.

'Then come with me,' she said, a grin on her face. He turned to her, without expression. 'We would be good travelling companions,' she went on, still playing with him. 'I can tell.'

'We barely know each other.'

'But we get along, don't we? You can tell these things in the first moment of meeting someone.'

'Please,' he said, 'enough.'

'Oh, you don't like the sound of it.' And she pulled a face.

'I think, right now, I would give anything to be able to do just that.'

The smile left her eyes. Nico felt the touch of her hand on his arm.

'Then what keeps you here? You are an apprentice, not a slave.'

'Because I owe Master Ash a great deal, that's why. We have . . . an arrangement, and I will not break it.'

'You think he would not release you, if he knew your true wishes?'

'I don't know what he would do,' replied Nico. 'He would feel wronged, at the very least.'

'Nico . . .' She sighed. 'Ash is a good man. You underestimate him. I have watched him when he and you are together. He cares for you.'

Nico stiffened, loosing her hand from his arm. 'I doubt that. He tolerates me, yes. Mostly though he avoids my company when he can.'

Softly, she said, 'For one so canny, you have something of a blind spot.'

He did not understand what she meant by that.

'It's his way to be reserved. Even those who have known him for a long time he keeps at arm's length. He has suffered much, Nico. All the old farlanders have. I think, even though he would deny it, he fears the pain of further loss in his life.'

Nico did not respond, and the sound of the splashing water filled the little garden instead. It had grown cool, meanwhile, so that he shivered, and realized that a dampness had taken to the air. Already, he could see hints of his own breath clouding before his eyes.

'It's getting cold,' he said.

'A fog comes,' she replied.

'Fog? Now? This place has some strange weather.'

'It's from the mountains on the mainland. We'd better head back if we do not wish to freeze.'

Nico took one last lingering look at the roof garden, and then he turned his back on it, forcing a smile on to his face. He said: 'Master Ash has a story about freezing. I will tell you it on our way back.'

*

The room offered a bleak welcome when he at last returned to the hostalio. It had taken his last remaining coin to open the door, and Nico fumbled in darkness within the washbasin for any remaining quarters that might still be lying at the bottom of it. He found one, fortunately, and used it to turn on the gas lamp. He then settled down on the top bunk with the thin blanket wrapped about him, thinking of the past few hours while his body slowly warmed itself.

Ash returned that night, seeming even more weary than before.

The old man bumped against the washbasin as though he did not even see it.

Another headache, thought Nico.

Ash merely grunted at him as he lay himself upon the lower bunk. Nico wondered what he had been doing all evening, and considered asking him outright, but Ash would most likely tell him to be quiet. Besides, he had other, more urgent, questions to press upon him.

'It is a cold night,' the old man said at last.

'Freezing.'

'Have you eaten yet?'

Nico realized he had not. 'No, but I'm not hungry. This place robs me of any desire for food.'

With care the old man raised himself from the bed. He rifled through his pack and pulled out some oatcake wrapped in wax paper.

'Master Ash . . .' Nico began, and waited for the old man to face him.

Ash offered him the oatcake. 'Eat,' he commanded, though Nico only shook his head.

'Master Ash, I wish to ask you something.'

'Then ask it.'

Nico took a deep breath, gathering his courage. 'I've been wondering. I'm not so certain I'm cut out for this – to be Rōshun.'

Ash blinked, as though he was having trouble focusing. He tore off the wrapping and bit off a chunk of the oatcake himself, still not taking his eyes from Nico.

In a torrent, the words tumbled from Nico's lips. 'I don't know if I have it in me. This work . . . it's worse than I expected it to be. And last night . . .' He shook his head. 'To fight as a soldier, to defend my homeland, perhaps that's one thing, but I'm not so certain of this.'

'Nico,' said the old man gently, his cheek stuffed with oatcake, 'if you do not wish to be my apprentice any longer, then tell me so, and I will settle things with you now so you may go home.'

Nico jerked upright. 'But what of our bargain?'

'You have seen it through as best you could. You have worked hard, and faced danger. Simply say the word. I will take you to the docks right now and find you a berth on a ship. You can stay onboard tonight, and by morning you can be sailing away from here. I will not hold it against you. I would do the same myself, if I could.'

Serèse had been right, he realized. This was a good man.

Ash wrapped up the rest of the cake and turned away, fumbling to stow it back in his pack.

'*Do* you wish to leave?' came the old man's words, absently, his back still to Nico.

Nico gazed down at the farlander. The old man seemed almost frail tonight in his weariness. The way he stood, slightly slumped over the pack, not moving, not even breathing it seemed, as he waited for a reply.

Ash's question hung in the air gathering in volume, creating a distance between them; they were strangers to each other in that moment, separated by diverging paths.

It came to Nico in a flash. *You're dying.*

He blinked at the old man, reflecting on the headaches, the constant use of the dulce leaves, the urge to take on an apprentice. Ash was ill, and knew it was only going to get worse for him.

It was suddenly too much for Nico. He thought: *I will never be able to live with myself, not for a second, if I leave this sick old farlander here, in this awful place, alone.*

'No master,' he heard himself say. 'I think this city is just getting to me, that's all.'

Ash remained a moment with his back turned to him, his shoulders swelling as he took a fresh breath.

When he turned around, the distance between them vanished; once again they were returned to their familiar roles of master and apprentice.

'You should get some sleep,' suggested Ash. 'It will be a long day tomorrow. We can speak more in the morning, if you wish.'

Nico lay down, his head propped on one arm. Ash assumed his meditation position on the floor. There he breathed silently, his eyes fixed on a particular spot on the door.

Nico gazed at the ceiling, not more than two feet above his head. He studied the cracks in the plaster, the warm light flickering against them, the dark patches where damp had taken hold. He listened to the occasional clatter of coins as they tumbled within the walls, deposited in the floors above, and finding their long way down the collection chutes to some secure vault in the hostalio basement far below.

He wondered how long the old man had left to him. It must be a disease of some kind, something terminal.

Nico would stay with him, despite his own doubts. Even though he knew this was really, a decision based on loyalty and compassion, rather than any real desire to remain.

When he fell asleep a short time later, he dreamed of burying the old man next to the grave he had made for Boon. Serèse was there, too. She spoke some words over the grave. Nico himself was silent: in place of a speech he lay the old man's sword against the packed earth. When they turned and walked away from the site, he felt a mixture of sadness and relief. It was as though with every step the heaviness in his stomach lightened.

He and Serèse carried packs on their backs. For an eternal time after that, Nico dreamed that they were travelling together, carefree and in love.

CHAPTER TWENTY-THREE

Ensnared

The sun sank fast in these mountains. By late afternoon the shadows they cast were already pooling into a bleak onset of twilight.

The column of Commandos made camp by a clear stream. They had been travelling hard for a full day now, on foot mostly, since they had left their zels in the coastal foothills along with a few of their men. Mules carried the heaviest of their baggage, more footsure in these mountains than the heavy thoroughbreds they had left behind. Purchased in Cheem Port with their imperial coin, men were unloading them now, mostly items of food and small disassembled pieces of artillery. Orders, when necessary, were given by silent hand gestures from the officers, who were distinguished only by the insignia of rank tattooed on their temples.

One by one the last of the purdas returned. These were the elite scouts of the imperial army, named after the hooded cloaks they wore, which were camouflaged with breaks of colour and featherings of grass and foliage. Each was accompanied by a large wolfhound, bred for this work. The purdas reported the surrounding area to be clear.

Regardless, a double ring of sentries was posted around the camp, squatting hidden from sight in their improvised hides. No fires were lit. The men's shelters were sheets of speckled canvas propped on sticks, each a lean-to just large enough for a man to crawl underneath and stay dry from any rainfall.

The Commandos worked smoothly and with little supervision. Their colonel, chewing on a plug of tarweed as he watched from the centre of the camp, gave a satisfied grunt before he left his men to it.

He headed away from the periphery of the camp towards the kneeling form of the Diplomat.

'This is it, then?' he asked gruffly, as he knelt beside the berry bush the young man was scrutinizing so closely.

Ché continued to stare down at the bush. He was dressed in simple leather armour beneath a heavy cloak of dyed grey wool. He wrapped it tighter about himself, and replied, 'It is.'

Cassus, the colonel, drew one of the black berries towards him, still on its branch. 'It looks remarkably like a skull,' he observed of the white markings upon it. 'I wouldn't wish to put such a thing in my mouth.'

'I don't eat it. I prepare it correctly, and smear some of the juice on my forehead. It is lethal to use it any other way.'

The colonel held the berry for a moment longer then released it, causing the small bush to quiver. Cassus stood and considered the man by his side. Ché did not look up.

'When will you take it?'

Some faint expression flickered across Ché's face, and was gone before it could be read. Again Cassus wondered what was troubling him.

The colonel liked to think of himself as a perceptive man. He knew this guide of theirs was struggling with something, some concern that was only worsening as they grew nearer to their goal. *He does not wish to be doing this,* Cassus often found himself thinking.

'In the morning,' announced Ché. 'The men will meanwhile need their rest. There's no telling how fast I may travel, or over what kind of terrain.'

'And you will be truly delirious the entire time?'

Ché's lips parted, showing teeth. 'Entirely out of my skull.'

The colonel did not like that, and he said as much. But he had complained before about this aspect of their mission, and the Diplomat had no further reassurances for him now. The man offered nothing but silence: it was not his concern.

Cassus turned and surveyed the camp, where the men had almost finished their preparations. Already, some were hunkering down beside their lean-tos to chew on their dried rations or talk quietly amongst themselves. Others had stripped off to bathe in the stream.

They had numbered eighty-two when they had first set out from Q'os: the colonel and eight squads of ten men each, a full company in all; plus one more to their number, this strange Diplomat sent to them from High Command. Two of the men had fallen ill during the voyage and therefore had remained on the ship; two more had been left behind to look after the zels; another had wrenched his ankle on the hike up into the mountains. Such losses were less than the colonel might have expected. That left him with seventy-seven men in all: not quite four platoons.

The colonel was worried, though. He had been worried even before they had set off on this hastily prepared mission. They faced upwards of fifty Rōshun, according to their Diplomat guide. Fifty Rōshun, on their own territory, defending their lives and their home. His Commandos might be the finest fighters in the imperial army, but he still disliked such odds.

Cassus had wondered why the Matriarch had not committed a full battalion of army regulars to back them up. A mission like this was surely best undertaken slowly, with large and overwhelming numbers. But he supposed the Beggar Kings of Cheem Port would have balked at such a force wishing to land at their docks, no matter how much gold was offered to them.

Besides, perhaps the rumours back home were true. Something was astir in the capital. Companies were being reformed out of the remnants of others; men from the quieter outposts of the Empire were being recalled to Q'os. The rumour-mongers had talked of only one thing, and Cassus judged them to be right. He had taken part in more than one invasion himself.

Ché rose from his study of the bush and met the colonel's eyes at last. Once more, Cassus felt himself stiffen under the young man's cold and empty gaze.

'The morning, then,' agreed the colonel, speaking around his lump of tarweed.

Ché nodded and walked away.

Cassus watched as the young man staked out a lean-to well away from the others, and threw his pack beneath it. The man sat in front of his crude shelter with his legs folded, facing the last of the light, his hands clasped together, his eyes closed.

He looked like one of those fool-crazy monks of the Dao.

A few of the men took notice of what he was doing, as they had back on the ship. They nudged each other, leering quietly.

He's a dangerous one, Cassus mused. *I wouldn't like to cross him.* The colonel turned away, spitting upon the grass as he did so. *Well, soon we will face fifty of his like.*

He filled his lungs with mountain air, scanning the snow-capped ranges around their camp. He knew they were out there somewhere, hidden in some high valley behind their monastery walls.

Surprise, he thought as he contemplated this mission once more. *It will all come down to surprise.*

*

Nico awoke with a start.

The room flickered with gaslight. Ash sat on the floor, still deep in meditation, his hooded eyes fixed to the same spot on the door. Nico rubbed his tired eyes. He had no way of telling how long he had been asleep. An hour perhaps?

Someone shouted outside in the hallway, complaining with the loud senseless words of a drunk.

It was the only warning they had.

The door burst inwards with a crash against the wall, sending out a puff of chalky plaster. Nico's body clenched with the sudden shock of it. He opened his mouth, perhaps to shout something, perhaps simply to gasp. Instead he found the strangest of things occurring: time slowed for him, hovering on the edge of that first instant.

From the corner of his eye, he saw Ash's hand reach for the blade by his side. But Nico knew that it would encounter only emptiness. The sword was stowed in a canvas roll beneath the bed, where he had replaced it earlier after his return. In the doorway, he saw the white press of Acolytes as they rushed through it one at a time. Their robes seemed caught in mid-motion, like a painting, the folds in them given depth with shadows and highlights, the curious silk patterns in the cloth shimmering in the light. He saw the naked length of steel in the grip of the foremost man, brandished like an extension of his arm. An oily sheen ran along the blade, sea blue, corn yellow, moist-earth brown; while a reflection of the gaslight shone close to the hilt, like a miniature sun. He saw the man's mask, and how its many apertures were in deep blackness save for the whites of his eyes – fixed now on the old farlander squatting on the floor, caught unarmed and unawares.

And then time whiplashed back to normal, and all was chaos and a great roar was filling Nico's ears, shocking the senses from him further, and he realized that Ash was the source of it, still squatting there and doing the only thing possible as the lead Acolyte lunged at him with his blade.

It was a primal shout, like nothing Nico had ever heard before, like nothing he would ever have thought possible from a human throat. It was shaped and directed with such commanding force that Ash's attacker was stunned for a moment, and dropped the weapon clean from his hand as though it had turned red hot.

It was enough to give Ash the second that he needed to jump up and grab the only loose furniture in the small room. A chair. He swung it full-force into the Acolyte's face. Bones cracked behind the mask, and the man reeled backwards into those trying to push in from behind. The farlander charged into him, shoved them all back, with his own momentum, through the doorway. Somehow he got the door closed against their weight. He rammed his back against it, holding it shut.

'Nico . . .' he said with a measure of coolness that frightened Nico more than calmed him. 'Throw me a coin, boy, quickly now.' And he jerked his head to the washbasin, now out of his reach, where they kept the change needed to feed the room's various coinslots.

Nico scrambled down from his bunk as Ash fought with the door, which shook violently and tried to jerk him out of its way. '*Hurry*,' Ash hissed.

Nico reached the basin. He fumbled for a coin, not seeing any, and suddenly he feared he had already used their last – but no, his fingers found one where his eyes had not, and he plucked it up, tossing it to Ash.

Ash caught it in one hand and in the same motion twisted and dropped it through the slot on the doorframe. He turned the key, and relaxed his stance only slightly as the lock clicked into place; hammering could be heard against the quivering wood, and Ash still pressed himself against it, clearly not trusting much to the lock's strength.

Nico took a pace towards him, then turned and took a step towards the shuttered window instead. He stopped there, paralysed with indecision.

Ash frowned at him just as an axe blade cut through the door beside the old man's head, spitting a shower of bright splinters. 'The window, boy. The window!'

Nico didn't have to be told twice. It was their only way out. He rushed over and pushed at the shutters . . . except they didn't open, and refused to budge in his hands. They required a coin.

Nico cursed as he again fished in the sink for another one, though this time he knew he had used them all.

He turned to Ash blindly, wringing his hands, too panicked to think straight.

'The purse!' Ash hollered. '*There! On the bed!*'

Sure enough, when Nico fumbled open the purse he found a quarter amongst the other coins, and he took it to the coinslot, and tried inserting it with shaking fingers into the hole; but then he fumbled and dropped it, and had to chase after the thing as it rolled back across the room all the way to Ash's feet.

Ash shouted something he didn't hear. Nico scooped up the coin and returned to the window frame. His aim was truer this time and the quarter rattled out of sight. Nico forced the shutters open. He took a vigorous breath of air. Outside it was dark and thick with fog. He stuck his head out to look down at the alley some four floors below. He couldn't see any way down, no fire escapes or nearby drainpipes.

'We're trapped!' he cried, and leaned his head back inside just as something shattered against the frame. He stared at the broken end of a crossbow bolt as it clattered off the sill. Someone was shooting down at him from the opposite roof.

Nico scrambled back from the window.

Ash was shouting something about making a jump for it to the window opposite. The window in question was shuttered closed – and in a building a good seven feet away. Nico knew he would never have it in him to try such a leap.

'*Nico!*' roared his master, and Nico looked back to see the door was beginning to come apart around him, the axe blade chopping the planking loose.

He regained his feet, discovered that he had grabbed the fallen chair in his hands. He ran for the window and tossed the chair out into the night. The fog swirled in its wake as it crashed against the shutters on the opposite side. 'Open up,' he yelled after it, hanging back cautiously from the window. 'Open up!'

The shutters parted just enough for a face to peer out. Nico saw an old man squinting across at him. It was the same old fellow he had seen on his first day here, constructing things from matchsticks.

'Please,' Nico shouted. He snatched up the money purse. With a heave, he tossed it across the alley and in between the shutters into the old man's room. 'Take it!' he told him.

The shutters closed firmly once more. Nico almost sobbed, though, in truth, part of him was greatly relieved. Another crossbow bolt shattered the frame an inch away from his hand. He darted further back into the room.

Suddenly the opposite shutters opened wide. The old man grinned a toothless grin and beckoned with one hand. Then shuffled aside to make room.

Nico's stomach dropped away. He thought of making that leap. It brought memories of his fall back in Bar-Khos, when he had pitched from the roof of the taverna. It was not the fall itself he recalled so vividly, because he had never been able to remember it much; it was the moment before he fell, when he had slid towards the edge and then hung there for an instant, scrabbling for a hold that never came to hand.

He could see Acolytes' masks through the widening gaps in the door now, and Ash risking his neck with every chop of the axe that came through it.

'I can't do it,' Nico told him.

Ash said nothing for a moment but, with the deepest understanding, he glowered. 'Our blades then. Throw our blades across.'

Nico frowned, but he did as he was bidden. He turned his back and scrabbled under the bed for their weapons, dragging the canvas rolls out into the light. He made for the window and tossed them across to the room opposite.

He failed to hear Ash approach from behind – the destruction of the door was too loud for that. It was a surprise then when the old man dragged him from the window back towards the door, or what was left of it, and even more of a surprise when he picked Nico up by the seat of his pants and the scruff of his neck. He growled some farlander words of encouragement and charged for the window, with Nico yelling and flapping his arms as Ash swung him hard and sent him sailing out into clear space.

Nico arced across the alleyway. For an instant, he even thought he was going to make it.

He didn't. The opposite window rose away from him before he could reach it, and all of a sudden there he was again, back in that nightmare moment he had feared most of all, falling fast to his death.

This time though, with sweet mercy, his outstretched hands clipped against something and managed to grab hold. It was the jutting windowsill, and he swung with a hard shock into the wall, and hung there by his fingertips, his bare toes scrabbling for a purchase against the coarse brickwork.

He glimpsed Ash leaping across the same space above his head, his cloak flapping as a flying bolt just missed him, diving headfirst into the room. And then he was there at the window, yanking Nico up and inside.

Nico lay panting on the floor. The old match man leered down at him, his gums chopping in excitement, as he sat on a bunk beside a replica ranch house built of matchsticks – and entirely ignored by Ash, as the Rōshun kicked open the canvas roll to unfold across the floor, before he yanked out their two sheathed blades. He tossed Nico his sword as he struggled up from the floor, levelled his own just as the first Acolyte leapt through the window behind them.

Ash shoved Nico out of the way, and ducked a fast swipe aimed at his neck. He thrust his blade through the Acolyte's belly, in and out, as quick as that. He kicked the man out of the way and lunged at another white-robed assailant, even as he, too, was leaping through. This one fared better. He batted Ash's blade aside with one hand, forcing him to swerve from a return jab to the face.

They struck and parried in a fast exchange, blades scraping and ringing, scattering Nico and the old match man towards the door of the small room, and destroying the furniture all around them in their frenzy. Remarkably, the matchstick ranch house remained untouched.

Nico struggled for the door of the room and pulled it open. He had to get out of there.

He stumbled out into a dark corridor with his blade drawn. Ash knocked into him, stepping backwards through the doorway too, still fending off the Acolyte. A quick glance showed more of the attackers leaping across and into the room. The toothless old man was sitting back out of their way, clapping his hands with glee.

Nico ran off along the corridor, Ash close on his heels. A startled face at a doorway; another door slammed shut; a stairwell leading up and down. Nico leapt down the stairs, three steps at a time. He hooked his hand on the banister and swung himself around each turn, down one floor after another until at last he had reached the bottom. He could see his way to the front door at the end of a long hallway.

Ash grabbed him as he fled towards it. The old farlander jerked him back, pushed him in the opposite direction while white flashes came flying down the stairwell they had just left.

Washrooms, dirty sinks and scrubbing boards for clothes and a harsh smell of starch in the air; he could hear the whine of his own breath in his throat, the slap of his bare soles against the tiled floor as he turned this way and that; a moment of elation, a gaslight on the wall illuminating the back door of the building, and then Nico went bursting through it into a fog-filled night – and into a sudden eruption of noise.

Chips of stone flew all around him. He stood fixed to the spot, unsure of what was happening, or why his ears pounded under a quick succession of deafening cracks. And then he realized he was being fired upon by a great number of rifles. More rifles than he had ever heard before.

He would have been perforated with shots if Ash had not tripped him and sent him sprawling to the ground. They both crawled out into the deep fog, well away from the light spilling from the doorway. The fog obscured them from sight as shots whipped above their scalps. Behind them, the pursuing Acolytes hung back inside the doorway of the building, not risking themselves to the maintained volleys of fire from their colleagues. Ash and Nico crawled along the street. Nico did not even feel the pain of its rough surface in his knees and elbows. When they were far enough away Ash tugged him up on to shaky legs, holding firmly to his arm.

They made a run for it. There weren't any street lights here, but still someone spotted them. Shouts rang out, and then the sounds of pursuit.

A shape challenged them from ahead, but fell in silence at a slash from Ash's blade. Nico leapt the body, not giving it a second thought. More shapes, and Ash flicked out with his sword again, never slowing in his stride. Nico had dropped his own blade somewhere along the way. He didn't care. A flyer passed overhead, just above the rooftops, black and fast enough to be seen through the fog, circling the immediate district.

The entire area appeared to be surrounded and they could spot movement whenever they passed better-lit streets than this one. As they came to a T-junction opening into a well-lit thoroughfare, the sound of firing brought them to a halt. They ducked back, seeing both ends blocked off.

Nico cowered against a wall, trying to find a hiding space that was not there. At every shot fired, his body tensed in expectation of instant pain. Ash pulled him roughly out into the street. They crossed it moving as low and fast as they could. Cries from both ends betrayed the occasional victims of friendly fire.

A building ahead, squat and uglier than most in this city. Its doorway was without a door, black as night. They fell through it into a stinking space without light, sparks flying and chips of stone raining down from the outer edges of the doorway behind them.

They stumbled deeper inside, the dimly seen walls covered in the faint impressions of graffiti. It was a public latrine, with a row of privy holes ranged against one wall.

Ash strode to the rear of the small building, where a few grimy narrow windows ran high up along the back wall. He smashed one with the hilt of his sword, cleared away the jagged edges.

'We must split up, boy. I am much faster on my own. If you hide I can lead them away from you.'

Nico cast a glance about him. 'Hide? Where?'

Ash swept his gaze along the row of privy holes, in a single wooden bench covered with dubious stains. The old man tugged at it till he had wrenched the bench up from its mounting. The smell was enough to make him gag. Beside him, Nico began to retch.

As his master confronted him, Nico backed away, appalled, from the expression on his face. He knew what Ash was proposing, and started to shake his head slowly, with determination.

'You want to die here?'

'Don't leave me then. We'll make a run for it together.'

'We are trapped, Nico. We must be creative and find a way out of this for you at least. Now, get in.'

'I won't do it.'

'*Please*, Nico. Listen, they come.'

It was true. The sound of footfalls could be heard, pounding along the street outside.

'Now!' commanded Ash, and entirely against his will, Nico felt his body step over to the gaping space of the exposed privy.

A hard shove sent him toppling into it, where he landed on his back. His body settled into a sodden, stinking mound which had the consistency of mud, and which tried to claim him. He retched again, and this time he vomited.

'Hush!' whispered Ash from above him as he lifted the privy bench back into place.

Nico clamped a hand across his mouth, gagging and shivering in silence. 'Make your way to the docks when it is clear,' instructed Ash through one of the holes. 'You will see a statue of one of their generals – you cannot miss it. I shall meet you there at dawn if I can. But if I do not return, Nico, then leave this city. Go home to your mother. Live a long life and think well of me.'

The old farlander tossed down a purse of coins. It clinked mutedly in the foulness next to him.

'Farewell, my boy.'

'Master Ash!'

But Ash was gone. Nico could hear him slithering out through the window, and then footsteps scraped by the entrance, and someone shouted, and they were after him.

Others remained behind. Lamplight flickered through the holes overhead; shadows passed by, the scuff of heavy boots and the closeness of shouted commands echoing in the reeking space immediately overhead. Nico closed his eyes and tried to breathe in without gagging. He tried, with all his will, not to think of what they would do to him if he was caught.

Light flickered against his eyelids, but by the time he had gathered enough courage to look upwards it was already fading.

The chase moved on. The room overhead became dark and silent.

He waited. He heard more shots in the distance. A scream. People shouting.

Nico lost track of time. He found that not moving at all was the best way to minimize the sensation of the ordure against his skin. He lay in perfect stillness, trying to breathe without actually breathing.

He wondered how Ash fared, and was certain, despite the sheer scale of the trap set around them, that his master would find a way clear of it. That at least gave Nico some hope.

Dogs barked. Again voices. Nico's heart stopped in mid-beat as footsteps returned to the entrance.

'They searched in there already,' came a woman's voice.

'Those idiots? They might be good at waving their swords around, but I doubt their skills at observation.'

Boots scraped overhead once more. A lamp flickered, casting shadows.

'Where is Stano? Did you see him?' The woman's voice sounded worried.

'Aye, the Rōshun ran him through in the fog. Bad luck, that.'

'Dead?'

'He looked it.'

The woman seemed displeased at that. 'When we catch these bastards, I will have first crack at them.'

'Be my guest.'

The voice was directly overhead now. Lamplight shone through the hole. Nico cringed away from it.

A face appeared. Its eyes met his.

Suddenly, teeth shone bright.

CHAPTER TWENTY-FOUR

Waiting by Mokabi

The fog had barely thinned by dawn.

It blanketed the streets like a layer of vaporous snow, obscuring everything within it and everything without, even the rising sun itself, which was just a vague glow without heat. Daylight, for those unfortunate enough to be up and about at this early hour, was nothing but a thin luminescence that added form to the morning chill. Pedestrians collided awkwardly on the pavements. Carts ran across the paths of other carts, while draft mules snapped teeth at each other in their nervousness. The fog reeked: it clung to the backs of throats, stung the eyes. It coated every surface with moisture, so that even the sagging flags of the district dripped wetly.

Ash hurried along the street. His cloak was sodden through, as were his clothes beneath it. He carried his sword with him still, though he kept it hidden from sight. Dried blood stained his hand where it had trickled from his reopened wound. The old farlander walked with a slight limp.

Ahead, the monument reared up through the fog, a huge spike rising into the murk. Struggling figures were spitted along its vertical length, their death throes frozen in skilfully cast bronze. Ash stopped beneath it: General Mokabi, three times larger than life, stood at the base of the spike, looking outwards. His expression was fixed in a victor's triumph, though it was a hard-won victory as seen in the weary lines of his flesh. He held arms akimbo, his head slightly thrown back: as though relishing the admiration of others at this his greatest achievement.

Nico was nowhere to be seen.

Ash released a breath and sat down heavily upon the parapet encircling the monument. He winced as he took the weight from his feet.

Dawn was turning to early morning. He wrapped the cloak tighter around himself, though the damp wool held little warmth. He did not stir again. After a while it was as though he became part of the monument itself, so that, as the traffic increased across the surrounding square, no one noticed him sitting there, waiting.

Mid-morning passed into late morning. Still no sign of Nico.

The old farlander stood up, and walked for a time around the base of the monument, to work some heat back into his legs. He scanned the surrounding fog as he went. In the distance, a clock chimed out the hour.

By early afternoon, Ash sat down again with his sword in his lap, courting trouble – it was against the law to openly bear arms within the city. His thumb stroked the leather scabbard, his gaze darting out from the folds of his hood. A breeze stirred from the sea, which lay somewhere off to his right. Autumn leaves scuttled dry and brittle along the ground, shed from trees he could not see. The fog stirred, creating spaces within itself, though it still refused to lift.

The clock chimed again. Slowly, Ash rose. '*Nico!*' he cried out.

The sound of his voice was muted, lost in the wrapping of fog.

Around his ankles the dead leaves swirled. The old man hung his head.

*

'Tell me, precisely now, what happened?'

It was Baracha, and he was losing patience with his comrade.

Ash sat for some moments in silence.

The boulders they all sat upon were slick with dampness, giving the appearance of black, volcanic rock. Here and there, within depressions on the rock surfaces, minute pools of brackish water reflected bands of twilight, breaking occasionally into free-running rivulets that ended in slow monotonous drips. Nearby, a gull pecked half-heartedly at a dead crab.

'I hid him away, and tried to lead them on a chase. It was a mistake.'

'You think so?' remarked Baracha, sarcastically.

'Father,' Serèse interrupted sharply.

Ash stared down at the wavelets lapping against the stones at his feet. The sea was out there somewhere, hidden and silent save for these fringes of itself.

Aléas tried to speak, but it emerged as a croak. He tried again. 'It's hardly Master Ash's fault. It's a miracle he got out at all.' Baracha glowered at his young apprentice, but Aléas spoke on. 'We would have been captured ourselves if not for Serèse's sharp eyes.'

He was the first to state aloud what they all knew must have happened to Nico. *Captured.*

'What happened to you?' inquired Ash, looking up from the water's edge.

'Serèse thought we were being watched when she returned to the hostalio, so we slipped out before they could make a move against us. If not,' and he met his master's eyes before he said it, 'we would have all been as geese in a bag.'

They were quiet for a time. It was not a comfortable silence shared amongst comrades; instead it was an individual isolation, each wrapped in their own concerns. The wavelets washed against the shore. Behind, the city murmured on, its sounds subdued and ghostly.

Baracha studied the old farlander perched on his rock. He shook his head again. 'You're pondering something. Out with it.'

'In the morning, we should proceed with the plan.'

'We should, should we? That would leave us little time to prepare, Ash.'

'These fogs tend to last for a few days. Tomorrow should continue the same as today. After that, who knows?'

Baracha stroked his beard, beads of water dripping from its frazzled ends.

'Plan?' inquired Serèse. 'What plan?'

'I have made some arrangements,' replied Ash, 'which might gain us entrance to the tower.'

'But what of Nico?' she demanded. 'Are we simply going to leave him in their hands? Sweet Erēs, what must he be going through even now, while we sit here glum and bickering between ourselves?'

Gently, Ash replied: 'I am well aware of what he will be going through, Serèse. We will not be forsaking him. By now he will be held within the Temple of Whispers, for that is where the Regulators work from. So. If we wish to save Nico, that is where we must go anyway.'

'Save him?' snapped Baracha, standing tall. 'We'll do no such thing! The boy is lost to us, and we all know it. We can risk no more lives on fools' errands. If we storm the temple, we do so to take down Kirkus. *That* is our mission here, nothing else.'

'And we shall stay true to our mission. But before we finish with Kirkus, he will tell us where to find Nico. You may do what you like then. I will go and find my apprentice.'

'And I, too,' agreed Aléas.

'You'll do as you're told, boy,' snapped the Alhazii. 'As soon as we finish our task, you'll be leaving along with me. For if you're even still alive by then it will be a miracle in itself, and I will risk you no further.' His bluntness stunned Aléas to silence. 'And you, daughter, all fired up and spirited, I know what you're intending, but I tell you right now, you will not be coming with us. I will not risk you at all.'

'You can't stop me, father.'

Baracha took a step towards her, his big fists clenched. He restrained himself with a visible effort. 'I can stop you,' he told her – and none doubted it.

Serèse flung herself to her feet, her own fists clenched, and glared up at his towering bulk. 'If it was your own apprentice, *father*, would you not attempt to rescue him?'

'Perhaps,' he admitted, while avoiding Aléas's gazes 'if there was any chance of success. But since when did I owe that boy anything? Ash should have taken better care at looking out for him. It's hardly my fault he has fallen into their hands.'

Serèse turned away in disgust.

'He is right, Serèse,' said Ash, raising a palm. 'You cannot come with us. We will need someone to remain outside, to provide a means for our escape. Getting in is one thing, but your father speaks the plain truth. It will be a miracle if any of us survive. If we do, then getting away will require yet another. We will need you for that most of all.'

His words placated her a little, and she slumped back against the rock.

'We must be quick,' continued Ash, 'if we are to procure everything we will need. I fear it will require most of our remaining funds.'

Serèse studied the old man's face. 'Do you really think you can save him?'

Before he could reply, Baracha spat on the shingle between them. 'We're not doing this to save the boy – will you get that into your skulls, all of you? For all we know he is dead already.'

They all turned away from each other once more. Ash stared out to sea again, studying it not by his eyes but by his ears. Baracha picked up a pebble, threw it clattering into the rocks nearby.

A flap of wings caught Ash's attention. He was in time to turn and catch the after-image of a startled gull, flying off; it was the emptiness mostly that he saw, the space it had just occupied. He looked up and saw the white gull gliding into whiteness.

A simple smile crept over his features. He threw his hood back, took a deep breath.

'He lives,' he declared.

Baracha frowned. Aléas and Serèse turned to him, expectant.

'How could you know that?' Baracha demanded.

'An intuition,' he said. 'The boy lives. And he is in need.'

*

Nico had no idea where he was.

Upon his capture, they had manacled his wrists together and shoved a hood over his head. It had been a terrifying experience – the dislocation of sight, the heavy cloth pressing against his face as he panted and struggled to breathe, the rough hands digging into his flesh, shoving and pushing him one way and the other, the slaps, the shouts, the disorientation. Voices had risen in excitement all around him. A rider had been dispatched, bearing the message that a Rōshun had been caught, the clatter of hooves fading away down the unseen street. Nico had been thrown into a cart of some sort, the smell of his own filth-smeared clothes gagging him as it rocked along over the cobbles. They had crossed a bridge, or else some other structure made of wood. After the iron-rimmed wheels of the cart trundled across it, the vehicle stopped for a heavy gate to be opened, and then it passed through a stone entranceway, and halted again. Nico had been hauled out and shoved roughly along a stone-flagged floor, up some steps, through another door.

He stood now in a room of some sort. He could tell it was large by the echoes heard through the heavy cloth of the hood. A woman shouted somewhere in the distance, the sound of her tirade terminated by a loud clanging impact.

The scent of hazii smoke filled the air. People were conversing in low voices somewhere off to his left.

'Keys,' the male Regulator demanded, by Nico's side.

'I'll need the contract if you still have it.' It was another male voice, a new one, breathy as from the lungs of a heavy smoker.

There was a rustle of crumpled paper being unfolded next to Nico's ear.

'You only lifted the one, huh?'

'One more than you ever caught, Malsh,' quipped the female Regulator.

The smoker chuckled like a cat hacking up a fur ball, as he approached the prisoner. Nico heard the metal rasp of scissors opening, and then someone was cutting the clothes from his body without further fuss.

'I'll need a name, too, for processing,'

The woman's voice was heavy with intent. 'Forthcoming,' she drawled.

*

Nico was led naked and still hooded through a series of iron doors that were opened in turn before him, and closed again behind, a collection of keys jangling each time. The stone floor felt gritty underfoot.

A man was talking loudly, directly ahead, his voice rebounding along the narrow passageway. He was reciting a verse or a poem of some kind, in a language only half Trade and half something else, and as Nico was manhandled onwards, the same voice neared until it seemed to be right next to his face, and then it was passing behind him, and fading faster than seemed right.

The passage veered in a gradual curve to the right. Soon it was sloping downwards, too, so that Nico stumbled along near falling each time his feet trod on air.

The Regulators stopped him with a crunch of halting feet, then turned him around.

The noise of an iron door opening on its hinges sounded like the panicked shriek of a young girl.

Nico was shoved through a doorway, his manacled hands flailing ahead of his tottering feet. The door closed with a crash, changing the sound of the confined space.

At first he thought he was alone, but then he heard the scuff of a boot, and then another from a different direction. He sensed the two Regulators breathing on either side of him.

'Lie on the floor,' ordered the man.

'What?'

'*Lie on the floor,*' repeated the woman.

Nico was trembling. He could hear, absurdly, his own teeth chatter.

His knees began to fold beneath him, and then he was getting down on the floor, his chin resting on the stone, his ribs pressing sharp against its hardness.

He heard the squeak of leather, as fingers flexed. He heard this sound four times in all.

The first kick was enough to loosen his bladder. His body clenched around itself, and he gasped at the howl of white pain deep inside him.

'He's pissed himself already,' observed the woman.

And then they laid into him properly.

Nico tried to crawl away from their blows. He could hear his own voice screaming out for them to stop. He would have told them anything at that point, for he could find no courage in this situation, stripped not only of clothes but of dignity, of spirit.

But they asked him nothing. They merely took turns at stamping on his legs, or smashing his head against the floor, or kicking his ribs; not in a frenzied way, but slowly, methodically, as though this was everday work to them, and they wanted to make a thorough job of it.

They were going to kill him eventually; he was sure of it. But as his head began to swim in a fog of darkness, the door squealed open, and the blows ceased without warning.

'Holy Matriarch,' panted the man with obvious surprise.

Footsteps and a swirling of robes.

'Let me see him,' came a different woman's voice.

The hood was pulled free of his face. Nico lay gasping for air and squinting at the brilliance of a single lantern set on the floor.

He opened one bloody eye just wide enough to take in the newcomers. The two Regulators were bowing low at the waist as they faced a tall woman of middle years. She wore the familiar white robes of the Mannian order. At her side stood a youth, even taller, trim and athletic, clad also in white robes.

'Have you administered the witspice yet?' inquired the Matriarch. They all looked down at Nico, bleeding on to the cool stone floor. 'No, we've been softening him up first.'
'Very well. You may administer it now.'

Orders were quickly given to someone outside the cell. An old priest appeared, holding a twist of white paper in one palm. He knelt beside Nico. Gently, he touched the boy's face until Nico looked up into his eyes. A healer perhaps, Nico thought. The old man unfolded the paper. As he blew across it, a fine white dust caught Nico full in the face.

He coughed, rubbed at his burning eyes. Then weariness seized hold of him, spread him out across the floor. His thoughts began to swim through a thick haze as though he was midway to sleep. Dreams surfaced occasionally, only to disappear again without trace.

Nico experienced only fragments after that.

*

Leave us, commanded a woman's voice.
    Matriarch? said another.
    I would speak with him.
    As you command.
Nico was walking along a narrow mountain path. Goats chewed on the sparse grasses above him, watching him from the corners of their eyes as he passed.

Baa! he cried out, letting them know that he was aware of their attention.

    Why does he make such a noise?
    It's the spice. He's partly in his dreams now.
Nico was thirsty, and he could scent water ahead. He crested a rise and looked down into a ravine. A river gushed along the rocks at its bottom. He grinned.

Boy! a voice commanded, from somewhere high.

Nico looked up into a woman's face. It was a plain face, but made ugly by the emotions shining through from behind. He was reminded of a bird, something black and malicious.

She was asking him questions, and he was talking . . . talking about his master and the city and what they were doing here. A young man stood by her side, staring down at him. His expression grew meaner as Nico talked, the lips curling back. A wolf making ready to attack.

The woman stared with eyes hard as glass, unblinking. It seemed that if he kept talking she might stop fixing him with that hungry stare. Nico wanted away from it. He wanted to return to his own private space. He talked of Cheem, and the monastery in the mountains there. He talked of Aléas, Baracha, old Oshō. He talked of the ancient Seer up in his hut, how he might scratch at his lice but could do things Nico still did not understand.

Stop rambling, demanded the woman, and she clutched his face in her talons.

She asked of his master again: what he was planning on doing next. Nico told her of the Temple of Whispers, how they had considered ways in which they might get inside it, so they could find Kirkus, and slay him.

She became angry at him then, though he didn't know why. Perhaps he had forgotten his chores again. Perhaps he'd had another shouting match with Los.

She squeezed his face hard, then stood up.

Perhaps your grandmother was right, she said to the young man by her side. *If this is what they're training to be Rōshun these days, there is little to be feared.*

She hovered over Nico. A drop of spittle appeared between her thin, ruby lips. It stretched and fell, plopped against his closed eye.

You came here to murder my son, little Rōshun. So I tell you now, your friends will soon be dead, your order destroyed, and you – she prodded him with a toe, and he flinched from it – *we will make an example of you.*

The young man was breathing heavily. He wanted to tear Nico apart. *I'll finish him now, myself,* he growled.

No. You may have some fun with him, but keep him alive. The games are to be held again tomorrow. We'll send him there. Are you listening, young pup? Again she nudged Nico with a toe. *We'll send you to the Shay Madi, where you can meet your death in front of the crowds. They can witness how fierce the Rōshun truly are, and how we must tremble before them.*

She swept away, her robe a billowing mass behind her.

The young man grinned with sharp teeth.

He stamped hard upon Nico's hand, so that something cracked inside it.

Nico screamed.

CHAPTER TWENTY-FIVE

Bravery of Fools

A procession was leaving the Temple of Whispers. It was a royal procession, a fact made apparent from its size and grandeur and the banners it displayed, those of the Matriarch herself, showing a black raven on a white background. From the rooftop, Aléas, Baracha and Ash watched as it crossed the bridge over the moat and wound its slow way eastwards, where the games were to be held today, in the Shay Madi.

Along the streets, red-garbed devotees rushed in their hundreds to see this unexpected procession of the Holy, crying out as though their wits had fled them entirely. Columns of Acolytes emerged and disappeared again in the thick fog like ghosts of men, some detaching in squads to hold back the press of devotees. Palanquins borne by dozens of slaves swayed past, one after the other, their occupants hidden behind heavy, embroidered curtains. Lesser priests pounded on drums, or gyrated in a rising frenzy, or whipped their bare backs with the branches of thorny bushes. Aléas watched closely, counting them as they went by.

'It might help us,' said Baracha, tensely, 'with so many gone from the Temple.'

Ash replied with a shrug, then he straightened up and began to sort items from a canvas bag that lay open on the concrete roof. Today he was dressing for vendetta, as they all were. He wore reinforced boots, tan leather leggings padded around the knees, a stout belt, a loose sleeveless tunic, and bracers. Over this he threw on a heavy white robe that reached down to his toes. Baracha donned an identical robe. They stood facing one another, flexing their limbs in their new garments.

'Stiff,' Ash grunted.

'Like wearing a sack of canvas,' Baracha agreed.

These priestly robes would have to do; they had been easier to replicate than the fully armoured dress of the Acolytes.

Beside the two men, Aléas tugged a cloak from his own bag and began to shrug it over his head.

'No,' ordered Baracha, 'not yet.'

The big man hoisted a harness of heavy leather, slipping it over Aléas's shoulders so that it was fastened in an X across his torso. To this, he and Ash began to secure the various tools of their trade, or at least those they had been able to gather together, throughout the night, from the various black-market traders they knew within the city. These consisted of a set of throwing knives, their blades perforated with a series of holes for lightness; a small crowbar; a foldable grappling hook and climbing claws; pouches of ground jupe bark mixed with barris seed, along with pouches of flash powder; an axe with separate haft extensions; crossbow bolts; two bags of caltrops; a medico, and a coil of thin knotted rope; a leather flask of water; two small casks of blackpowder, air-tightened with tar, more difficult and expensive to procure than all the rest of the equipment combined. It was a ridiculously heavy burden, and Aléas soon felt his legs buckle beneath the weight.

'You're going to be acting as our pack mule,' his master explained. 'Which means you stick to us no matter what, and whenever we call out for something you pass it to us quick.'

Baracha hefted a small, twin-firing crossbow. 'When you're not passing us gear,' he said, thrusting the crossbow into the young man's arms, 'you'd damn well better be shooting at someone.'

Aléas jerked his head, straining a nod. The tension was growing in him.

Ash helped get the robe over his sudden additional bulk.

'You look like a pregnant fishwife,' he said, clapping a hand to the lad's shoulder.

Aléas frowned, and waddled around, making exaggerated movements. He could tell from their expressions that he wasn't a pretty sight.

The temple bell struck eight o'clock.

'Your army is late,' commented Baracha.

'Have faith. It will be here.'

Ash returned to the parapet. He set one foot up on the ledge, supporting his crossed arms on his raised knee. He watched the last of the royal procession pass by. He looked up at the tower. For a time, he simply stood and took it in.

They were located on the safest vantage point they had been able to find, the high-up roof of a casino built on a street that ran along the perimeter of the moat. The premises were still open at this early hour, if the lights and sounds pouring from a few open windows below were anything to go by. Aléas shifted his weight from one foot to the other, afraid to sit down, in case he could not get up again unaided. He joined Ash at the parapet, though after a moment of looking at the tower he gazed out instead over the rest of the city, the merest outline of it visible through the fog.

I might die today, echoed his mind, as though detached from the fact.

His stomach seemed on fire.

Behind him, he heard his master reciting the morning prayer. He knew, without looking, that Baracha would be kneeling with his arms folded across his chest, his face turned towards the faint hint of the sun. Today he would ask for courage in his prayer, and the blessings of the true prophet Zabrihm.

Ash, too, knelt on the flat rooftop, and assumed a posture of meditation.

'Come,' he said to Aléas. 'Join me.'

Why not, thought Aléas, and struggled with his load until he was kneeling beside him.

Aléas breathed deeply, seeking stillness. It would not come easily, though, for his body was agitated, tense. It was at times like this that he wished he genuinely believed in the power of prayer like Baracha. Instead, he performed his own litany: his own private call for meaning.

I do this for my friend, he asserted. *Because he deserves my loyalty, and because I was born of Mann, and have much to redeem for my peoples' ways. If I die, I do so with righteousness.*

If I die, I –

Footsteps, sounding from across the rooftop.

'Your army,' announced Baracha dryly, climbing to his feet.

Aléas turned his head, as a man appeared out of the fog and stepped towards them, his eyes goggling as he took in their attire.

'So you crazy fools really mean to go through with it, eh?'

'You're late,' responded Baracha.

The man plucked the tattered top hat from his head. 'My apologies,' he said,' and he bowed so low that the hat in his hand almost scraped across the concrete roof. 'The directions your girl gave me were somewhat scant, but I'm here now, and I have what you need.'

As they all gathered to face him, Aléas could smell the man's stench even across the distance of several feet. His thinning hair hung in lank strings from his scalp, flaked with dandruff, and his scrawny body hunched unprepossessingly beneath a soiled flapcoat. When he scratched at himself, Aléas could see the man's fingernails were caked with dirt. When he grinned, his teeth resembled a brown mush.

The newcomer exhaled wetly as he extracted something from the deep pocket of his coat. It was a rat, and the creature began to struggle as he held it out by the tail. The animal was entirely white, its eyes pink.

From another pocket the man took out a sachet of folded paper. He opened it up with one hand to reveal a minute amount of white powder.

He blew it into the face of the rat. The creature twitched and made a sound that might have been a sneeze.

Fascinated, Aléas watched as their visitor began to swing the rat to and fro, the animal struggling all the while. At a certain moment he exaggerated the swing, so that the rat sailed upwards, around, and right into his gaping mouth. He clamped his mouth shut, the pink tail dangling limp from between his lips.

The man looked, in turn, at each of their faces, registering shock save for Ash, who had known what to expect.

The rat man hunkered down on his hands and knees. With his chin almost touching the roof he tugged at the tail, drawing the white rat from his mouth. He lay it out upon the concrete, where it appeared to be dead.

He blew air against its tiny face. The rat stirred, twitched its whiskers: its eyes cracked open. It rolled on to its side and gazed at him as if mesmerized. The man gathered up the creature into his hands, then he climbed carefully to his feet. He next approached each of the

Rōshun in turn. At each one, he squeezed the animal so that it ejected a squirt of urine on to their clothes. The stench of it filled Aléas's nostrils.

The stranger drew a canvas bag from another deep pocket. He dropped the rat inside it, then with great care he plucked one of his hairs from his own head and used it to tie the bag closed. The rat started to struggle within, the bag hardly seeming secure.

'Here,' he said, offering Ash the squirming bag. Ash squinted at it. He gestured to Baracha, and the man offered the bag to the Alhazii instead.

Baracha was even less keen. 'The boy can take it,' he decided.

And so Aléas was burdened with yet another item to carry: this time a sack containing a struggling rat.

'He is a king amongst rats,' explained the man to Aléas. 'They will come for him, when he calls them.'

'And when will that be?'

'Right now.'

Aléas looked about him. He could see nothing, certainly no rats.

'Our thanks,' said Ash gruffly, and handed the man a purse of coins.

The man bowed again, less pronouncedly this time. He tapped the top of his hat after he had replaced it upon his head. 'I would wish you good luck, but that seems a rare commodity these days. Anyway, it's hardly worth squandering on fools. Goodbye, then, Ash. May your end be a glorious one.'

With this final blessing he hobbled away.

*

'When I said we required an army,' muttered Baracha, as they crossed the street and approached the bridge, 'I was talking in a literal sense. Men and such. Men with weapons. Armour. Discipline.'

From the edges of their vision they could see shapes emerging and scattering in the fog. The rats were coming out.

'These are better,' said Ash.

The Rōshun stopped before the squat sentry post that barred their way on to the bridge. A masked Acolyte stepped out, hand resting on his sword hilt. He began to speak, but stopped abruptly when Ash thrust a knife into him, twisting it up into his lung.

Ash withdrew the blade, air whistling from the gaping wound. The man toppled on to his side, gasping like a fish out of water behind his mask.

Baracha stepped over him. A brief scuffle sounded from within the sentry post. He emerged grim-faced. They stepped on to the bridge.

Aléas still carried the bag in his hand, limp now. The king rat had stopped squirming. He cast a look over his shoulder and saw a shapeless mass following behind them. The tower loomed overhead, hidden eyes watching their approach. Loopholes ringed the lower reaches of the temple, jutting out from its sheer sides so that archers could fire straight down. Aléas tried to walk normally in his robes and with his heavy burden.

They halted at the base of the tower itself, in front of the massive iron gate. A grate slid open, at waist level, revealing only blackness beyond.

Aléas moved as instructed. He pulled open the neck of the bag, easily snapping the hair which bound it, and emptied the animal through the hole.

Almost immediately its fellow rats emerged from the fog and rushed for the gate. The three Rōshun swung away to either side, batting the swarming creatures from their legs. Against the gate, the rats piled upwards like a drift of leaves until they were able to squirm through the open grate.

'Smoke,' demanded Ash, flapping his open hand. Aléas fumbled beneath his robe for one of the small bags filled with jupe bark and barris seed, and tossed it to him.

Shouts sounded from within. An alarm went up, a bell clanging fiercely.

The farlander bent and lit the bag's fuse with a match. He tossed it to the ground, where it began to spew clouds of white smoke that helped to augment the natural cover of fog. A bolt shattered at Aléas's feet and without even thinking he raised his double crossbow to aim at a loophole some twenty feet above his head, and snapped off a shot. From a different loophole a rifle spurted a blast of smoke and a hurtling lead shot, which couldn't be seen save for its bloody and instantaneous progress through Baracha's left ear.

'Aléas!' bawled the Alhazii. Aléas twisted and fired again.

While he was at this business of returning fire, Ash and Baracha were working to free one of the two small casks of blackpowder that hung beneath his robe. Baracha ignored the ruin of his ear, which hung in tatters, dripping blood. 'You tie knots just like my mother,' the Alhazii grumbled to Ash, both of them struggling to get the cask loose. More shots crashed down. The noise was deafening, shards of wood flying up around their feet. The cask finally came loose. Aléas reloaded his crossbow and huddled by the side of the gate, knowing they would be shot through in no time like this, smoke or no smoke. But he could hear shouts from the loopholes now, and guards yelling in panic. The rats had reached them.

His master's gruff voice could be heard above the gunfire: 'We need to use more,' he was shouting. 'We need to use both casks.'

Ash wasn't listening, though. He laid the wooden cask by the gate, soaked its fuse with water, scurried away.

'Clear away!' hollered Baracha, and all three jumped down from either side of the bridge on to the concrete foundations beneath it.

The fuse was a short one, though it seemed an eternity as they waited for it to soak through. The blackpowder cask was constructed from a single piece of wood, with a finger-wide hole at its top filled with thick, semi-hardened tar. The fuse poked through this, and when it sucked the water to the contents within, it would ignite from the sudden contact with moisture.

It exploded suddenly. An ear-jarring rush of air crashed overhead, followed by reeking black smoke and portions of wood and rat that splashed into the water of the moat in a brief shower of debris. Coughing, they poked their heads back up. The gate was still intact.

Baracha yelled as he jumped back on to the bridge. He waved his arms at the gate. A shot raced past his head, though he didn't flinch. Instead he straightened and looked up with a scowl.

Ash leaped up, too, and helped Aléas back on to the remnants of the bridge. Aléas's ears were still ringing from the explosion. No time to think, though. Through the smoke he could see that planks of the bridge had blown away to leave only the concrete foundation, exposed and blackened; the gates too were blackened, badly buckled, but seemingly intact. Before them Ash stood stroking the scabbard of his sword. He exchanged a glance with Aléas, his eyebrow raised. Aléas bent to reload his crossbow. More shots crashed out. One took the skin from Baracha's shoulder, before it skipped off the concrete, sailing past Aléas's right knee.

'By all that is holy!' Baracha bellowed up in rage. 'Will you aim at someone else, just this once!' He snatched the crossbow from Aléas and aimed at a loophole still boasting a cloud of drifting smoke. He fired twice. A shout of pain rang out. He tossed the piece back to his apprentice.

'Now what?' he demanded, rounding on Ash. 'I told you we needed to use both casks.'

Ash held a finger to his lips, attempting to hush the big man. He stepped through the clearing smoke and placed a palm against the smaller door set into the gate, which was now warped and partly ajar. He tilted himself forwards, pressing hard.

The door fell inwards. It clanged to the ground without any hint of a bounce. Within lay only smoke and darkness.

The pair of them swept through. Behind, Aléas hobbled under his load. An Acolyte lay writhing on the ground, smothered in a carpet of rats. They trod a path around him, not looking.

A wide entranceway lined with murder holes. Another gate at its end. But it lay open.

Beyond was a large, starkly gas-lit chamber, where several riding zels stood with their reins tied to posts, and next to them a few empty carts. Troughs of water lined two walls and a stable was close at hand, if the smell was anything to go by. Passages led off from the open space. The Rōshun chose the one directly ahead, Ash going in front, Aléas taking the rear.

This passage led into the lower sanctum of the Temple of Whispers, the largest open area to be found within the tower. The walls of the space were the same colour as exposed flesh; a sacrificial altar, of pure white stone, stood at its far end in a pool of gaslight turned low. Columns of pink marble ran in two rows the entire length of the sanctum, rising into the dimness of a ceiling arching high overhead, which was covered entirely in friezes of Mann – images that reflected much of the chaos to be found on the floor below.

The chaos was one of panic: a desperation to escape the torrent of crazed vermin now converging on everything that moved. Acolytes struggled across the open space as though they were on fire, each enveloped in a mass of writhing fur. Some rolled on the floor, trying to crush their attackers. Yet the three Rōshun stood amongst it all, unmolested.

'I did not expect this to be so easy,' quipped Baracha, which only an Alhazii could say while his ear dangled loose from his head.

The rats cleared a path for them as they trod through the mayhem. An enclosed spiralling stairwell occupied each corner of the temple space, three of them leading upwards. The nearest one, on their right, led downwards, however. The Rōshun hovered next to it, peering into the gloom below.

'Slave quarters,' announced Ash.

'How can you tell?'

'The stink.'

The Rōshun converged on the far end of the sanctum, before a shallow pool of water that extended across the entire floor, and separated the rest of the temple from the altar. They stopped to confer.

'You think Kirkus is still in the Storm Chamber?' Baracha asked, as an Acolyte charged past him and dived into the water. They all ignored him.

'We have no choice but to assume so.'

'There should be a climbing box,' said Baracha. 'All of these towers have one. Can you spot it?'

'There,' said Aléas, motioning to a door he could just discern in the wall behind the altar.

'We try the climbing box, then,' said Baracha. 'We'll never make it if we have to fight our way through every floor to get to the top.'

'Agreed.'

Ash mounted the thin bridge that vaulted the pool, his sword, even now, still in its sheath. Baracha stepped straight into the water and waded across. Aléas chose the bridge.

The twin doors of the climbing box were small, cast-iron, and firmly shut. There appeared to be no hole for a key, or any other obvious way in which it could be opened. 'Crowbar,' demanded Baracha with a snap of his fingers, hand outstretched.

Aléas began fumbling within his robe, till Baracha impatiently tore the front of the garment open to expose the harness. He snatched the crowbar from it, and set to working on the doors.

Still, they wouldn't open.

'We need to blow them,' he grunted, handing back the crowbar. Ash consented, and they took the remaining keg of blackpowder, set it against the door, soaked the fuse.

'Clear away!' bellowed Baracha as they scurried for cover. This time they had the good sense to cover their ears.

As the smoke cleared, a shaft was revealed through the blasted doorway. It soared straight upwards through blackness, as did the metal cable hanging taut to one side, and an iron ladder next to it.

'I was rather hoping we could hitch a ride,' observed Aléas drily.

'We climb,' rumbled Baracha.

*

Aléas went last, and he gritted his teeth with effort as he hauled his weight, hand, by hand up the rungs of the ladder. The shaft was illuminated partway by the light from below, but already he had lost sight of Ash in the murk above him, leading the way with Baracha some distance behind, climbing more slowly, because of his bulk. The shaft reeked of grease and was full of dust, so that Aléas stopped to sneeze more than once.

After a time, he was forced to stop and rest. The air rattled in his throat. His lungs were burning. He wiped his nose clean on his sleeve, and then crooked an elbow around a rung and locked himself in position by clasping both hands together. Aléas was strong and fit, but he wondered whether he could finish this climb. They were too far up now for the light penetrating the open door below to reach them, but his eyes were adjusting to the darkness, and he could see his master vanishing up ahead.

He had no choice but to follow, so he began to climb again.

It took him another four rests, with a great deal of hauling in between, before he rejoined his master. Baracha hung on the ladder in the dimness, waiting for him.

'What took you so long?' he hissed down.

'I was enjoying the sights,' said Aléas. 'And then, for the fun of it, I got to talking with a pretty girl from Exanse. Or was it Palo-Valetta? You know, I don't recall.'

'Pass the crowbar,' mumbled Baracha's voice.

Aléas did so, no easy manoeuvre with them both perched precariously on the ladder. He watched his master pass the crowbar on up to Ash, who was blocked from further progress by something solid spanning the shaft. Before long, chips of wood cascaded from above.

Aléas caught a fragment in his eye, and cursed as he blinked to clear it. For a moment his legs dangled freely.

'Aléas!' hissed his master in remonstration.

An entire plank of wood tumbled past then, bouncing off the side of the shaft as it disappeared beneath his feet. Two more followed, and then Ash was clambering up through the hole he had made, with Baracha following soon behind. Aléas, half blinded, pulled himself wearily up the final stretch. He grasped the edge of a jagged hole which had been hacked through the floor of a climbing box. Next moment, Baracha clutched him by the harness and heaved him right through, so that he hung there in his grasp, facing the big man, before his feet were set on the floor. He rubbed his afflicted eye, though that only served to make it worse. He could feel grime in his nostrils, sweat pouring from his skin.

The carriage was sealed with iron doors, a curved handle on either side obviously intended to slide them apart. Through them they could hear the muffled sound of bells ringing, and a voice barking orders.

Again, the crowbar failed to prise the doors open.

'Stuck fast,' gasped Baracha, while Ash studied a metal lever sprouting from one side of the cubicle. He pushed it up: the climbing box shuddered and rose by a centimetre. It clunked to a stop, then dropped back to its original position.

'We are not at the very top yet. This climbing box goes further.'

'So why doesn't it move?'

Ash stroked at a brass plate fixed immediately beneath the lever. All three peered closer, and saw that embedded in the plate were four brass tumblers, each stamped with a series of digits. Ash tried them with his thumb. They rotated, like tiny wheels on an axle, revealing different numbers as they moved.

'I've heard of this,' piped up Aléas. 'It's a number lock. You need to set the correct number on all four tumblers.'

Ash, thumbing through them, gave up with a wave of his hand. 'It would take a miracle to chance upon the correct sequence. I fear we are stuck.'

Even as he said this, the doors slid apart.

A dozen startled Acolytes stood blinking at the Rōshun, who blinked back at them just as surprised.

Baracha, growling, grabbed the Acolyte closest to him and yanked him into the carriage. It broke the spell.

Ash and Aléas each grabbed a handle and began to close the doors, while the other Acolytes struggled to push their way through the narrowing gap. Fists crashed against Aléas' head, clawing hands grabbed for his hair.

Aléas strained against the handle while fending off an Acolyte; with blows impacting against his head, he saw glimpses of bared teeth, eyes widened in anger, a backdrop of bobbing heads and blades manoeuvring for an opportunity to strike. The doors were almost closed now. They were blocked by the shoulders and legs of a single Acolyte, who snorted through his nostrils at the effort of it, but still would not pull back.

'Arm yourself,' ordered Ash, as he wove his head back and forth from a lashing fist. The old man drew his blade at last as he jerked his head back from the point of a sword, and hacked down with his own. Blood shot into the climbing box, unreal, ghastly, bright.

Aléas struggled to draw his own steel. The sight in his left eye was bad – there was a splinter there for sure, which he could feel every time he blinked. He freed his blade and jabbed without aim.

Behind, he heard Baracha shouting at his captive. 'The number!' he was demanding.

'Push,' Ash encouraged the young apprentice, leaning into the effort. The door closed by another fraction.

More hands gripped at the closing edges. The Acolyte in the gap was either unconscious or dead, and those behind were using him now as both shield and leverage. Ash was meanwhile making a fine mess with the point of his blade. Blood jetted and pooled on the floor; Aléas slipped on it, fumbled to stay fixed to the door handle, dropped his sword in the process from his greasy hand. A burning pain slashed along one cheek, and he dodged his head aside, feeling wetness there. He tightened his grip against the door handle. and instinctively batted aside a blade he did not even see.

'Master!' he hollered, turning his head to the Alhazii.

Baracha had a hold of the man he was interrogating and was panting deeply only a millimetre from his face. The man was no Acolyte at all, but a priest of elderly years, with a bald pate and white hairs sprouting from his flaring nostrils.

'You'll get nothing, I tell you, nothing at all out of me.'

'No?' replied Baracha, as he hiked up the priest's robe and worked his hand beneath it.

Across from Aléas, Ash tumbled away from the door.

Aléas yelled as his hand lashed out to grab the suddenly vacated handle. The doors slipped wider again, allowing more shoulders and arms to gain leverage. Aléas roared for new strength, fought to keep the gap from widening any further. *This is it,* he thought, expecting a knife in his ribs at any instant. *We never stood a chance.*

The priest bumped against his back in his struggle with Baracha. 'Stop that,' the old man was shouting in a clipped accent.

'Master!' Aléas tried again. A face cursed at him, thrust so close he could smell the garlic on its breath. Above it, a length of wood was being forced between the doors, then someone else began to lever them open.

Baracha ignored him. 'The number, or I rip them right off of you.'

Ash was down; he was conscious, but moving as though drunk.

'Stop it!' shrilled the priest in a voice that verged on hysteria. Then he screamed with all his might.

'The number!' Baracha raged.

'Four-nine-four-one! Four-nine-four-one!' The priest's awful squeal filled the small space, and then it ceased abruptly. Aléas felt him slide down against his legs.

Baracha tossed something ragged and bloody to the floor. Bile rose in Aléas's throat. He didn't have time to linger on it, though, for a knife was snaking about his stomach, trying to find a way through all the gear slung about him.

Baracha leaned over Ash and thumbed the number lock on the door. 'Hurry,' Aléas growled.

'It doesn't work. The fool lied to me.'

'The lever! Push the bloody lever!'

With a shudder, the climbing box began to rise. Shouts of pain accompanied the sudden withdrawal of limbs from the doors, which did not move along with the carriage but fell away as they rose.

Aléas sagged back against one of the walls. He was sheeting sweat. Three gulps of air and then he pushed himself off the wall, and knelt down beside Ash.

'What's wrong with him?' Baracha asked.

Aléas saw the knife dangling from the old man's thigh, and

inspected the gash. 'It's only a flesh wound,' he announced. Carefully, he drew the blade free. Ash gasped.

Baracha sniffed at the blade.

'Poison,' he said. 'Hurry boy, an antidote.'

Aléas gathered his wits. This was no time to fall apart.

He grabbed the medico hanging over his hip. 'Which one?'

'All of them.'

Aléas lifted all four vials of antidote and poured a few drops from each one between Ash's lips.

The climbing box clattered to a stop. Baracha jumped over to the new set of doors, grasped the handles to keep them closed. No one attempted to open them, though.

Aléas rubbed at his inflamed eye. He lifted the flask of water he carried and tilted his head back to wash it clear. He blinked, and repeated the treatment. It seemed to work. He then took a long drink.

'Rush oil,' Ash rasped from the floor.

Aléas knelt. He took a small clay pot from the medico, peeled off its paper stopper, dabbed some of the waxy cream on his finger, and smeared it on to Ash's lips.

The sparkle quickly returned to the old man's eyes. 'Help me to my feet,' he ordered.

'Easy,' said Aléas, helping him up. 'You've been poisoned.'

'I know. I can feel it.'

Baracha was listening against the double doors. 'How do you feel?' he asked quietly, turning. Ash offered a quick shake of his head.

'I think it's crushed hallow seed,' said Aléas, holding the poisoned blade close to his nose.

'Very rare,' commented Ash.

'And difficult to flush. We must purge you, once we get out of here.'

'Are you both ready?' asked Baracha.

Ash recovered his sword from the floor. He cast free his heavy robe and used it to clean the hilt, and then the curved length of its blade. He looked like a farmer cleaning his scythe.

A sharp pain struck the old man as he finished. He stooped, clutching his side as he sucked in a lungful of breath. It took an obvious force of will to straighten his back.

He finally nodded.

Baracha slid open the doors.

CHAPTER TWENTY-SIX

A Killing

Kirkus felt sick. He stood by the heavy vault door, his ear pressed against it. He could hear only silence beyond.

They were coming for him, and he knew it, and the knowing made him want to run. But run where? He was at the very top of the sky-steeple here; the only way out was down through the very people who were trying to kill him.

He could only hope the Temple guards would stop them. They *would* stop them, he was certain of it, for they had been trained since childhood for such an event. But how, he wondered again, had these people even made it so far?

Kirkus pushed away from the door and strode back into the Storm Chamber. He held a short-sword in his hand. He hefted it, swung it once, twice, through the air.

He would not need it, Kirkus told himself. They would never get inside.

Manse, the old priest, stood waiting in the centre of the room with hands in sleeves and head bowed. A mute servant tended the fire, though occasionally she glanced towards Kirkus.

'Both of you, to the door,' Kirkus instructed. 'Inform me if anything occurs.'

He ignored them as they scurried past him. He prowled the room, stopping before the window glass. He pressed his forehead against its coolness. At this height he was above the fog; the effect was that of the tower rising above a sea of clouds, with other towers elsewhere, poking through here and there, like islands.

He heard a shout even through the thick glass, carried up from one of the windows on the floor below. Again his stomach quailed.

Kirkus had only truly feared for his life once before now, and that had been several years ago during his first purging. He had broken halfway through that week-long ritual; in no way had he been able to summon the will to carry on.

His grandmother had come to him then, offering water as she sponged the foul mess from his face. At last he had stopped shaking. His tears had ceased to flow. He had looked up at her, still seeing phantoms. He knew he was close to losing his mind.

Why is the divine flesh so strong? she had whispered into his ear.

He had only croaked in response, unable to speak.

Tell me! she demanded, her voice lashing him like a whip.

Because . . . it does not suffer . . . from weakness, he had recited, barely able to breathe the words.

Good. Now tell me of such weaknesses.

He felt then as though he was high on narcotics and his thoughts refused to focus. He fought to gather them by holding fast to his grandmother's words.

Conscience, he gasped.

Good. And why do we consider conscience to be a weakness?

He had faltered at that. He knew the answer, but in his broken condition, his mind shattered, he was unable to frame it into words.

The old crone smiled. *Because, my child, it is not our natural condition.* And then her smile faded, for his head had dropped again in exhaustion. *Listen, this is crucial!*

With all his strength he lifted his head once more.

Even the Daoists know this. There is no natural sense of right or wrong in the world, no inherent laws of justice. Does a she wolf feel guilty when she comes upon something young and vulnerable, and devours it? No, she does not, for she needs to live and feed her pups. Conscience is a concept know only to man. People teach their children such notions, so that they might know from right and wrong, but no one is born with these beliefs within them.

Kirkus had frowned. He knew all of this. Why was she wasting what little time was left to him?

Now tell me. Why do people instil such ideals as conscience in their young. Hmm?

Because they're weak, he said, recalling the words he needed. *They need rules to protect themselves from the strong.*

Indeed. For they look at the world around them, and they see the cruelty of it, the death and injustice, the blind chance, the struggles for survival and dominance, their own ever-closing mortality, and they quail. They cannot face the bitter truth of it; to do so would be to drive them mad, even as they call us followers of Mann mad. And so, they invent ways to protect themselves from the realities of life; conscience, laws and justice, right and wrong, the World Mother. In these things they seek sanctuary, huddling together against the coldness of the world while they share in the warmth of their own delusions.

But we are Mann, Kirkus. We are not so weak. You and I, all of us of Mann, we have been instilled since youth with a more honest set of rules. We have been forced to look upon the world and accept it for what it truly is. This is our power. This is *your* power. Never forget that, child. Never forget your power, for you are strong boy, strong.

Now survive this. Summon your will. Push through.

It had been enough, at that time. He had made it through the purging.

Kirkus exhaled. His breath clouded the glass and obscured the world of fog beyond. For a moment he thought of Lara. He wondered where she was today, if she had gone to watch the games perhaps.

He knew that Asam and Brice would be there by now. He imagined the three of them meeting in the imperial stand, their talk made easy by their years spent in tussle and play as children together, in the quiet halls and dark dens of the Temple of Whispers – they and Kirkus. He pictured Lara's small face as they told her that Kirkus would not be coming today, that he was imprisoned in the Temple until his mother decided otherwise. The slow blink of her eyes as she heard this. Her words that changed the subject entirely, and had nothing to do with Kirkus save in the absence of any mention of him.

Lara, said his inner voice.

Kirkus pulled his forehead away from the window. He circled the room, making a conscious effort to focus his will. He stopped at one of the steaming bowls and bent to inhale deeply, feeling the rush of the narcotic coursing through his body. Strength flooded into his muscles and he straightened up. He swung the sword again. It whistled through the air.

He had been trained since youth in how to use such a weapon.

If they made it this far inside the temple, he would kill them all. Every last one of them.

*

It was oddly deserted on this uppermost floor. They stepped into a high-vaulted chamber which led through to similar chambers, all lit by low-flickering gaslights. The air was warmly oppressive. Tendrils of smoke curled across ceilings covered in decorative plaster. Doors lined the walls to left and right, muffled voices audible behind them, the occasional angry shout.

The three Rōshun stayed close together as they moved through the long chamber. The floor of polished wood echoed under the fall of their boots.

A white-robed priest scurried past an archway, some fifty feet ahead. He glanced at the intruders but did not stop. They heard a door shut behind him, a key rattling in its lock. They moved through the same archway.

There were two Acolytes posted here, each guarding a single door. They drew their swords as the Rōshun appeared, but did not budge from where they stood.

'Aléas,' prompted his master.

Aléas lifted his crossbow, and hesitated for only a second. Once, twice he fired and each time took an Acolyte in the chest. They both fell in gasping heaps, clawing at the embedded bolts.

'Keep moving,' suggested Ash.

As they approached the next chamber, they saw masked Acolytes fanning out with pistols in their hands. The Rōshun took cover on either side of the archway leading into the chamber. Baracha tore free his robe. Aléas knelt to place his crossbow on the floor, then lit a pouch of flash powder with a carefully struck match. Something was dripping on to the floor – blood, Aléas realized, from his own cheek.

He tossed the burning bag inside the chamber beyond and drew back, ramming fingers in his ears. The instant it exploded in a bang and a searing flash, Baracha and Ash rushed into the chamber, Aléas lumbering only a few strides behind.

A dozen Acolytes reeled blindly with their hands pressed to their ears.

Ash broke the spell, running with a sudden lunge and slash. His blade sang. It seemed to miss the Acolyte who faced him, but then the man's head tilted backwards and toppled to the floor along with his hands, and the open stumps of his neck and wrists began to broadcast jets of blood which sprayed on to all of those nearby. A shot went off as Baracha cleaved a second man's belly, the puff of smoke fading into a bitter reek as the white-robes began to cast aside pistols in exchange for their swords, swinging them wildly in the general direction of their assailants. Another shot rang out, the sound lost in the chaos of the fighting.

Ash worked his way into the centre of their opponents' line, ducking and weaving, striking one and fending off another. Baracha moved behind him, covering their flanks by battering left and right. A white-robe lunged to pierce Baracha's exposed side, a crimson handprint stamped above his heart as though for the perfect target marker. Aléas shot the man spinning him to the floor. His master failed to notice.

As the fighting intensified, Aléas glanced up over the heads of the combatants and noticed a flight of steps, and at the top of these steps a female Acolyte of middle age standing tall and unmasked as she reloaded a pistol.

Coolly, Aléas took aim with his second shot and fired straight at her chest.

The crossbow string snapped just as it released the bolt, the ends of the string flapping backwards as the bolt clattered futilely against the stone wall behind his target. She looked up, and flashed him a smile with a mouthful of dyed-red teeth.

Aléas struggled to reload the crossbow with the last remaining string, and followed, from his peripheral vision, the motions of the woman raising her pistol to fire at him.

He saw smoke then flame, and was struck on the side of the head, and staggered backwards, and fell. Blood gushed from his scalp. Lying shakily on his back, half stunned, air hissing through his teeth, Aléas still fumbled to reload.

The Acolytes, as if regaining their senses, converged on Ash and Baracha in a concerted counter-attack. Ash moved too fast to be surrounded; Baracha had a more difficult time, his blade being much heavier. He took a slash across the back which opened up his leather jerkin, and the skin immediately beneath it.

Baracha cried something in Alhazii and swung his sword around without looking, staving in his attacker's ribs – where the blade stuck, forcing Baracha to pause in order to free it. The big man's head flicked up, just in time to see another Acolyte's sword sweeping down from above. It chopped through Baracha's left wrist before striking the wooden floor and sticking fast.

Aléas wiped his eyes clear as he finally slotted the trembling string into place. His master was hollering in a great gust of rage and pain while his eyes fixed on his severed hand lying on the floor. Baracha hefted his sword with his other hand, and opened the Acolyte's throat with it.

He went into a frenzy after that.

'Aeos, Toomes, bullshorns,' shouted the woman, still fumbling to reload her own weapon. 'Flank and take the young one.'

Two Acolytes broke off from their engagements and headed towards him.

Aléas, still on the floor, pushed himself backwards as he hurried to place a bolt against the now-drawn string. He launched it into the stomach of his nearest attacker. The second jumped forward, and then Aléas was suddenly in his own battle, fending off blows with the unloaded crossbow. For a moment he panicked, as a slash knocked the weapon from his hands. Aléas rolled clear. He struggled to his feet, his load of equipment slowing him, and his balance all wrong. He drew his sword.

The Acolyte was good, but then so was Aléas. It was instinct that made him duck beneath one unexpected sweep; he came up with the point of his blade lunging at the man's neck, which the Acolyte barely avoided. They were both panting hard, one in armour and the other weighted with equipment. Aléas was fitter, though. He swiped aside a riposte and stepped forward, cali style, his outstroke taking the man in the side. He twisted the blade. Slipped it out. Allowed the man to fall to the floor.

He glanced up to see the fight was theirs. Only two Acolytes remained on their feet, both confronting Ash. Baracha was striding towards the woman who stood upon the steps, bellowing words whose sense was drowned by their own volume.

The woman fired her pistol but missed. She tossed it aside and drew her blade, assuming a wide-footed stance on the topmost step.

'Come then, you big bastard,' she declared.

Baracha climbed six steps then flicked the stump of his arm at her. Blood lashed across her eyes.

His next move drove his blade cleanly through her abdomen. He dragged her, impaled, from the top step to stand beside him. He used his foot to push her free of the blade. She clattered down the steps and lay still.

A sense of calm fell upon the scene. The last Acolytes had fallen. Moans, coughs and retching echoed against the high ceiling above them.

Baracha sagged to one knee. 'Aléas,' he groaned.

Aléas wove his way through the carnage and went to the aid of his master.

Baracha looked to the top of the stairs, where a heavy vault door blocked the way. 'To the top, boy. Take me to the top.'

Together they struggled upwards. It was a slippery business, though, since Baracha was losing blood fast. Aléas helped to lower him to the floor, propping his back against the door. They had a clear vantage point from there, difficult for anyone to surprise them.

'Tourniquet,' his master rasped. He had turned bone-white, and his teeth were beginning to chatter. With haste, Aléas threw open the medico and set to work.

Ash stumbled up the steps and collapsed against the door beside Baracha. He was covered from toe to scalp in blood, though fortunately most of it appeared not to be his own.

'How are you?' he gasped.

Baracha looked down at his stump. With the tourniquet in place, the flow of blood had decreased, though it was still looking bad.

'I lost my hand,' was all he could say.

Aléas stopped his master from further chatter by shoving a strip of leather between his teeth. He tore open one of the bags of flash powder, sprinkled some on to the stump without warning. Baracha bit down on the strip in his mouth; the leather he wore creaked. Aléas fumbled with lighting a match, then held it against the stump. The powder went up in a flash, instantly cauterizing the wound. Baracha rolled his eyes upwards and passed out, whereupon Aléas set about wrapping a bandage around it.

Beside them, Ash was fumbling through the medico. He took out the pot of rush oil and dabbed more of the white cream against his tongue. He shook his head to clear it.

'We're in bad shape, Master Ash.'

'Hoh,' exclaimed the old man. 'I did not expect us to make it even this far.'

Aléas motioned to the door. 'Well, we go no further. Even with blackpowder, I doubt we'd make it through this door.'

'Nonsense,' said the old man. 'We still have our wits.'

Without standing, Ash reached up and hammered the hilt of his blade against the iron door. He waited, then he hammered some more.

'They are finished!' he shouted through it. 'It is safe to come out!'

Aléas frowned, spoke quietly: 'You really expect them to be so foolish?'

'Always expect foolishness,' Ash answered just as quietly, 'when minds are scattered by fear.'

As if to prove his assertion, a muffled voice replied through the door. 'Who speaks this?'

'Toomes!' Ash responded without a pause.

There was no reply. They waited for some minutes but nothing happened.

Aléas wondered how they would ever find Nico now, in their current condition. They didn't even know where he was being held. It seemed hopeless.

A clunk sounded through the door. Then another. It began to open.

Ash leaned on his sword and rose swaying to his feet. He met the old priest's face with a toothy grin.

Before the priest could react, Ash shoved past him. A woman stood just within the doorway, hands pressed to her mouth, her eyes gaping.

'Do nothing,' Ash instructed them. 'Aléas,' he called over his shoulder. Aléas was checking his master's pulse which was proving difficult to find. There . . . a faint beat against his finger. Well, he supposed, there was nothing more he could do for him now, anyway.

He followed the old farlander inside.

*

Birds sang from silver cages. The air reeked so thickly of narcotics that Aléas felt giddy with it. He suppressed an impulse to giggle.

The chamber was bright compared to the dimness they had just left, a result of the high windows that ran entirely around its perimeter. The sky was blue out there above the fog, the sun too bright to look at.

'Kirkus!' demanded Ash.

The old priest lowered his head. The woman, a servant of some kind, glanced for a mere instant up towards the raised section above.

They passed a crackling fire in the centre of the room, moved swiftly up the wooden steps that led to sleeping quarters separated by walls of thin panelling. Each of the four rooms there was empty.

Ash stood for a moment. He raised his nose in the air, sniffed.

He spun around, then returned to the bedroom they had just checked.

Ash ducked beneath the massive bed, snaking a hand under it. He began to pull, till a leg emerged, then naked buttocks, then an entire body.

It was a young priest, his lower lip pierced with golden spikes.

'Kirkus,' announced Ash triumphantly to the terrified, drugged eyes of the young man, who held up his hands like a boy shielding his eyes from the morning light.

'Nico. Where is he?' demanded Ash.

Kirkus blinked, finding focus at last on the face of the Rōshun. Ash shook him with a snarl.

'Gone,' Kirkus panted, a hand casually gesturing at the air. 'To the Shay Madi.'

He told the truth. Aléas could see it in his eyes.

Their hung heads, on hearing this, seemed to lend the young priest strength. He dropped his arms, used his palms to raise himself up. 'You're too late,' he announced. 'He's well broken, as you will be, too, if you cause me harm.'

'Finish him,' said Aléas, with ice in his voice. 'There might still be time to save Nico.'

Ash shifted his stance and set his blade against Kirkus' white throat.

'Hold!' wailed the young priest. 'You do this for gold, yes? Well I have gold, more gold than you could spend in a lifetime.'

'Then what good would it be to us?' replied Ash, and with an almost gentle motion flicked the tip of his blade across the young man's throat.

Kirkus goggled. His tongue emerged from his gaping mouth. He reached a hand to his throat, trying to fix it. A dark crimson appeared suddenly between his fingers. As it spurted, he slowly choked to death.

They watched until the Matriarch's son lay lifeless.

When they returned to him, Baracha was conscious and trying to get to his feet. Aléas marvelled at the man's resilience.

'Is it done?' he asked, as Aléas helped him up. Aléas nodded.

'What of the boy?'

'The Shay Madi,' said Aléas grimly.

'Perhaps he lied,' the Alhazii offered, more to Ash than to his apprentice. But Ash ignored him, and descended the steps.

They rode the climbing box back down.

CHAPTER TWENTY-SEVEN

A Day for Rejoicing

Bahn was glad of the incense that drifted through the dim atmosphere of the inner temple. He stood beneath the high windowless domed roof of the building, in a silence permeated by the low murmurs of the Daoist monks performing their ritual, swaying only slightly in the armour he had been wearing for twelve hours altogether, and which by now weighed like an extra man upon him. The rigid, contoured plates and sheaths were coated in a fine grey dust streaked with sweat, and it itched where the leather insides pressed against his tacky skin. He was aware of how badly he must smell to those around him, but he was almost glad of that, too. It would help to mask any lingering scents of sex.

His wife seemed glad merely that he had made it at last, even if their daughter's naming ceremony had already begun in his absence. Marlee knew to appreciate these chances Bahn snatched of returning home from the Shield, not least because it signified a lull in the fighting.

Part of Kharnost's Wall had collapsed during the previous week, heralding another round of infantry assaults from the Mannians as they attempted to exploit this sudden weakness in the city's defences. The Khosians, in return, had struggled to hold the invaders off long enough to repair the breach as best they could. Bahn himself had so far not fought during the week-long defence of the wall. He had been there merely in his usual capacity as General Creed's aide, his role to observe and to stand back from the fighting. When the Mannians had attacked again last night, Bahn had been stationed with the field-command team on the second wall, from where he had watched through the long darkness as the battle ebbed and flowed around the latest breach and upon the far parapet. He had perceived only dimly

336

the fighting taking place in the flame-lit darkness, and in sudden spells of brightness made stark by shadow and light as flares had drifted from the sky, like a dream he had once had of burning mis-shapes of men tumbling from the stars.

Bahn had done nothing all night except for this silent watching and the regular despatch of runners to the Ministry of War with reports relating to the ongoing defence. Occasionally he had replied to one of the comments of the command team, or had shown his acknowledgement of some black joke they had made in their attempts at relieving the tension. Still, it was the sixth prolonged assault in as many nights, and Bahn was exhausted from it. As the sun had risen in the east, across their left shoulders and over the skirting wall that protected the coast of the Lansway on that side, the enemy had with-drawn, bearing their wounded with them, and the assault had at last, and with sweet mercy, faded away.

A new landscape emerged in the aftermath of withdrawal: a broken and twisted one with movement dotted all about it, though move-ment ragged and spent and without much direction. Bahn observed the city's men staggering around with comrades, as though drunk – most likely they were – or sagging to their knees in the mud or on the blood-slick stones of the parapet. Some called out to the dawn sky, or called out to others, or laughed, simply laughed. With the din of battle now gone, Bahn felt as though a harsh wind had been battering his flesh all these long hours of darkness and vigilance, and then had suddenly vanished. He listened to distant gulls cry out in their eternal hunger. He looked at the other haggard faces of the command team, and returned their hollow gazes with his own.

Cold without and numb within, Bahn had climbed the Mount of Truth to report to General Creed, the old man awake in his Ministry chambers with the curtains still drawn, oil lamps flickering in the corners, looking as though he had not slept. The enemy had been repulsed at the cost of sixty-one defenders dead, Bahn informed him. Some were still unaccounted for. Countless more had been wounded. Repairs on the breached wall were now resuming, though it was still doubtful they could seal it in any way save for a makeshift one.

'Very well,' Creed's tired voice had replied, his back turned to Bahn in the deep leather armchair he sat within.

Knowing he was late, Bahn had stayed only long enough in the

Ministry to wash his face and hands free of grime. He had also begged for some bread and cheese from the kitchen, and eaten that on the trot as he hurried down off the hill to the nearby Quarter of Barbers, the dawn streets lively, almost festive, as was their wont in the aftermath of such an attack.

His family temple was to be found in this quarter – Bahn's side of the family, in this area where he had been born and raised. On Quince Street, the prostitutes were still out from the night before, tending to business with those soldiers still drifting out from the walls, made lustful with relief and the shedding of blood.

As Bahn passed the women, a few called out to him by name, the older ones who still remembered him as a youth. He nodded with a tight smile, kept marching. At the corner of Quince and Abbot he caught the eye of one girl in particular. His stomach clenched at the sight of her. She recognized him, too, and not from long ago but from only recently, from mere days ago, as she curved her spine to pronounce her small bosom and peered out from under her heavy lashes.

So young, Bahn thought, with something close to despair in him.

He had made a promise to himself, that first and last time, that he would not do this again. Bahn strode onwards with every intention of passing the girl by. He turned his head only to nod a greeting, but then the girl's lips parted to speak, and he saw the colour of them, the soft red blush of them, and he halted.

Close up, he could see the red soreness around her nostrils from inhaling dross, and the sunken look of the addict in her eyes. She appeared thinner since last he had encountered her.

'How are you?' Bahn asked the girl, his words sounding gentle enough, though his voice was tense from the blood pulsing through him.

'I'm well', she had replied, and her look of hunger reached out to his own, stirring deep eddies of need.

His gaze roamed over her pale shoulders, the smooth skin of her chest under her low-cut dress. For a delicate moment he thought of savouring her small breasts in his mouth.

Bahn had taken her in an alleyway behind the side-street tenements, his sense of time suddenly diminished to a series of images as fractious and disconnected as in battle; consumed in all entirety by a need to empty his frantic lust inside her, along with incipient self-loathing certain to rally in strength later on, and those sights and sounds and scents that had surrounded him all through that awful bloody night and the ones before it, and the guilt too – shame even – at his pampered role in this war, the awareness of his own self-preservation as he looked down at men, at comrades, hour after hour, dying, while he did nothing but watch.

He released it all in those precious moments of squander, and afterwards, overcome by a hollow exhaustion, he pressed into her hand his purse which contained all the money he carried on him. Bahn wanted to say something more to the girl. She offered a brief smile, knowing the rhythms of men. For a moment Bahn felt he was a boy again.

Now, as the monks continued their chanting, and with the feel of the girl's body still impressed against his own, Bahn found that he was shivering slightly, perhaps from some form of aftershock from the night before, perhaps from the events more recent than that. He trembled in the stale temple air next to his wife, his son, the other family members who had come today to watch his daughter be bestowed with her name, and thought, in something of a panic, *Merciful Fool, what was I thinking?*

It had occurred in broad daylight, in an area where he was still well known by the locals. Anyone might have noticed him walk away with the girl, anyone who might know Marlee too. What would he do if he had caught some disease off the girl? How would he explain that away?

I am in the grasp of a demon, Bahn thought to himself. He looked about as though he had startled himself with this thought, and saw across the way, in the dim alcove of a wall opposite, a golden statue of the Great Fool kneeling in contemplation, thin and bald and handsome, grinning at him from ear to ear.

Bahn inhaled the pungent spiciness of the atmosphere, as it took long moments for his shaking to subside. *Never again*, he swore to himself, and in meaning it he felt his pulse begin to lower.

It is this war, he thought. *It corrupts my spirit as it corrupts all things that it touches.*

As though in some tacit agreement, the guns on the Shield opened up just then in a ripple of distant concussions. A few of the children's heads turned in interest; the rest of the congregation remained unmoved. Perhaps the guns heralded another Mannian assault after the brief respite. Perhaps it was simply the resumption of an ordinary day at the Shield. Bahn did not feel inclined to concern himself with it just now. It was hardly as though he was badly needed on the walls.

Before his gathered family, three monks of the Way stood around the cut-stone edges of a sunken fire. It was only a small fire, a handful of coals with soft red underbellies, barely smoking. Upon the coals lay a pile of mymar leaves, yellow and crisping inwards from their serrated edges, their smoke tinged blue and rising to curl around the coddled form of his daughter, who was held by the monks above the same fire, as they chanted and moved their hands in a circular motion so that she was borne with it, wrapped in a bundle of linen. *She does not cry*, Bahn observed, and his daughter coughed a tiny-lunged cough from the smoke wafting about her, and blinked up at the oldest of the three monks – old Jerv who had been here even when Bahn was a boy – and studied the white wisps of a beard that sprouted from his chin.

His daughter had made it through her first year, and was fit and well. For Mercians this meant a time for rejoicing, the time when the child would finally be bestowed with its name. For his daughter – who, ever since learning to crawl, had tended to rush around everywhere at a fast trot – this name would be Ariale, after the legendary zel with wings on its hooves. Marlee herself had announced this was the perfect name for her, but then Marlee thought all things that were humorous in life were apt and good. For Bahn it had taken some time to come around to the idea of naming his daughter after a zel.

Ariale Calvone. It was a good name, he decided now, smiling, and with that smile he felt more himself than he had done in many days.

The assemblage of people today was mostly from Marlee's side of the family: her mother, her aunts and uncles, shopkeepers and military men in the main, some of them people whom Bahn hardly knew at all, and who he had barely met since the day he and Marlee had first been bonded. As a family they looked well in their fine-stitched clothes, each standing with the same straight-backed dignity of Marlee herself.

In comparison, his own relatives were few in numbers, and looked at odds with the others in their casual stances and their well-worn temple-best clothing. His mother was not there, no doubt already busy mending shoes and leatherwork in her small dwelling-cum-workshop on Adobe Street, not far from here in fact. Bahn had not expected her to come, nor had it been for her benefit that they had chosen his family temple of boyhood for the ceremony. Their own local temple in the north of the city had simply been fully booked long in advance.

His aunt was in attendance, though, Vicha with her wild black hair barely tamed for the occasion, and her two daughters, Alexa and Maureen, both as blond as she was dark, all of them still officially in mourning after the death of Hecelos, husband, father and master carpenter, lost at sea when his grain convoy – the one that the Al-Khos shipyards were working so hard to replace – had been sunk on its return from Zanzahar five months previously. A good man, Bahn had always thought.

Reese was there too, striking in her red-headed beauty, though her eyes were lined with darkness as though she had not been sleeping much. Los was not with her, thank Erēs.

A young monk emerged from the shadows and began to shuffle around the family members with a wooden aeslo in his hand, letting it ratchet open before flicking his wrist to clap its two boards together like the jaws of a mouth, over and over again, in a rhythm that was slow and brooding. His other hand bore a plain begging bowl, seeking alms in return for the service they were performing on this day. With solemn faces the congregation dutifully emptied coins into the bowl passing by.

When the monk came to Bahn, he realized he had given all his money to the street-girl, and was now without coin. He was forced to mutter an apology to the shaven-headed young man. It irked Bahn, anyway, this needless interruption to the ceremony. In his youth, they had simply allowed you to leave what you could on the way out after the service was finished. But times had changed it seemed, even here.

Marlee produced a coin from her own purse and offered it instead. Her eyes inquired if he was all right, sensing the tension in him, and he nodded, placed a palm against her back, drew her closer.

The monks bore the couple's daughter high in the air now. Their chanting was in old Khosian, sounds as smooth and fluid as water sluicing over stone. They recited her given name and prayed that she would receive the Nine Deliverances during a long and fruitful life-time of good work. Little Ariale giggled as they lowered her again, kicking her legs within her bundling garment. The old monk Jerv smiled down at her.

In another life, Bahn might have been performing this ceremony for someone else's child. His mother had always wanted him to become a monk, being the youngest of three sons, his elder brother Teech already committed to their craft of shoe and leather mending, and the middle brother Cole enlisted young in the army against her wishes.

Bahn might have made a fine monk, too, for at heart he was a gentle man. The result of too much mothering, his father had always declared in his own, quiet way. But Bahn's love for Marlee had swayed him from that course.

In the proceeding years, his eldest brother had died of unknown causes, suddenly dropping dead as he sat eating his supper. A heart defect, the local healer had suspected. It was not long after this that his other brother Cole, Reese's husband, had deserted his family along with the cause of Bar-Khos. With two sons so quickly gone from him, his ailing father had wasted away from grief within the space of a year. Bahn's mother had struggled on alone, her sim-mering, unvoiced resentment towards Bahn, her only remaining son, turning in the months following into open animosity towards him. She cut him regularly with remarks aimed at provoking a sense of guilt. She compared him constantly with those sons she had already lost. It was as though she believed he was in some way respon-sible for his brothers' plights, and had brought down on them the injustices of Fate for his shunning of the cloth.

And now what was he? Bahn wondered. A soldier, yes, though certainly no warrior.

Only his own little family offered Bahn a sense of having achieved something right on this path he had chosen with Marlee. He worked hard at being a good husband, a good father, so it cut him even deeper than his mother's words did when he failed them.

Well, no more, he thought. *I will hold this family together no matter what the cost.*

*

Once the ceremony was over, and his daughter returned to them flushed with excitement, the smell of smoke still lingering in her fine hair, the family gathered in the small square outside the temple in the bright sunlight they had almost forgotten during their time inside. They would return to his aunt's house only a few streets away, where she would hold a family reception with food provided by all, in whatever meagre spread they had been able to fashion together.

Reese walked together with Bahn and his family. She fussed over Ariale and Juno, equally playful with them both. She and Marlee chatted about the ceremony, small things inconsequential, while the sound of the guns roared to the south so steady and regular that Bahn could tell it was merely the daily exchange between the opposing sides. Perhaps the Mannians had given up for the time being, Bahn thought, and truly wished for it to be so.

He and Marlee walked arm in arm while Reese carried their daughter, and their son trailed behind. Marlee looked to him, as though to say, *Well then, ask her*. He nodded.

'Have you heard from Nico yet?' he asked Reese, and she hefted Ariale more firmly upon her hip before she replied, 'A letter arrived last week, half drowned in the sea by the looks of it. I couldn't make out what it said but, yes, it was from Nico. I could tell that much from the terrible handwriting.'

'Good news at least,' said Marlee. 'Even if you could not read it. I'm sure he's thriving . . . wherever he might be.' And Marlee left her words adrift in the hope that Reese might tell them more about where her boy had gone, but she did not.

As they left the square, they saw a hedge-monk squatting on the ground with a bowl sitting before him. The man was of middle years, and he stood up as he saw the group approach, then stepped before them, offering his blessings and shaking his bowl. Save for his grubby robes, he barely even looked like a priest. A livid scar ran down his face from forehead to chin. His skull had not been shaved for days.

Another fake monk, Bahn realized. Ever since the council had decreed all begging illegal save on grounds of religion, men in desperation had donned robes and shaved their heads and pretended to be monks such as this one.

The sham of it, Bahn thought, simmering anger suddenly arising inexplicably within him.

'Blessing be upon you,' the man in the black robes declared kindly enough, a few coins clinking in his bowl.

Bahn shoved his way past him, pushing harder than he had intended. A yelp of surprise come from the fake monk's throat, as his bowl went tumbling to the ground and the coins scattered, spinning sunlight.

The family, all of them, stopped to stare at Bahn. Even his son Juno blinked up at him.

I'm sorry, Bahn thought of saying to them all. *I watched our men die last night while you all slept in your beds safe and sound because of them. And then, this morning, I ploughed a young whore likely riddled with infection, driven to this condition by poverty and the warped needs of wayward husbands like myself.*

But he did not, not on this day. Instead, Bahn performed the apologetic smile of the good husband, the good father, and took his son by the hand, and walked on.

CHAPTER TWENTY-EIGHT

Shay Madí

The chief whip enjoyed his job. At least it seemed that way to Nico, as the stocky man dragged him roughly from the holding pen deep beneath the stadium floor, occasionally spitting the word *'Rōshun'* from his plump, stained lips as though it was the worst of curses. Twice his whip lashed out against Nico's back, though Nico barely felt it. It was merely one more pain to add to many.

'In you go,' he snarled as he shoved Nico through a rusty barred door. Nico stumbled into a narrow caged passageway which he saw led some six feet to another sliding door, now also being drawn open from the outside.

A guard stabbed at him through the bars with a pronged stave, blunt but painful, forcing Nico through it into the cage beyond.

He tripped over a prone body and sprawled to the floor, crying out as fresh agonies shot through his shattered hand.

Nico could feel pain everywhere, and he was increasingly feverish from it. His left eye had swollen shut; he couldn't even tell if the eye-ball was still there. His lips were a swollen mush. Most of his front teeth were broken or missing. It hurt even to breathe.

The door clattered shut behind him and was locked by one of the guards, while the chief whip laughingly called out to the rest of the unfortunates confined in the cage.

'Make way for the mighty Rōshun,' he declared. 'Perhaps, if you're kind enough to him, he will save you all.'

Nico curled into a ball and lay shivering. He could smell his own stench and, above it, that of many others. The cage was crowded with men and women waiting to die.

He felt a hand settle on his arm. He peered up from his one good eye to see a man's face looking down at him with concern.

'Here,' he said softly, as he offered a ladle of water. Nico sipped, instantly choked it back up. 'Easy,' soothed the man. Nico drank some more.

With care he tried to sit up, if only to breathe a little better. Almost instantly his ribs were suffused with white heat. Nico gasped.

The man helped him along, and a few of the others cleared a space so he might rest his back against the bars of the cage. He noticed the man's head was shaven and he wore a black robe.

'Yes, I'm a monk,' said the man, in response to Nico's surprise.

Nico merely nodded. It was the only thanks he could offer. He looked around the enclosed space, saw that everyone was now observing him. He let his gaze drop to the straw-strewn, earthen floor.

A roar rose from the arena outside, the muffled sound passing through a heavy gate at the end of another barred passageway. A woman lying on the floor moaned into the dust.

'May you be with the Dao,' said the priest to Nico, touching him lightly again on the arm. The touch was comforting, human. The monk turned away to see to the woman, and to offer her what little comfort he could.

Nico wrapped his arms about himself, moving the limbs with a delicate slowness. He forced his mind to focus on his breathing. Every time he exhaled, he thought of the agony releasing itself from his body. When he inhaled, he thought of stillness.

It seemed to work, after a while – or at least enough for him to think straight. Thoughts were good now. They could take him away from this place.

So he allowed his mind to drift. He thought of sunny Khos, the cottage, his mother. He wished he could see her now more than anything else in the world.

Time passed unawares. The bars of the cage clattered behind his head. It was the chief whip again.

'That one next,' the man decided, and pointed out the woman being comforted by the monk. 'And that one, the monk, too.'

Other guards prodded the chosen captives with their pronged staves, though keeping at a safe distance behind the bars. 'Up – up!' they shouted.

The monk helped the woman to her feet, still holding her close to him. An outer door slid open in the cage. Together, they stepped into the passageway leading to the gate.

'Stop,' said the chief whip.

The guards pressed against the barred passageway and reached inside with leather-gloved hands. They yanked away the woman's clothing until she stood there exposed to their stares. Purple bruises covered her flesh. Bite marks, too. The monk for his part, was allowed to keep his robe, so that the crowd could tell what he was.

A sword was passed to the monk, and then a small round shield. He dropped them both to the ground. 'I won't fight,' he stated flatly.

The guards cursed and prodded him some more. Still he refused to hold either weapon or shield. Beyond the gate the crowd bayed restlessly. The guards gave up on their persuasions, and tied the sword and shield to the monk's wrists, where he let them hang there uselessly. The man's hands were trembling, though he stood tall.

The gate swung open and thin daylight flooded through. Nico could see nothing beyond outside, blinded by the sudden illumination.

Both woman and monk were prodded out through the gate. Then it closed behind them and the crowd roared.

Nico felt the noise deep in his stomach. It almost loosened his bladder. He clenched inwardly, resisting its urge to empty itself. Blessedly, after a few moments, the sensation eased.

'What will happen to them?' asked another young man, his voice dead of emotion. He did not direct the question to anyone in particular.

Yet it hung in the air, calling out to all of them.

'They will die,' came another voice. A middle-aged man, sitting with three others – soldiers if the scars and tattoos they bore were anything to go by, and the way they sat impassively, as though they had often waited together like this for the arrival of death.

They looked Khosian.

Specials, Nico guessed. He knew from his father's accounts, how those underground fighters were often captured when the tunnels collapsed behind them.

Without pity the soldier stared at the young man sitting across from him. 'Men armed with steel will slaughter them like cattle. Or they may be eaten by animals driven mad by hunger.'

The young man turned his head away, biting his lip.

'There's always a chance,' said another, a woman with the old scars of a branding iron evident on both her cheeks. 'If you fight well enough, the crowd might spare you.'

The soldier snorted, and Nico swallowed around a hard lump in his throat. He thought of the young woman out there now, not more than twenty years old, terrified out of her wits. It could be Serèse, or any other girl he had known back home. What kind of world was this, where people hungered to see a human being hacked to pieces for sport?

A scream sounded from outside. The woman. The stadium fell silent.

Her sobs for mercy echoed into the cage – then ceased abruptly. Everyone in the cage looked to the floor to avoid each other's eyes, even the bitter soldier.

The monk was shouting something. Nico couldn't make it out, though the words were angry and passionate. A sound followed, like that from a butcher's stall, and then another. The crowd didn't roar this time.

Nico covered his head with one arm, and cowered beneath it. With every beat of his heart he could feel the pain pulsing from his injuries. Again he sought out other things to keep his mind occupied.

He thought of Ash, and how his master had not come to rescue him from this horror.

Perhaps he had, considered Nico, and he lay dead now in the trying.

But Nico refused to believe that. In reality, he considered the old man to be invincible, a force of nature – and you could not kill a force of nature, merely wait for its passing. *Where are you, then?* he demanded of his master.

Perhaps Ash hadn't tried at all. Maybe some aspect of the Rōshun code had stopped him from attempting a rescue. The code did not allow for personal acts of revenge, so perhaps, too, it did not allow for personal acts of rescue, not when the needs of their vendetta were more pressing.

I should have left you when I still could, Nico reflected. *I should have taken my chance, and returned home to Khos and my mother.*

For a moment he cursed the day that Ash had walked into his life. But in truth it was a superficial emotion, and he cast it away quickly. He did not wish to be bitter about such things now he was so close to his own end. Ash had been good for him. It was Nico's fault he had allowed things to go this far.

Serèse came to his mind. Nico would never have met her had it not been for his master. But again Nico's thoughts twisted inside him; he imagined his friend Aléas dazzling the girl with his charms and good looks, sweeping her off her feet after Nico was gone. He imagined how they would both remember poor Nico – how he had been a friend once, long ago, a strange lad, but with a good heart; and how it was a bitter memory, even now, to think how he had died in that terrible way. *We should have tried harder to save him*, they would say, before returning to their fine bed to sweat away their regrets.

More bitterness, Nico realized. It wasn't like him, or so he had always thought. But his mother could be like that sometimes. Maybe it was true what people said, and your parents rubbed off on you, no matter what.

Someone was addressing the crowd outside: a woman's voice, loud and imperious. It was the Matriarch herself by the sound of it. She was telling them something about *Rōshun*. Nico realized she was telling them about him.

Sweet Erēs, he wasn't ready yet. He wondered if he ever could be. A guard approached and prodded his damaged ribs through the bars. He flinched from the touch, still covering his head with one arm. Another guard jabbed his back.

'All right!' Nico snapped as he struggled up.

They forced him into the passageway, where a black robe landed at his feet. They forced Nico to put it on, the effort almost causing him to black out.

Next, they gave him a short-sword and shield. A guard buckled the shield to the forearm above his useless hand. The men were quiet and professional as they worked, like weary drovers glad to be near the end of their day. None would meet his eye, he noticed.

'Don't put up much of a fight,' suggested one of the guards, speaking close to his ear. 'Let them finish you quickly.'

The entrance yawned before him, fat with the bright daylight. Nico shielded his eyes. Terror surged through him, chilling him with uncertainties, as they prodded him out through the gateway.

*

The sun shone overhead, weakened by a thin layer of cloud. The fog he had glimpsed on his journey to the Shay Madi was gone now, though the sand still lay damp beneath his bare feet. A smell of carnage hung in the air: it clung to his tongue, to the back of his throat. He could see trails of blood in the sand, leading to different closed gateways positioned around the walls.

Nico gazed around at the thousands of faces waiting expectantly in the stands. For a breathless moment their stares devoured him where he stood. Someone laughed, and then they were all laughing, a cacophony of howls that was like some awful nightmare come real. Nico shrank into himself. Shame overwhelmed his panic.

'You came to kill us, little Rōshun,' called out a voice, and he turned to face the Matriarch herself, who stood in the royal box flanked by Acolytes and priests. 'Now pay for your failure.'

A hush descended across the vast bowl of the stadium. A shadow passed across the sand: birds – black crows – wheeling overhead.

Slowly, a gate began to open on the opposite side of the enclosed space. He heard the snap of firecrackers. Flashes lit the dim interior of the gateway.

A pack of wolves raced out on to the sands.

Nico took an involuntary step backwards.

Soldiers lined the stone walls of the arena, which were too high to climb. The gateway ahead was now closed tight.

Nico counted six wolves in all. At first they moved in some confusion, but then they began to take notice of him. They ranged outwards, around the arena, but closing the distance.

Nico gripped the short-sword tighter. He hefted the blade, trying its weight. It was a hacking weapon, weighted towards its tip. Baracha had made them train at times with such simple blades.

Movement caught his eye and he turned to see a wolf darting in towards him, kicking up sand from its feet, its tongue lolling loose.

There was nowhere for him to run.

Nico spread his feet for balance and raised the shield. It took all of his nerve to stand and face the charging animal; it was, very possibly, the single most determined act of his life.

He swung the blade, almost unbalancing himself with the force of the movement. The wolf snapped its teeth and darted away, its animal reek lingering behind it.

Another sped in from his right. Again, frantically, he swung the blade, just missing as it dodged out of reach.

Three were now approaching him slowly from directly in front. Sweat began coursing off him as though someone had doused him with lukewarm water. Nico backed up against the closed gate. The crowd howled in anticipation.

In the back of his mind a quiet place suddenly appeared, a corner of detachment that he retreated into without question. He took a mental breath, and it provided enough of a space for Nico to wonder what these people could possibly gain from such butchery as this.

Echoes of the crowd's laughter still occupied his mind. He recalled those bitter times as a youth at the schoolhouse, when children had laughed at another's misfortune. Cruel, cutting laughter, without compassion. At times he had even joined in himself.

He thought, too of the monk calling out in anger to this crowd, earlier. All these thousands of people, and that man had been the only sane one here.

It was true and, as he realized it, the shame of their mockery left him. It turned outwards, directed on to the crowd themselves, so that he felt shame for them instead – for their desire to watch the murder of another and take delight in it.

We are all cruel children at heart, he reflected.

Blood flushed to his face. His jaws clamped tight, shooting spikes of pain through his head from his ruined teeth. It came to him, then, that to be terrified of this situation, to cringe away from it, was only to allow it to win, to be right. Better to be angry, he decided. Make a stand.

The six wolves charged.

Nico hesitated for an instant, and then something vital occurred within him. His training suddenly connected with his despair.

With a grunt, he pushed off from the gate and staggered forwards to meet the animals head on – just as Ash would have done.

A wolf raced in from his left, so fast that it left spouts of dust trailing in an arc behind its feet. He smashed its muzzle with the shield, both of them rebounding from the collision, Nico gaining only strength from the agony that burst from his broken hand. He slashed out at another wolf coming in to his right, air whooshing from his throat in rapid pants. The blade opened up its scalp.

As he closed on the group of three, he skipped in his stride and kicked deep and hard into the sand, spraying a cloud of it across their eyes. It blinded them enough that, for a moment, they faltered, shaking their heads – and then he was in amongst them, stabbing and hacking with his blade, smashing with his shield, mercifully feeling nothing as their teeth and claws raked him.

Nico was conscious of very little after that, for he was in a red frenzy. He was aware of stopping one of the wolves in its tracks by uttering his own animal snarl. He was aware of chopping at another until it was no longer of one piece. He was aware of getting bitten deep in the thigh, and biting his attacker in return just as fiercely, his sword stabbing and stabbing.

And then Nico was on his knees in the sand, sucking air into his heaving lungs, and he was done for, his strength utterly spent.

All around him, the wolves lay either dead or dying.

Not a sound stirred in the stadium save for his own gasping and that of one adversary nearby, panting as it lay on its side. An image of doom flashed in his mind, and then it was gone.

Nico was unaware of his own wounds as he looked up to see the Matriarch staring at him across the distance between them. Even from here he could see that her mouth hung open in astonishment.

Nico heard a chant rise from the crowd. He had no idea what it meant.

He spotted an Acolyte hurrying through the press on the stands to reach his mistress. He shouted something into her ear and again her gaze flicked towards Nico. She took a curved knife from her belt and even as he watched, she plunged its blade deep into the messenger's belly. Blade still in hand, now darkly wet, she turned back to face the arena.

'Burn him,' her voice rang out. 'Burn him alive.'

A storm of protest rose up from the crowd. She stood against it, unswayed.

Acolytes appeared from the various gateways around the walls.

They converged on Nico, pointing their swords at him so that he would not move.

Not that he could have moved. He dropped his own weapon and rocked back on the sand. He put his face between his knees and sucked in air. He could think of nothing but regaining his wind.

When next he looked up, he saw men busy erecting a bonfire in the centre of the great arena. In relays, guards and soldiers ferried armfuls of planking and chopped wood towards it. Around the stadium people still shouted their dissent. They pushed against the ring of soldiers, some even hurling missiles at them.

The bonfire grew higher.

CHAPTER TWENTY-NINE

A Storm in the Mountains

Ché awoke to a foul taste in his mouth and a pounding in his head as though he had been drinking hard liquor, though he knew he had not. It was the after-effects of the berry juice he had smeared on his forehead all those days before.

He heard a sharp crack in the distance, and then another. Rifle shots. He opened his eyes, saw it was evening. Early stars hung, brightening, overhead.

Ché groaned and forced himself up. He swayed on his feet, stumbled, toppled on to his back. He groaned again and looked about him. He knew this place.

He was at the foot of a high valley. By his side a bush swayed in the breeze, heavy with plump berries. Ché blinked his eyes clear. The daylight was fading fast, though he could just make out the course of the broad stream that twisted up the valley floor. His gaze followed it upwards, scenting the breeze as he did so: blackpowder and burning wood. He knew what he would see there.

The monastery, surrounded by its forest of mali trees.

The building was aflame.

As Ché looked on, flashes of fire sped towards the monastery from different directions: artillery shooting through the dusk to impact against the buildings in gouts of flame and debris; and snipers, armed with long-rifles, firing down from high bluffs over to the west.

The flames were catching hold fast. Silhouetted against their light, Commandos were moving by platoon into the forest of malis. A bell was ringing.

Ché's stomach growled in hunger. It was the memory of mealtimes spent here, the same bell calling out for supper.

*

Clouds scraped over the mountain peaks, blotting out the stars one by one.

Ché paused at the edge of the mali forest.

In the shadows beneath the trees men fought in grim struggle. He saw firelight flash against blades, and a black-robed figure cutting his way through a line of Commandos, as their lieutenant yelled for them to close in and take him down. To the left, towards where he judged the main gateway to be, he could hear a larger action taking place. Steel clashed above the uglier clatter of rifle shots. Men hollered.

He flinched as a great explosion tore half the evening gloom away, and looked up in time to see the upper portion of the tower – where he knew old Oshō to live – disintegrating in a cloud of dust. Someone screamed in the distance; from pain or rage, he couldn't tell.

Ché retreated from the treeline. His eyes refused to consider any more of the destruction. He stared fixedly at the ground before his feet, lit occasionally enough to show clumps of grass, stripes of shadow. He skirted the treeline, came to the stream again.

Ché turned and followed it upwards, leaving the monastery behind him.

Soon he saw it: the little shack of the Seer.

'Hello, Ché,' said the Seer, in Trade, squatting in front of the shack.

At least Ché's name had been real, while he had lived here, even if he had not been.

He stopped. He looked for weapons on the ancient Seer, or any sign of Rōshun lurking inside the hut.

'How are you?' asked the Seer, his tone gentle.

Another whumpf of artillery sounded from below. The ground trembled beneath Ché's feet. It shook him to answer though his response was a mere shrug.

Ché didn't really know how he was.

The ancient farlander nodded, and patted the grass by his side. Ché hesitated, as though the grass itself might contain hidden dangers. Delicately, he sat down beside the old Seer.

Together, they faced the battle below.

'We wondered where you had vanished to,' said the Seer in his thin, weak voice. 'But now we know.'

A tightness in Ché's chest. 'It was not of my own choosing,' he said.

'I don't expect that it was. I would have seen it in you, if you had been the type for easy betrayal.'

Ché dropped his gaze.

'I do not judge you,' said the Seer, patting his hand. 'We do as we must do. But tell me, please – how have you been, since we last sat and talked like this?'

Ché scratched at his neck. He considered what to say to this man he had known so well in another life. For a moment, Ché wondered what he was doing here, talking with him like this so casually, like friends. But then he heard the crack of shots fired below, and he remembered why he was here, and not there.

'When I lived here,' he said, 'I would dream, every night, of being a different person. Now I *am* that person, and every night I dream of being who I once was before. I am split in two by my past. I cannot escape it, however much I might try to flee.'

'You have it wrong, Ché,' said the Seer. 'You cannot run from your past.' And the ancient farlander leaned closer, so that Ché caught the reek of his breath. 'You can only sit until you are still, and wait for it to leave you.'

'I try.' Ché sighed. 'I meditate, as I was taught here, but still I am torn.'

'What of your Chan?' asked the old man, as though that was somehow relevant. 'Is it as strong as I remember it to be?'

'My Chan?' Ché's voice was heavy with disgust. 'If I once possessed such a thing, it was long ago squandered by my own hand. I am not who you think I am, old man.'

'I know who you are,' asserted the farlander. He sounded so certain.

'Then tell me,' said Ché.

'You are a laughter, from deep within you.'

'I haven't the patience for riddles tonight.'

The corners of the old man's lips twitched. He gazed down on the burning monastery, and his mouth stiffened.

'When you first came here, I did not notice you. I pay no mind to such things, for you young ones are like the butterflies of summer, always coming then going. But I noticed, on certain days, when the air was still or the wind was playing in the right direction, snatches of laughter coming from the grounds of the monastery. Most laughter that I hear from there, it is restrained, you see, or courting an audience. This, though, was not, and it would always catch my ear. It was – how do you say it – so natural, *spontaneous*. Like a child experiencing joy.' And the Seer nodded as if in agreement with himself.

'So I asked myself . . . I asked myself who is it that I can hear laughing so well? And I thought of all who were there as Rōshun, all who I knew of, and I did not know.

'So I waited. The answer always comes if you wait long enough, have you noticed? And it did. One day, your master brought you to me, so that I would look into your heart and tell him what I saw. Straight away, I knew you for the creator of that laughter. You had a humour in you, Ché, that made spite of your demons.'

Flames now sprouted from the roof of the north wing of the monastery. The dining hall was on fire, and Ché thought of the thousands of mealtimes he had spent there, chatting or listening to his peers.

Softly, he asked: 'How is my old master?'

'Shebec? He is dead.'

Ché stiffened. Felt a cold numbness wash through him.

The fire was spreading fast; sparks flew wild through the air. The stand of mali trees in the centre of the courtyard caught alight. From here, two men could see their upper branches wreathed in smoke. The trees themselves swayed in the waves of heat.

'Will they win, your people? I cannot see clearly with these poor eyes of mine.'

'You are the one who is the Seer.'

A faint smile passed over the farlander's lips.

'The Rōshun,' said Ché, 'they are making a fight of it.'

'That is good.'

'Will you not join them?'

'Me? I am too old to fight.'

They fell to silence. With glazed eyes, Ché watched the reflections of flames as they were cast against the underbelly of low clouds. He thought: *This was home to me once. I think it was truly the only home I have ever known.*

'They will kill you, if you stay here,' he warned.

'I know.'

Part of the roof collapsed. The flames leapt higher.

'And my people,' said the Seer. 'They will kill you, if they win through.'

'I would expect so,' replied the young man.

The old Seer chuckled drily to himself. He patted Ché's hand once more. 'Then sit with me a while longer,' he said, 'and let us see what happens.'

*

He was too late, and he knew it.

Ash clambered higher, breaking away from the rearmost tier of crowded seats, the highest and furthest from the stadium floor. He climbed a rusty iron ladder bolted into the outer wall of the stadium, passing guano-stained gargoyles and statues of imperial celebrities. Soldiers had been stationed here only moments before, but now they had left to converge on the more troublesome elements of the crowd, as people began throwing missiles and demanding that their calls for mercy be recognized.

He was weak with sickness, and long past the last of his strength. Still he climbed, forced on by the dread of what needed to be done. There was only one thing he could do for the boy now, and the knowledge of it sat like a heavy certainty in his guts.

Nico had fought well, Ash having arrived just in time to witness his fight against the wolves. All the while, he had scanned the stadium for some inspiration to strike him, a way to save his young apprentice. Nothing had come to him.

Hope had flared when Nico, against every expectation, had somehow fought through to win the crowd's approval. But now all that had changed again, reverting to a nightmare once more. The Matriarch had heard of her son's death, that much was clear, and she wished to wreak her vengeance on this boy in front of all. Such was the way of grief, the spoils of violence. It was his own fault, Ash realized. He had brought this fate down upon the boy.

Below, on the stadium floor, they had erected a post atop the pyre, and Nico was being tied to it even now. He seemed oblivious to what they were doing to him, his face tilted to the sky. The ends of three long chains had been looped over the top of the post. Acolytes stood with their hands wrapped in rags, holding the other ends slack. Others doused the pile of wood with oil.

Ash knew how the Mannians did such things. Doused in oil like that, the pyre would catch fire fast, offering little chance for the victim to pass out from the fumes. They would scorch him alive, then drag him out just as he stopped screaming. If timed right – and they considered this a form of art in Q'os, such was the nature of the place – their victim would still be alive, his flesh livid and exposed. He would then be nailed up for public display and left to die pitifully, suffering in agony.

Ash could not allow that to happen.

As if on cue, more white-robes appeared around the pyre, holding unlit brands. They set about lighting them as the soldiers stationed along the walls fought to push back the surging crowds.

Ash finally reached the top of the wall, and for some moments lay on the hard parapet. His skull felt as though it was trapped in a vice, sending nausea cascading through his body.

The wound in his leg had reopened, and he could feel his strength trickling and pooling in his boot, squandered out through the leather. Ash rummaged in a pocket, moving his arm and nothing else. He pulled out his pouch, drew some of the dulce leaves from it. He stuffed them into his mouth, rested his head against the stone once more. Immobile, he waited for the sickness to subside.

For as far back as Ash could remember, people had always complained that life was too short. He had often wondered at that because to him, for many years now, it had seemed life much, much too long. Perhaps he had simply experienced more incarnations than most – as some Daoist monks would have people believe – and the sheen on this game of life had simply worn thin for him, so that he could see through it too easily. Perhaps it was time to transcend this wheel of life for good, as those monks would say.

In his own questioning way, Ash did not know whether to believe in any of that. How could one know?

But he did know, now more than ever, that long ago he should have retired from this business, and taken himself to some distant mountain and built himself a hut there, to live out the rest of his years in simplicity. It wouldn't have brought him happiness – happiness was still part of the game after all. But perhaps, by setting everything aside, it might have finally brought him peace.

Ash lay his cheek against the cool concrete and closed his eyes. He could let it all go now, and never face what he would need to face any moment from now.

The boy had fought well.

Ash used his sheathed sword to help him rise unsteadily to his feet. He swayed, blinking to clear his vision. He turned to face the arena floor, distant from here, almost unreal.

Smoke already spilled from the base of the pyre. Acolytes stood around it, prodding it with burning brands as they set it to further life. The tethered young man began to struggle.

Ash hauled out the crossbow he had taken from Aléas. Carefully, he slotted the two bolts he carried into its grooves. It was a short-range weapon, but the bolts were heavy. From this height that might suffice.

Ash took another sighting of Nico, then hoisted the crossbow and aimed it high. He inhaled deep into his belly, concentrating on the flow of air through his lungs. His body slowly relaxed.

A moment arrived, and it still seemed strange to him, even after all these years, that moment in which he no longer felt that he was breathing, but being *breathed*. Slowly he exhaled and he felt his finger tighten against the trigger.

The bolt shot out faster than sight could follow. Ash didn't move from his posture, but stayed fixed like that as his eyes picked out the dark bolt falling in an arc towards the sand of the arena.

It struck the post just above Nico's head. Ash blinked away sweat. It was gushing now from his scalp like blood from an open wound, carrying his tears away with it.

Flames licked around the boy's feet. Smoke billowed about him. Nico was choking, and fighting to free himself.

Ash inhaled again. He lowered the crossbow by a fraction of an inch. Exhaled.

Released.

*

The more Nico struggled to breathe the more his lungs burned. He coughed and fought to break the chains that held him to the post.

The smoke was making him light-headed; his bare soles flinched against the touch of flames. For a moment, he was back in Bar-Khos, on the hot tiles of that roof, with Lena cajoling him from behind. It seemed as though his whole life revolved around that single mistake.

Nico would have done it all so differently, had he the choice.

He was close to his own death now. Strange how life seemed so vividly real near its end. Colours bled in tones he had never before noticed; even the tan sand was an infinite variation of light and shade, captivating his eyes. He could taste smells that went far beyond pleasant or unpleasant. He could hear individual voices in the great wash of the crowd; words even, tones of meaning. Why could it not always have been this way, so rich and vibrant? He could have sat for days on end and simply rejoiced in it all. Perhaps, he thought, this is what it is like, too, when we are born.

What a shame, then, to lose this brilliance of life until the very moment of our death. This was what the Daoists talked so much about, he realized. His master had certainly talked of it: the way the world stilled when you yourself became still, so that at last you could see it, sense it, capture it as it truly was. Real and infinitely uncoiling.

He heard something strike the wood above his head. Nico paid it no mind. Instead he looked down at his feet, and saw the pit of flames gathering force beneath him. A surge of heat billowed around him like scalding water. He was going to burn to death. He was going to be eaten alive by those flames.

Nico had heard a story once of the time the Mannians invaded the country of Nathal. A monk in the city of Maroot had sat in the street in front of the High Priest's manor and doused himself in oil, and then set the oil alight, and burned himself alive without the merest flinch, in protest at the crimes the Mannians were still perpetrating against his people.

How had the man done that, Nico now wondered. How had he found such stillness?

The heat was engulfing him. He blinked, trying to see. It was too real, all of this. Part of him refused to believe it was happening. It was not the part of him that mattered, though – not the part that recoiled from the flames and choked on the smoke and the smell of cooking meat, and began to scream and struggle in animal panic.

Nico rolled his eyes, desperately seeking something to grip his mind upon. The Acolytes stood with their burning brands, their eyes behind their inhuman masks narrowing against the drifting smoke.

The pain rising from his feet was quickly edging towards agony, an agony that he knew he could not bear. The smoke obscured everything now.

Nico tilted his head back in an attempt to draw air. A blue sky, the clouds breaking to the east and etched by sunlight. Amongst them, between spaces in the smoke, a sudden dark motion. Something falling towards him.

He gazed at it, mesmerized by its spinning flight.

He was shocked by a sudden impact. Began to choke again on a sharp taste of blood. His vision faded into itself, fixed blurrily upon the sun or something else that burned just as brightly. Then, even that faded to nothing.

CHAPTER THIRTY

Rites of Passage

His snoring woke her early that morning. The light was still grey in the crack between the curtains hanging over the one small window of the bedroom. The air of the room was still, and stank of sex. Reese lay there in the dimness, watching Los sleep: the thin creases on his cheek against the feather pillow, his boyish open pout as he breathed, his blond lashes. She considered waking him with a probing hand in his lap. Some love play to ease the tightness in her chest, the anxiety coursing in her blood. But she made no move.

Instead, Reese studied the beams of the ceiling, and tried to make sense of her dreams of her son until the room became infiltrated by the first warming tones of the sun. Then she rose in silence.

She opened the back door and let the cats into the kitchen, simply to fill the cottage with some life, and pretended annoyance as they curled around her bare ankles as she washed and prepared herself for the day ahead. Los had stopped snoring now that she was up and about. She picked up his discarded clothes, reeking of wine and fragrances and smoke, and went out to the yard and threw them in a wooden tub next to the big stone trough full of rainwater which she would use to wash them later.

Birds sang out their rich melodies above the dumb clucking of the chickens. From out of the east, the fan of daylight was spreading into the sky above the trees and the swathes of canegrass standing still in the breathless morning. Reese stood with one arm cocked and a fist on her hip, looking out over it all. She tried to think of nothing. She wished only to breathe in the soft clarity of the world as it rose from the memory of night, and with that clarity dispel the nameless sorrows that had come to her in the form of her dreaming. She felt tense, as though she would cry if only she would allow herself to.

Inside again, Reese busied herself with chores until she came to Nico's room. She opened the rickety door with its pale scratches at waist height, and glanced about her on the floor of the empty room for something to pick up or straighten out or put away, until she stopped, and put a fist to her hip again, and wondered what she was doing.

I have become like Cole's mother, she thought in annoyance. *Banging my stick at the silent walls all night long, to scare away mice that no one else can hear or see any sign of.*

Reese could not recall when she had last entered this room. She hadn't felt sure what to do with it since Nico had run off to live in the city, whether to leave it be and allow herself the hope that he might some day return to her, if only for a short visit, or whether to face a harsher reality, one that Los had been keen to impose on her since Nico had departed with the farlander – and now her own dreams too, it seemed – that her only son was gone, and gone for good.

The room was bare beyond the mere absence of Nico's belongings. It had never remained this clean and tidy when he had lived here, though he had, to his credit, been tidy enough. A few things of his still remained: his tin bird whistle on top of the windowsill, which he had lost long ago and she had found again after he had left; next to it some smooth, mottled pebbles from a streambed; his fishing rod and tackle propped in the corner, in their canvas wrapping. The bed was made as Nico himself had left it so long ago; the edges of the sheets tucked into the straw mattress, folded over the pillow.

Dust everywhere, though, she saw now as she looked long and proper.

Reese hurried out and filled a pail with water and vinegar and returned to her son's room and began to wipe everything clean. She worked until her forehead was greasy with sweat and the sun had risen above the line of trees visible through the watery window glass. Occasionally the urge to cry welled up in her again, and she would work all the harder until it had passed, her knees aching as she washed the creaking boards of the floor, her back complaining as she stretched to reach the beams of the low ceiling. She left the sweeping until last; on lifting Nico's few belongings to brush beneath them, she was sure to place them back precisely as they had been before.

At last Reese straightened up, wiping the damp curls away from her face with the back of her hand. She stood and scrutinized the polished surfaces until she was satisfied the room was properly clean.

The window faced her, now bright with sunlight.

Reese unlatched it and pushed open the frame, and stood back with her hands clasped together as though she was waiting for something to enter. A moment passed, and then a sudden breeze blew into the room, and Reese inhaled deep and long as the morning air caressed her face and filled her lungs from the bright world beyond.

'My son,' she whispered, as tears ran inexplicably down her face.

*

A body lay naked on the marble altar, its arms folded neatly on its chest. Its eyes were closed.

The corpse had been ritually cleansed by the grim, silent priests of the Mortarus, the secretive death cult of the Mannian order. For an hour they had carefully sponged the body with cloths bleached white by the bile of living sand eels – the same bile that had whitened their priestly robes, their stiff masks, the banners of Mann that hung on the high walls around them. In the silence of the Temple the bright cloths had been dipped into a bowl of blood-warm water, the ripples disturbing the fresh petals drifting around the brim, the cloths raised dripping into the air and throttled almost dry in fists. With a hiss of ritual words the priests had then drawn the cloths across the lifeless skin.

When this work was complete, and the priests of the Mortarus departed in a shuffling procession of chants and rustling robes, a scent of wild lotus lingered about the corpse, and the wound across its neck had been stitched, a black line barely noticeable beneath their skilful applications of paste and powder. They had been unable to do anything about the expression fixed to the corpse's face though.

It was this that Sasheen was finding most difficult to bear.

'What are your commands, Matriarch?' came a soft voice from behind her.

The priest Heelas, Sasheen's personal caretaker, stood a dozen feet from the altar with his head bowed. He kept his eyes fixed on the marble floor, as though unwilling to look at the kneeling form of his Matriarch, or at her mother perched on a wooden stool by her side.

Sasheen did not hear him, though the echoes of his voice lingered, finally whispering their way through her grief.

'What?' she said, in a distant voice.

'You called for me, Matriarch.'

Sasheen wiped a hand across her eyes and, for a moment, her vision cleared. She took in the still form of her son as though for the first time, a mere husk now, empty and bereft of meaning. Only for a moment could she look into his face fixed in a strangled contortion of horror.

Something stirred within her. Her back could be seen to stiffen.

'Stop everything,' she said in a cold whisper.

'Everything, Matriarch?'

'*Everything*,' she repeated, and there was a rising force to her words, a hard strength that contradicted the weakness of her tears. 'The ports and bridges. All transportation. Fountains. Temples. Entertainments. Business . . . If a mere beggar reaches out for money, have his hands removed. I want it all to stop, do you hear me?'

Sasheen inhaled a shuddering breath, scenting the lotus in the air. 'My son is dead,' she said, 'and they shall show their respect.'

Caretaker Heelas clenched his hands together, and allowed a few heartbeats to pass before speaking. 'What of the Augere, Matriarch?' he asked carefully.

She had forgotten about the forthcoming week of celebrations.

'Yes,' Sasheen said darkly. 'That, too, all of it. We shall commemorate the Augere at a more fitting time.'

The caretaker's silence was one of stunned astonishment. He remained composed, however, and bowed his flushed head low.

'Is that . . . all?'

'All? No, it is not all, Heelas. I want this city torn apart. I want these people found and brought to me alive. Explain to Bushrali that if his Regulators do not accomplish what I ask of them, he will find himself beginning a new career – as a eunuch in one of our Sentiate harems. Is that clear?'

'Perfectly, Matriarch.'

'Then go.'

The man left with uncharacteristic haste.

Sasheen's fists were shaking, she discovered. She clenched them tight.

'Calm yourself, child. Calm yourself.'

Matriarch Sasheen turned on her mother. 'Calm myself? My son lies dead and you tell me to calm myself? I should have you dragged from here and burned alive for those words.'

The old crone sat on a simple wooden seat, her translucent hands folded together. 'If it would make you feel any better, my dearest, then order it so.'

For the space of a heartbeat Sasheen truly considered it.

Her hand dropped limply to her side. She turned back to her son, lying on the altar within an arm's reach before her, his final resting place before he was interred in the dry vaults of the Hypermorum.

Sasheen spotted something lying on his chest. She reached for it, her long nails hovering for a moment. Delicately, she plucked something from the bare skin, catching one of the wispy hairs on his chest as she did so. She inspected her fingertip. An eyelash.

It trembled against her breath, fluttered free, falling from sight.

My son is dead, she thought.

Sasheen had never known pain like this before. It was a kind of madness, like that lurching of the stomach when you realized you had forgotten something vital, but it was much too late to correct it – except that sensation was now prolonged and constant, so that it consumed her every waking moment, and every sleeping one too; a screeching, tearing, animal terror that threatened to choke her if she did not release it in some way.

A wetness tickled her palms: her nails digging hard enough into her flesh to draw blood.

'Soothe yourself, child,' came the old crone's voice once more from her side. 'You are the Matriarch. You are the highest example of Mann. You cannot afford to be seen this way.'

Sasheen shrugged off the withered hand that settled on her shoulder.

'He was my son. My only child.'

'He was weak.'

The words hit her like a slap.

'Daughter,' soothed the old woman. Her tone might have been mistaken for an apology though it was not. 'Come, sit with me a moment.'

Sasheen glanced about the chamber. No one was in sight, save for the Acolyte guards posted at the distant entrance. All of them had their backs turned to her.

Sasheen shuffled across to sit before her mother.

'I cherished him too,' said the old woman. 'He was my grandson, my own blood. But it isn't Kirkus you grieve for, Sasheen. He died swiftly, and no longer does he suffer. You grieve only for yourself.'

Sasheen looked down at her clenched hands. She could not pry apart her fingers.

The old woman scowled. 'You must adapt to this loss, my child. Even a wild animal grieves for the death of its young. But like any animal, you must adapt and move on. You can bear another child, still. Rest assured, this grief is a passing weakness. You must hold fast to who you are.

'My son was not weak.'

'But he was, Sasheen, he was. How else could he have fallen without even a struggle? We pampered him, you and I. All these years we thought we were teaching him strength, when in truth he was merely learning how to hide from us his own deficiencies. If we had not been so blinded by our affection for him, we would have seen that – perhaps corrected it.' She held up a palm before Sasheen could protest. 'We must take from this lesson what we can. We have each become pampered in our own ways, daughter. We are rulers of the world, after all. But for our own sakes we must consider this as a warning. We are surrounded by enemies every moment that we breathe, and we will fall to them in the same way, to the knife, to the poison, if we fail to show them our fortitude. You wish to fall like your son, hmn?'

A silence, Sasheen's eyes staring at the floor.

'No, I thought not. So I will make a suggestion. We shall inform Cinimon of a new purging – for ourselves, for the order at large. We will cleanse the flaws from ourselves, and at the same time rid the order of those who do not deserve to follow the calling of Mann. Perhaps, in its own way, it will help you through this loss.'

Sasheen blinked, barely seeing at all. 'Perhaps,' she answered in a small voice, and it was a release, in a small way, to relinquish her will to that of her mother, even if it was only for the moment. 'Perhaps,' she breathed again, as she folded herself on to the cool floor of stone, and wept.

The old woman rose. She wore a heavy cloak over her robes, and paused for a moment as she removed it. With stiff limbs she knelt next to her daughter, as though intending to offer comfort. Instead, she lay the cloak across her daughter's head and body, so that she resembled nothing more than a shuddering mound on the floor.

The old woman frowned.

*

It was four in the morning, according to the bell that chimed from the Mannian temple at the southern end of the great square. On cue, a patrol of city guards marched into the plaza, wielding shuttered lanterns and long, studded clubs. Their captain scanned the area for signs of disturbance, but no one was in sight in Punishment Square at this hour of curfew. All was quiet save for the distant barking of a dog.

A shadow drew further back into an alley. It waited until the patrol had passed. A movement followed: a hand motioning for someone to come forward. Together, two forms loosed themselves from the murk and padded silently into the square.

They rushed across the marble flagstones in bare feet, barely making a sound. At the very centre they paused, looked up to take in the horror that hung there – the burnt corpse of a young man nailed to a scaffold. A wooden board hung about his neck. It was branded with a single word, though it was too dark to make out now. They already knew what it said.

Rōshun.

Quickly, one of the figures hoisted the other on to the scaffold. The climber set to work with a knife. The body dropped an inch. With a moment's more work it fell free and crashed roughly to the ground.

'Damn it!' hissed Aléas, still balancing on the scaffolding. 'Could you not have caught him?'

Serèse looked up from the corpse, her face twisted in a grimace. In a whisper she said, 'This is a little difficult for me, all right?'

'Fine,' replied Aléas, swinging back to the ground. 'And it's the easiest thing for me.' He stooped and pulled free the board from about its neck, then wrapped the body in thick sacking. With a grunt, he hoisted it on to his shoulder.

Quickly, they hurried from the square.

*

Patrols were everywhere. A curfew had been declared, no one to be allowed on the streets after midnight. Earlier, they had heard talk of the ports being sealed. No one was being allowed to leave the city.

It took over an hour to track their way across Q'os to the industrial areas on its south-eastern coastline, where they were to meet with Master Ash and Baracha. It was mostly wasteland here. Vast warehouses lay slumped beneath the faint light of the stars, sinister in a way that reminded them of the dark entrances to caves. Aléas and Serèse avoided these structures by crossing a strip of marshland, at times wading up to their knees through cold, sucking water. Beyond, they struggled up the face of a dune stained with soot.

The night sea shone before them with scuffs of luminescence. A breeze blew against their faces, salted and fresh. Aléas panted for breath, the weight of Nico's body now a burden he could barely continue with. Serèse did not offer to help him.

Together they descended the other side of the dune, and made their way down into a secluded cove that was all but hidden from sight. Baracha sat there by a small fire, chewing tarweed and nursing the bandaged stump of his left arm. He lifted his blade with the other as they approached.

'It's only us,' said Aléas, and his master relaxed and returned the blade to his lap.

A dark recumbent form shifted to acknowledge them: Ash, lying on the sand on the other side of the fire, head resting on his pack. He grunted, forcing himself to sit up.

They had spent the day gathering driftwood into a pile on the sand of the little cove – or at least Aléas and Serèse had, for the two Rōshun were barely fit to stand. With care, Aléas now lay Nico's body on top of the pile, a few sea-smoothed logs tumbling loose. Ash limped over as he did so. Clumsily, the old farlander began to yank off the sacking.

'I think perhaps it's better left alone,' suggested Aléas, placing a hand on Ash's shoulder. Ash shrugged free of his grasp. He only stopped when the body was uncovered and he could gaze down on it by the light of the fire.

The old man drew in a sharp breath. He swayed for a moment, enough for Aléas to steady him.

Gently, Ash's fingers dabbed at the blackened flesh. They brushed against the end of the crossbow bolt buried in the boy's chest. Ash did not move for many minutes.

Baracha stumbled over with a burning length of wood. Without ceremony he stuffed it into the inner depths of the pile, twisted it as though stoking an already lit fire. The pyre began to smoke. They stepped back from it and after a time caught sight of the first sparkle of flame.

Baracha picked up a handful of sand. He cast it on to the new-born flames, reciting words beneath his breath. Aléas comforted Serèse; both cried freely now, for the first time that day. The flames crackled higher, twisting through the crisscrossing of logs to take hold of the body on top. Colours danced amongst them: vivid blues and yellows and greens from the sea minerals that caked the wood. Fat spat from the pyre. A smell of burning meat came with a shift of the breeze.

After a while the pyre collapsed into itself, consuming Nico.

In the distance, far out to sea, the sun's first light leaked into the predawn sky. Shadows shafted across the horizon as the castings of unseen clouds.

Ash recited something in the farlander tongue. He repeated it in Trade, perhaps for the benefit of his young apprentice.

His eyes, though in shadow, were alive with two pinpricks of flame. He declaimed: 'Even though this world is but a dewdrop . . . even so . . . even so.'

*

Ash had instructed them to obtain a clay jar wrapped in leather to hold the ashes. Wearily, but with much presence, he raked the grey dust until it lay in a flat bed across the scorched sand. He paused. For a moment, he watched particles of dust playing in the remnants of heat.

For his mother, he thought, as he scooped ashes into the jar with the aid of the stick. Portions of bone lay scattered amongst it, and he scooped the smallest pieces up too. Once it was full, he stoppered it, and lay it carefully in his canvas pack.

He had a smaller jar too, a clay vial really, the length and thickness of a thumb, to which was fixed a loop of leather twine. Into this he scraped some more of the burnt remains and plugged it with its wooden stopper. He slung it around his neck, so that it hung there against his chest like a seal. It felt warm against his skin.

In standing up, a sudden pain flashed through his skull. Ash swayed. Someone was talking to him, though he could not see the owner of the voice. He teetered backwards, fell.

Sprawled on the ground, barely breathing, hands tugged at him. A voice asked if he was all right, could he hear them? The pain stabbed again, deeper than ever. Ash gritted his teeth, cried out in the harsh farlander tongue. And then unconsciousness took him.

CHAPTER THIRTY-ONE

Consequences

There was no way out.

All the ports had been closed following the death of Matriarch Sasheen's only son. Checkpoints were set up on the city's main thoroughfares and in many of the lesser side streets. The city guards compared the faces of passersby with sketches they held in their hands. People gossiped that Rōshun had come to the city – one of them a farlander – and killed the boy priest, and were still here amongst them. Some said it had been an act of revenge for the young Rōshun burned to death in the Shay Madi. Patrols roamed everywhere. At night a curfew was enforced under penalty of execution. Squads of soldiers, led by grim-faced Regulators, crashed into hostalio rooms, or illegally open taverns, brothels, private apartments, demanding answers by force, dragging away suspects, searching always for someone.

As though that wasn't enough to disturb the regular life of the city, speculation on the imminent military campaign began to pass freely amongst its populace. Soldiers had been flooding into the city for weeks now. Sprawling encampments had grown up on the northern and western edges of the city, along with shanty towns of hangers-on – pedlars, prostitutes, craftsmen, vagabonds – all massed on their outskirts. In the First Harbour a vast fleet was gathering. It was larger than anything seen in living memory: men-of-war in the main, but sloops and transports too.

Some said these were going to Lagos to replace the Sixth Army there, but they were considered fools and quickly shouted down as such – for all knew that only a token garrison would be needed on the island now. Lagos was a name spoken only in a hush these days. In the aftermath of its failed insurrection, it had been laid to waste at the personal command of Matriarch Sashseen herself. The stories that came from the island told of desolate killing fields without sign of life, dotted occasionally by mountainous funeral pyres where once towns and villages had stood – for every man, woman and child of the island had been put to the torch. New settlers from the Empire's crowded cities were being offered parcels of land there. They were emigrating in their thousands.

Wiser heads considered Cheem a more likely target for the forth-coming invasion. Perhaps the Matriarch had finally grown tired of her trading fleets falling prey to the inhabitants' piracy. A less likely option was the Free Ports, though that would be a risky undertak-ing, since their navy remained the finest in the world; it must be, for even outnumbered, it had held off the predations of the Empire for over ten years.

Perhaps, then, they were to attack Zanzahar, offered the obliga-tory jokers in such conversations. They joked about that because it would be the greatest folly of all.

Q'os was a city astir then with uncertainty and speculation, and while it may have been safe enough for those who claimed it as their home, its streets were treacherous for those who could not. Baracha, with his apprentice and daughter, and a still unconscious Ash, knew well that they were being hunted by their enemies. It was vital that they left, and sooner rather than later.

But the ports were closed.

With no other options available, they sought out a place to hide. They planned to wait for shipping traffic to begin again, a matter of weeks at most they believed. After all, the city relied on sea commerce for its survival. It couldn't choke its trade for long.

They found a deserted warehouse not far from the cove where they had cremated Nico's body. The wooden structure had been partly cremated itself in an old fire that had destroyed most of its north and west sides. But the parts of it to seaward were still roofed and, in amongst the blackened ruins, they found some corner offices that remained relatively intact.

It was there they holed up and waited, and looked after Ash as best they could.

The old Rōshun was lost in some form of unconsciousness. His breathing was shallow but regular and he uttered no sounds, and did not ever move. Occasionally his eyelids flickered as though he dreamed.

Most days, Baracha sat within the warehouse staring through one of its gaping windows out to sea. When not doing this, he paced about the confined space of the inner office, swearing under his breath at the loss of his hand. Whatever pain he suffered, immense as it must have been, he covered up in his own Alhazii way. The stump, at least, appeared to be healing well.

He rarely even looked at Ash, lying lifeless and gaunt on his pallet. Instead he seemed to entirely avoid the old man in his present state of weakness, seemed somehow appalled by it.

'I hope I never fall ill when it's only you to look after me,' admonished Serèse one morning, noticing his lack of concern, the old Rōshun lying on one side of the room, Baracha sitting by the window on the other. She was dripping water into Ash's mouth from a sodden rag, so she did not see her father turn and regard her with eyes hooded by a frown.

Perhaps she had been too young at the time, Baracha reflected, to remember how her own mother had lain like this, unconscious for a week, before she had passed away.

And perhaps, said an echo in his mind, *she remembers it only too well, and is simply stronger than you.*

And Baracha recoginzed it for truth, and felt lessened by the realization, and looked away.

The days turned into weeks. They were restless and tense and suffering from grief, all of them, in their own way. They began to snap at each other. Often, they had to hush their sudden arguments for fear of betraying their presence. They wrangled over who was eating the most food, drinking the most water; they fought over who should empty out the bucket of slop at night, or keep watch for unexpected visitors, or cook, or wash up, or who should sleep where. They even argued over their daily card games of rash, using chores and food instead of coins to place bets, until at times they almost came to blows over these games, hurling accusations of cheating or collusion, everyone disgusted, the loser skulking off feeling sore.

It was in the middle of one of these heated debates, right at the very end of the second week, all three of them shouting red-faced at each other, when a voice sounded from the far corner of the room and asked them all to kindly shut up.

It was Ash, sitting up in his pallet, his eyes screwed in annoyance.

'Master Ash!' exclaimed Aléas.

'Yes,' replied Ash, as though agreeing that it was, indeed, he.

*

With the ports still closed and no ships allowed to leave, fewer captains were willing to approach to the island of Q'os with their cargos, and those that did sail into the harbour inevitably sold their goods at exorbitant rates.

As a consequence, food prices in the city rose to levels that only the wealthy could afford. By the fifteenth day of the self-imposed blockade, riots broke out over the desperate shortages of food. A warehouse district in the north was razed to the ground. Elsewhere fires raged throughout the city, and streets were barricaded. In Punishment Square a cavalry charge cut down two hundred people demanding bread: the majority of them hungry women and children.

The ports were reopened the next day.

*

The temple of the Sentiates was deserted today save for those who lived within its walls, for it had been shut down like all other entertainments in Q'os while the city properly mourned the loss of the Matriarch's son.

Ché, for his part, did not consider Kirkus much of a loss. He knew the young man's form only too well. Kirkus had been a spoiled lout with delusions of greatness, wreaking havoc wherever he went while he waited for his mother to move aside and allow him to assume the throne. Who knew what monstrosities he might have unleashed on the world, had he ever attained the position of Holy Patriarch? If he had lived to achieve such a position, he would have been the first Patriarch born and raised for the role – all previous rulers having clawed their way to the top, and having clung there by tenacious fingertips for as long as they could. None yet had survived long enough to pass on the throne to any descendants. Such was the constant dogfight for the throne.

Ché had been stunned by the news of the young man's death, on finally returning to Q'os – not by the death itself, but the success of the Rōshun in achieving such a feat. Professionally, he could not help but admire them: a direct frontal assault on the Temple itself? He had marvelled at the sheer audacity of it upon hearing the reports. No one had foreseen it, certainly not Ché himself. The imperial Diplomats were trained in more subtle methods; they did not plan in such direct terms.

Here at the Temple of Sentiates, Ché's mother had been aghast at what she considered a tragedy for the Empire. In some odd way she considered herself to be personally involved in the affairs of the Temple of Whispers, especially when they involved the Matriarch herself. No doubt it was a result of the pillow talk she so often engaged in with priests from the Temple. Ché knew that she attracted a higher class of customer than most.

'Your skin looks terrible today,' she admonished, as they sat by the fountain on the seventh floor of the Sentiate temple.

'Thank you for reminding me, mother.'

'You haven't been taking care of yourself. You look exhausted.'

He leaned his face away from the soft play of her fingers. 'I've been away,' he said, 'on a matter of diplomacy. It proved difficult.'

'Yet you have been back for days, for I have my sources. You should be well rested by now, surely?'

The air was cool here, freshened by the gentle cascades of the fountain. Ché could see a reflection of himself upon the surface of the pool, but it was dim, shadowy, without detail. He trailed the tips of his fingers through the rippling water, scattering himself.

'I've not been sleeping well,' he confessed.

She studied her son more closely. He felt uncomfortable under her gaze, and refused to meet it.

'Something troubles you?'

Ché looked up. On the other side of the chamber a group of eunuchs sat gossiping amongst themselves. He could barely hear their words over the splashing of the fountain, but he still lowered his own voice as he spoke.

'Mother . . .' he began, and paused, struggling with the words he wished to say. 'Have you ever thought of leaving this place?'

'Leave the temple?' She blinked in surprise.

'Q'os, mother, and the order of Mann. Have you never thought, perhaps, that we might leave it all behind and make a life for ourselves that is of our own choosing?'

She glanced quickly towards the eunuchs. 'Have you lost your mind?' she hissed, leaning closer. 'Leave the order? What would possess you to say such a thing? Why would I wish to leave my home, my friends?'

Ché turned away from her eyes blazing with indignation. She composed herself.

'My son, whether you like it or not, this life suits me. I feel safe here. Whatever I desire, I may have. And in return, I can contribute in my own small way to the greater good of Mann. I'm needed here. I am considered of worth.'

'You are a whore,' he replied, before he could stop himself.

He felt the sting of her hand across his face. The eunuchs stopped their chatter to stare at them across the playing of the fountain.

'Mind your own,' Ché warned them, and they looked away quickly.

'Mother,' he tried again, even more quietly. 'You're in danger here. Surely you must know that. You are the means by which they keep a leash on me.'

'Nonsense. I have made many friends over the years, Ché – people in high positions. They know my loyalty to Mann. They would not allow any harm to visit me.' She paused, narrowing her eyes. 'But why? Do you plan something that may anger your superiors?'

Ché saw the danger he was in then, and held his tongue.

He scooped a handful of water over his face. It helped revive him, though the liquid tasted oddly sour against his lips.

'I'm merely tense,' he said at last. 'Perhaps I need to find a more peaceful line of work.'

He stood up, his chin still dripping water. 'I must leave you now.'

All trace of suspicion fell from his mother's features. 'So soon? You have only just arrived!'

Ché nodded. For an instant he wanted to reach down to her and rest a hand against her face – to touch, connect, feel close to this woman who remained a stranger to him, even now. But he knew she

378

would find that gesture strange, and that it would only betray him further.

'I shall see you soon, mother. Take care.'

*

The voice reeked of spices today. It was not the same high-pitched, whining voice that had spoken to Ché just before he departed for Cheem, nor the brusque baritone one he had delivered his report to upon his return. This was a female voice, the one he heard least frequently of all.

Even so, he did not like this voice. He did not like any of them, but especially not this one. Ché was always unsettled when he heard it come drifting through the wooden panel facing him in the wall of the shadowy alcove – muffled as it was, it sounded dark and ancient, like death.

'I have a new assignment for you,' it said to him now.

'I'd assumed as much.'

A wheeze, dry as tinder. 'You forget yourself, Diplomat. Restrain that arrogance, or I shall see it clipped from you.'

She mistakes my resentment for arrogance, thought Ché. *How typical of these people.*

Ché composed himself, enough at least to mutter an apology.

'Very well,' she said. 'Now, your assignment. The Holy Matriarch will be leaving Q'os soon. She will require a Diplomat to accompany her on her forthcoming campaign, as is our custom. In case, as it were, some diplomacy is required within the army itself.'

In other words, Ché mused, in case one of the generals refuses his orders or tries to seize power for himself. Ché was to serve as the Matriarch's bully boy, then – the threat that would keep everyone in line while in the field.

'The invasion, it goes ahead then?'

'Of course it does. The Matriarch has been politically weakened by the death of her son. A military victory in the field would do much to reinforce her position.'

'What do you need of me?'

'Ah, I sometimes forget how your instructors teach you on a need-to-know basis. Perhaps it is my age, and my faculties fading.' Again that wheezing sound. Ché suddenly realized that it was a chuckle. 'I shall explain to you then. You see, we have a tradition in our order, a tradition which stems back to our earliest days of empire. When a Patriarch or Matriarch takes to the field, they in turn take with them a chosen Diplomat.'

'Why me?' he asked bluntly.

'You have never asked such a question before,' murmured the voice.

Ché held his tongue. It was starting to disturb him, these things emerging from his mouth before he knew of them. His façade was fracturing; though, worse than that, it seemed that he could not bring himself to stop it from happening.

'It is you,' said the voice, 'because most of your fellow Diplomats have already been despatched to Minos to begin our early negotiations – and also to reinforce the belief that Minos, not Khos, is our intended target. You, Ché, are the best that remains behind.'

Perhaps that was even the truth of it. 'My orders?'

'Simple. Obey the Matriarch in all things.'

'That is all?'

'There is one more thing.'

He waited, knowing by now that his handlers liked to leave the most important aspect of his mission to the very last.

'Matriarch Sasheen takes a great personal risk in this venture,' continued the voice, then hesitated, as though bolstering its will to say what must be said next. 'If it becomes apparent that she is about to fall into the enemy's hands . . . or, likewise, if she decides that all is lost and tries to flee for home . . . then you, young Diplomat, must kill her.'

'Kill her?'

'Kill her.'

Ché glanced over his shoulder, as though someone might be listening.

'Is this a test?'

'No, it is an order. We cannot risk a Holy Matriarch of Mann falling into the hands of the Mercians. Nor can we have her turn tail and run. The prestige of the Empire would suffer too greatly from either occurence. Either she is victorious or she is to die a martyr's death. Is this clear?'

His breath had caught in his throat. He wondered how many previous Diplomats, accompanying a Holy leader in the field, had been given the same instructions. Perhaps all of them, he realized – for never had one of their leaders fallen into enemy hands, or for that matter fled from a battle.

Suddenly, everything Ché had ever understood about the Empire's structures of power – and who truly ruled it – shifted in a fundamental way.

'Yes, it's clear.'

'Good. Then be on your way, my child.'

CHAPTER THIRTY-TWO

The Ministry

For all the great size of the Ministry of War, its corridors and halls tended to have a deserted feel to them, so that one could make the long walk from one end of the building to the other and barely lay eyes upon another person. It was quiet like the hush of a museum or library. Occasional murmurs could be heard through thick doors of tiq, and in the halls the heavy strokes of clocks ticking. Dogs barked and children shouted in the park outside, though the sounds were muted as they passed through the white-framed windows that flooded the interior with light, the hundreds of glass panes shivering now and again with the distant rumble of cannon.

Guards were stationed at sensitive areas throughout the building. They stood as unmoving as statues, contributing little by way of presence, watching the rare passerby with slow, unfocused eyes.

Two did so now. They knew the man who strode towards them and the general's chambers, for he was Creed's chief aide and disposed to visiting the chambers several times in the course of a day, though this morning his face was paler than usual, and his steps hammered to the pace of a fast heartbeat. As he approached the men on sentry duty, they could see the small green squares of graf leaf still stuck to his face where he had cut himself shaving, and the rough shambles of his dark hair that had yet to be combed through with any order.

The general's personal secretary, young Hist, looked up as the man swept past his neatly ordered desk. The secretary opened his mouth to speak, but the two guards blocking the door intervened first.

'Your business, Lieutenant Calvone,' one of the guards intoned as the man came to a breathy stop before them.

'Not now,' Bahn snapped, and pushed through even before they had time to step aside.

*

'Urgent despatch, General,' Bahn announced as he entered the room with a slip of paper clutched in his hand.

General Creed, Lord Protector of Khos, did not respond. He sat instead with his eyes closed, on a reclining leather chair, while his ancient concierge, Gollanse, plaited his long black hair for the day.

'General,' tried Bahn again, and when again the general still did not respond Bahn sighed, and reminded himself: *You cannot rush this man.*

Gollanse hummed something tuneless as he finished braiding the man's hair. In the sunlight it looked black as crow's feather, only succumbing to traces of grey at the temples. The general was proud of his mane. He wore it loose during action, for he knew it lent him a youthful flair despite his advancing years. He sighed as Gollanse patted his shoulder to inform him he had finished.

General Creed rose from his chair and looked at Bahn for the first time.

'Report,' he said, from across the room.

'Despatch from Minos. From one of their agents, sir. In Lagos.'

'Read it for me.'

Bahn coughed to clear his throat. ' "From the Ministry of Intelligence, Al-Minos, Overseas Section. General Creed, be advised we have learned that one of our agents has been successful in the interception of an imperial despatch in the vicinity of Lagos. The despatch congratulates Admiral Quernmore's part in quelling the island's recent revolt, but rescinds his previous standing orders relating to the speedy return of the Third Fleet to Q'os following such an outcome. Instead, the fleet is ordered to remain at Lagos for now, pending further instructions. We believe this may relate in some way to the Free Ports." '

Bahn had already read the letter several times. Still, his fingers began trembling again. *Steady yourself, man. It might mean nothing.* 'It was sent to us by carrier bird four days ago, sir. We received it this morning.'

General Creed betrayed no outer signs of alarm, though Bahn had been expecting such calm. Since the death of his wife three years earlier, the general had ceased to be startled by anything that occurred in this never-ending war with the Mannians. It was as though nothing, ever again, could be as bad as the news he had received on the day of her death.

'I thought they were being overly quiet of late,' General Creed murmured from across the room, where he had turned to the windows overlooking the Shield, his hands clasped behind his back.

Somehow, in spite of the words, the general's calm tone settled Bahn's nerves. He realized once more how much store he placed in this old man's abilities as a leader.

He has turned into my father, mused Bahn, *and I the young boy.*

His hand sought out one of the two wooden chairs before the desk and he sat himself down heavily. Bahn was of a different cut to the general. He had been awoken shortly after dawn by Hanlow, of the Khosian intelligence corp, after a long and sleepless night in which his thoughts had refused to settle. At the door of his townhouse he had accepted a dispatch from the early-morning visitor, a decoded version of the message already scrawled down one side of it. Creed would still be asleep, Hanlow had said, and he did not wish to simply leave it on a desk. After Bahn had read the note his eyes had flicked to meet Hanlow's and he had cleared his throat. Very well, he'd said. He would take it to Creed himself.

Once the messenger had gone, the simple business of finding his left boot had turned into a one-sided argument with his wife. Marlee's patient decorum had only worsened his sudden bad temper, and he stomped around the house flinging items about in search of the errant boot. In gradual measures a black rage had descended upon him, a mood new to him, and wholly foreign.

Bahn had turned and shouted at Marlee at the top of his lungs, an occurence as shocking as striking her a blow. His son had fled the room; Ariale began to wail from her bedroom upstairs.

Marlee followed after her husband, talking to him calmly, allowing him no room in which to breathe. He watched himself, as though a passenger inside his own body, aware of his voice ringing loud and sharp in the ever-brightening rooms of their house, shocked by the things he was saying to her, to himself; by the outrage that coursed through him without reason.

At last Marlee had seized his arm in a sharp grip. 'What is it?' she had hissed. Bahn had forced himself to look her in the eye. At once the spell left him.

What am I doing? he had wondered, as he returned to his normal self.

Breathing out a long sigh, Bahn had caressed her arm as an apology. 'Maybe nothing,' he said softly, and he drew her to him, smothering his face in her berry-scented hair as he pressed her hard body against his own, her slender waist clasped within his hands. And in that embrace he felt all the weariness of the war rush into him like the years of an old man suddenly being poured into someone young and undeserving, and he thought again, trembling, *What am I doing?* – for it seemed in that question that everything he had ever loved or had offered purpose in his life lay furled within its answer.

Marlee held up his missing boot in one hand, which she had discovered a moment earlier. Their eyes glittered as they rested the bones of their foreheads together. He kissed her face while in his hand he still clutched the crumpled despatch.

'What do you make of it, sir?' Bahn asked, as he licked his dry lips. 'It sounds like an invasion to me.'

The old warrior was standing close enough to the window pane to mist the cold glass with his breath. He wiped it clear with a single noisy smear of his sleeve.

'Yes, it does, doesn't it?'

'To Khos?'

A moment of consideration. 'Perhaps – it would not surprise me.'

At those few words, Bahn felt the blood drain from his face. 'Sweet mercy. I pray to Fate it is not so.'

Creed said nothing for a moment, his eyes squinting as he took in the Shield stretched out below.

'As do I,' he murmured. 'We must inform the Council.'

Bahn stared hard at Creed's profile, silhouetted vaguely in the daylight. For a moment, just a second or two and no more, a tremor ran through the general's jaw. And then it was gone.

CHAPTER THIRTY-THREE

Farlander

'This is all our doing,' said Serèse, looking out of the carriage's window at the passing destruction, the bloodstains on the streets, the blackened buildings still leaking smoke.

Baracha peered at her, perplexed. He did not understand his daughter these days. By his side, Ash appeared lost in his own world. He had spoken little since his seeming recovery.

The carriage turned east towards the First Harbour, following the wide, meandering thoroughfare known as the Serpentine. Ash stroked the small jar of ashes that hung about his neck, unconsciously it seemed, as he pondered something.

They had deemed it too risky to book tickets for a passenger ship straight to Cheem; the Regulators would be watching the ports closely, hoping the Rōshun would emerge from hiding now that the ports had reopened. Instead, they had met with an Alhazii smuggler known to Baracha, and had offered the man a large sum of money for berths on his fast sloop. He was intent on shipping a cargo of dross down to Palo-Fortuna; whence they could easily find transportation back to Cheem. It was a safer option. They would be avoiding customs altogether, by rowing out to the ship in a small boat from the wharf fronting a private warehouse.

The driver pulled the zels to a stop. To their right, the wharf led to the open bay where the fleet lay at anchor. The carriage rocked on its suspension as the four cloaked and hooded figures stepped out from both sides. Baracha paid the man and followed the other three to the edge of the wharf, where a large rowing boat bobbed in the water. Six bearded sailors sat at the oars, restlessly eyeing the vicinity. They held their oars vertical in the air.

Momentarily, the Rōshun stopped to take in the sight of the great fleet.

'I wonder where they will make for,' mused Baracha.

'Wherever it is, I feel pity for them,' responded Aléas.

The sailors were waiting impatiently. They had no wish to linger here with their ship already loaded and ready to sail.

'Remember,' said Baracha in a hushed voice to his daughter and Aléas, 'we are escaped slaves, and Ash is a monk escorting us to his mission in Minos. Speak only when spoken to, and keep well out of sight.'

Aléas and Serèse were first to clamber down into the boat. No greeting came from the sailors, save for sharp orders to sit quickly and stay out of the way. Ash held back, still fingering the jar suspended at his neck.

Baracha moved to step down behind them, then stopped, a foot still resting on the wharf side. He muttered what sounded like a curse, and turned back to Ash.

'You're not coming with us, are you?'

'No. I do not think that I am.'

The Alhazii strode off a short distance from the boat. Ash slowly followed him.

They halted together under the pale morning sun.

'You can't do this,' declared Baracha.

'Yet I must.'

'Speak plainly, you old fool. You wish revenge for your boy. You want to race off and slay the Matriarch herself.'

Ash did not deny it.

Baracha spoke low, though the words were spat with force. 'And what example do you set by such actions? Our oldest Rōshun running off to seek his revenge?'

'It is justice that I seek. It is the very least the boy deserves from me now.'

Baracha snorted. 'You bandy with words. If you commit this act, you break the code that we live by. It is a personal vendetta you are speaking of, and it goes against all that the Rōshun stand for. Even I can appreciate that much.'

'Then I am no longer Rōshun,' replied Ash coldly, 'and I break only my own code, not that of the order.'

Baracha grasped his arm. The old farlander looked down at the hand that gripped him, then up to the angry eyes. 'Rōshun or not, you set an example to us all. You have reached the end of your wits from grief, that's all. You're not yourself.'

'No, I am not. I have lain for two weeks in the sweat of my own nightmares. Yesterday morning I awoke, only to discover that those nightmares are real.' He reached for Baracha's restraining hand. He plucked it free without effort.

'Alhazii . . . I know nothing, anymore, except that I cannot live with myself, not a second longer, if I do not see this through.'

For a moment, Baracha trembled on the edge of a great rage. His fists clenched, blood inflamed his face: it was what always happened when he failed to get his own way.

Quite unexpectedly, the words of the Blessed Prophet came to his mind.

Do not judge a man for the path that he follows. Unless you have walked each and every step in the same direction, you cannot tell another where he is headed, nor what he leaves behind.

Baracha looked to the sky, then down to the ground, then back to the wizened farlander broken with grief before him.

He blew the frustration from his lungs.

'Then blessing of Zabrihm be upon you, you old fool,' he said. He held out his hand, and Ash squinted at it for a moment, then clasped it.

Baracha strode back to the boat, shaking his head.

'Baracha,' barked Ash.

The big man turned. Ash tugged the urn of ashes free from his pack. He approached and handed it to Baracha.

'Keep this until I return,' he said. 'If I do not make it back, see that it gets to his mother. Aléas will know of her.'

Baracha nodded. With the urn in his hand he jumped into the boat. The sailors pushed off from the wharf side, began to pull at the water with their oars.

As the boat cut through the swell towards the waiting ship, and the salt water slapped and hissed against its sides, Baracha twisted around on the plank he sat upon. He thought, perhaps, to give a final salute to Ash, for he knew then that he would likely never see him again.

But already, the old man had turned to face the city.

Stands a Shadow

Turn over to read the prologue of *Stands a Shadow*,

book two in the Farlander novels . . .

The Shining Way

It was like being at sea, this plain of grasses that stretched to the brink of the horizon and beyond; the eyes filled with sky wherever they looked. In the milky brightness of day the twin moons hung lonely and high, the smaller of the two a pale white, the larger a pale blue, cupped in darkness and clearly spherical in form; reminders, to any observer with knowledge or imagination, that the world of Erēs too was a monstrous ball tumbling through the nothingness, and that they were spinning with it.

'Thank the Fool there's no wind today,' remarked Kosh, sitting poised in the saddle of his prized war-zel. 'I haven't the stomach for another burning.'

'Nor I,' replied Ash, and tore his gaze from the far moons, blinking as though returning to himself and the world of man. The air lay thick and hot today, shimmering above the stubby grasses that stretched between the two armies. The heat waves were causing the dark, glittering massif of enemy riders to loom with an unreal closeness.

Ash clucked his tongue as his own zel tossed its head again, jittery. He was a lesser rider than Kosh, and his zel was young and still untested. Ash had not given this one a name yet. His previous mount, old Asa, had fallen with a ruptured heart in their last skirmish just east of Car; a day in which the smell of roasting meat had hung like a pall above their fighting, while the enemy Yashi were burned alive in the great wind-driven conflagration Ash and his comrades had sent gusting into their ranks. Later, his soot-stained face streaked with tears, he had mourned for his dead zel as much as for his comrades fallen that day.

Ash bent forward and stroked his young zel's neck with a gloved hand. *Look at that pair*, he tried to communicate to the animal by thought alone, eying the still form of Kosh and his trusted mount. *See how proud they look together.*

The young zel skipped once on its hind legs.

'Easy, boy,' Ash soothed, still stroking the muscular neck of the animal, flattening the grain of its coarse hair, black as pitch between the bands of white. At last the zel began to settle, began to snort the fear from its lungs and calm itself.

Leather creaked as Ash straightened in his saddle. Beside him, Kosh uncorked a waterskin and took a long drink. He gasped and wiped his mouth dry. 'I could do with something a little stronger,' he complained, and pointedly offered none to Ash. Instead he tossed it back to his son, his battlesquire, standing barefoot next to him.

'You're still sore at that?' asked Ash.

'You could have left me some, is all I'm saying.'

Ash grunted, leaned between their mounts to spit upon the ground. Blades of tindergrass popped and crackled as they absorbed the sudden moisture. It was the same all across the plain; a constant background noise could be heard – like uncooked rice raining down on far shingles, as the secretions of the two armies wrought a chorus of similar minute reactions from the grasses beneath their feet.

He looked right, over the head of his own son and battlesquire Lin, the boy standing there in his usual quiet absorption. Along the line, other mounts were prancing edgily beneath their riders' attentions. The zels could smell the enemy war-panthers in the odd scrap of breeze, leashed within the distant ranks facing them in this nameless spot in the Sea of Wind and Grasses.

The People's Revolutionary Army were outnumbered today. But then they were always outnumbered, a fact that hadn't stopped them from learning how to win against an enemy overly reliant on grumbling conscripts and the established hierarchical forms of warfare as laid out in the ancient Venerable Treatise of War. Today, the confidence of the old campaigners was apparent as they waited for the fighting to begin. This was it, they all knew, the big throw of the die; everything that either side could muster had been committed to this final confrontation.

A cry rose up and spread along the ranks; General Oshō, leader of the Shining Way, cantering on his pure black zel, Chancer, past the lines of the Wing, the men who today would anchor the left flank of the main formation. A lance bobbed upright in his hand, a red flag trailing from it above the dust that coiled from his mount's hooves. An image was stitched across the cloth: one-eyed Ninshi, protectress of the dispossessed. It was snapping and fluttering like a flame.

Oshō rode with the easy grace of a man taking an early morning ride for the pleasure of it, as confident as the rest of the veterans of the Wing. Their strategy for this battle was a sound one, and it had been proposed by General Nisan himself, overall leader of the army and military hero of the revolution. They had voted overwhelmingly in its favour when the army had held its general assembly during the night.

With the main body of their forces acting as bait for the overwhelming numbers of enemy Pulses, and with feints to the flanks designed to entangle the overlords' predictable Swan's Wings, the real killing stroke would be delivered by the heavy cavalry of General Shin's Wing, the Black Stars, hidden in the long grasses to the south-west, directly behind the position of the Shining Way. With every Wing of the enemy engaged and ensnared in the action, they would sweep around long and fast, and in all the confusion take the centre of the enemy from behind, hoping to create the type of rout they had seen countless times before.

'Today is the day, brothers!' General Oshō roared with passion. 'Today is the day!'

Men raised lances and hollered as he passed by. Even Ash, not one for outward displays of enthusiasm, felt a rousing of pride as the men cheered and pumped their fists in reply. His son was one of them.

A plume of dust rose around the general as he drew his war-zel to a halt. With dancing steps he turned the mount to face the far ranks of the enemy. At the sight of them the zel snorted and swiped its tail. Together, Oshō and Chancer waited as silence fell.

'By the Fool's balls I hope he's right,' grumbled Kosh with a nod to their charismatic leader. 'It's time we brought these boys home to their mothers, don't you think?'

It was a question hardly needing a reply.

Around them, ranging through the ranks, the daojos whipped at the rumps of zels and shouted for the men to draw tighter in their formations, reminding them of their orders and the basic preparations for the fight.

'I hear the overlords offered a casket of diamonds to any general willing to turn tail.'

Ash flicked a grassfly from his cheek. '*Phh*. When haven't they tried to buy us out? Today is hardly different.'

'Ah. But today is the day.'

They both chuckled, their throats hoarse from the smoke of the pipes and the campfires of the night before.

It was true, what Ash had said. In the early days of the revolution, when the People's Revolutionary Army was little more than a rag-tag force lacking confidence, cohesion or any notable victories to call its own, the overlords had offered each fighter in the army a small fortune in unchipped diamonds if they would desert to the other side. Some had defected to the overlords' ranks – a great number in fact. But those who had refused the offer, who remained to fight on despite the sudden impossibility of their position, had found an unexpected strength in their collective refusal to sell out to those who would own and exploit it all. Amongst the ranks, where many had become demoralized by hunger, bitter losses, and the constant threats of capture or death, a renewal of spirit came upon them all, a sense of righteous brotherhood. It was the true beginning of the cause. From that time onwards, slowly but surely, they had begun to turn back the tide.

'It does feel like an end to things, don't you think?' Kosh asked.

'One way or the other,' Ash replied, glancing down at his son.

Lin was unaware of his scrutiny. The boy supported the upright bundle of spare lances in his hands, and the spare wicker shield upon his back. His eyes were wide with a fourteen-year-old's sense of wonder. Specks of reflected sunlight shone in his dark pupils, the whites bloodshot from the heavy drinking of the night before. The boy had sat up late around one of the campfires, joking and throat-singing with the older battlesquires of their Wing.

A different person, Ash now thought, to the half-starved urchin who had stumbled into their base-camp two years ago, having run away to join his father as his battlesquire. The boy's bare feet had been shredded from a trek that most grown men would have baulked at.

And for what? For the love and respect of a father who could no longer tolerate the sight of him.

Ash felt a sudden kindling of pain in his chest; a sense of overwhelming shame. In that moment he felt the need to touch his son, to reassure him with the press of a hand, as he had with the zel a few moments before. He lifted his gloved hand from the pommel of the saddle and reached out with it.

Lin glanced up. Ash gazed down upon the heavy brows and the turned-up nose that reminded him so much of the boy's mother, and of her family, whom he'd grown so much to despise. Features that seemed not in any way to be his own.

His hand stopped halfway towards the boy, and for several heartbeats they both stared at it, hovering there, as though it represented everything that had ever stood between them.

'Water,' Ash muttered, though he wasn't thirsty. Without comment, the boy hefted up the bulging skin.

Ash took a sip of the tepid, stale water. He rolled it about in his mouth, swallowed a trickle, spat the rest out again. Where it fell the tindergrass hissed and crackled. He returned the skin to Lin and straightened in his saddle, angry at himself.

'They come,' announced Kosh.

'I see it.'

Across the entire enemy front, a roiling carpet of dust began to rise into the air. The Yashi trotted forwards in their formations, high banners bobbing from the backs of riders, flying the colours of Wings and their shifting locations of command. Horns sounded; windwhirls wailed like calls to the dead, the sounds washing slow and rhythmic over the ranks of the People's Revolutionary Army. Ash's zel snorted, becoming lively again.

On this flank alone, the overlords' forces numbered twenty thousand at least, a deep mass stretching to the right towards the haze of the battle line's distant centre. Their black armour soaked up the harsh daylight; helms bobbed with tall feathers. Sunlight sparkled from thousands of metal points, a bright dazzle amidst the dust raised by the advancing army, as the hooves of their zels crunched the tindergrass of the plain into pieces fine as powdered talc.

Before the advancing Yashi, clouds of moths and flies rose up from the short grasses, and birds too in their thousands. They rushed over the heads of the People's Revolutionary Army in a great crying wave of flapping wings, so many in number that the air cooled for a moment in their shadow.

Below, the zels snuffled and rolled their eyes as a hail of loose feathers and guano droppings fell upon them. Lin hefted the wicker shield over his head to protect himself. Others along the line did so too, so that it appeared as though they were sheltering from sudden missile fire. Jokes sounded from the veterans, laughter even, the rarest of sounds this close to a fight.

Ash wiped his forehead clear and surveyed the hardened men of the Shining Way, this Wing of the army in which he had fought for over four years now; an old veteran himself now at the age of thirty-one. The Wing numbered six thousand in mounted infantry. They wore simple leather skullcaps tied down around their ears, white cavalry scarves knotted around black faces and wooden goggles to mask their eyes from the sunlight. Many of their armoured coats had long ago been painted with stripes of white like the zels the men lived and fought upon, and ornamented with the teeth of their enemy as lucky charms. Squinting, peering beyond these men, Ash could make out the great curve of the rest of the army, this great conglomeration of Wings.

He wondered how many would return to their families and their old lives if they won here today. The revolution had become a way of life to them over the years, bloody and cruel as it was. The People's Army was a home and family to them all. How would they cope with giving up the freedom of the saddle, the bonds they had formed with each other, the highs of action, when they returned to their farmsteads and their regular, mundane lives armed with nightmares and faraway stares?

He supposed he would find out himself. If they won here, and Ash and Lin survived, he would return with his son to the northern mountains and their lofty village of Asa, to their homestead and his wife whom he hadn't seen in years; try to forget the things they had seen and done in the name of the cause. Yet he would miss this life too. In so many ways, he knew he was better at this than he had ever been at supporting a family.

Ash could feel the prayer belt wrapped tight like a linen bandage around his abdomen, its ink-brushed words pressing against his sweating skin. Within its bounds he carried a letter from his wife delivered to him only a week before. Her words, carved into a thin sheet of leather, had pleaded once more for his forgiveness.

'Father,' said his son by his side as the enemy grew nearer. The boy was holding aloft one of the lances, his face slick with sweat. Ash took it, and the shield too. On his left, Kosh's son did the same.

'Are you ready?' Ash asked his son, not unkindly.

The boy frowned, though. He leaned and spat in the same way as his father sometimes did. 'I'll stand, if that's what you mean,' he declared maturely, but he said so in a voice still unbroken with age. There was anger in his tone, at the perceived insinuation that he might run on this day, like he had in his first real battle, overcome by it all.

'I know you will. I only ask if you are ready.'

The boy's jaw flexed. His stare softened before he looked away.

'Stay in the rear, close to Kosh's boy. Don't come to me unless I signal, do you hear?'

'Yes, father,' answered Lin, and then waited, blinking up at him, as though expecting something more.

The thin leather of his wife's letter felt cool against Ash's stomach.

'I'm glad you're here, son,' he heard himself say, and his throat clamped tight around each of the words. 'With me, I mean.'

Lin beamed up at him.

'Yes, father.'

He turned and sauntered away, and Ash watched him leave as other battlesquires filtered back through the ranks. Kosh's son joined him, slapping the boy on the back; a joker like his father.

A soft thunder rumbled across the heat of the plain.

The Yashi were charging.

Ash pulled the goggles down over his eyes and the scarf across his face. Beneath him, he could feel the tremor of the ground transmitted through the bones and muscles of his zel. He glanced to General Oshō, as did every other man of the formation. Still the general refused to move.

'With heart,' he told Kosh.

Kosh pulled his own scarf up. Some kind of awkwardness kept his gaze clear of Ash. One way or the other, they would probably never fight side by side like this again; comrades, brothers, crazy fools of the revolution.

'And you, my friend,' came Kosh's muffled reply.

They gathered their zels' reins tighter in their fists as General Oshō levelled his warhead at the approaching enemy. Ash lowered his own lance.

Oshō's zel sprang forward.

As one, the men of the Shining Way followed him with a roar.

The Black Dream

As the empire of Mann threatens the world with enslavement, only a single island nation continues to stand in its way – the Free Ports of the *democras*. For ten years they have held their own, but now the empire draws its noose even tighter around them.

Rallying to its defence are those from the secretive network known as the Few, including the cripple and troubleshooter Coya Zeziké. Coya has hopes of enlisting the forest Contrarè in the aid of the besieged city of Bar-Khos. With him is Shard, the only *Dreamer* of the Free Ports, a woman capable of manipulating waking reality or the strange dimensions of the Black Dream.

The Rōshun order of assassins have also engaged in the war at last. But Ash, their ailing farlander, has more urgent business to overcome. Facing him is a skyship voyage into the Great Hush, then further journeying to the fabled Isles of Sky, where he hopes to bring his dead apprentice Nico back to life. Yet his voyage into the unknown may save more than just Nico . . . it may save the Free Ports themselves.

Book three in the Farlander novels

March 2015

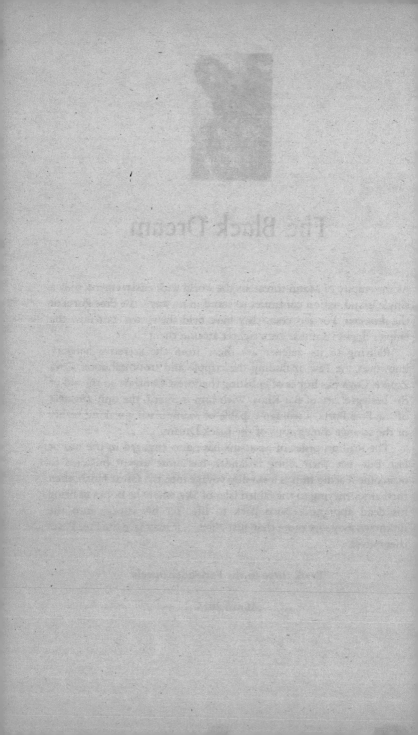

extracts reading groups
competitions books new
discounts extracts
extracts
competitions
reading groups
discounts
books
new
events
extracts
discounts
events
reading groups
events books
extracts
new titles reading groups
interviews
reading groups
extracts
new
books
events extracts
extracts
books
discounts
new books events
events
books
interviews
new books
extracts
events new
new
discounts extracts discounts

www.panmacmillan.com
extracts events reading groups
competitions books extracts new
books